When W

© 2019

This collection is a compilation of separately published Books 1-3 in Steve Milton's series *Three Straight*. The books as they appear in this collection are identical to the separately published books.

We Three

We Three

© 2019 by Steve Milton

Book 1 of the series **Three Straight**

This book is a work of fiction.

Steve Milton's spam-free insiders' club: http://eepurl.com/bYQboP

One

"Faggots!"

The shout came like a wild bark.

It echoed between the skeletons of abandoned downtown department stores. The sound chased Colin and Matias into stomach-tightening terror.

"Just fucking run," Matias blurted. His face flushed red with fear. It seemed to be the first time Matias had been afraid of anything.

By the time he'd said *run*, Matias was already running himself. Colin ran alongside him, gasping for air. The faster he ran, the deeper he had to breathe the alley's rancid garbage smell he'd been avoiding. *No matter how much money you have, this is still Miami*, Matias had always warned Colin.

Colin concentrated on running faster, any faster he possibly could. Super-turbo mode, if he had one. "Come back here, fags!" the voice echoed again, this time accompanied by running footsteps behind them. The footsteps were getting closer.

A lifelong Miami resident, Colin had been mugged once already. That hadn't been so bad. He'd handed over his wallet and gone home to replace his cards. Those were easy to replace, with private bankers and family concierges and all. The scariest things, though, were those that even his family's bankers can't help with.

That voice screaming somewhere behind Colin and Matias wanted more than their wallets. They could only run faster.

They weren't even gay. They were just two guys taking a shortcut through an alley. There was nothing gay about two buddies hitting the clubs on a Tuesday evening then walking home together.

Whoever was screaming didn't care about logic, of course. There was no reasoning with hate.

Colin gritted his teeth. He put the turbo-boost in his legs and feet, right through to his Tod's driving shoes. Matias was already running a good two steps ahead of him. Despite being kind of chunky, that Matias kid was always faster than Colin.

"Where you going, fags?" The taunt was closer. It had almost caught up with them.

It wasn't just an echo off of brick walls. Their night had gone from uneventful, leisurely, to grossly terrifying.

Matias ran faster. His red-and-white Chucks pounded on the pavement, quicker and quicker. Colin did all he could to keep up with him, even if he was running out of wind, even if breathing felt like sucking on a snorkel, one that had been taped shut.

Streetlights of the main road shone ahead of them like the Promised Land. Colin ran faster, pacing his feet to the rhythm of Matias's fast breaths.

A foot-high pile of garbage blocked the end of the alley. Beyond the pile of garbage was the main road, the streetlights, civilization, maybe even the police.

At his last step before the garbage pile, Matias leapt up into the air, sailing over the banana peels and cardboard boxes. Colin took a deep breath, as if the air was going to help him levitate, and followed Matias's leap over the garbage.

In that moment, soaring across a foot-high pile of trash in a Miami alley, Colin's life felt like a video game. It was exciting. For once.

"Next time, fags!" the voice boomed behind them, sounding less menacing for once.

Colin stopped. Catching his breath, he leaned down and braced his arms on his knees.

Matias patted Colin's back. His brown eyes carried Matias's usual gentle mockery, the kind of half-insults that bromances were made of. "You're pretty winded after like thirty seconds of running."

Colin glanced up at Matias, staring into the orange glow of a street lamp, the Miami Tower vaguely growing out of Matias's curly brown hair. Matias's round face was also soaked in sweat, even if a bit less so than Colin's own. "Yeah, Matias, you're no Usain Bolt either."

Matias shrugged. He used the back of his hand to push an avalanche of sweat off his forehead. "I'm more like Usain Dawdle."

Colin honored Matias's comedic talents with a golf clap.

"So do you agree with me?" Colin knew to work the situation to try to push through his agenda. It was just as his dad had always told him: *when everyone else is shell-shocked, that's when you take charge.*

The car-ride thing was a start to Colin's perennial list of Matters To Be Discussed With Matias. Maybe Matias would finally agree to stop walking around the city like a couple of plebs.

"Do I agree with you what?" Matias stood with hands on hips, gray half-lit Miami skyline behind him. He was beautiful, in a classical sort of way.

"Do you agree with me," Colin said, clearing his throat the same way his dad did when giving a speech, "that we should stop walking around the city like a bunch of — a bunch of *itinerants* — and start taking Uber, Lyft, anything other than our feet?"

"We're twenty-three and totally out of shape, and your solution is that we become more sedentary?" Matias sounded like a professor of logic sometimes. Colin loved and hated that about him.

"We're Miami millennials who go clubbing and shopping." Colin shook his head. "Be realistic. We're not training for a triathlon here."

"Reductio ad absurdum." Matias shook his head and kicked a piece of stuck plastic off his shoe. Then he started walking again. "Nobody mentioned any triathlons. Not even biathlons. Not any kind of thons. I just think walking isn't bad for us."

"I have two Amex Black cards with no spending limit, and a Visa with enough credit on it to buy a Miami condo — okay, a small condo, no ocean view, but still, a condo." Colin looked up at the dark sky that had given him all this fortune, as if he was pleading not to be misunderstood, not to be taken for a regular person who needed to walk. "And you, Matias over here, you insist that we fucking walk everywhere!"

"Walking is healthy." Three words. Three words were all Matias needed. He'd made his point. That was how Matias rolled.

"Getting gay-bashed in some alley doesn't seem healthy at all." Counterpoint, Colin. "I'm not much of a believer in leaving a good-looking corpse."

"You know we could take defensive measures against that shit too." Matias scanned the street and the alley and the buildings around them as if he were about to command a SWAT team.

"No, man. No guns." Colin almost wanted to throw up just from saying that word. "No fucking guns in my home, in my life, anywhere."

"Not guns. I've had enough guns around me." Matias winced a little while shaking his head. "I just mean physical training. Joining a gym. Hitting the weights. Getting in shape." Matias flexed his arms in a ridiculous-looking muscleman pose.

"This isn't a fucking Popeye cartoon, man." Colin rolled his eyes. "Urban safety isn't a matter of having muscles."

"Did I open a can of spinach that I'm not aware of?" Matias stared wide-eyed at Colin. His huge brown eyes looked like they could consume oceans.

"I just mean — this is real life." Colin made his best face of the world-weary adult. "Not a cartoon."

"You're gonna tell me about real life, Colin Warner?" Matias smirked.

Matias was probably going into one of those *real life* speeches of his he felt he was entitled to deliver from having grown up in Hialeah and attended the University of Miami on a scholarship. As if that somehow made him an expert on everything from hand-to-hand-combat to, well, anything and everything else that he could construe as "the real world."

Colin never said it out loud, but he wasn't all that clueless. His upbringing had given him the chance to see more of the world than most twenty-three-year-olds had seen, that was for sure.

"Being physically fit isn't a be-all end-all defense, Matias." Colin sighed. "No matter how much you're about to mock me for *not* having grown up poor, for *never* having gone dumpster-diving — I'm sorry, I admit I never had that experience — I do have some concept of reality."

"Reality, Colin Warner style!" Matias yelled out. He spread his arms wide like wings and ran down the sidewalk, then banked his whole body to the right and ran back to Colin.

"What is that even supposed to be?" Colin couldn't help but grin as he shook his head in disapproval. "An airplane?"

"It's you. With your head in the clouds." Matias triumphantly outstretched his arms and wiggled his head as if he were somehow making his way through a cloud.

"And it's your private jet!" Matias shouted again. "Or your dad's private jet. Doesn't really matter which, does it now?" Matias broke out in laughter and took off for another round of wings-outstretched flying down the sidewalk.

Matias knew Colin's secrets. After having lived with him for five years, Matias was as familiar with Colin's family wealth and status as he was with the sight of Colin's bare ass.

"You don't have to announce that so loudly." Colin sighed. Matias was allowed to know Colin's wealth, but it wasn't such a great thing to shout from the rooftops — especially when standing on a Miami street corner at midnight.

"Why not, man?" Matias Air Flight 1 suddenly stopped in its tracks. Matias even retracted his wings. His lips tightened and he looked a little bit embarrassed. "Isn't it obvious from looking at you, Colin, Colin Warner—" Matias very obviously looked Colin up and down— "that you're a rich kid? Like they say, a child of privilege?"

At least Matias didn't start singing that awful song, "Fortunate Son." That song, with its lyrics about being a senator's son, had been written just to torment Colin.

"Some private matters are just better not to announce on dark street corners at night, alright?" Colin sighed and shook his head. He played up at being the streetwise and world-weary one of the two. That was a pretty good feeling, even if it wasn't well founded in reality.

"Alright." Matias extended his wings again. "Stealth Gulfstream 6 private jet ready for departure. Let's go home, shall we?" He shook his wings like a duck shaking off water, then pointed his head and whole body toward the phallic hulk of their condo building up ahead.

Chucks shuffled and scuffled on the pavement. Wings still extended, Matias ran toward their building. Or actually, it was just their condo, not their entire building. Or actually, it was just Colin's condo, but Matias had lived there with him since their third year of college, so it was pretty much Matias's too.

They'd been university-assigned dorm roommates for their first two years, so why not keep a good thing going?

Colin had talked Matias out of insisting to pay some rent back then, and he was going to talk Matias out of this dumb Luddite "let's walk" idea now.

Matias was only jogging toward their building, not running full-speed, but Colin struggled to keep up. Maybe joining a gym wouldn't be such a bad idea.

Two

"I fucking love how you still wear your gym shorts for this." The man's soft, fat hands ran over Duke's legs.

Duke shut his eyes just enough to see what was going on down below his waistline, but not see enough to make it too traumatizing.

He knew what to do to earn his keep. He pumped his dick in and out of the man's face.

The man moaned and sucked and slurped hard on Duke's cockhead. The man's cologne and office sweat almost smelled stronger than the gassy stink of the gym's parking garage.

The man spat Duke's dick out of his mouth and looked up at Duke's face. He reached down inside the pants of his tailored suit and started jerking his own dick. Then he spoke up to Duke: "Now slap me. Tell me I'm a cocksucking fag."

Slapping was out of the question. It triggered Duke the wrong way. There was all that stuff about his past. And it gave a self-hating, closeted, usually rich and powerful dude a bit of pretty horrible blackmail material against the semi-homeless guy whose dick he'd just sucked in a parking garage. A guy like that could accuse Duke of assault or worse. People would do anything. They did.

"Cocksucking fag!" Duke yelled down at the man, trying to sound convincingly hateful and homophobic.

The man was jerking his dick frantically now and sucking Duke's dick even harder. He grabbed at Duke's ass with one hand and gave a thumbs-up with his other hand. That was usually the signal for more verbal humiliation.

"Suck my dick, faggot," Duke growled. That sounded convincing. One day, if he got his life together, maybe he could be a Hollywood actor, the one who always played the pissed-off homophobe.

The man gasped, sucking harder on Duke's dick. His hand under his pants sped-up its jerking and his face flushed red with orgasm. Their faces would always stay just as red after orgasm, once the shame set in. Duke just had to collect his money before they ran away.

The man's whole body pulsed in orgasm. He twirled his tongue on Duke's cockhead. Duke moaned in feigned ecstasy.

When the man breathed a hot, exhausted breath onto Duke's cock and let it slip out of his mouth, Duke knew to broach the question. He extended his open palm downward and said as nonchalantly as he could, "Hundred dollars, please."

He tried to act like a tollbooth employee. Or a bottled water vendor. He wasn't judgmental. He wasn't going to make anybody feel bad about what they were buying and why they were buying it. He just wanted the money.

It was only a hundred bucks for these guys. Maybe fifteen minutes of their billable time. An hour of it if they were really "poor." When they ran away without paying, it wasn't the money that they didn't want to spend. It was the rubbing-it-in that got to them: the confirmation that not only were they sucking dick voluntarily, but they were paying money for it. The money they paid was the uptight, suit-clad, girlfriend-and-wife-having, deeply closeted men's tangible, monetary confirmation that they were nothing more than cocksucking fags.

A hundred bucks went far for Duke. If he sucked ten dicks, a thousand was the monthly check he sent for Sam. Or for the woman to deposit in her bank account, anyway — and for Duke to hope it was for Sam. Even if Duke wasn't officially Sam's father, even if his son had never heard of Duke, even if Duke's biological fatherhood was only by virtue of a desperate trip to a strip club thinking he could make himself straight, supporting his son was the least he could do.

The soft fat hand reached into the charcoal-gray suit pants pocket and put a hundred in Duke's hand, together with putting a blank nod in the direction of Duke's face. Eyes firmly downcast, the man got up from his crouch and got the hell out of that parking-garage bathroom, probably back to his Tesla, his Boca Raton four-bedroom, and his wife.

A hundred dollars richer, Duke breathed easier. His evening shift upstairs was starting soon. Eighteen bucks an hour, but there was a free shower before and after, some high-end toiletries he could indulge in like a feted prince, and most importantly, a lot more closeted dudes who'd ask him what it would take for them to suck his dick. "Fitness" clients: some of them even dropped the fitness training part, because the dick was all they were after.

Early mornings and late evenings were the time to get male clients. Mid-day, Biscayne Fitness was full of women — women who just wanted to get in shape. Female clients would ask him out for coffee, but would never, ever, offer to pay a hundred bucks to suck the trainer's dick. Women were better than that.

Upstairs, the shower washed off the nasty feeling of some Bvlgari-smelling real estate broker's hungry mouth. Hot water felt amazing. Miami was always hot, ambient hot, but still, a hot shower wasn't free to come by.

The shower faucet labeled H sat there glistening, heavy and ornate like a ship's wheel, the kind of ship's wheel Duke had imagined steering as a kid. He cranked it all open and let it pour down.

Showering was Duke's regular moment of respite, between living in the parking garage, sucking dicks for money, and soliciting clients out on the gym floor. In those moments, he could pretend he was a normal person. He could pretend he was on his way home from a respectable job, that he had a respectable husband, that he was alright with himself. With his eyes half-closed and water splashing down, he could almost wish it into being. Almost.

His phone alarm chimed. Five minutes to go before his next training appointment. That was plenty of time to dry off, throw on his clothes, put on socks and shoes, and go out to the gym floor with a friendly, slightly solicitous smile.

A wall of cooled air hit him when he walked onto the gym floor. The locker rooms were temperature controlled to a good five degrees warmer than the gym floor, because of course they were.

This was Biscayne Fitness. These people's lives were perfect.

"I'm Duke Jones." Duke contorted his face into his realest fake look of fitness enthusiasm. He needed to look like Mister Motivation for helping spoiled gay men get into shape. "So who's got the training appointment with me?"

Of the two specimens standing all pussy-footed in front of Duke, the browner, beefier one looked like he'd actually been to a gym before. His pretty-boy boyfriend or sponsor or whatever looked like he might've seen a gym from the window of his favorite nail salon.

Whatever. He'd train them one and train them all. The only problem was that if these two were together, they were already getting their willies suctioned, and there wasn't much chance of them engaging Duke's services downstairs.

"Both of us," the beefier dude said. Apparently he spoke for the both of them. The other one was probably his bitch-boy.

"Alright. That's cool." Duke nodded. Sure. That was cool.

The gym paid Duke the same eighteen bucks an hour for training two dudes instead of one, even if they charged each of the dudes the same hundred bucks an hour each. Two hundred an hour for the gym, eighteen an hour for Duke. But that was business or capitalism or whatever they were calling it.

Duke hadn't gotten paid any more in his MMA days when they sold more t-shirts or packed the crowd, and it was the same now at the gym. Bonuses were for bosses.

"We're just looking to get into better shape," the blonde, blue-eyed one pleaded.

It was like he was trying to justify himself, justify being in a gym. He didn't want anyone to think that his body wasn't already perfect.

Blondie was infatuated with his own looks. He probably would have hired himself as his own rentboy. He was getting Duke's training at a hundred bucks per hour per person, times two.

On top of that he and his boytoy had to pay a five-hundred-dollar monthly gym membership, each. Blondie would've been able to afford whatever he would've charged himself for his own presence.

"I mean we go walking, but—" Brownie blurted out. Seriously, these dudes are what, twenty, and they go walking, and then get personal trainers? They must've fast-forwarded thirty years to the lifestyle of rich fifty-year-old gay dudes, Ritter Lehman grade. "Yeah. Some strength training wouldn't hurt."

"Alright!" Duke clapped his hands together. "How much athletic experience do you have? What's your fitness level?"

"I played high school soccer." Brownie shrugged. "Not the major leagues or anything, but we did some weights and stuff. Of course, that ended five years ago."

"Cool." That was the most neutral thing Duke could say. It was the usual story of an aging gay dude wanting to get back into high school athletics so he could fuck as much ass as he'd fucked back in high school. Except Brownie was like twenty-three.

"My name is Matias, by the way." Brownie stuck his hand out. That arm definitely had some muscle. He pronounced every letter in *Matias*, probably because he thought it was exotic or some shit.

"Cool." Duke said it again. He was on personal-trainer autopilot. His words were whatever sounded the most professional and was the least likely to cause some uptight client a boatload of offense and get Duke fired.

Duke looked over at Blondie with a plaintive smile aimed to get his name.

Blondie was socially skilled enough to get the message. "I'm Colin." Blondie smiled big. What a perfect fucking name for such a perfect specimen: Colin. "And I played lacrosse in high school." Of course he played lacrosse in high school.

"But that was a few years ago, I assume?" Duke grinned. That blond little twink probably went around claiming to still be in high school. "You've been out of high school a few years?"

Matias smirked at Colin. It was the same smirk Duke would've given Colin if it had been allowed. "This dude actually graduated!" Matias punched Colin's shoulder with the gentlest, softest of play-punches. "He must've bribed the principal."

"Ah, Matias—" Colin shook his head. His discomfort spoke of the joke's proximity to reality.

"Sorry!" Matias covered his mouth primly with his hand. What a little queen. "Your high school didn't have a principal. It probably had a *headmaster*." Matias smiled knowingly and rolled his eyes.

"We had both, actually." Colin smiled in a way that owned the situation. That was admirable. "The headmaster is the boss of the principal."

"Like Mister Duke here is gonna be the boss of both of us." Matias smiled eagerly. He was getting into this. "Right, Duke?"

"Well, the trainer and the client are a team, working together to—" Duke recited the speech he'd had to memorize in his state-required personal trainer class.

"Just play along, man!" Matias gave Duke exactly the same play punch he'd given Colin.

"Alright, alright. I'm gonna whip you both into shape, hard." Duke tried to sound stern, without letting on that he was all too good at that kind of talk from his second career downstairs.

"That's kind of hot," Colin whispered with a half-smile.

"Oh." Duke always waited for some explicit confirmation of his male clients' homosexuality before acknowledging it himself. It was always obvious they were gay, but it wouldn't have been becoming of a fitness trainer to say anything until they said it themselves. "So you guys are getting in shape to spice up your sex life?"

"Yeah—" Colin started to answer and nod.

"What? No!" Matias's face turned to a disgusted frown as he shook his head in a hundred denials, first at Colin, then at Duke. "Our sex lives, plural, sure, maybe. But we're not gay. No, sorry. I mean I know a lot of guys here are gay. But we're straight."

"Yeah." Colin's eyes suddenly opened wide, as if he'd just woken up. "I mean working out might help us, you know, with the ladies." He sounded like a closeted twink trying to sound like a frat douche. "But no, noooo, no way, not like that. We're not gay or anything."

"Sorry." Duke tried to sound apologetic instead of amused at their typical closeted denials. "What's *or anything* though?" Was he overstepping by asking a dumb question like that? He was just breaking the ice with his clients. And he wanted to hear this guy talk.

"I mean we're not like, bi." Colin's last word was by far the quietest. He held up two fingers to illustrate exactly what he wasn't. "We're not any of that." Colin pursed his lips and nodded confidently, like a man who'd just finished a massive mental workout, or an act of self-delusion.

"That's cool. Some straight guys come to this gym too." Duke smiled. The paucity of heterosexual men was a running joke in all of Miami. "A few. I think. They must be somewhere around here." Duke looked all around the gym floor and laughed. Colin's face only locked into a cold, mortified stare.

"Ha, right!" Matias seemed to be forcing himself into a jolly chuckle to break the otherwise awkward moment.

"So. Let's get started and assess your fitness before we develop a plan."

"Cool," the millennial duo nodded in unison. Agreeing to this kind of thing was a lot easier than doing it.

"Colin, you wanna go first?" That was for Duke's own voyeuristic pleasure. But there was always a respectably trainer-like excuse for Duke's own urges. "Since you've been out of the fitness world longer."

Duke smiled. Colin returned the smile.

"I'm always the guinea pig." Colin looked around the gym floor.

"More like the canary in the coal mine." Matias gave Colin a shoulder-punch that looked more like a caress. If these guys weren't gay, every small interaction of theirs at least revealed the intimacy of their relationship.

"Canary?" Colin asked. His face looked as confused as it must've been if he'd ever stepped into a Gold's Gym. "Like a bird?"

"Since you're blond," Duke said to Colin while sending a small, cheesy wink to Matias. "Get up on the shoulder press now."

"Sure!" Colin nodded. His smile was too cocky. He jumped up on the machine's seat like he was about to ride off on his beautiful horse. "How high does this thing go?" Colin glanced behind him at the weight settings.

"Three hundred," Matias said before Duke could answer. Matias's face looked like an *LOL* emoji as he said the *three hundred*.

"Let's start with a few reps at twenty pounds." Duke walked over to the weight settings. "Then we'll see how you do and whether you want the weight higher."

"Don't insult me now." Colin shook his head as if twenty pounds wasn't worth his time.

"Not an insult." Duke tried to look particularly nonthreatening. "Every athlete starts out at the low weight settings, then—"

"Start me at a hundred fifty." Colin punctuated his request with a tongue-snap and a glance back at the weight settings bar. "Pounds."

"This is just a little fitness evaluation, not the Olympics." Duke laughed at Colin a little nervously. There was really no point to the kid humiliating himself in front of his trainer Duke and his body-double Matias.

"Yeah, I'm your client here." Colin nodded.

"Alright man." Duke sighed. He set the weight to a hundred fifty. He could've set it lower and Colin never would've known, but that would've established the wrong precedent for their relationship. Trainer and client needed to be honest with each other. Always.

"Here we go!" Colin lifted his arms and wriggled his fingers over the lift handles as if he were an Olympic athlete.

"Just don't push too hard." Duke patted the part of Colin's smooth, muscular arm just below the sleeve of his t-shirt. His skin was warm and innocent, childlike. "You're not supposed to be at a hundred fifty, I'm reminding you. So don't overexert yourself."

"Alright, here we go!" Colin shouted out again, still hovering his hands over the handle grips.

"He thinks he's Rocky." Duke sighed and shook his head like a trainer who'd seen it all. Duke's job was to make sure the Rocky types stroked their cartoonish masculine egos and had their fun without injuring themselves.

"Rocky? Colin's more like cocky," Matias stage-whispered to Duke loudly enough for Colin to hear. A bald-headed dude over on the leg press looked over and grinned.

"Gym banter. Good start." Duke nodded reassuringly. "So Colin, you wanna lift?"

"I was just waiting for you to get out of the way." Colin's grin was probably sarcastic. He seemed like the kind of trust-fund kid who at least had some self-awareness and could laugh at his own ridiculousness.

"Well, we're out of the way!" Matias shouted out. He clapped his big meaty hands together the same way Duke did to provide his clients with encouragement.

Colin inhaled. He spat on one hand, then the other one.

"FYI, for the future." Duke sighed. "Don't spit. It's against gym rules. We'll have to sanitize. Once again, you are not actually Rocky." Duke couldn't help but smile.

"Cocky," Matias whispered again.

Colin nodded to Duke and Matias, as if taking notice of the general din of a crowd of cheering fans while not bothering with the specifics of they were saying to him. He adjusted his hands on the machine's handlebars. He half-closed his eyes. And growled, pushing up against the handles. The more Colin pushed, the more the handles didn't move.

"Alright, man." Duke nodded in acknowledgment of Colin's valiant effort to lift a hundred fifty pounds. "Good try. I can decrease the weight for you now."

Colin eased up on the handlebars. "I can lift it. I'm strong enough. Don't stop me."

"If you really want." Duke shrugged. He kind of didn't give a fuck. It was his eighteen bucks an hour no matter what the clients were doing, even if it was a one-percenter millennial pushing and grunting against a weight he couldn't move. The only worry was if clients thought they weren't getting much out of their hundred dollars per hour per person.

"Go for it, Sisyphus!" Matias shouted out.

"Did you just call me a sissy-fuss?" Colin's face pouted into exaggerated rage.

"No, I mean the Roman god—" Matias looked at Colin with pity.

"Greek, not Roman." A triumphant smile broke across Colin's face. "And he was a disgraced king being punished by the gods, not a god himself."

"Sorry." Matias shrugged.

"I went to private school, as you keep reminding me." Colin snapped his tongue again and flashed a shit-eating grin. "It does have its benefits."

Duke stepped in between Colin and Matias. It didn't feel quite like he was interrupting them; it felt more like stepping into their shared light. "Can we switch from Greeks and Romans to weightlifting please?"

"Right!" Colin said. "Let me lift this thing!" Colin leaned his head back and again rested his hands on the handlebars.

As Colin pushed against the handlebars he tensed his face into a look of extreme consternation. Drops of sweat seemed to be pouring out of his pores on sight. He was actually trying to show off a bit harder than most out-of-shape guys did on their first session.

"Icandoit!" Colin grunted through clenched teeth. He pushed against the bar again. He breathed in and out quickly. His forearms quivered.

"You can do it, Colin." Matias was the calm coach-like figure in encouraging Colin's Rocky fantasies. Duke would've joined in, but he didn't want to say Colin could do it when clearly Colin couldn't.

"I!" Colin grunted. "I!" It looked as if there was some vanishingly small chance of Colin actually moving the hundred fifty pound weight. It wasn't a superhuman amount of weight. But it was still beyond Colin's ability. "I—"

Colin let go of the bar. He hadn't lifted it at all, so it didn't have any distance to fall.

Colin's pretty-boy face turned to panic. He ducked his head under the machine and sprinted away from it, back toward the locker room.

"The fuck?" Matias said. It sounded more like a statement than a question.

"My educated guess here would be—" Duke had seen it all before, especially from macho dudes who'd just eaten a big macho meal before overexerting at the gym.

"Hold on." Matias took a beeping phone out of his pocket. "Urgent message from Colin."

Those two had their own urgent-messaging system. They were like Batman and Robin. Except purportedly straight.

"Do you guys sell—" Matias's face broke into a half-embarrassed, half-mischievous grin. "Do you guys, Biscayne Fitness, do you guys sell, like, workout shorts and pants and underwear?"

"Yeah, we do." Duke nodded. It was pretty obvious what had happened. It wasn't uncommon among untrained dudes trying to show off. "Let me guess. Colin had a big lunch before coming over here?"

"Yeah. We ate at Blue Collar." Matias's smile was a little bit guilty. "Loaded burgers and stuff. Like an hour before we came over here."

"Alright, alright." Duke shrugged. "I've heard of that place, Blue Collar, from some of my clients who like to eat there."

"Yeah, Blue Collar's pretty awesome, isn't it?" Matias's eyes lit up. The kid obviously loved to eat. The mention of that restaurant

24

had probably made him forget all about his shitstained buddy cowering in the locker room. "Crowded though."

"Can't say I've eaten there." Duke shrugged. He eyed the gym's in-house cafe, where he also couldn't afford to eat, but where the employees usually saved him a few unsold chicken wraps at the end of the day. "I'm a bit too, you know, blue collar to afford Blue Collar."

"Huh." Matias looked puzzled. "I hate to pry, but dude, two hundred bucks an hour and you can't afford Blue Collar? I don't even know anybody who makes that much."

"Who am I?" Duke asked, grinning.

"Umm. Duke? The trainer?"

"Right."

"And who do you pay your two hundred bucks an hour to?" Duke seldom had to explain this point to his clients — the basic fact of the exploitation of labor, or of the boss's markup, or the pimp's cut, and the fact that Duke didn't take home that money they paid the club for training — but Matias was young.

"Uh, Biscayne Fitness?" Matias looked puzzled. Then his face lit up in sudden recognition. "Oh! I see. They don't pass on that money to you."

"They hardly pass on any of it to me," Duke whispered. "Anyway. You should go buy some new pants for your buddy. The clothing shop is just under the escalator there. We can start the session again once he's all clean and dressed. I'll get the cleaning crew to sanitize the machine."

"Yeah." Matias looked up at the skylights in the ceiling: the smoky orange of Miami at dusk and the sun setting over the swamps and trailer parks off to the west where Duke had grown up.

"You guys, you and Colin, are really great at taking care of each other." Duke surprised himself by how openly he'd blurted it out. He'd thought it, but it wasn't meant for public release. It was released now, and he had to roll with it. "It's just nice to see that."

"Yeah. We watch out for each other. I mean, we got thrown together as college roommates, and then we just stuck together, even when Colin moved off-campus, and even after we graduated." Matias looked into Duke's eyes. His words sounded like a confession. "It's like, it's like family, it's better than family. Colin is great. He's an idiot sometimes, but he's great."

"Yeah. That's awesome." Duke tried not to envy. "Hey go get him some new pants and we'll start training again."

"Yeah." Matias walked off.

If his buddy Colin had even a single gay cell in him, he must've noticed that meaty steak of an ass.

Better than anything served at Blue Collar. Duke couldn't afford it either. Colin certainly could.

Three

"The fuck?" Matias stared at the figure slumped on the garage floor. Colin didn't seem to be able to provide any explanation. "Isn't that—"

"Our trainer?" Colin squinted into the corner of the parking garage, behind a row of parked SUVs.

"He probably had a tough workout or something? Or had a few to drink afterward?" Matias shook his head. There were reasonable explanations for why their trainer Duke was sleeping on the floor in a parking garage below Biscayne Fitness. There weren't many of them. "The fuck. What the fuck."

Colin's eyes suddenly opened wide in concern. "Don't tell him we're using the gym's parking validation."

"I don't think he cares." Sometimes Matias's job was putting things in perspective to Colin. Whatever circumstances had put Duke on that concrete parking-garage floor, they would concern Duke more than Colin leaving his Tesla in the Biscayne Fitness garage beyond his gym stay.

"Duke." Colin wasn't shouting it, but he wasn't exactly whispering. Still, Duke didn't budge.

Matias lay his hand on Colin's shoulder in gentle reprimand. "Don't yell at him across the garage, man. Let's come up and see what he's up to."

"Yeah." Colin put his Tesla remote fob back in his pocket. They weren't getting in the Tesla anytime soon. This wasn't going to be just a thirty-second greeting of a familiar acquaintance in a parking garage. "He doesn't seem like a drinker," Colin said, still squinting in Duke's direction.

"And you were able to ascertain that from what exactly?" Matias said, shaking his head with just the slightest, barely perceptible eye-roll. "A one-hour training session? At the outset of which you shat your pants?"

"Don't roll your eyes at me like that." Colin snapped his tongue. "My uncle drank too much. I know the type."

27

"Yeah?" Matias sighed as they walked toward the yellow-painted wall that supported Duke's sleep-slouch. "You think every alcoholic is CEO of First Miami Bank and gets his nightly drunken penis-hunting exploits published on the front page of the Herald?"

"My uncle's homosexuality was never proven." Colin suddenly sounded defensive. "Anyway, Duke just seems like a healthy, healthy kind of—"

They stepped up to drooling Duke sleeping propped against the wall. Colin had actually been right. That didn't look like a blackout-drunk sleep, and Duke really did not look like a drunk.

Matias crouched down next to Duke. He lay his hand on Duke's bare arm and spoke to him gently. "Hey, man. What's up?"

Duke woke up. He was beaming a smile. "Hey guys! Colin! Matias! What's up?"

"Umm." Matias leaned in to smell for booze on Duke's breath. There wasn't any.

"Yeah, what's up, guys?" Duke was fake-perky. And he definitely wasn't drunk. "I thought you left the gym a long time ago!"

"Uh, we were just wondering." Matias stopped himself from finishing the thought.

"We were wondering why you're sleeping on the floor of the parking garage." Colin seemed to have no compunction about finishing Matias's statement. Maybe Colin didn't know that someone might have been embarrassed to have been caught in that position.

"Oh yeah. You know. Tough workout. Just took a break here." Duke propped his head up in his hands. He'd obviously been sleeping pretty deeply.

"I don't want to pry, but is there anything we can do to help you?" Matias was echoing what he'd always heard every counselor and other professionally concerned person say. Except it was *we* whose help he offered. Matias more or less couldn't do shit without Colin, at least if the shit that needed doing involved spending any money.

"Oh, I'm fine, guys. I just—" Duke's face was turning more red.

"You need a ride home?" Matias asked. "We've got our car here. Colin's car." When Matias wasn't watching himself, he always fell into that habit of calling it *their* car. It made him and Colin look like a married gay couple. Which they most definitely weren't.

"I'm fine, really." Duke was shaking his head awake.

"Really, no problem to drive you home. Or wherever you need to go. Or whatever." Colin flashed his Tesla fob at Duke, as if Duke had questioned Colin's access to transportation.

"I think he knows you've got a car, dude." Matias tapped Colin's hand that held the car remote. Colin put it away in his pocket like his hand had been scalded by Matias's touch.

"You're just gonna sleep here?" Matias asked Duke.

"Y- Yeah." Duke's reply wasn't even evasive.

"Is this where you normally sleep?" Matias crouched down again next to Duke. Colin followed along, crouching alongside Matias.

"Yeah. It's no big deal. I mean, it's not what it sounds like. Or not what it looks like. I'll be fine." Duke gave the most forced, artificial smile ever.

"We have a place. A condo." Colin was doing the *we* thing again. It was Colin who had the condo. But Matias had always lived there with him, so there was kind of a *we*. Matias was eternally grateful for that. "It's like ten minutes away. You're welcome to stay."

"Ah, no." Duke's forced smile stayed glued on his face. It looked like someone had Photoshopped a smile onto his otherwise sad face. It didn't match his otherwise unhappy expression. "I mean, I'm used to this. I'm fine here."

"So, like — this is where you normally stay?" Colin asked. Colin did sound like he was auditioning for the reality TV show *Trust Fund Kid Meets A Homeless Person* — but Matias didn't actually know any homeless people either.

Duke sighed wearily. "My clients come early in the morning and late in the evening. Any apartment I can afford is at least an hour

29

and a half away. So when I had an apartment, I was getting home from work at one A.M., going back out to work at four A.M. And I needed a car and insurance and gas and toll money. It wasn't worth it, being broke to pay the rent on a place I was in for three hours a day."

"That's rough. Sorry." Matias lay his hand on Duke's muscled forearm for a good three seconds. It was more than a momentary pat. After that revelation from Duke, it felt like they were closer than just a momentary pat.

"It's not so bad. It's a sleeping place like a sleeping place. When I'm asleep I don't even know." Duke's eyes darted around, as if looking for more reasons he could name to justify sleeping on a concrete floor. "And I'm always close to work. And I can use work's shower and bathroom."

"Dude." Colin flashed his best, most socially outgoing smile. He was working hard, obviously. He was making progress on the talking-to-people thing. "Our place is way too empty. Seriously. Just come over and sleep. It's really way, way too empty now. It's four bedrooms and a balcony and shit."

"And shit?" Duke looked at Colin knowingly.

"Not literally. I mean—" Colin stumbled through his words. "Not literally shit."

"I'm just teasing you, duder." Duke laughed, genuinely. "A dude who sleeps on a concrete floor is still allowed to tease, right?"

"Yeah. But you're not that dude anymore, ok, duder?" Colin smiled.

"It's fine, guys." Duke shook his head. "I need to get to work in the morning anyway. I sold my car when I gave up my apartment. I sent my son to private school— ah—"

"You have a son?" Matias asked.

"Not living with me. Long story." Duke shook his head. He definitely didn't look like he wanted to talk about it.

"Our place is like a fifteen-minute walk from here." Colin pointed off in some random direction with his eyes. "Or a five-minute jog, for you."

"Or a one-hour drive, for Colin during rush hour." Matias precision-dropped a play-punch on Colin's shoulder.

"I never like to impose on people." Duke's head-shake looked like he was in pain. "I never accept anything. But you know—"

"Just come stay with us. Even if just tonight." Matias stood up, then held his hand out for Duke. Of course it was symbolic. There was nothing wrong with offering someone a helping hand, and nothing wrong with accepting it.

"I can't even begin to say how grateful—" Duke stood up, after a steadying tug on Matias's hand. He was so much bigger standing up. He hadn't even seemed that huge in the land of giants that was the Biscayne Fitness gym floor. In the parking garage, wearing only his t-shirt and shorts and running shoes, surrounded only by parked cars, Duke was a giant himself.

Duke glanced behind a column and lifted out a big blue backpack. "I hope that fits in your car's trunk."

"My car even has a back seat." Colin held up his key fob again. He thought that back seat made him more down-to-earth than most of his family friends, who tooled around in Ferraris and the like.

Matias glanced at Colin: "Now you can thank me for making you buy the Tesla instead of the Aston Martin."

"Matias keeps me in line." Colin clicked his tongue and glanced off to the red Tesla parked in the corner.

"I can help you with your bag." Matias sounded like a hotel bellman.

"At least let me be the muscleman here." Duke grinned. It was another real smile from him.

"Sure, sure." Matias clapped Duke's full backpack. "Just trying to be hospitable."

Duke sighed. "You've been — way more than hospitable. You've been great already."

"That's nice and all—" Matias said. "But— shotgun!"

"I guess you got it." Duke nodded at Matias. "This time."

Duke bent down to clear his head below the car's roofline. He contorted himself into the Tesla's back seat. It was a roomy enough seat for regular-sized adults, but Duke was a lot bigger than regular-sized.

Four

"Wow." Duke had promised himself not to say that when he saw Colin's condo. He had his dignity. He'd lived in downtown Miami, even if only on a concrete floor in downtown Miami.

He wasn't some ingenue who'd never seen a high-end condo. But there he was, saying "wow," like a gaping hayseed.

Miami's one-percenters had their condos. Duke had seen their insides, at least on the internet. He had prepared himself to see an expanse of space, wall-mounted LED TVs, and Sub-Zero appliances.

He wasn't prepared for floor-to-ceiling ocean views, balconies with more floor space than his former apartment, and pizza boxes and takeout food litter everywhere. Apparently even high-end condos weren't self-cleaning.

In its airy, uncrowded expanse, Colin and Matias's condo looked like the gym floor at Biscayne Fitness. Random pieces of furniture apparently had been dropped in by an interior designer, or maybe a parent, and never used since. Huge TVs hung on the wall. The ambient smell was a mix of ocean air plus whatever detergents the maid used, whatever air fresheners they had around, and for the most part, a mix of the familiar smells of pizza, cookies, and beer.

"Feel free to look outside." Colin said it almost anticlimactically, motioning Duke toward the patio doors. "Just push the touch button on the glass."

Colin's advice was helpful. Duke might've destroyed the door otherwise, trying to slide it apart manually.

Duke walked toward the city lights visible outside and the glass doors separating him from the outdoors. He touched his finger to the beige nipple on the door's edge and the doors electrically parted. Nocturnal Miami salt air swept over him like an ocean wave.

He stepped out onto the balcony. Flickering beachfront hotel lights stretched up to Broward and down to South Beach. The beaches themselves were mostly clear at night. It was only the true vagrants out there at night: those who didn't have even a garage floor to sleep on.

"Pretty quiet up here." Even at night, Miami at ground level had its normal sonic signature of car horns, motorcycle engines, blasting radios, and drunk tourists. In the rarefied space of that condo balcony, Duke was in the middle of the city, but floating above it.

"At midnight, we hang out in the hot tub a lot and look over the city." Matias sounded wistful when he said it. Not many twenty-three-year-olds could manage wistfulness. But not many twenty-three-year-olds sat around in a hot tub looking out over Miami.

"At the health club downstairs?" Duke asked.

"Uh, yeah, there's a hot tub there too. But we have one of our own up here." Matias's thumb vaguely pointed to another side of the condo. "And the view's better up here."

"Oh. Oh!" Duke did his best not to act too surprised or impressed. He nodded his best everyday nod.

"So —" Colin cleared his throat to make his presence known. "Shall we recess to our respective bedrooms, then reconvene here in fifteen minutes for hot-tubbing?"

"I think so." Duke couldn't help but smile. "If you can show me my respective bedroom."

"That one's mine and that one's Matias's." Colin pointed with two fingers like pistols at two doors, then moved his pointing to the two other doors. "Those other two bedrooms are free. You can inspect and choose."

"Is there a goat behind one of the doors?" Duke asked. Colin looked at him in mild disbelief. Too young, or hadn't watched enough TV reruns while home alone in a trailer park, or most likely, all of the above.

"I got that joke!" Matias waved his hand up in the air like an eager student. "My parents learned English from *Let's Make a Deal*."

"Good job." Duke nodded. "You and them both."

"Yeah." Colin nodded, in half-comprehension.

"Not to spoil the moment or anything." Duke sighed and looked down at the floor, then touched his hand to the pocket of his gym shorts, the one that held his very thin wallet. "But how much do I owe you guys for bedding down here? I've only got a few hundred on me. I have a feeling this costs a bit more than my usual Motel Six."

Duke had no compunction about charging, or letting his employer charge, Colin and Matias for fitness training. Colin and Matias could just as well charge Duke for room rental.

"Only one request, alright?" Colin held up his finger in the air.

"Yeah, what can I do for you? A tap dance? A little soft-shoe?" Duke tapped his foot back and forth on the hardwood floor.

"No tapdance." Colin snapped a finger in the air. He was the choreographer now. "Serious for a second now. Don't try to pay for staying here, alright? Don't even bring it up, please. Seriously. I just have a thing against it. I can accept money for work or whatever, but just don't mention paying to stay here, ok?"

"Uh. Yeah." Duke had to overcome all his instincts about never accepting anything for free, because the most expensive things always start out free. "I mean — I can help you guys with your fitness or something? I can clean this place up, for one."

"Our place is a fucking sty." Matias sniffed at the air and made a face of disgust at bad smells that were most likely imaginary. All Duke could smell was the fresh ocean air. "Feel free to clean up as you wish, but not any more than either of us does. You're not the janitor. I mean we get a maid up here every week or so, if we don't forget."

Colin cleared his throat and announced: "Enough with the prolegomena."

"The what?" Duke asked. *Prolegomena* sounded like the name of a microbe that lives on gym equipment.

"*Prolegomena.*" Matias rolled his eyes, then rolled his eyes some more for more effect. "The word means introductions or lead-ins. Colin got that word from his dad and likes to show it off."

"A lot of guys inherit something long from their dad and like to show it off." Duke shrugged.

"You've definitely got the right sense of humor for living here." Colin gave Duke a thumbs-up. "Our brains pretty much stopped developing in junior high."

"I'm not sure if I even got as far as that." Duke shrugged. The reality was that Duke already had adult problems in junior high. He hadn't had much of a childhood, nor the luxury of teenage years spent joking around about dick sizes. But that wasn't something to bring up in this idyllic oceanfront condo moment.

"Am I recalling correctly—" Colin spoke grandiosely to Matias and, by extension, to Duke standing near him. "That the three of us were preparing for a little hot-tub splish-splash? That we were somehow unjustly delayed? But that we should return to that path forthright?"

"If your dad wasn't a senator, Colin." Matias shook his head with a shit-eating grin. "If your dad wasn't a senator, I'd think these verbal ejaculations of yours were abnormal."

"Your dad's a senator?" Duke did his best to be nonchalant. That was the way to act like just one of the guys. Is your dad a senator? Do you have a jet? Will it rain next Wednesday? Mundane sorts of questions, no big deal.

"Um." Colin shrugged. "As long as he keeps winning elections, yeah, I guess he's a senator."

"Senator Warren Warner of Florida!" Matias's voice suddenly sounded remarkably adult.

Colin smirked and nodded at Matias. "You've got a job at C-SPAN if medical school doesn't work out."

"I actually like your dad." Duke wasn't lying. He wasn't going to come out and admit the reason he liked Warren Warner — because Duke was a flaming homosexual and Warren Warner was a flaming supporter of homosexuals — but he could say he liked him. It wasn't wrong to vote for a politician, was it? That was how they won elections.

"Yeah, that's cool. Most people like my dad." Colin took a step toward the patio and stared off into the dark ocean. "Or at least hate him less than they hate his opponents. He wins elections. That's what matters."

"Man, he really stood up for—" Duke started to say. He cut himself off because most of the things Senator Warner had bravely stood up for were pretty fucking gay.

"Hey this isn't fucking C-SPAN!" Matias clapped his hands into the air. "Go to your bedrooms, take your showers, come out here and let's continue the conversation in the hot tub!"

"Yeah. Before we run out of time." Colin's grin oozed smug satisfaction.

"Run out of time?" Duke asked. Did private hot tubs have operating hours or something?

"It's a running joke we've got." Matias sounded almost wistful. "Up here, it's like time stops still. We're never out of time for anything." Matias half-shrugged at Duke and then at Colin, and retreated to what must've been his bedroom: a heavy off-white bedroom door at the end of the hallway.

Colin jauntily stepped toward the next door on the hallway. He beamed like he was about to open a Christmas present.

Two more doors lay in front of Duke. Sure, the guys had told him to inspect the two free bedrooms and figure out which one he prefers. That just sounded tacky. It would've been not just looking a gift horse in the mouth; it would've been comparing two very expensive gift horses' mouths to check with had the shinier teeth. Or something like that. He was never very good at metaphors.

He pushed open the door closer to Colin and Matias's rooms. Inside was a bed, perfectly made. It wasn't king size. The lack of stuff, crap, chairs and condom wrappers and dirty socks in that bedroom made judging scale difficult. It was like judging the picture of a cock taken with no background. There were definitely floor-to-ceiling windows, letting in the night's sparkling blackness as a counterpoint to the room's bright white walls and hyper-bright lighting.

A touchscreen. A control panel. Buttons. Duke wasn't going to make an idiot of himself by trying to open the glass door with his mere hands. He knew to click through a few menus. The balcony doors opened, like the Red Sea parting. Then they closed. There was music. Pandora. There were some buttons with abbreviations he'd never heard of. And the bed was huge.

When Duke lay back in that bed, his body went catatonic. He didn't want to move anywhere. It wasn't even a matter of it being better than a concrete floor or a Starbucks sofa. It wasn't just that it was better than any apartment Duke had ever lived in. It was better than any bed Duke could have ever imagined. It was like sinking into the Everglades, on his back, sinking in and never wanting to leave.

Duke shut his eyes. For just a second.

"Dude!" That was Matias's bassy voice just outside the bedroom, and definitely Matias's hairy fist banging on the door. "You've been in there for an hour!"

Even through the bedroom door, Colin clearing his throat was a distinctive sound. "There will be time later for self-abuse!" Colin announced while clearing his throat. Duke wasn't jacking off, but just the sound of Colin clearing his throat was sexy enough to give him a bit of an itch.

"Yeah, man." Matias's more mature voice rose again. "You can jack off later. Shower and get ready for the hot tub for now."

"Oh yeah. I just fell asleep." Duke lifted his head from the all-consuming vortex of softness that was the down pillow. "I'll shower and join you guys in a minute."

"For real now, alright?" Colin sounded harmlessly testy, like a frat boy telling a bartender to hurry up. "No more naps!"

Leaving that bed required superhuman willpower and Herculean strength. Duke did it. He marched to the shower — the luxurious, high-pressure,   everywhere-spraying,   toiletries-filled shower that could've detained him for another hour.

But he had places to go. He toweled himself off, as silly as it was before going hot-tubbing, and put on his same gym shorts and t-shirt. He didn't have a swimsuit per se, but those gym shorts were clean and good enough to wear in a pool.

More knocks at the door. Duke was fully dressed and ready to go. He pulled it open, to the sight of Colin and Matias, shirtless.

Colin's muscles wound around his torso like armor. His body was an exercise in minimalism: every ounce was lithe, lean muscle. His skin was lightly tanned, with no tan lines on the arms, like the body of a man who always went out naked.

Matias was only an inch or two taller than Colin, but he dwarfed him overall. He was all body mass. His huge pecs and triceps counterbalanced the dad-bod aspects of his furry chest and paunchy belly.

"Done staring?" Matias grinned like he wasn't unaccustomed to attention.

"Oh. I wasn't staring or anything." Duke wasn't much of a liar. "Yeah. I mean. Uh. Let's go to the tub."

Colin led the way, his lithe legs stretching and undulating with every step. Even his bare feet were tight and graceful. Barefoot, he moved across the hardwood floor like a ballet dancer.

Matias was Colin's backup and cleanup, the heavy artillery. Duke could only imagine what kind of dick Matias was packing under his basketball shorts — even if it was unprofessional of him to think that way about his personal-training clients.

They led Duke to the other side of the condo, rooms and windows and balconies he hadn't yet seen. Chlorine smell blew in from somewhere, along with the sounds of bubbling water.

Colin pointed with his entire palm. That sliding glass door was already open: a narrower balcony, off to the side, that held a hot tub. From inside the condo, the hot tub resembled a neon-lit UFO floating in the sky outside the window.

"Ahhhh." Colin exhaled as if he'd just come home from a long day at work. Of course he hadn't.

If Colin had the money to live a life of leisure, then so what? Duke wasn't fond of envy or of begrudging those who had more than he did. Most anybody had more than Duke did — especially his clients at the gym.

"Yeah, aahhhh." Matias grinned. He stuck a finger in the hot water and nodded his approval. Somehow the gesture looked sexual, as if he was about to suck his finger dry after having poked it into the hot water.

"Smell that chlorine, dude?" Colin asked. "We keep it pretty strong in the hot tub."

"It can bleach your clothes." Matias eyed Duke up and down, as if Duke was transgressing some unspoken rule by wearing a t-shirt and shorts.

"We've got a rule around here." Colin grinned, a little bit salaciously. "We've always got a sale going on at the hot tub."

"Yeah." Matias snapped his own waistband against his belly.

"Sale?" Duke asked, a little bit wide-eyed. It was turning into some sort of weird ritual.

"Sale." Colin nodded. He slipped both hands under his waistband and slid his shorts down. His long pasty white dick flew out of his shorts, semi-erect. "The sale is, all clothes, one hundred percent off."

"Yeah, it's just us up here." Matias pulled his shorts down, exposing his filet mignon of an ass. It was like pulling a sheath off a mountain.

Duke couldn't help but gulp at the totally unexpected sight of Matias's bulbous ass. It was that much better in reality than Duke had chance to imagine it in the few seconds he'd allowed to consider what Matias's ass might look like.

Still breathing hard, Duke forced himself to look away from Matias's ass. That only brought him to the sight of Matias's low-hanging nuts. Matias's big firm balls looked like they could fuck an army.

Colin raised his leg to step into the tub. His leg was shaped like the Mona Lisa: a study in perfectly beautiful proportions. His legs, his ass, and his freshly scrubbed, pasty white dick disappeared under the hot tub bubbles. Colin sat down and leaned his back in some sort of beatific hot-water ecstasy.

Matias turned his bare ass toward Duke. He stepped into the tub backwards. Why did he need to do that? The meaty mounds of his ass cheeks disappeared into the water like sinking sex glaciers. He kneeled down on the hot tub floor, face toward Colin, and splashed water on his shoulders and face.

Matias got into position across from Colin. Then he corrected himself: "We have a guest today. How could I forget?" He slid down to the tub's side to prepare for a three-man equilateral triangle.

"Yeah. A hundred percent off." Duke said it nonchalantly. He lifted up his shirt over his head. Everybody wanted to see his muscles. There was nothing new in that.

Nobody expected the scar on his chest, but he could always explain it as an old MMA injury. That sounded a lot manlier than having been gay-bashed in South Beach.

"Do you even lift, bro?" Matias called out to the sight of Duke's muscle.

"Just a little." Duke laughed. Modestly. He pulled down his shorts and stepped out of them.

"Holy shit, man." Matias laughed and shook his head at Duke's dick. "Forget about lifting. Was your dad a horse?"

Colin squinted at Duke's crotch. "Maybe it's professional equipment on loan from John Holmes."

"Don't worry." Duke stepped into the hot tub. "It shrinks down to a respectable size in hot water."

The water was hot, as hot as it could be without becoming uncomfortable. Bubbles and foam erupted to the surface. It looked like a colorless volcano, and Duke's body was parting it as he stepped in.

This tub was that much smaller than big gym tubs. With three male asses perched on it, the bench was downright snug. If Duke didn't keep his feet perfectly planted on the floor, they'd drift over to touch Colin's and Matias's feet.

"Is that a manly gym scar?" Matias's eyes were fixed on the top of Duke's chest. The attack had been almost a decade back, but the physical scar was still there. The psychological scar, maybe. Duke stuck a bandage or surgical tape over the gash if he knew he was going to be out shirtless. But if he had the opportunity to explain it away as an MMA fight scar, that was even better than a bandage.

"It's from my MMA days." Duke stared nonchalantly into the foamy water and three sets of legs and dicks.

"No, really." Matias smiled.

"Seriously. I used to fight MMA." Duke looked at Matias and nodded. "No joke."

It was true that Duke used to do MMA fighting. It was even true that he'd gotten the scar during his MMA days. That the scar it was from some knife-carrying gay-bashers in a Miami alley and not from an MMA fight — let them contemplate that part themselves.

"Oh wow. We're getting trained by an MMA dude." Colin lazily raised his hands above the waterline and gave two thumbs up.

"I guess you don't do MMA anymore?" Matias asked. "I wouldn't want to pick up any more scars like that."

"This kind of scar isn't a big deal." Duke splashed hot water on his scar and slapped it to show the world how much it wasn't a big deal. "I didn't quit MMA for that."

"So why'd you quit? Couldn't stand the attention?" Matias smiled, with an obvious stare at Duke's shoulders and pecs.

"Too many knocks to the head." Duke finger-tapped his forehead to demonstrate. "Not good for long-term. Too many of the MMA guys end up brain-damaged. And I've got a son to take care of."

"Yeah, you mentioned your son." Colin looked at Duke expectantly, like he wanted to hear more. Duke didn't mind indulging Colin's curiosity. Sam was Duke's favorite conversation topic anyway.

"I've never met him. I never saw his mother after we conceived him."

"That's tough, man." Matias grimaced. Had the kid ever known tough? Had he ever had to sleep on a concrete floor and suck dicks to feed a son he'd never see? It didn't matter though. Most people hadn't.

They could still feel something for Duke. Their empathy was still valid.

"Thanks." Duke nodded, with a little bit of the longing for Sam — and for a normal, loving life — weighing upon him.

"I'm sorry to intrude." Colin sounded so much like his famous father. "His mom was your girlfriend?"

"Uh." Duke laughed nervously. "She was my girlfriend for an hour."

"Oh I see." Colin was trying hard not to be embarrassed by the subject.

"Strip club." Duke nodded at Colin and Matias, as if they might have never heard of a strip club. "I was in a low place, trying to get something out of myself, trying to change myself, trying to be — trying to be something I'm not. Anyway I had sex with her and a month later she called me saying she's pregnant."

"And she wanted to keep the baby?" Colin's face and voice had turned remarkably mature in his line of questioning. Maybe that too was his father's influence.

"Well, the other option—" Duke shook his head. "The abortion thing was not going to be an option. She was against it too. So I just told her I'd do what I could to help out. Money. Money, money, and money."

"Just money? You don't see your son at all?" Colin's questions came as sharp as his blue eyes staring at Duke. Colin would grow up to be one of those second-generation senators, definitely. There was a razor edge to his twinky ditziness.

"She's dating some dude. She doesn't want me involved at all. I don't know where the guy thinks Sam comes from." Duke looked out, northward along the coast, up toward Broward, where eight-year-old Sam was somewhere. "They live in Fort Lauderdale. But I'm persona non grata. I just stay away."

"You've never met your son?" Matias's face tensed in pain. "Not even once?"

"Only in my dreams. A lot." Duke stared down into the hot bubbling water. It definitely would not have been a good time to cry. "Otherwise, no. I've never met Sam. Not for the eight years he's been around. Can we talk about something else please?" Duke smiled plaintively. He was there to be the cool fitness trainer, not the quivering triggered fountain of tears that talking about Sam always made him into.

"I'm the social media coordinator of my dad's reelection campaign!" Colin announced, appropriately apropos of nothing, just as Duke had requested. "And Matias is preparing for the MCAT."

"MCAT. That's hardcore." Duke nodded all his respect Matias's way. He mentally kept sentry on his tear ducts, should thoughts of Sam suddenly return.

"MMA is a lot more hardcore than MCAT." Matias laughed. "Like, we don't have to kick anybody's ass on the MCAT. Just have to kick some equations' asses."

"Speaking of kicking asses." Colin, unlike Matias, still sounded like he was in a perfectly serious congressional inquiry mode. "Other than general fitness — sometime, when you have a chance, can you teach us some self-defense? Like how to protect ourselves? Not get our asses kicked in some dark alley?"

"I can teach you the world's best self-defense technique right now." Duke sighed wearily and shook his head. "Walk away from any fights. Run away from any fights, actually. Just don't get involved in that stuff." Duke shook his head some more. He punctuated the seriousness of his advice with a few seconds of eye contact with Colin, then Matias.

"Yeah, but didn't you, in MMA—" Colin looked like he believed to have found an inconsistency in Duke's story.

"Yeah. That's a show." Duke shook his head. "MMA is entertainment. Fighting under spotlights in front of an audience, for sick bloodthirsty people's entertainment. Humans aren't any better now than in the Roman gladiator days."

"Didn't you enjoy it?" Colin asked.

"Uh, no." Duke exhaled deeply. How could anyone have enjoyed getting beaten up a few times every evening, for money that wasn't much better than minimum wage? "Would you enjoy getting punched and kicked for a cheering crowd?"

"No, but I'm a wuss." Colin smiled, genuinely.

"Yeah, so is everybody else with a brain. I was just as scared as you'd be"

"So you just did MMA to make money for your son?"

"Bingo." Duke patted the scar on his chest. "This scar is my reminder of him."

The scar did always remind Duke of Sam. That was true, but not in the way Duke was implying. Getting gay-bashed was what had sent him to a strip club, as if he could gain attraction to women through some practice, the same way he could gain strength through weight training. Those thugs knifing him in an alley had at least, indirectly, given him Sam.

"And now you're doing personal training to make money for your son." Matias sighed. "Money that you'd otherwise be spending on rent."

"Yeah, but no pity party needed." Duke shrugged. "It's my choice to sleep on a garage floor. Nobody is forcing me." Duke playfully splashed hot water on himself. "I could stop sending Sam money and move in with a roommate in Miami. Or I could go back to living two hours away in an apartment I could afford and getting an hour of sleep a night. But I choose to live the way I do."

"Past tense, I hope. Past tense." Colin shook his head.

Past tense? Were Duke's problems suddenly resolved? Were Miami apartments now free? Was Sam's private school now offering free tuition for children of self-hating homosexuals?

"I mean, I hope that's the end of you living on a fucking garage floor, man. I hope we can help you out here." Colin swept hot water on himself as if bathing himself in Duke's troubles.

"I really appreciate it. Thank you so much." Duke sank down with his chin in the water. During his brief stay, he could soak up all the warmth, the feeling of abundance, the sheer *normalcy* of staying with Colin and Matias. "But once I leave your condo — there's no magic new life appearing for me or anything."

"We're saying, like—" Colin looked over to Matias, as if he needed his approval. "Matias agrees with me, I'm sure. We're saying like you can stay with us. Permanently. Or a long time at least."

"No, no way." Duke was reacting impulsively to an offer of free help. It wasn't even that he didn't want to impose. Nobody would've let him impose in the first place. Any offer of "free" help was bound to end badly and leave Duke in an even worse place than he'd started.

Staying for a night or even two nights, fine: he could believe that was a free offer. Duke was enough of a novelty to be welcome for a night or two. He was the homeless man they'd brought in from the parking garage. Colin and Matias could make a great story of it when they met their real friends down at the craft beer pub or mustache waxery.

Beyond a couple of nights, though, nothing was free: not in this world and not in any other one.

"Seriously, dude." Matias shook his head. He lifted a thick, wet finger out of the bubbling water and pointed it at Duke. "You'll be a lot comfier here than on the garage floor. We're not gonna charge you anything. Shit, Colin hasn't been charging me anything."

"I haven't?" Colin laughed. "I'll have the accountants check on that." Colin glanced over into the condo, as if held an office full of green-visored accountants. Maybe it did.

"But Duke's such a nice guy," Colin said to Matias. "Even the accountants would want him to live here gratis."

Gratis. What twenty-something said *gratis*? A senator's son, maybe.

"Yeah. Really, dude." Matias made his hands into two fists, then pumped water into upward fountain streams. His smile opened into childlike glee. "Gratis."

"My worry is." Duke stared down into the water, at his dick — the dick that might very well be taken out of service if Duke abandoned his parking-garage charcuterie. "That by the time you tell me I've overstayed my welcome, it will already be too late. I'll have ruined my friendship with you. I won't have a fallback on the garage floor. I'll lose—" Of course he couldn't say he'd lose his little black book of paying cocksuckers "--I'll lose my survival skills, stuff like that."

Matias stretched his beefy arms outward like a floatplane's wings over the hot water. "Your implicit metaphor here is that you're a wild animal who'll become domesticized and then be unable to survive when released back into the wild? I mean that seems to be the model behind what you're saying."

Colin pointed his thumb at Matias. "Dude's a philosophy major. He won't let us mortals forget it."

Matias rolled his eyes, then pointed his finger directly at Colin. "Dude's a one-percenter, and never lets us mortals forget it!" Matias disappeared under the bubbling water and blew out some big breaths, bubbles running to the surface. Maybe Matias had kept his eyes open underwater. There was definitely a lot to see.

Colin watched Matias rise above the water and wipe his eyes dry. As soon as Matias looked at Colin, Colin asked him, "Did you see the Loch Ness Monster down there?"

"Two Loch Ness Monsters, dude." Matias nodded knowingly. He said it so familiarly that dicks were probably a running joke between them. How could they not have been? Two horny young dudes with nice bodies and big dicks, living together — if they had even a single gay gene between them, they would've been fucking like caffeinated rabbits already.

"Yeah, that's how rumors of the Loch Ness Monster start." Colin was making his best faux-thoughtful face. He looked like a teenager giving a report in history class. "Someone sees something really big. Tremendously huge." Colin spread his arms apart to purportedly show how big it was. "They see it underwater and they just don't know how to explain it." Colin smiled in mock wonder.

"Yeah?" Matias grinned. Then I saw one Loch Ness Monster, and one baby flobberworm." Matias broke out laughing, looking directly at Colin.

"Don't insult Duke's cock size like that." Colin grinned proudly. It was a somewhat clever reversal on his part.

"It's not opposites day, dude," Matias said through his eruption of laughter. "The Loch Ness Monster was definitely Duke's. Stand up, Duke. Seriously, I just wanna catch another view of that thing."

"Dude, no offense, but did you hear what you just said?" Colin asked Matias. "You want Duke to stand up so you can get a better look at his big dick?"

"Yeah, so what? Nothing wrong with a dude wanting to check out another dude's meat." Matias made a fast jerking-off gesture, his hand splashing the water.

Colin shook his head at Matias. "Whatever you say, Liberace."

"What's Liberace?" Matias asked.

"Shut up and enjoy the show," Colin said, like an impatient theater usher.

The show was on. Duke stood up. Hot water dribbled down his body and tickled his asscrack. His dick just hung there, with only the slightest hint of erectness to it. The bootleg Viagra he took every evening to stay hard through multiple disgusting encounters must've been wearing off.

If they wanted to see his cock, they were welcome to it, certainly. They wouldn't be the first men to fetishize the size of Duke's penis. At least Duke counted these guys as his friends, not just parking garage randoms who suck off and forget.

"Oh fuck, man. Fuck. Damn." Colin wiped his lip. He must've been drooling. "I was all laughing at you wanting to see that dick better, but shit, man. That's nice. Not just huge but just nice."

"Dude, did you just hear what you said?" Matias was laughing ecstatically, with high-pitched squeals. He must've relished the moral victory of not having been the only man in the tub who was eager to check out Duke's cock.

"Nothing wrong with curiosity." Duke ran his fingertip from the base of his dick all the way to the tip. It grew hard instantly.

Colin stared at Duke's now fully erect dick. "Jesus Christ."

Matias grinned. "Nah, Jesus wore a fig leaf."

Duke wrapped his right hand's fingers around his dick shaft and used his left hand to pull at his foreskin. Being uncut always felt special. Duke bounced his dick up and down in his hand. "And don't forget: unlike me, Jesus was circumcised."

"He was?" Colin stared wide-eyed again at Duke's ten inches.

"Yeah." Matias made a *snip-snip* gesture with his hands. "Levitical law and shit like that."

Colin nodded at Matias. "He's always the smart one."

Duke shrugged. "Both of you guys seem pretty smart." That was true, even if in different ways.

"Aw thanks, man." Colin nodded. "I gotta say though, Duke: around here, you're definitely the well-hung one."

"You guys are no flobberworms. It's cool." Duke gave two thumbs up.

"Nothing like what you're carrying." Colin shook his head and stared at Duke's erect dick pointing in his face. Maybe he even smacked his lips.

"Yeah?" Duke sat back on the hot rub's outside edge. His legs dangled in the water, his balls hung off the edge, and his dick pointed hopefully at the sky. "Let's see what you've got, then."

"I'm always up for a dick-waving contest." Matias laughed and shook his head. With a slightly pained look, he hopped up out of the water and sat on the tub's edge. Matias's thick uncut dick hung down like a full tube sock.

Good thing Duke was already hard. One look at Matias's veiny dick would've made him rock-hard. The secret would've been out, or at least Matias and Colin would've suspected something about his sexuality.

49

"Alright, just so nobody calls me a spoilsport." Colin took one step up and backward to stand on the hot tub's seat. His long, compactly lean dick swung up out of the water.

For some reason, Colin was rock hard. He sat down on the tub's edge.

"Shit." Duke shook his head. "Looks like we're building a fucking teepee."

A few hours past, he'd been sleeping on a concrete garage floor. Now, he was having a dick-showing contest with two dudes in a luxury condo, where he was apparently welcome to live for free. *Just don't fuck this up* was all Duke could tell himself.

"Except." Matias waved his half-hard dick in the air, the same way he'd usually wave his finger to illustrate a point. "Except Colin's side of the teepee won't meet building codes."

"Excuse me?" Colin was really a body-double for Senator Warner asking questions in a congressional hearing. He looked and even sounded just like him. Except Senator Warren Warner wasn't sitting naked on the edge of a hot tub and waving his hard dick around. "I do believe, in good faith, Matias, that that the length of my penile instrument exceeds the length of your penile instrument."

"Senator Colin Warner, may I offer a rebuttal?" Matias asked. They really looked like college kids at play, ornate titles and all — but then, they were just barely out of college.

"I'll take your rebuttal." Colin grinned, again very satisfied with his own wit.

"My rebuttal — and it's a big fat rebuttal — boldly challenges the relevance of penile length as a metric." Matias held his hands out in front of him like a lecturer making a point. His fat cock, which had grown erect, made more of a point. "Indeed, I propose a revolutionary alternate metric."

"Oh shit, man." Colin shook his head and waved his hand in front of his face. "I'm not wrapping measuring tape around my dick to measure how thick it is. Not that again."

"Nay!" Matias called out.

"What, you're gonna measure with your tongue?" Colin smirked.

"Nah, man." Matias shook his head sternly. "I'm not gonna measure dicks with my tongue. This isn't Congress."

"Whoa!" Duke yelled out viscerally. Not only were these two dudes sitting in a hot tub on top of Miami. They were also giving each other sick burns. This must've been the life — so distant in every way from everything Duke had ever known.

"Gentlemen. Call to order." Colin stood up on the hot tub's bench seat. "Please allow my colleague Matias to describe his proposal for evaluating our penile fortitude."

Hot water bubbled at his tight, toned, muscular calves. The rest of him was naked: pale flesh scorched just right by the sun, with enough muscle to suggest he'd done a sport in high school, but not an ounce more than that. His dick was the long, lean centerpiece, the representation of his whole physicality.

"Yes, old chap." Matias held an imaginary pipe to his lips and took a few imaginary puffs. "I dare say, old bean."

"Shit! You always fuck it up!" Colin winced. "This is supposed to be Congress, not the fucking House of Lords!"

"Oops." Matias shrugged. When he lifted his arms, hints of his underarm air peeked out from under his triceps. Sexy as fuck. "Anyway, I'm suggesting we measure dicks scientifically."

Colin snickered at Matias. "What, yours with an electron-scanning microscope?"

"Let's progress past the puerile humor and get to the meat of the question, shall we?" Matias smiled broadly. His eyes lit up with mischief. "It's elementary knowledge that penile fortitude is best measured not by the metric of dick length but rather by the accurate assessment of cock mass."

"Mass? You're gonna weigh our dicks?" Duke laughed and shook his head. These guys really had a lot of free time. They were sitting on top of a luxury condo skyscraper at one A.M. casually discussing weighing their dicks. Duke was now with them.

"We've got electronic scales at the gym," Duke helpfully remarked.

"No need to go anywhere," Matias shook his head again, mischievously again. "We've got that scale hidden away somewhere."

"Oh shit." Colin shook his head. "You mean the electronic scale we bought for weighing our—" Colin made finger-quotes "tobacco?"

"Yes." Matias rolled his eyes. "When you were going through your stoner phase."

"Don't mention that." Colin laughed.

Matias laughed back at him and kicked some hot water into the night air. "I and I will zip my mouth, mon."

"Every college student goes through a Bob Marley phase, right?" Colin gestured lighting an imaginary bong.

"If you say so." Matias laughed and splashed water in Colin's direction. The way it splashed across Colin's tight stomach and pubes reminded Duke a little too much of a cumshot. He was already hard, so there was no harm in imagining. "Anyway, we still have that scale."

"Go get it then!" Colin's face brimmed with enthusiasm. "Go get that scale and we'll compare dicks for real."

Matias made a cartoonish stoner face with both his hands flashing *peace* signs.

"Legalize it and I will advertise it!" Matias shouted, then hopped up out of the tub. He ran into the condo, gleefully skating with his bare feet on the hardwood floors.

Colin smiled and without any trace of shame stared Duke's body up and down. He looked like he was about to feast on Duke. "So how much do we have to work out to have a body like yours?"

"Ah, you know." Duke's training clients always asked him that, as if he had a magic formula for getting ripped. "A lot of it is genetics."

"Yeah, genetics." Colin grinned and pointed at Duke's dick.

"Yeah, everybody's different," Duke said. It was his best noncommittal conciliatory response, one that didn't scare his clients away from at least aspiring to be ripped with muscle.

"Some are just a bit *more* different." Colin's eyes were still locked on Duke's half-hidden purple dickhead and the monster-size shaft it was attached to.

"Here we go!" Matias came back. He was only slightly less dripping wet and not any less naked. But now he was carrying a small digital scale. "This thing's waterproof. Really convenient for our purposes here."

As the Miami shoreline twinkled down below and people went about their very serious lives, Matias set down the digital scale on the hot tub's edge. He pressed a button and the scale turned on with a beep.

"You'd better tare it!" Colin broke out into laughter at the word *tare*. He acted as if taring a dick-weighing scale at the edge of a hot tub were a hilarious matter. It was a hilarious matter actually.

"Tare it using a micro-dick?" Matias glanced at Colin.

"Yeah, you won't need my help for that task!" From the opposite edge of the tub's ledge, Colin kick-splashed water directly at Matias's fat dangling dick.

"Alright, alright." Duke raised his hand, volunteering as the voice of mature reason. "Enough prolegomena, as Colin would say."

Duke hopped into the tub and walked a step so he'd face the electronic scale. He held down the *tare* button. The scale beeped. "Alright guys. Instead of talking about taring, I just went ahead and did it. See how that works? Man of action right here." Duke nodded mock-triumphantly. Maybe at twenty-eight he was too old to be playing like this with these twenty-three-year-olds. But if he'd never had that kind of playful fucking-around in his life, was it too late to have it at twenty-eight?

Colin cleared his throat. He must've had a big announcement in store. "Weigh 'em and weep." He swept his hand grandly, like an auctioneer. "And Duke goes last. In case he breaks the scale."

"I guess we can start with Colin, to make sure the scale it works at low weights." Matias pointed down at the scale.

"How am I gonna?" Colin walked over to the scale on the tub's ledge. "Oh, yeah, like this."

Colin kneeled on the hot tub's seat. His ass just cleared the waterline. His dick, dripping wet, was at the perfect height to be weighed from the scale on the ledge. Colin positioned himself and slapped his dick down on the scale's plastic surface like he was weighing a cut of ham.

"No fucking way, man!" Matias yelled out. "It's wet! Nobody's gonna believe that."

"Yeah? I'm kneeling in a hot tub." Colin looked back over his shoulder, as if verifying that he was in fact still kneeling in a hot tub. "It's kinda wet in here."

"Alright." Matias grabbed a thick white bath towel from the stand next to the tub. "Let me pat it dry."

Matias wiped the scale's plastic weighing surface. He tossed the towel's edge like a fire blanket over Colin's dick, then wrapped it from above.

Colin gulped hard. He stared at Matias's hand toweling his dick. His eyes were locked on the spectacle and his jaw dropped open. His breathing grew heavier.

"I've never dried anything so tiny!" Matias laughed. Still gripping the towel, he teasingly pumped Colin's dick.

Colin turned bright red. His breathing turned to a gasp. HIs arms and torso shook. He looked like he was about to collapse, even just kneeling on the seat.

"Oh fuck." Colin stared down into the towel. That towel was all that separated the grip of Matias's fingers from the hardness of Colin's dick.

"Aw." Matias grinned, looking down into his hand. "Something's warm and sticky."

Colin's expression of terror turned into an expression of mirth. His face still flushed, he stared down at the towel-wrapped, flaccid dick in front of him.

"We gotta clean it again now." Matias shook his head as he unwrapped Colin's dick.

Duke nodded at the unfolding situation at the tub's edge. "Seems Colin has some trouble containing his body functions when he's excited."

"Excited?" Colin asked in a quietly ashamed voice.

"Just a technical term." Duke worked to minimize any embarrassment. "I meant *physically stimulated.*" Colin nodded in acquiescence.

Matias stood up enough to grab the extendable shower head hose and turn it on. "We don't wanna wash that stuff back into the hot tub." Matias took away the towel and stared down at Colin's half-flaccid naked cock lying on the scale.

Colin looked up at Matias with a look of *What happens next?.* Matias pointed the shower hose down at Colin's dick at squeezed the handle. Colin's hips and ass shook as the water spray hit his half-flaccid dick and the scale under it.

Colin folded his hands behind his back. He could've washed his own dick. He didn't even try.

Matias lay his right hand under Colin's dick. He held his hand flat. When water spray hit Colin's dick, Matias jerked Colin's dick — or just innocently washed the cum off of it. He held the spraying shower head closer to the cock's base. He directed the spray up and down, like he was massaging Colin.

Colin's face went blank again. As the water spray touched up and down along his shaft, his whole dick visibly hardened, like an inflating balloon.

Matias worked it up and down with his hand some more. Then he casually said, "I think it's clean now," and wrapped it in the towel again.

"I guess it would weigh more when it's hard," Matias said, looking down at Colin's hard cock. "Good strategy, man."

"Yeah, thanks." Colin could barely speak through his quick breathing. His hands were now on his own hips. HIs fingers were white from digging in to his hips in nervousness.

Matias wiped the scale dry. He unwrapped Matias's cock and let it drop on the scale. "You watching this, Duke?"

"Yeah." Watching those two have their first touches of dick was such a voyeuristic thrill that Duke had almost forgotten that they knew he was watching. "I'll make sure the weighing is fair."

The scale beeped. "Eight point five ounces!" Matias shouted. "Colin is packing eight point five ounces!"

"That's respectable." Colin nodded and stared down at his hard dick on the scale like a deli salami.

"Eight point five ounces. When he's hard," Duke said. Colin's hardness was very much in Duke's thoughts.

"Your turn for the weighing station, man." Colin pointed at Matias standing above him. "Hop in the hot tub and kneel down." Colin took his dick back from the scale as if he was picking up his pet from the vet's office.

Matias nodded and stepped into the hot tub. Colin climbed out. His long, lean, hairy legs were gorgeous. Colin's legs climbing up out of the tub up on that night balcony were even sexier than the gleaming Miami skyscrapers behind them.

Colin lifted his whole body out of the tub and squatted next to the scale. His wet dick and balls dangled down below his super-tight ass.

Matias was arranging himself exactly in Colin's previous position, kneeling on the tub seat. His dick lay like a fat wet fish on the scale. His meaty ass pointed directly at Duke. Its slightly hairy rim looked like an entrance to the most exclusive club of pleasure.

"Ready?" Colin asked Matias.

"No way, man." Matias shook his head indignantly. "How can I get a fair weighing? I'm not even hard yet."

"Matias has a good point." Duke nodded, trying to look understanding. "He's gotta get hard for a good reading."

"Yeah." Matias gripped his own dick and stroked it up and down. It grew thicker and the engorged cockhead popped out from the hold of Matias's hand. "Aren't you gonna dry it in a towel?"

"Oh yeah." Colin wrapped the same towel around the dick. "And we gotta make it fully dry. Or fully hard." Colin grinned and jerked the dick up and down with the towel. It grew even fatter, thicker, and longer.

"Ready to get weighed?" Colin asked.

"It's still not fair, man." Matias shook his head. "I'm still not fully erect. Not ready for competition yet."

"You have a hand, don't you?" Colin laughed. "Just jerk it some more."

"Hey Duke." Matias looked back over his shoulder. For a split second, Matias's gorgeous dark brown eyes were above his gorgeous brown ass cheeks. "I need some inspiration over here."

"Yeah? You want me to do a Tony Robbins motivational act over here or something?" Duke grinned with a bit of disgust.

"You do kind of look like that dude." Colin laughed.

"Yeah, you do look like him." Matias looked Duke up and down back over his shoulder, as if he hadn't had any previous opportunities to look Duke up and down. "I don't need any life coaching though."

"I'd be a shitty life coach." Duke shook his head. His life had been so full of fuck-ups. A guy sleeping on a garage floor didn't have the right to be life-coaching anybody.

"I just want you and your dick over here." Matias did a little wave, as if it wasn't clear where in the hot tub he was. "So I can look at you. For inspiration. For dick size."

"Sure." Duke had been jerk-off fodder for more than a few guys, but none as hot as Matias. He took a big step through the center of the hot tub and ended up at the edge next to Matias. Matias was kneeling, facing out to the dick-weighing scale. Duke sat at the tub's edge, facing the tub side. Matias could get a clear view while he jerked it.

"Shit, man." Matias drooled a little as he stared Duke up and down. "I wish I had muscles like that. I wish I had a dick like that." Matias stared hard. He pumped his dick. His eyes explored every square inch of Duke and he jerked his cock in unison with the visual exploration.

"Don't be so hard on yourself." Duke smiled at Matias's delicious body and dick. "Oh wait, you're trying to be so hard."

Duke idly played with his dick. Matias was obviously enjoying it. He stared like his eyes were deepthroating Duke's cock.

"Is this role model helping you?" Duke leaned back on the tub's ledge and opened his legs wider. He palmed his balls and raised them in his hand to show off to Matias. He kept stroking his right hand over his dick. Precum oozed from the dickhead and Duke diligently spread it over the entire shaft.

"Fuck, man." Matias was jerking himself harder and faster. "You're making your whole dick fucking glisten with your precum."

"Yeah?" Duke kept pumping. He swept his fingertip over his dickhead and licked off his own precum. It tasted the same as always: honey-sweet. "I love my precum."

"Oh fuck." Matias's eyes grew more desperately hungry as he stared Duke up and down. Matias pumped his dick frantically. It was already as hard as it could get. He seemed to have forgotten all about the weighing.

Matias breathed hard as he stared lasciviously at Duke. He jerked his dick frantically with his right hand and grabbed at his own balls with his left hand. His thighs and ass were making thrusting movements, like he was fucking the side of the tub.

Colin stared in awe as he squatted next to the scale. Colin's rock hard shaft pointed at Matias's face.

Duke ran his finger from the base of his dick up to the dickhead. The tip of his finger glistened with precum. He held his precum-stained finger up in front of Matias. "You want a taste?"

Matias breathed hard and heavy. His mouth quivered. His eyes flitted between his own engorged dick and Duke's entire dick and body, and Duke's precum-stained finger in front of his face.

Matias opened his mouth and breathed through it. His lips quivered. He looked at Duke's body, Duke's dick, and Duke's finger. Then he looked back down with a little bit of shame.

When Matias's eyes returned to Duke's upheld finger, he put his tongue out. He half-closed his eyes, like he was about to receive a sacrament. Duke put his glistening fingertip over Matias's mouth. Matias licked the precum off Duke's finger, then sucked the rest off the fingertip. He sucked hard, like he'd been waiting his whole life for that drop of precum, that sacrament.

As soon as Duke's finger was in Matias's mouth, Matias's whole lower body shook. He thrust against the edge of the hot tub like he was fucking his hand.

Matias gasped and sighed. His hot breath ran over Duke's finger, and Matias' licked and sucked it again. He threw his head back, still holding Duke's finger in his mouth.

A rope of cum flew from Matias's dick. It splattered on Colin's thigh. Colin only looked at it with a grin. He grabbed the towel again and wrapped it around Matias's still-throbbing dick.

Colin "dried" Matias's dick with the towel, jerking it up and down. Matias was still shaking and thrusting. Tightening his thighs and ass with each pump, Matias fucked Colin's toweled hand while sucking Duke's finger.

Duke ran his tongue up and down the entire length of Matias's finger. Matias sighed and whimpered something like "oh, fuck." He frantically pumped his dick at Colin's toweled hand.

Matias's cum oozed out the edge of Colin's towel. The smell was even stronger than when Duke had orgasmed in that same place. Colin looked at it and smiled, as if in commiseration.

Matias inhaled deeply and opened his eyes. Duke pulled his finger out of Matias's mouth. Matias's eyes stared in disbelief at Duke, then Colin.

"So are we almost ready to do some weighing here?" Duke asked. He leaned over and took the shower handle.

Matias sighed and nodded. He looked like he was struggling to keep his eyes open.

Duke put his hand over Colin's hand. He raised the sticky, cum-soaked towel off of Matias's fat cock.

Duke sprayed the dick with water and ran his hand up and down its full fleshiness. Matias and Colin both stared down at it as Duke squeezed and groped Matias's dick while supposedly washing it.

Matias's girth was impressive. Even after cumming, his dick grew thicker and harder again when Duke handled it. Young dudes like that could cum a few times a night.

Duke tossed Matias's thick dick up and down in his hand, like a tennis ball. It filled and hardened every time it landed.

"I think this one's ready to weigh," Duke said to Colin and Matias. Colin grinned. Matias nodded, still bleary-eyed from his climax.

Duke tossed the dick up and down in his hand a few more times, to give Matias a fairer weighing; it seemed to grow fuller and harder every time.

"Yeah, I'm ready." Matias smiled. His eyes flitted between his own dick and Duke's exemplar.

"Alright, come one, come all," Matias announced, then guffawed. Colin and Matias laughed too. "Time to weigh this monster."

The scale beeped. "That's zero point six ounces!" Duke announced with a laugh. "We can mail Matias's dick for fifty cents!"

"You fucker." Matias shook his head at Duke. "You're reading it upside down. It's actually, uh, it's uh — nine point oh ounces!"

"Oh yeah." Duke shook his head with a smile. "Honest mistake." Duke laughed at Matias's still-indignant face.

Bantering with these dudes was everything Duke had missed out on in his teens and early twenties. Struggling to eat, struggling to come out, and getting the shit kicked out of him in the MMA ring every night: those years hadn't exactly been conducive to exchanging light-hearted banter.

"Nine ounces of pure man-meat!" Matias shouted, probably loudly enough to be advertising his dick to the entire building. He grabbed his hard, thick dick and slapped it against the scale's weighing platform.

"Alright, man." Colin shook his head dismissively. "So you've got a nine-ouncer. We heard you. You can simmer down now."

"Future senator Colin Warner." Matias loudly cleared his throat. "May I ask you a question?"

"Yes, I accept questions, even from short-dicked dudes." Colin snickered.

"Ah." Matias held up his hand like some sort of parliamentarian. "That's the meat of my issue. The thrust of my argument. The very point of the matter." Matias was giggling like a first-grader who'd just learned the word *abreast*.

"Just don't cock it up," Colin said. His radiant smile shone like a sun above his angular shoulders, his tight pecs and abs, and his long, slim dick.

"The weighty issue here, Sirs—" Matias was giggling so much that he had to wipe spittle from his mouth. "The weighty issue is that my phallic instrument seems to weigh a full half-ounce more than Colin's!"

"Yeah, big deal." Colin shook his head. "Your dick's half an ounce heavier than mine."

"Well, it would be no big deal, Sirs." Matias sighed with a gravely serious look. "Except that our colleague Colin has lorded his superior penis length over me just about as long as I've known him."

"Sorry, man." Colin laughed and shook his head in a way that made clear he wasn't serious. But neither was Matias.

"The meat of the matter here is that we still have one more dick to weigh." Matias stared at Duke's dick. If Matias wasn't actually drooling, his face definitely looked like he was drooling.

"And it's big one." Colin nodded at Duke's dick as if it was a separate individual entitled to its own respect.

"A dick like that kind of gives you perspective." Matias, too, paid his respects to Duke's massive schlong. "What before you thought was big—" Matias looked down at his own dick, "--turns out to be tiny in comparison."

"Yeah, man." Colin nodded wistfully. "Seeing a dick like Duke's is like staring into the vastness of the universe." He again nodded deferentially at the topic of discussion. "Makes me feel like I'm Carl Sagan."

"What I'm suggesting here." Matias cleared his throat and stroked his dick a few times until it grew perfectly hard. "Is that we allow Colin to apologize for his past misdeeds, and in particular, for his excessive and unwarranted claims, over the course of the many years I have known him, about the superiority of his wiener."

"I apologize." Colin sighed and shook his head. "And I recognize and fully acknowledge that your dick is indeed half an ounce heavier than mine."

"Mister Warner." Matias sighed theatrically. "Words are not enough to make up for your years of serious misdeeds. We will need you to complete a task of unpaid labor as your penile penance."

"Alright, Matias. Alright. I'll complete a task of unpaid labor." Colin laughed and made a gesture of jerking off a dick into his mouth.

"You're not so far off the mark, my good man!" Matias smiled like a man quite sure of his plan. "I was thinking you could help our colleague Duke get ready for the weighing of his massive schlong."

"You mean like—" Colin broke down in giggling laughter. "Like I'm gonna be a fluffer?"

Matias giggled, then regained his composure, at least for the few seconds necessary to speak. "I suppose you could call your mode of employment by that name, if you so chose."

"Whatever it takes to contribute to the effort." Colin folded his hands in front of his hard dick and put down his head very seriously. "You know you can depend on me to help."

"Assume the weighing position." Matias pointed Duke to kneel on the hot tub seat. Duke did as told. He kneeled on the seat, facing out, and lay his half-hard dick on the tub's ledge.

With a grin more mischievous than he'd ever had, Matias pointed a finger at Colin. "Colin, get to work."

Colin hopped into the tub. He smiled at Duke like what he was preparing to do was not at all a punishment.

He sat down on the tub seat, alongside where Duke was kneeling. He stared hard at Duke's dick. He giggled again and told Duke, "Let me help you with that."

Duke turned on his knees to face Colin. Colin brought his head down toward Duke's dick. He looked up again, then over to Matias. "This thing is huge, man. I don't even know what to do."

Matias shrugged. "Just suck it. See what happens."

Duke was already growing harder from all the attention Colin and Matias were giving his dick. Now Colin was breathing his warm twink-breath on it and staring directly at its engorged tip; that was fucking hot.

Colin opened his beautiful pink-lipped mouth a little and looked up at Duke, as if for approval. Duke gave him a quick thumbs-up and said, "It's all you, man."

He lay his palm under Duke's dick. He bounced it up and down, just as he'd done with Matias's dick. Then he opened his mouth wide. He looked up at Duke again. Duke again told him, "It's all you."

Colin opened even wider and surrounded the dick with his open jaw. It looked like a lion trainer's trick — except after one more glance of Colin's beautiful blue eyes up at Duke, Colin closed his mouth around the dickhead, as much as he could.

His virgin mouth was so fucking hot and tight. He just held Duke's dick in his mouth, without doing anything to it. It was like Duke's dick was a chewable vitamin and he was waiting for it to dissolve to get all the vitamin D. He'd obviously never sucked dick.

Colin sealed his lips tight around Duke's dick and sucked. He just sucked at him like Duke was a beverage.

It didn't feel bad at all. The visuals helped: the blond twink in the hot tub of his condo balcony getting his first taste of dick. Duke relaxed to enjoy the fluffing instead of immediately blowing a load down Colin's throat.

Colin must've suddenly remembered what he'd seen in porn. He bobbed his head up and down on the dick, like a chicken. His pink little lips were sliding up and down on Duke's shaft and it felt great.

His blond hair glistened, reflecting the moon and the balcony lights. If it was a guy Duke liked who was sucking his dick, Duke loved to run his hand through his hair. He liked Colin. Colin was great. As great as Colin was, Duke knew not to do anything like running his hand through Colin's hair or grabbing at his tight, muscled arms. That might've been "gay." It could've rapidly ended the fun. It might have even endangered Duke's having a place to sleep. It was a careful line he had to toe.

"Yeah." Duke said it in the manliest possible growl. Nothing gay about enjoying getting fluffing.

"How's Colin doing on his task?" Matias asked from his perch outside the tub. "Is he doing a passable job?"

"Fuck yeah." Duke gave a manly thumbs-up. Matias spat onto his hand and jerked his own dick while staring wide-eyed at Colin sucking off Duke.

Matias's thick, manly hand roamed over his dick. His nipples were visibly hard, even in the darkness. He breathed hard while watching Colin suck. The sight of it all was almost too much for Duke.

As Colin bobbed his head up and down on Duke's dick, his back muscles rose and fell in ripples. Colin moaned in excitement and the vibrations went through Duke's whole body.

Duke couldn't hold it anymore. His whole lower body spasmed. He grabbed at the side of the tub. The sight of Colin's hard dick sticking up through the waterline made Duke shake even harder.

Duke grunted and shot a huge gob of cum into Colin's mouth. Colin looked up at Duke, shocked. He opened his mouth a little and cum oozed out.

Duke shot another rope deep into Colin. Then another. Colin kept the rhythm of his head bobbing up and down as duke emptied his cum into him.

"Fuck, Colin." Matias was shaking his head only slightly slower than he was stroking his dick. "You had Duke all hard and now you messed it up."

Without taking the dick out of his mouth, Colin looked up at Duke and Matias's conversation. Duke moaned in satisfaction after his last spurt. His skin was awake and tingling all over.

"Clean up that mess first," Matias said to Colin. Colin was already slurping the cum off of Duke's dick.

Colin let Duke's dick fall from his lips. His face looked like he wasn't sure whether to be ecstatic or ashamed about his discovery.

Matias waved Colin aside: "You had Duke's dick ready to weigh, but then you ruined it. Let me do it now."

Without waiting for Colin's reaction, Matias stepped into the tub. He sat on Duke's right side, with Colin still on Duke's left.

"Let me finish the job," Matias announced to Colin and Duke.

Colin's face was still red and he had a blank look of still processing the loads of cum he'd just taken into his mouth.

"Like this." Matias opened wide and moved his open mouth onto Duke's dick. He kept jerking himself as he did it.

Maybe Matias had never sucked a dick, but he must've been preparing for the moment, because he was all tongue and lips and sucking and slurping. Colin watched him in awe.

Duke might've cum right away from skill like Matias's, had he not already cum once into Colin. Duke did his best to breathe deeply and enjoy Matias's eager tongue and lips roaming over his dick. It grew rock hard again, just a minute after Colin had sucked him off. It had been a long time since he'd been able to recover his erection that quickly — but it had also been a very long time since he'd gotten his dick sucked by someone he actually liked.

"You're pretty good at that, man." Colin was staring at the scene of Matias working Duke's dick. After his orgasm, he looked like he was being woken up by smelling salts. His eyes were opening to the sight of Duke's dick in Matias's mouth. His pasty white dick was getting harder too.

Matias's mouth was full of dick, so Duke had to speak for him. "I don't think Matias can speak with you now. Can I take a message?" Duke pumped his dick just a little bit deeper into Matias's mouth: enough to probably put his virgin mouth at the boundary of what it could take.

"Well, just that—" Colin was mumbling almost incoherently as he stared at the dick. Only the first quarter of the shaft was inside Matias's mouth. The rest of Duke's length and girth glistened outside Matias's mouth, untouched unencumbered by any man's lips or tongue.

"Just that—" Colin coughed out some chlorine smell and stared at the dick. "Just that this was supposed to be my task, wasn't it? I mean here's Matias stealing all my glory, just because his dick is heavier than mine."

"I got some life advice for you, Colin." Duke felt like he was breathing and talking on manual mode. Matias slurping his dick was not conducive to having a running conversation with Colin.

"Yeah? I just need to have a huge dick like yours and then everything will be ok?" Colin stared down at Duke's equipment again, and stroked his own cock a few times in seeming appreciation of what he saw.

"No, man." Duke inhaled a big breath of air so he could sort of talk while Matias was bringing him higher and higher with his cocksucking. "My life advice is that if there's a task you're interested in, just jump in and do it. Don't wait to be invited. Just do it. If you can help out and provide value—"

Duke was still talking. Colin's lips were already closing in on Duke's shaft.

This time, Colin knew what he was doing. He put his thin pink lips to the veiny side of the shaft, while the tip was still submerged in Matias's mouth. Colin sucked on it like it was a corn cob.

Maybe it wasn't obvious. But Colin figured it out. He used his tongue on the shaft. And it felt amazing. He licked the shaft up and down, from the base to the part where Matias was sucking it. He looked at Matias nervously when their mouths were close together. They didn't kiss, but maybe they thought about it.

Colin dove under Duke's dick. Craning his head down, he pushed his face into Duke's nutsack. His tongue was now running up and down on Duke's nuts while Matias was still head-bobbing and slurping on Duke's dick.

Duke groaned in pleasure and nodded his approval to his two cocksucker friends working his dick. He probably couldn't cum again. Probably. At least not for a while. And if he did cum again, he probably couldn't get hard a third time. At least not for a while.

He'd never before encountered good luck. His life had always been, at best, just no better and no worse than fair.

Sometimes worse. Never better.

Now he was on a condo balcony, getting his dick worked by two gorgeous guys who were apparently going to give him a new life, one with a bed and a shower. Knowing that they cared about him and for him even made their two-man blowjob feel a lot better.

Matias let Duke's dick slip out of his mouth. He was still chasing it with his tongue as it left his mouth, giving the cockhead a final lick as it fell from his lips. Colin's lips and tongue were still roaming Duke's shaft.

Matias looked at Duke and palmed his cheek. "My jaw's getting sore." His face was apologetic.

"Guys." Duke shook his head. His body tingled from arousal, but he forced himself to at least sound level-headed. "I'm already plenty hard and ready to get weighed."

67

"Oh yeah?" Colin rose up from feasting on the shaft as if his favorite meal had just been taken away from him.

"Let's weigh it," Matias said, still massaging his jaw.

Duke lifted his dick out of the tub and put it on the ledge again. He shook it dry. Matias quickly took a towel and toweled it off, then turned on the scale. His eyes were a bit glazed and his motions were a bit uncertain.

Duke lowered his dick down onto the scale.

"Shit, man." Colin shook his head, staring down in awe. "We need a crane for that thing."

"Hey now!" Matias squinted down at the scale as it beeped. "We have established the weight of the Loch Ness Monster to be — eleven point zero ounces!" Matias tapped the scale's display for confirmation. "Duke's dick weighs exactly eleven ounces."

"Holy fuck." Colin laughed and shook his head. "I've never even eaten a steak that big."

Matias splashed some hot water on Colin. "Didn't you just chow down on an eleven-ounce steak?"

"Oh." Colin flushed even brighter red. "Oh yeah."

"Alright, guys." Duke exhaled deeply. The sexual tingle was slightly leaving his body. "We've weighed our dicks. I hope everybody is happy now."

"Yeah, that was—" Colin shook his head. He looked up into the sky, as if recollecting something. "It was something. It was definitely something." Colin winced very slightly.

"I am sensing some humiliation here?" Matias kicked up some hot water like he was trying to swim away from the balcony. His thighs, his calves, even his feet were beautiful. "Since formerly proud Colin is now certifiably the smallest dick in the tub?"

"I think we've got *bigger* things to think about." Colin glanced at Duke's face, then Duke's dick.

"Like that it's two A.M. and I have to report for work at Biscayne Fitness in four hours?" Duke asked. He had a place to live, but he still wasn't idle rich. "I do think I'll shortly be retiring for a slumber." Duke mimicked Colin and Matias's faux-formal turns of phrase. He was even pretty good at it.

"Alright, man." Colin looked in Duke's eyes. Then he obviously looked down at Duke's dick. Then he very obviously looked away, his face full of embarrassment.

"I've got MCAT practice tests to take." Matias's face turned from embarrassed to slightly worried. "And Colin's got — whatever it is that he does for his dad on Facebook." Matias made a dick-jerking masturbatory hand gesture.

"Yeah, yeah." Colin rolled his eyes. He was beautiful when he rolled his eyes like that. Colin had the biggest eye roll of any man Duke had ever seen. Colin probably had no idea how stereotypically gay it made him look. "Let's retire back to our respective quarters, Gentlemen."

"Hey Colin." Matias looked down at his feet as he spoke. "You have a bedroom. I have a bedroom. Now Duke has a bedroom too."

"Yeah?" Colin asked. "Something wrong with that arrangement?"

"That fourth bedroom. It's got a bed and everything." Matias shrugged. "And we're not even using it. And it's just really nice when the three of us spend time together."

"You suggesting we pull the hot tub into the fourth bedroom?" Colin smiled like he had no doubt what Matias actually meant. He made a gesture of pulling a very heavy thing.

"No, Sisyphus. I'm suggesting—" Matias started to say, his eyes still locked on his feet.

"I know who Sisyphus is, and I know what you're suggesting." Colin beamed a smile. "And it's an awesome idea. That bed is definitely big enough for three."

Matias pointed his thumb at Duke. "Even if one of them's got an eleven-ounce dick?"

Colin stared at Duke's dick again and smiled like he was recalling a particularly delicious meal. "If it can fit in your mouth, it'll fit in that bed."

"Oh yeah." Matias nodded slowly.

"That's a slogan for the ages." Duke smiled as non-threateningly as he could. He was about to get in bed with two horny purportedly straight guys, and he had to act totally nonchalant about it. That wasn't easy, but it was a lot easier than sleeping on a concrete floor.

"I've just gotta put on my Spiderman pajamas." Colin said it so offhandedly that it might've been true. "See you guys in the Unwanted Room in five minutes."

Duke had a place to sleep. He had two guys with him who wanted to sit and banter with him and even bed down with him, not just worship his cock and then run away.

Miami's skyscrapers twinkled in the wee hours. A few hotel windows were still lit. Cruise ships bobbed in the distance. Fresh salt air blew over Colin, Matias, and Duke: air that was all theirs to breathe and thrive on.

Duke was one of them. The air was his to breathe. The bed was his to sleep on. Life wasn't perfect, it was closer to perfect than it had ever   been.

Five

A ray of hot sunlight burned across Colin's sleeping face.

Why did the sun have to be such a bitch?

Colin half-opened his eyes. Duke's shirtless torso stood between the bed and the window. Matias had muscles, but not like that.

"Getting up to go to work?" Colin mumbled. It was the best small talk he could think of that didn't involve the alternating waves of desire and shame he'd fallen asleep to.

"Coming back from work, dude." A pillow flew on a precise trajectory from Duke's hand to the spot on the headboard immediately next to Colin's head. It was the most precisely aimed pillow-toss Colin had ever seen. "It's almost noon already. Shouldn't you be doing whatever it is that you do?"

"Oh." Colin leaned up and took a look around the room. Matias's backpack was gone, and he normally left home around eleven. It really was late in the morning. "How did you get back in?"

"Matias gave me an access card before I went out this morning." Duke slipped his hand into the pocket of his fabric shorts and waved a building access card at Colin. He definitely wasn't wearing any underwear under those fabric shorts. Duke's glutes could have powered a jackhammer.

"Matias is a cool guy." Colin smiled. If it hadn't been for Matias, Colin never would've had the confidence to invite this near-stranger into his condo.

If not for Matias, Colin would've lived in that condo totally alone — without Matias's gentle smile, supportive small talk "intellectual" lectures, and occasional takeout food gifts. Colin would not have survived post-college life without Matias, not any more than he could've survived college dorm life without Matias.

Colin was no genius as life choices went. Inviting his college roommate join him off-campus had been one of his better decisions. Colin had never been close to anybody until he met Matias that first day of college.

71

"Mind if I—" Duke started to say.

"I don't mind if you anything and everything." Colin shook his head. "Just feel at home here. My casa, your casa."

"Well you've got quite a nice casa." Duke smiled. His eyes seemed to be sparkling more at Colin than at Colin's casa. "I was just going to go to my bedroom to sleep some more before I go back to work at five."

"It's your place, man. Your bedroom. Your sleep." Colin gave a thumbs-up. Of course Duke was welcome to sleep. He was even welcome to sleep in his own bedroom, not their newly designated common sleep room. Colin had to go post some Facebook ads for his dad's anyway. But it was uncomfortable to think about Duke being *away* somehow, even if just across a few walls inside the same condo.

Duke slipped away, out the bedroom door. His face did look exhausted. He'd probably gotten no more than an hour of sleep before meeting his morning training clients.

Colin sauntered over to the desk in his own bedroom. The *Warren Warner For Senate* banner over the desk reminded him of his task: promoting his father's political campaign. Not just promoting his father's political campaign, but also being his father's son.

He had it easy, kind of. At least Colin didn't have to promote some caveman candidate, and at least his father ran pretty clean campaigns. Colin wouldn't have to make up memes accusing the opponent of being a Satanist or a Jew or a homosexual.

Especially not a homosexual. Senator Warren Warner prided himself on his support of gay rights. His South Florida constituency was heavily either gay or pro-gay, and his constant challenger in the Democratic primaries was Clint Braver, an openly gay young lawyer. Any hint of homophobia would've been political suicide for Senator Warner.

That was Senator Warner's public life. Warren Warner, like most politicians, drew a sharp distinction between his public and private opinions: between what he said at campaign rallies and what he said at home to his son.

Colin, thanks to his lack of interest in football, quail-shooting, and strip clubs, had grown up being called every anti-gay slur from the Great Big Encyclopedia of Homophobia.

It wasn't so bad. At least Colin wasn't gay, probably.

"Harvard is my dream med school. Everybody's dream med school." Matias gazed out at the beach down below, the stars above, and Colin and Duke lounging on the balcony. He was on track for Harvard, if his MCAT score the following week was as good as his practice tests.

He could also hope that the interviewers in Cambridge liked him, even if there was a slight culture clash. Matias wasn't from the typical rich, intellectual background of a Harvard student, but living with Colin had actually given him the confidence that he wasn't any worse than rich people.

Sometimes it was difficult to remember that this idyllic life was going to be only a stopping-off point in his life. After Duke had moved in, especially, the three of them in the condo felt so settled and permanent. It took mental self-discipline for Matias to remember that they'd be parting ways soon.

"At least no one will fault you for not reaching high enough." Duke's nod seemed to convey that he knew how hard that shit was. "I didn't have the chance to go to college, but shit man: I'm almost glad I could use being poor as an excuse for not going, because I don't know if I'm smart enough for that."

"Hardest part about college is getting in." Colin smiled. "That's what my dad always told me. I don't know if I believe it though."

"I wish I could give Sam college advice." Duke sighed.

"You can't?" Colin asked.

"I don't have any advice to give. Number one, I dropped out of high school." Duke shrugged and his eyes wandered down to the slats of his lounger chair. "And number two, I'm, you know, not allowed to contact. I'm estranged. Whatever you call it. Sam doesn't know I exist."

"But you care about Sam." Colin sat up slightly. "You care a lot. That's obvious."

"I'm— I'm sending him to private school. The best private school. He has a scholarship, actually, and then I pay the amount the tuition doesn't cover, a thousand a month."

"Up in Fort Lauderdale?" Colin asked.

"Yeah."

"Pine Crest School?" Colin's fingers tapped on his lounger's armrest.

"Yes! How did you know?" Duke looked shocked.

"There aren't many private schools that expensive." Colin looked off, up the coast, his eyes wandering to Fort Lauderdale to the north. "And also, I went to Pine Crest."

"Oh!" Duke shook his head. "Then you and Sam are, uh, what do you call it. Schoolmates. Co-alumni. Something like that."

"I don't know if Sam would want to be associated with my shitty academic performance." Colin shrugged. "But sure."

"Supposedly—" Duke's eyes looked dreamy again. "If you graduate from Pine Crest, college is a shoo-in. Whatever you want to do is a shoo-in. That's what I'm trying to get for Sam. So he doesn't have to sleep on a concrete floor like his dad. Or strip like his mom, for that matter."

"A thousand bucks a month is not small money." Colin sighed. "I'm going to be bluntly honest and say that if I weren't funded by my parents, I have no fucking idea how I'd even come up with anything like a thousand bucks a month."

"You might have to suck dicks for the money," Matias called out. "You've shown talent at that at least."

"Not jokingly." Colin shook his head. He was supposed to be the ditzy one, but his thoughts often held impressive gravitas. "Seriously, I mean, if I had a son who needed tuition money, and I didn't have rich parents? Seriously, maybe I'd suck dicks for money. I certainly wouldn't be able to earn much fucking around on Facebook, for which my dad's campaign currently pays me ten thousand a month."

"You get ten thousand a month for that online campaign job?" Matias asked, surprised. Colin was always as open as he wanted to be with Matias. He seldom mentioned exact numbers, though. Colin seemed to have become more open since Duke had moved in.

"Yeah. The pay is all like, symbolic, you know. It just goes straight to my investment funds. My spending cash is all from my trust fund distributions anyway. But yeah." Colin smiled a little bit uncomfortably. "The more you know."

"That's awesome." Duke nodded. "I mean, it's awesome that your parents can provide for you like that. I try to do, like, one percent of that for Sam."

"Shit, man." Colin sighed. "Obviously you're putting yourself out for Sam. Obviously. My parents are great for me, but it's not like it's a difficulty for them to fund me. For you, you're like — that's love. That's commitment."

"I do what I can. Like anybody would." Duke lay back in his lounger. He seemed to suddenly remember the opened bottle of beer Colin had put at the side of Duke's lounger, for his consumption. Awkwardly, he sniffed it and took a swig.

Colin's gaze drifted from the far distance to Duke's face. "Hey. Duke. I was thinking."

"We gonna have a penis-weighing rematch?" Duke took a deep breath and grinned.

"No, man. You're undisputed." Colin made an exaggerated gesture demonstrating Duke's penis size. He looked like he was describing a huge trout.

"Then I'm all out of guesses." Duke stretched his arms up to the sky. "What were you thinking, Colin?"

"Hear me out." Colin cleared his throat. His face went into Senator Colin Warner mode, even if he was still shirtless and sipping a beer on his balcony. "Tuition for Sam at Pine Crest is what, twenty five thousand a year?"

"Yeah." Duke winced a little. Those big numbers would've been painful for anybody. "Though he gets a need-based fifty-percent discount. So it's twelve thousand a year."

"And you just pay the bill every month or something?" Colin asked. It was vaguely apparent where his thoughts were going.

"Sam's mom does. Tricia. I transfer a thousand a month into her checking account, and then she does the actual monthly tuition payment. Why?"

"Duke. I don't want you to take this the wrong way." Colin bit down on his lower lip. He was thinking hard.

"I've been tossed around by life enough, man. I don't take anything the wrong way." Duke laughed, like a man trying to laugh off an injury.

"My point though." Colin sat up completely. "I could write a check for twelve thousand for a year of Sam's tuition. I mean, honestly, I wouldn't even notice the money was gone. It would take a big burden off of you, wouldn't it?"

"Well—" If there was an emoji for *flabbergasted*, Duke's face was it. "I mean. It would take a big burden off. But why would you even do that?"

"Why would I not do it?" Damn. Colin really had a way. Whether it was from his father or not — he had a way.

"Um, why would you give twelve thousand dollars to someone you've known for three days?"

"What does three days have to do with it?" Colin shook his head. "I can see who you are. I can see what you're doing for Sam."

"If I may interject here, Duke." Matias smiled at him. "Colin's generosity to near-strangers is legendary."

"Are you making fun of me, man?" Colin asked. If Colin was blind to something because of his own wealth, he was mostly blind to the extent of his own generosity. It was all small stuff to him. He didn't quite realize how big it was to people in the cheap seats.

"Dude." Matias shook his head. "First day in the dorms, right? Colin and I just met. I tell him he's got a nice Macbook Air, right?"

Duke smiled at Matias. "Yeah, and then?"

"Next day. Next day!" Matias shook his head and lightly clapped Colin's back. "Mister Amazon Prime delivery man comes to our dorm. With a Macbook Air for me."

"Yeah, I had one and you thought it was cool, right?" Colin shrugged. "I thought it would be nice if we had the same laptop."

"That's like what?" Matias asked, counting imaginary figures in the air. "Twelve hundred bucks? Fifteen hundred? Colin?"

"Something like that." Colin shook his head to convey the trivial nature of the money involved.

"Yeah, see?" Matias said to Duke. He glanced over at Colin as if Colin were an item he was promoting. "Like, the money didn't even matter for Colin. He just wanted to get me a nice laptop."

"You make me sound so generous." Colin looked at Matias deadpan, then stared out into the ocean. His eyes wandered slowly across the coastline, as if he was considering his life's legacy.

Maybe Colin needed a bit of a teasing prod. Only Matias knew him well enough to do it. He grinned at Colin mischievously. "Duke already knows that you're orally generous."

"I didn't hear anything." Duke covered his ears, then uncovered them. "Anyway, there's nothing wrong with being orally generous."

"So? Tomorrow? We can go to Pine Crest together and I'll write them a tuition check? I don't feel like driving up to Broward today."

"You are serious about this?" Duke shook his head.

"Deadass." Colin showed two thumbs up.

"What?" Duke squinted.

"How old are you, man?" Matias asked Duke. *Deadass* was one of those words.

"Twenty-nine." Duke sighed just a little bit. "That means I should still know what *deadass* means, right?"

"Debatable." Colin seesawed his hand in the air.

Duke beamed a smile: a smile of knowing that the most serious problem in his life at that moment was that he'd never heard of the term *deadass*. "I mean, don't turn thirty until next month. That's when I'm supposed to stop knowing."

"I think you're mistaken there." Matias made his best scornful face. Duke was getting his kid's tuition problem solved. They could tease him a bit about his advanced age. "I think the cutoff age for that word is twenty-five, not thirty."

"And you guys are what?" Duke's smile was still beaming his general satisfaction with the turn his life had taken. No sight could have been happier than a huge smile on a huge dude. "Barely twenty-one or something?"

"We're both twenty-three, we'll have you know." Colin cleared his throat. "Old enough to drink."

"Alright. Old enough to drink." Duke snickered just a little. "So *deadass*, Colin, you're gonna pay my son's Pine Crest tuition for a year?"

"Deadass." Colin shrugged. "Totally deadass."

"Just because?" Duke sighed and shook his head as if trying to wake from a dream.

"Not *just because*." Colin's voice turned serious again. Senator-like, like his father. He stood up and folded his hands behind his back. He scanned the horizon again as he spoke. "But because I like you. Because we're housemates. Because I want to take the financial stress off of you. Because anybody who sleeps on a concrete floor to send his son to private school deserves at least my attempt to help."

Matias provided some backup. Contextualization as it were. "I can't speak for Colin here. But you care about Sam. I can see how much you care about Sam. That's how much Colin cares for us. For me and now for you too."

"I've just never met or seen anyone like that." Duke exhaled deeply and shook his head. "Not in real life. It's not like real life."

"So, tomorrow we'll go there?" Colin made a car-driving gesture in Duke's direction.

"I've got the MCAT tomorrow." Matias sighed a little. He was supposed to dread the MCAT. That's what was expected of him. But actually, he'd studied hard and he'd one well on practice tests. And the past few days, he'd been feeling on top of the world. He was actually looking forward to the MCAT. "Gonna be just you two studs road-tripping up to Broward."

"I mean — yeah." Duke breathed in deeply. His eyes were opened big. He looked overwhelmed, like a child on Christmas morning. It was like the expression he had when Colin had first offered him a place to stay. "I'll be back from my gym clients around eleven A.M. I guess you're even gonna chauffeur us up there?"

"No, man." Colin looked down on the floor and made an exaggerated, emoji-like frown. "My car's all out of gas."

"Your car is—" Duke started to say, then broke out in a smile. "It's a Tesla, dude! I'm not stupid."

"Good catch." Colin shrugged.

"Tomorrow." Duke nodded slowly. "Eleven o'clock. Up to Broward. For Sam."

"You got it." Colin gave a double thumbs-up. "For Sam."

Seven

Sam's school campus swept without compunction or reservation across swampy west Fort Lauderdale. This place was worthy of its cost and reputation. The fountains sprayed up like there was no question about their right to do it, with no worry about the cost of water or electricity or anything else.

At Pine Crest School, worries disappeared. Maybe they never even surfaced to begin with. That was the life Duke wanted for Sam.

This school that Duke was paying for was, unlike Duke himself, well able to pay the bills. In that kind of environment, not having enough money seemed alien: unthinkable. The buildings, gardens, and fountains appeared to be right out of an old-school Flagler-era resort.

Colin parked the Tesla in a spot marked *Parents*. His smile at Duke conveyed enough: Duke was the parent. Maybe by some weird stretch they were both parents.

Sam's photo, birth certificate, school enrollment form, and tuition statement were all ready to go on Duke's phone. Colin had reassured Duke against all his perfectly reasonable doubts: Colin would indeed pay the twelve thousand, twelve thousand something, thousand dollars. Duke didn't even need to bring his wallet or checkbook — not that Duke had a checkbook.

"I'd like to — we'd like to pay a tuition bill," Duke proudly announced to a uniformed man hedge-trimming around a Victorian column.

"Bursar's office. That way." The man pointed to a grim wooden door down an outdoor hallway.

There was an actual office for paying tuition bills. A bursar's office.

Maybe Duke should have made Colin believe that bursars were nothing new to him and that yes, of course, Duke had been looking for the bursar's office all along. Why though? Colin already knew Duke well enough. Colin was going to be writing the bursar a check that Duke couldn't afford to write. That was way beyond Duke needing to fake his background.

Duke walked into the bursar's office. Colin trailed him.

"I'd like to — we'd like to pay a tuition bill." Duke was just stating facts. But saying it felt so good. Duke was being useful to Sam. DIrectly. Sure, he'd been sending money to Tricia, but it somehow felt more real if he showed up at Sam's school himself and paid the bill himself.

"Student name please?" The woman behind the desk looked like she'd processed a few thousand tuition payments just that afternoon.

Duke answered eagerly. "Last name Erlea. E-r-l-e-a. First name Sam. Samuel." That was his boy. Sam used Tricia's surname, and Sam had never met Duke, but that made Sam no less Duke's son.

The woman at the desk clicked her house and typed. "Student's date of birth please?"

"January first, two thousand eleven." Easy question. One one, one one. Duke had that tattooed on his shoulder.

"Hmm." She clicked again. "Do you have his student ID number?"

"I might—" Duke paged through his phone's folder of scanned Sam-related documents: mostly bank payment and deposit receipts.

"It would appear on any tuition statement or invoice or receipt from the school."

"Ah, I've got that." Duke scrolled to the tuition statement. "His student ID number is E-L-6-5-5-1."

"That doesn't sound right." The woman behind the desk wrinkled her nose. "Our student ID numbers—"

"It's right here." Duke lay his phone on her desk, the PDF scan of the tuition statement prominently on the screen.

"Are you sure this is a—" the woman wrinkled her nose again. "That doesn't look like— this is — this doesn't look like our statements at all. That's not even our logo."

"It says *Pine Crest School*. It's got your address." The alternative was impossible. How could it not have been the right tuition statement?

"I'm sorry." The woman's head-shake went from mild concern to serious discomfort. "Did you receive that in the mail? I don't think it came from us."

"I got that from— long story— but—" It was too much to explain, and this school administrator had done nothing wrong. She was doing her job. "Let me call my ex wife."

"Sure." The school employee gave them a forced smile and a wave. That made it clear that any ex-wife calling would have to be done outside the confines of her office.

Colin held the door open for Duke. As Duke stepped out of the office, Colin gently tapped his shoulder.

It was too early to console Duke about anything. There must've been a mixup with Tricia. Tricia wouldn't — not that Duke really knew Tricia, other than having had sex with her in a strip club and sending her money for the past eight years— at least he did have her phone number stored in his phone.

The phone rang. Once. Then again. It would all get cleared up. Tricia wasn't the most reliable person, but she loved Sam too.

"Duke? Yeah?"

"Hey. Tricia. I just need your help with something."

"I'm busy."

"I'm here at Pine Crest."

"You're where?"

"At Pine Crest."

"What's Pine Crest?"

"At Sam's school."

"You went there?" Tricia's voice rose.

"To pay his tuition."

"Didn't we agree? You send me the check and I do the payment?"

"Yeah. I found a way to pay for a whole year up front. I wanted to surprise you."

"You got twelve thousand dollars?"

"Uh kind of."

"Did you steal the money? What the fuck?"

"Tricia. Not important. For now. I'm trying to figure out how to pay Sam's tuition bill. They said the bill you sent me doesn't look right. The student ID number isn't the right format. The letterhead doesn't look like theirs."

"Why did you go to the school? Didn't we agree?"

"Tricia. Do you need to tell me about something?"

"You need to tell me why you went to the school. When we agreed that you'd be out of the picture."

"Fine." Duke's hands shook. "I'm sorry. I did a bad thing. I shouldn't have gone to Sam's school."

"Is this conversation over now?" Tricia sighed. As if Duke had been the one in the wrong.

"Tricia. I'm here at the school and I need to know—"

"This conversation is over." There wasn't even a click. At least in the old days they slammed down phones, or clicked to disconnect, or something like that. In 2019 there was only silence.

Eight

That was easy.

Nobody was supposed to call the MCAT easy.

Matias had crammed for that fucker for years. He'd never worked that hard on anything. And after all that, it really was easy.

The two hundred thirty questions had flown by. Each question was a well-rehearsed movement that Matias had already practiced dozens of times. Now Matias was the happiest man in the world.

"Who's home?" he yelled out to whoever might be listening in the condo. He slurped his durian smoothie, bought on a whim on the Uber ride home from the MCAT.

He'd aced the MCAT. It was the moment he'd spent at least the past few years — or maybe his whole life — preparing for. And now he would be the most desireable of med school candidates. He could have as many durian smoothies and Uber rides as he wanted.

"Who's homo?" Matias yelled out again. He hadn't invented that little vowel bend, but he and Colin had practiced it often, at least until that still-undiscussed night in the hot tub with Duke made gay jokes unbearably awkward.

"The world's most famously infamous medical school applicant has entered the building!" Matias shouted, this time craning his neck around to make sure his voice penetrated the condo's every corner.

"Hey. Matias." Duke's voice came weakly from their newly designated common sleeping room.

"Yo. Matias." Colin echoed Duke's voice. Colin's faint call, like a sparrow's, didn't sound any more enthusiastic than Duke.

"Guys. I aced the MCAT." Matias felt as if he was dropping a smoke-bomb of happiness to clear any unhappiness that may have been lingering in Colin's and Duke's world.

"Great job, man!" Colin called out first. "We knew you'd ace it!"

"You're an ace, Matias!" Colin followed up, again just a little bit weakly, from inside their shared fourth bedroom.

"Guys." Matias pushed the door open. Something obviously wasn't right. But whatever it was, he could cheer them up.

Duke's tremendous body lay face-up, diagonally across the double-king bed. Duke's head lay in the crook of Colin's lap. His big beautiful eyes stared up at the ceiling.

Colin sat up, his shirtless back pushing against a body pillow. Colin's hand ran through Duke's hair, tracing a line across Duke's temple and ear.

Duke looked in Matias's direction. Duke's mouth scowled as if he'd splashed strong soap in his eyes. Two laptops sat on the bed, both screens sleeping.

Matias sat down on the bed, between the laptops. "I'm sorry. Is something wrong?"

Duke exhaled deeply and shook his head. "I should've suspected something, but—"

"No, man." Colin lay both his hands on Duke's shoulders. "That's victim-blaming. You weren't supposed to suspect anything."

"Some mommy blogger in Tampa." Duke shook his head, staring straight up at the ceiling. "For eight years. She was sending me pictures from some mommy blogger in Tampa."

"Did you guys go to the school today?" Matias was just trying to open with the obvious question.

"Yeah." Colin answered the question with a face that didn't invite further questions.

"I'm guessing it didn't go well." Matias looked at Colin and Duke for some kind of confirmation. Whatever it was, it was bigger than Matias's having aced the MCAT.

"I guess I shouldn't be hiding anything from either of you guys." Duke wiped a stray tear from his jaw. "It's just really difficult to talk about."

"I can understand that." Matias nodded at Duke. "Do you want me to go to my room and we can talk more when you're ready?"

"No. No." Duke tapped the bed with his hand. "Sit down here. With us. We missed you all day. Well I missed you all day. I'm not sure if Colin did." Duke flashed a mischievous smile at Colin.

"Yeah, I missed you pretty bad, Duke." Colin nodded and stared off into the distance just a little bit. "Deadass."

"Wow, deadass?" Matias laughed. "That's a lot of missing."

"Deadass. We're all here together. And we should share in this." Colin handwaved for Matias to sit closer in. Matias folded his legs so they just barely touched Duke's body.

"So." Duke sighed again. He half-closed his eyes as he started speaking. "It was all a lie, man." Duke spoke softly, still shaking his head as if begging for mercy from an invisible sky. "All I've lived for for the past eight years. All a lie."

"What was—" Matias started to ask. Was it the son? Was the son not really going to private school?

"Sam." Duke shut his eyes hard, like he was trying to shut out the world. "There's no Sam."

"What do you mean there's no Sam?" Matias had been expecting some kind of statement about the school bills.

"Well." Colin ran his two fingers away on each side from Duke's nose. He traced both of Duke's eyebrows with his fingertips, then brought his palms down to hold Duke's jaw. "You guys say I'm too nice and I'll get taken advantage of. But it seems Duke was too nice. Way too nice. And got taken advantage of."

"Not even too nice." Duke swallowed hard. Maybe there were a few tears in that swallow. "It's just a matter of accepting responsibility. I fathered a son, so I'm going to support that son. Basic responsibility, you know? But she took advantage of that."

"How?" Matias reached out to Duke's muscled, hairy arm. He squeezed Duke's wrist, then moved his hand down to hold Duke's thumb and palm in his own hand.

Duke was near-whispering. His eyes were closed. A tear pooled at the bottom of his right eyelid. "Forged documents. Photoshopped stuff. At least she didn't Photoshop all the photos. Real photos, even if there's no Sam."

Colin clicked his tongue. "She was sending pictures of some kid named Tyler from Tampa. Sending this kid's photos for eight years. Pictures she got from a mommy blog. I already emailed the blogger. She doesn't know anything about this shit."

"Yeah, I'm not a tech expert like you guys." Duke folded his legs up a little bit. His knees protruded upward in his dark jeans.

"Colin, did you Google image search or something?" Matias asked. He spoke quietly. It certainly wasn't the time to dwell on Duke's naivete.

"Yeah." Duke interjected. "I never even knew about Google image search. Or Tineye. The stuff you guys learn in college — pretty useful." Duke bit his lower lip.

"You got scammed, dude." Matias clasped Duke's hand. "But it happens to everybody."

"Ever happened to you guys?" Duke asked with a grin.

"Sure." Matias was first to answer. "Maybe on a smaller scale. Just because I"m not as generous as you. And not as much of an adult. Haven't been out in the world. And shit, I don't have any money for anybody to take."

"Remember this feeling." Duke nodded at Matias with a smile.

"What feeling?"

"The feeling of not having any money." Duke smiled. "You aced the MCAT. That feeling's not gonna last very long." Duke managed to laugh a little.

"Oh yeah. I'm gonna be rich real quick." Matias sighed. "Just need to get into medical school, spend four years there, five years of residency, three years of fellowship — I'm counting my billions right now!"

"Hey now." Duke play-squeezed Matias's wrist. "Don't be complaining about having to go to Harvard Medical School. There are worse fates in the world."

"Not disputing." Matias laughed. "Not disputing. Just saying I'm not getting rich quick, that's for sure. And anyway, I'm not going into medicine for the money."

"Yeah. There's a better way to make money." Duke closed his eyes again. The smile drained from his lips. "Scam confused closeted gay dudes into paying child support money for kids that don't exist."

"You're gay?" Colin asked Duke. Looking down into Duke's face in his lap, Colin's eyes opened wide, as if he'd discovered something new about a familiar touchstone. Colin sat up straighter, his torso taut against the pillow behind him.

"I—" Duke's face flushed. His breathing quickened. "I mean — at the time — when I —" Duke shook his head. "This is a lot for me to deal with right now."

"It's alright if you're gay." Colin nodded down into Duke's face like he was staring down into a well.

"I hated myself because — I got gay-bashed. That's how I got this scar." Duke winced with recollection of pain. He patted his chest through his shirt. "I always say I got the wound back when I was an MMA fighter. Technically true. I was an MMA fighter back then. But I got the scar from some street thug with a knife gay-bashing me in an alley."

"So back up here a little bit?" Colin's voice rose. He'd been in the room already with Duke, but he still sounded confused about the travails Duke described. "You fathered a child because you got gay-bashed?"

"More or less." Duke sighed. "As stupid as it sounds. I hated myself for being gay. Getting beaten up and stabbed for it just made me hate myself, my sexuality, more. Pretty dumb of me, right?"

"Everybody's got a different story." Colin stared blankly. "No such thing as dumb."

"Yeah, man." Matias reached out for Duke's other hand. He held it: clammy and uncertain. That was the hand of a man who was at least half-broken, not a fighter or a trainer, not the invincible Duke who'd strutted around the gym musclebound.

"I've gotten my share of gay-bashing." Colin shook his head. "Shit."

"That guy yelling at us in an alley—" Matias started to say.

"No." Colin raised his eyebrows. "Not even that. On my own. With my dad."

"Senator Warren Warner?" Duke chuckled. "Florida's most famous advocate of gay rights?"

"That's my dad's name." Colin spoke in a pained monotone. "Don't wear it out."

"You got gay bashed by Warren Warner?" Duke's face filled with shards of disbelief. "How is that even possible? Are you even gay?"

"Yeah, not everything is what it seems." Colin sighed.

"You mean?" Matias started to ask; even he wasn't sure which part he was asking about.

"The point isn't if I'm gay." Colin suddenly grabbed his t-shirt from the side table and put it on. "People thought I'm gay. My own father gay-bashed me. Some dumbass in an alley, because Matias and I were walking out late at night, thought we're gay. That's all that matters. People think."

"So—" Duke nodded slowly to himself, still lying in Colin's lap. "When you guys wanted to get personal training from me, it was because—"

"Yup." Matias squeezed Duke's wrist to emphasize. "We got threatened in an alley. We didn't want to tell you the details."

"You didn't want me to think you guys are a couple of faggots?" Duke clicked his tongue, a little bit angrily.

Colin gasped. "That was the very word."

"Yeah, that's the word they always use." Duke pulled down the front of his shirt. The scar lay under there, collecting his shoulder blade to his chest like a dried river the color of brick. "That was the word they used when they knifed me."

"You?" Matias rubbed at Duke's bicep, then his tricep. They were strength distilled into physical form. "You got gay-bashed? You got called a fag?"

"Maybe I wasn't as strong back then," Duke said quietly.

"Weren't you into MMA—" Colin looked at Duke.

"Physically, physically I was strong." Duke nodded. "But I just wasn't as strong in general. The whole Sam thing. Shit." Duke shook his head again.

"Made you stronger?" Colin asked.

"Right now it just hurts like hell." Duke inhaled deeply and stared up at the ceiling. "But sleeping on a fucking garage floor. Sending all my money to my ex. Taking money from dudes who wanted to play with my dick. Yeah that made me stronger."

"Wait. You—" Colin looked down at Duke again. Colin's eyes were surveying a man lying in his lap who'd suddenly become at least slightly unfamiliar.

"Feel free to eject me from the apartment. Or send me to the quarantine kennel. Yeah, I made cash with my dick." Duke slowly, almost shamefully, rested his hand on his crotch.

"You did it all for your son." Colin inhaled and exhaled deeply. "That's really love. That's, like, the definition of love."

"A nonexistent son." Duke coughed and covered his mouth. "A son that doesn't exist, never existed. Is it still love then?"

"Tree in the forest problem." Matias blankly squeezed at the thickness of Duke's arm. "If Duke loved his son but his son wasn't around."

The question wasn't just theoretical. It wasn't like one of those classroom philosophy discussions. This time, tears streamed down Matias's own face, not only Duke's.

Matias wasn't even Duke. It was better not to even think about how much this affected Duke.

"Duke." Matias slid his legs out and lay down on the bed, alongside Duke, facing him. He reached behind and held himself close to Duke, their chests touching. Colin lay one hand on Duke's back and the other on Matias's.

Duke whispered: "This is the worst thing that's ever happened."

Matias held him closer. Duke's body radiated that sweaty, flash-heated warmth of a man in panic and sorrow. Matias wrapped his arms, then his legs, around Duke's huge body: Duke's shallow breaths, watery eyes, and all.

"But as bad as this is." Duke spoke up toward Colin above him, then to Matias alongside him. "This is the most support. The most love. The most support and love I've ever received. From anybody."

"You mean us?" Colin scooped Duke's head into his hand and stretched out his own legs. He cradled Duke's head in his palm as he tilted his whole body to lie down at Duke's side, on Duke's left side while Matias lay on Duke's left. "Silly, stupid, us?"

Duke tilted his head toward Matias. Beads of sweat dotted his hairline. His face gleamed with tears and sweat. Matias brought Duke's head closer into the crook of his neck. Colin pushed his body closer into Duke's back.

Duke spoke into the crook of Matias's shoulder and neck. "That feels really good." He pulled his head out a little bit and tilted it up, then said the same thing again to Colin behind him.

"I heard you, man." Colin's voice filled the room, crisp and strong. He was taking on his role as a bulwark of stability in this storm. Colin's body had never looked as beautiful as it looked with his arms wrapped around Duke.

Matias stretched out his arms so he could hold Duke and Colin in one embrace. Where Matias's arm extended past Duke's body, he lay his hand under Colin's bare shoulder.

Colin softly moaned his approval. "I can't believe how good this feels."

Duke and Colin at Matias's side were the world's most beautiful men. Their faces, their physiques, and even their voices complimented each other. Wherever Duke was thick, Colin was thin. Lying side by side, Duke and Colin fit like a jigsaw.

Matias couldn't see himself from a bird's eye view, but he could imagine how he looked from how he felt: he and Duke fit together perfectly. He and Colin had always fit together perfectly. Some violent homophobe in an alley had seen it even before Matias could.

Duke pushed closer into Matias, chest to chest. Duke's pecs were heavy and warm. Even through two t-shirts, Duke's chest scar made itself obvious. His massive thighs wrapped around Matias's legs in a tight hug.

A hot, thick bulge in Duke's pants pressed against Matias's crotch. It was too heavy to be a dick. It felt more like a hot water battle, firm and radiating warmth. But Matias had seen Duke's dick in the hot tub. It was the size and hardness of a hot water bottle.

Duke's dick was the symbol and meaning of everything good: what had brought the three of them together, how they'd found a way to give one another pleasure, even how they could now comfort one another. In carefree, closed-eyed oblivion, Matias pushed himself closer toward Duke's dick, until its push on Matias's crotch was almost painful.

If loving Duke's hardness on his crotch was gay, if embracing Duke and Colin in bed was gay, if comforting and loving one another was gay, then Matias could be gay.

Gay. That word had been thrown violently against the two of them in that alley. That word had even scarred Duke in some other alley. Colin's father used it to win votes in public, then again to disparage his own son in private.

Fine. Matias grinded his own dick against Duke's massive cock. He had the power of making Duke feel good.

Duke moaned. He silently nodded every time Matias's crotch grazed Duke's dick. Duke's face was hot. His lips quivered. Every time Matias touched him, Duke gasped a little. The heat, energy, and closeness were pure fire — and that was through two layers of clothes.

"Stuff happens, man," Colin mumbled. His blond hair was buried somewhere in the small of Duke's back.

Colin stared past the back of Duke's head. Colin's sea-blue gaze shone into Matias's eyes.

He moved fluidly, smoothly like the future politician he was, rubbing his nude chest against Duke's back. His hands roamed up and down on Duke. Duke opened his mouth in a gasp and a sigh of overwhelmed pleasure.

Matias nuzzled his face down to Duke's collar, then his shirt buttons. "May I?" Matias poked the tip of his tongue at Duke's topmost shirt button as if it were a part of his sexual anatomy. He drew a circle around its outer edge, then licked across the center where the thread was attached.

Duke's fingers rushed in to help. He popped the topmost shirt button, the one that gave just the beginning of a view of his hairy chest, his beautiful chest, and of course the scar that started everything.

"You may continue," Duke whispered to Matias. "Not just *you may. You must.*"

Matias sniffed at the top of Duke's shirt. He needed to breathe in the aroma: soap, tears, and a little bit of manly sweat. It was how men smelled, how men's gyms and locker rooms smelled. It was how Duke had smelled during that first training session, during those few moments when he'd gotten close enough to Matias to give him shivers.

Once Matias's nose got close, Duke's skin smelled like nothing he'd sensed before. It was delicious, a little bit salty, and overwhelmingly, viscerally alluring. It urged Matias's hands to hurry up to unbutton Duke and peel the shirt off of him.

With gasp-sniffs of Duke's smell, Matias opened the front of Duke's shirt and lifted it off of him. Colin stared wide-eyed at the expanse of Duke's muscular back in front of him; it was the wonderfully expectant Christmas-morning look.

Colin's hands fell in front of Duke's shoulders. Colin's arms were completely wrapped around Duke. Colin's mouth and tongue dove into making love to Duke's muscled back. With every kiss, lick, and nuzzle of Colin's on Duke's back, Duke only moaned in appreciation.

Duke had had a shitty day. He deserved some pleasure. Matias could only attempt to join the project of making Duke happy. Or at least alleviating Duke's pain.

"My God." Duke threw his head back. The top of Colin's blond hair danced below Duke's shoulderline as Colin made oral love to every inch of Duke's back.

It was Matias's turn to make Duke happy. He drew closer and planted a wet kiss on the side of Duke's neck. Duke moaned and his shoulder shook. Matias had the power to make this hulk of a man happy, so happy that he was quivering in ecstasy. That felt great. It actually felt amazingly great.

"I'm wondering." Duke spoke between gasps of air. "Should I feel bad about feeling so good right now?"

"You should feel good about feeling good," Colin answered, between kisses of Duke's shoulder blades.

Matias dove down for a slow, wet lick of Duke's right nipple. Matias's tongue drew a circle. Duke groan-shivered. "Oh fuck."

Duke pushed his chest to Matias's mouth. He must've wanted more.

Matias had that ability, newly discovered, to make Duke feel good. He slurped Duke's hairy pecs and his hard, beet-red areola and nipple.

Duke loosened his leg grip around Matias's hips. He moaned as he lifted his legs apart. Colin's hand was between Duke's legs. His fingers danced on the underside of Duke's crotch, kneading his dick and balls through his pants.

"You gonna take off those pants, Mister Fitness?" Colin punctuated his question with a long, slow kiss of Duke's hip, just above his waist. Matias had never thought of that as an erogenous one.

"If I can hold my hands steady enough." Duke spoke through quick breaths. He unbuttoned his pants. He grabbed the pants and wriggled his legs frantically, like a man running out of a burning building.

He managed to get his briefs off together with his pants.

There was Duke's dick, thick and purple-headed, lying almost in Matias's lap.

There was Duke's ass, turned toward Colin. Matias could be a little bit envious, but at least the view wasn't going to waste.

There was Matias, feasting on Duke's neck and chest. Duke was returning the favor to Matias as best he could, groping Matias's arms and shoulders and kissing the top of his head.

All or nothing. There wasn't anything wrong with doing what he'd always meant to do. Matias rose up and brought his lips up to Duke's.

Matias pushed his lips against Duke's. Duke sucked Matias's lips and threw his tongue into Matias's mouth.

Ferociously, they kissed. Matias pushed his tongue into Duke's mouth.

Had Matias really been scared of rejection? Did he really fear that Duke might've drawn away from a kiss? What could've been farther from reality? Duke was kissing, licking, and sucking Matias's mouth and tongue. Every hot breath of Duke's blew over Matias's face as testimony to his power to give Duke pleasure, to love and be loved.

"Fucking hell!" Duke yelled it out when he didn't even have any air in his lungs. It sounded deflated. He was bright red. He inhaled and he said it again. "Oh my fucking God!"

"I just did some cleanup." Colin tossed a handful of baby wipes into the trash can. His tongue was tracing lines along Duke's ass cheeks. Duke was pumping his ass cheeks in ecstasy like he was fucking the air. Matias's t-shirt had raised itself up; as Duke air-fucked to Colin's licking his ass cheeks, Duke's thick cock slid over Matias's belly.

"Are you actually gonna—" Duke gasped again. Colin moaned. Colin's mess of blond hair disappeared down at Duke's ass rim.

Colin moaned again. Duke gasped again.

Breathing hard and fast, Duke writhed his ass into Colin's face. At the same time, Duke lunged into Matias with his own lips and mouth, kissing and licking him.

"I've never — nobody's ever —" Duke gasped, then exhaled, then gasped again. He grabbed Matias's hand with one hand. With the other hand it looked like he was drawing his ass cheeks to open wider.

Duke's dick pushed against Matias's leg like it was bolted hard to a wall. It had no give. Matias hadn't felt a lot of dicks, but it had seemed pretty clear that dicks were supposed to have some up-and-down sway. Duke's had none, like a hard, thick bolt emerging from the beautiful dunes of his pubes.

Colin moaned almost as vocally as Duke did. His lips and tongue were buried in Duke's ass crack.

"It's polite to slurp that ass," Matias said down to Colin. "Like ramen. Just slurp it."

"Fuck" was all Colin said back. The top of his blond hair bobbed up and down, his tongue pleasuring Duke's rim.

"Did someone say *raw men?*" Duke smiled directly into Matias's face. The gloom was gone from Duke's eyes. He drew his lips toward Matias's mouth.

Matias kissed Duke again, breathing all of Duke's tongue and breath into himself. He embraced and brought Duke closer to himself. He wasn't just making love or getting off; he was healing Duke's deepest being.

"Are you guys punning without me?" Colin spoke up from down below.

Duke made a sound like a squeal in response. "Just don't stop what you're doing down there."

"Yeah." Matias could play boss. "You keep slurping that delicious ass and I'll keep kissing this gorgeous man."

Matias laughed a little at what he'd just said. *Delicious* and *gorgeous*. They were like purple prose, overused superlatives. But this time it was real. Duke, all of him, was *delicious* and *gorgeous* like nothing else in Matias's world had ever been.

Matias drew Duke's shirtless torso closer to him. If this chest wasn't delicious and gorgeous, nothing was. Duke's chest scar tickled Matias's nipple. Matias drew his mouth away from Duke's lips and moved down to kiss Duke's chest, running his tongue along the length of his scar.

If Duke's eyes had been ninety-five percent sorrow, the sorrow was now five percent, at most. The rest of his gaze screamed of sexual excitement, the pleasure of a wet tongue in his ass, and the joy of being loved.

Duke whispered and whimpered. "This is torture."

"I can think of worse places to be," Matias said up to Duke's eyes. "Colin and I making love to you is torture?"

"It's torture for my dick." Duke grinned and looked down. "I've never been this horny in my life."

"Really?" Colin asked. He loudly licked and slurped Duke's ass rim. "This makes you horny?" He slurped again. "For reals?"

"You're cruel," Duke said through short breaths.

Matias whispered to Duke's ear: "I think I'm being paged to go downstairs."

Duke thought about it for half a second. His eyebrows jumped up as he understood what *downstairs* was. He echoed the call: "Stat," Duke barked at Matias, through his hard breathing. He pointed his engorged cockhead at Matias's face.

Matias grinned. "You think I just aced the MCAT but I can't find the eleven-ounce dick in your crotch?" He said it with a laugh, but he couldn't take his eyes off of the dick.

Duke's shaft smelled innocently fresh like soap and fresh laundry. The tip smelled sweet, like a cotton-candy machine.

Matias inhaled deeply from Duke's pubes and shaft. He let the shiny, sweet-smelling dickhead slip into the cradle of his lips. He sucked it further into his mouth like a lollipop.

The dickhead was huge enough on its own to press hard against the roof of Matias's mouth. The rest of Duke's shaft followed the dickhead in. It was big, too big maybe, but Matias wanted it badly.

Colin was still feasting on Duke's ass, groaning little Colin-groans in small bursts of satisfaction. Those little groans were exactly how he'd sounded when he was lifting weights.

Duke swayed his hips in rhythm to Colin's licks and slurps. Occasionally Duke whimpered and shivered as Colin fingered a particularly sensitive spot in his ass.

Matias would do the same thing for Duke that Colin was doing: make love to him, give him love, make him happy. He and Colin together could save Duke from a very bad day.

Matias opened wide and let Duke's dick slide into his mouth. He wanted all of it inside him, even if that was physically impossible. He sucked hard and tried to take as much of it as would go in.

The dickhead slipped past Matias's tongue. He sucked hard to take it even deeper. It was already down his throat before Matias had the conscious realization that he was actually deep-throating Duke. He was actually doing this most intimate thing with this hot stud whom just maybe he was starting to love.

Duke's fingers landed on Matias's shoulders. He groped, or massaged, or both. Duke squeezed his hands firmly on Matias's shoulders at the same moments when Matias sucked harder on his cockhead.

Matias tried to half-open his lips to leave a little bit of air so he could actually slurp Duke's dick instead of just sucking it like a straw. Duke moaned in response to Matias's slurps of his dick, or in response to Colin's slurps of his ass, or both.

Duke cradled Matias's neck and head. He comforted Matias in his hands the same way Colin had comforted him in his lap.

Matias wasn't normally a person craving of attention or devoid of love. Even if he'd never been in a romantic relationship, and even if he'd never been close to any of his family, he'd never felt anything missing.

Duke's hands cradled Matias's temples. The gesture was pure love. There could have been no other purpose to it but love.

Duke's loving gesture gave Matias fulfillment and emotional satiation. But it also showed him what he'd lacked all along.

Maybe you don't know what you have until it's gone.

But you also don't know what you've been missing until you've had it.

Matias sucked and slurped on Duke's dick to return love with love. He couldn't put all of it in his mouth, but he could at least have a goal of Duke's balls touching Matias's chin. The way Duke chuckled when Matias rubbed his stubbly chin against Duke's balls: he must have liked that.

How had Matias spent twenty-three years without this, without even having anything resembling it? How had he lived?

Colin had been there with Colin for the past five of those years. Neither Matias nor Colin had allowed what they needed to come to fruition. Not until Duke had shown up.

Duke grunted. His dick pushed harder against the roof of Matias's mouth. He bent his body to better expose his ass to Colin's hungry mouth.

Duke's dickhead crowding up against the back of Matias's throat should have been painful, or at least uncomfortable. Matias should have had a gag reflex, or at least some discomfort. His hands should have been pushing Duke away.

Matias's hands only pulled Duke closer. Matias only wanted more of Duke, deeper in him. Nothing hurt.

Here Matias was. Doing something gay. That he'd never, or almost never, done before. And it felt so fucking good.

Between Duke's legs, Colin reached out to Matias's shoulders and tugged on his shirt. "Hey, this is a no clothes zone. Take off that shirt."

Without slowing down making oral love to Duke's dick, Matias followed directions. He unbuttoned himself and tossed the shirt off into the pile at the end of the bed.

Colin reached out again to Matias. His finger landed on a bead of sweat on Matias's chest. He traced it slowly, staring at Matias's eyes and chest.

Matias knew it as well as Colin did. He and Colin were roommates, but they'd never touched each other. Not like that.

Matias had been there for Colin. Colin had been there for Matias. But not like that.

Colin had never looked so handsome as he did now that Matias allowed himself to see Colin's beauty. Matias reached out in reciprocation and fondled Colin's shoulder, his bicep, his chest, his belly. He'd known Colin for five years, but everything was completely new.

Colin dove back into pleasuring Duke's rim with his mouth while fondling and caressing Matias's chest with his fingers. Duke's dick grew even more engorged in Matias's mouth. It filled like an already over-full balloon. Having gone from rock-hard to diamond-hard, it pressed hard against Matias's teeth and was becoming girthy enough to challenge how wide Matias could open his lips.

Matias made love to Duke's entire shaft. Its ridges and veins cradled and tickled his lips and tongue and even the roof of his mouth.

The part of Duke's shaft that wouldn't fit in his mouth, the very base, Matias pleasured with his fingers. He ran fingertip-circles around the base where Duke's dick met his pubes. He stuck his tongue out as far as he could beyond his lips so its tip would caress Duke's nutsack.

Duke's ballsack was almost hairless. As Matias's tongue approached it, there was only one stray, wispy hair. Duke's balls were hot and firm. His nutsack's skin tickled Matias's tongue like velvet.

Matias made his tongue flat and pressed it against the full surface of Duke's balls. Duke grunted. It was almost a howl. He pushed himself hard into Matias, then pushed himself up and down in Matias's mouth. He grunted again.

Duke's thighs bucked. His whole dick jerked, so hard that it almost threw Matias off of it.

Hot sperm gushed out, all over Matias's tongue and down his throat. Matias sucked down its gooey, sticky warmth. In his mouth it was sweeter, stickier, and warmer than Matias had imagined it being.

Duke bucked again. Another rope of nectar shot into Matias's mouth: this one more liquid than the last, like Duke was quenching Matias's thirst for cum.

Duke was pushing back. He grinded and pumped his ass back against Colin.

It wasn't just Colin's tongue that Duke's ass craved. Colin was fingering Duke's ass, pumping his middle finger in and out of it like a jackhammer.

Duke yowled with pleasure at every thrust of Colin's hand. Every time Colin's hand slid into his ass, his hips bucked and he shot another rope of cum into Matias's mouth.

"Wanna give me a hand?" Colin asked, with a light, playful squeeze of Matias's nipple, and a look toward his finger pumping in and out of Duke's ass.

"Oh fuck." Matias grabbed and groped Duke's ass cheek and thigh. That was already hot enough.

He had no idea how to put a finger into an ass. It was supposed to be slow and cautious or something like that. But Colin's finger was already in there. Maybe Matias could just join in.

He made his pointing finger erect and edged it over Duke's smooth, sweaty ass cheek to his textured rim. He pushed it in. Duke gasped. The inside of Duke's ass was warm and moist, and Duke was clenching his cheeks onto it, grabbing Colin's and Matias's fingers. Where their fingers were, how their fingers felt being clenched by those ass muscles — that must've been where a dude's dick would go and how a dude's dick would feel in the grip of those ass muscles.

"Fuck," Duke mumbled. His hands frantically roamed over Matias's face and shoulders, caressing and fondling him.

Duke clenched his ass hard on their fingers. Duke's dick was no longer pumping out cum. He was catching his breath.

Colin smiled. That "I done well" smile of Colin's was exactly how Matias had felt after the MCAT — and exactly how he felt now after having taken Duke from despair to pleasure.

Duke pulled his dick out of Matias's mouth. It felt missing something after that; indeed, you didn't know what you were missing until you had it once.

Duke flipped his whole body on the bed. He stared at Matias's dick. His hot breath coursed by Matias's engorged cockhead.

Warm lips held Matias's dickhead, then the entire shaft. Duke's warm lips and tongue were frantically working Matias's cock.

Matias had never felt anything like it. It was like Duke knew exactly every ridge and vein of Matias's dick, and was going to milk it to bathe him in pleasure.

Duke's face was even more beautiful than his body. Matias stared into Duke's eyes. Duke looked back at Matias with a look of affection and gratitude.

That did it. Duke's eyes did it. Matias's orgasm was coming.

His cum welled up in him. He couldn't hold it any more. He shook and bucked. He pushed forward into Duke and shot into his mouth.

Duke frantically sucked and licked Matias's shaft and dickhead. Matias kept cumming as long as Duke kept stimulating his dick.

Matias shot more cum and harder than he'd thought possible. His thighs hurt from bucking during that orgasm.

When his cum was finally spent, he only felt Duke's warm, loving mouth wrapped around his deflating dick. Matias's eyes were already closed. He just wanted to sleep.

Duke let Matias's dick out. He wiped off the string of sticky cum on his lips. He softly kissed Matias's thigh. It was just a kiss after a blowjob, but it felt like a love story. Matias answered by wrapping his leg around Duke's torso.

Colin reached out and wrapped his arm around Duke's waist. He moved his hand to hold Matias's hand.

Colin was moaning. Duke was licking up and down Colin's long, skinny dick.

"You sniffing my dick, man?" Colin asked. His bright white teeth beamed from beneath his smile.

"Maybe," Duke answered, his eyes as bright as Colin's smile. He kissed Colin's dick lengthwise, like it was a corn cob. He rubbed his facial stubble on it. "I might be kissing your dick too. And licking it."

Duke wrapped his hand around Colin's shaft and started slowly pumping it up and down while staring into Colin's eyes. While he jerked the dick he licked and sucked on its tip. Then he cupped his palm under Colin's balls.

"I wanna milk all the cum out of you," Duke whispered up to Colin, and smiled. "For how good you've been to me. For how much you care." Duke drew his tongue out and with his tongue tip drew a circle on Colin's dickhead.

Colin gritted his teeth and blinked. He couldn't hold out long. A gob of cum shot from Colin's dick up into Duke's mouth. Duke caught it, swallowed it, and grinned at Colin. Colin only sighed: "Damn."

Duke brought his mouth down to cover Colin's dick. After he mounted Colin's dick with his mouth, he caught and swallowed rope after rope of Colin's orgasm.

Colin's eyes turned tired. He inhaled deeply and looked across at Matias, then down at Duke. "Hey Duke. Flip over and get up here."

Duke flipped his body around. He lay down on his back, head on the pillow between Matias and Colin.

Duke smelled like sex and sweat. Matias hadn't known that smell before, but he was starting to like it.

"You guys are amazing," Duke murmured through half-closed eyes. He softly held Colin's and Matias's hands.

"Before." Matias felt like he was babbling, but maybe what he said would make a little bit of sense. "Before all this, I really didn't know what love was."

"Duke. Dude." Colin was whispering too. "I hope you feel better."

"Damn." Duke sounded so sleepy that laughing and sobbing would've come out all the same. He turned his head left and right. The hurt was gone from his eyes. "I love both of you guys. I love you guys. I love the three of us."

Nine

"Clicks are up four percent month over month." Colin's audience nodded approvingly. Colin's PowerPoint report flickered in front of them.

Colin's dad, Senator Warner for the purposes of the meeting, was part of the audience. He nodded in rhythm with the rest of the campaign team.

Colin clicked to the next slide. "Online donations are up thirty percent month over month. We brought in over a hundred thousand dollars in online donations in the past thirty days."

Colin's dad tapped his finger on the conference table. "Average donation size?"

"Well, online, it's, um," Colin clicked on his spreadsheet. He stopped himself from giggling when thinking about that night in the hot tub with the digital scale. "Online, fifty-seven dollars and eighty-three cents is the average donation size. Twenty dollars is the mode, the most common donation amount."

"I know what a mode is. The argmax of the probability mass function." Colin's dad rolled his eyes at Colin with just a bit of disdain. "I'm worried that we're not attracting the big money here. We might need to shift the messaging."

"The Medicare-for-all blog post brings in the most donations." Colin looked back at his spreadsheet. "Most of them only for five dollars. But lots of donations and supporters."

"Good voters, but they don't have any money." Colin's dad sighed and shook his head. "We might need some messaging on the opposite side of that issue."

"Like, against Medicare for all?" Colin opened a new document on his laptop, ready to take notes.

"Yeah. Attacking Obamacare works pretty well dollar-wise too." Colin's dad looked at something in the stack of papers he held. His finger traced a row of polling numbers.

Nate the data guy tapped a pencil erase on the table and raised a finger in the air to make a point: "Messaging against quote unquote *socialist medicine* polls well with likely donors of net worth above one million."

Colin coughed a little bit uncomfortably. Providing healthcare for the poor had been a bulwark of his father's political campaigns as long as he could remember.

But then, he hadn't really seen inside the campaign until he'd started working on this campaign. Before that, Colin had heard his dad's campaigns only through the Facebook and YouTube debates they ignited.

Colin looked around the room. All eyes were on him again. "Um. So. Back to the online campaign report. Twitter followers are up ten percent since last month. Instagram followers up twenty-two percent." Colin smiled proudly. Sure, he had gotten the online campaign manager only because he was Senator Warner's son, but he also was doing a good job of it.

"Good. Good." Colin's dad leaned back in his chair. "But don't forget: this is still a money game."

"Yes." Colin nodded. He wasn't the money guy. He was only the online campaign manager.

"We've got a good update." Colin's dad sat forward and upright. "Let's adjourn for now."

When Colin started to stand up, his father's eyes shot at him like a watchtower's spotlight. "Colin, stay a bit please. Let's have a tete-a-tete." Colin nodded agreement. Agreement was his only option with his father, after all.

The rest of the staff shuffled out. They kept their eyes on the ground, seemingly aware of the discomfort between Colin and his father.

"Shut the door, Colin, will you?"

Colin shut and locked the door of the windowless meeting room. Whatever this tete-a-tete was, it was going to be serious business.

Dad pulled a pack of cigarettes from his slacks pocket, together with a lighter. He lit one, in the most offhand manner possible, as if it were 1963 and no big deal.

Senator Warner's smoking was a secret. He never did it when anyone unrelated was around, never at his office, almost never even when his family was around. He smoked, but as far as how much and how often, only he himself knew. But this was the first time Colin had seen him smoke at his office.

"I'm a senator." He took a puff and blew smoke at the ceiling, then shook his head. "I hear things. People tell me things. People talk to me."

"Yeah." Colin slid his chair closer to the table and put his elbows on the table and hands under his chin. He was trying hard to understand the significance of what he was being told. "Definitely."

"I'm not flying around Miami in a spy helicopter. I'm a thousand miles away, in DC, most of the time anyway. But I hear about things." Colin's dad stared at the *Warren Warner For Senate* banner hanging on the wall, as if the angles of its letter font held deep answers.

"Yeah." Colin shrugged and nodded. His father was stating the obvious. "Anything specifically you're thinking of?"

"People know you're my son." Colin's dad took a hungry puff from his cigarette, as if it was about to be taken away from him. The tip shone apple red. "Everybody knows you're my son."

"Sure." Colin smiled. His life had been built and defined by virtue of his being Warren Warner's son. Few people ever referred to "Colin Warner," just Colin Warner. It was always "Colin Warner, Warren Warner's son."

"Look." Colin's dad blew smoke at the ceiling, then angrily put out his cigarette in his styrofoam cup of water. He seemed to be punishing the cup, or the water in it. "I've heard about your little workout sessions at the gym. With Matias, whom by the way I have always liked and respected, whom I would never suspect of such

108

things, and with some other dude, some fitness trainer who's notorious for this sort of thing."

"This sort of thing?" Colin shook his head. Caustic cigarette smoke reached him and burned his nostrils.

"The LGBTQA, gender diversity, marriage equality, whatever they're calling it now." Colin's dad shook his head as if shaking a fly off his face.

"What specifically—" Colin leaned in closer. His father's lips and teeth were stained with smoke, and his eyes alternated between staring at Colin's neck and at the wall behind him.

"You're apparently in some kind of homo relationship with these guys." Colin's dad inhaled and sighed loudly. He looked like he'd just caught his son being naughty. "My contacts have seen you at the gym, at restaurants, even in Coral Gables, acting like a fucking homo."

"*Acting like a fucking homo?*" Colin shook his head. "Is that the term you used when you were the headline speaker at Miami Pride?"

"Don't bring politics into this, Colin."

"I'm not talking about politics. I'm just saying you don't sound like that when—"

"You're my son, not some fag voter whose marriage I have to applaud for." Colin's dad pulled the cigarette box out of his pocket again and used his teeth to pull out a stick. He lit it and sucked on it like expected it to make his son straight. "I have higher standards than what I say out in public. This is my son we're talking about."

"Alright. Whatever." Colin shook his head. It wasn't his job to counsel or even evaluate his dad's two-facedness. "The point is, when we met Duke, the fitness trainer, Matias and I realized we're gay."

"No way. No fucking way you're gay." Colin's dad stood up at the last word, *gay*, and towered over Colin, looking down on him like an angry god. "You're brainwashed. Or on drugs. There's no way."

"I'm sorry for the anguish it might cause you." That was the line Colin had mentally prepared should his father confront him about his sexuality. He hadn't expected it to happen that soon, and maybe if he'd had more time, he would've been able to come up with a better line. But the *anguish* line was all he'd had a mere two months after Duke moved in.

"If you're sorry about the anguish you're causing your own father, then why are you living your life as a faggot?" Colin's dad threw his arms in the air. He was making a show of his exasperation. Colin was supposed to feel like a bad son.

"Dad. There's genetic — physiological — I mean, I can't control who I am inside."

"You were always normal until now."

"What? I was always—"

"Remember Senior Prom back at Pine Crest? You and Stacey? How can you be gay now?"

"Yeah, I and Stacey." Colin's thoughts flashed back to memories of high school awkwardness, of just not finding himself drawn to girls the way other guys were. There was nothing wrong with girls, but to the teenage Colin Warmer, they'd seemed kind of overrated. "Our, mine and Stacey's, Ritz-Carlton room for the night. As soon as we were in the room I took out my PS4 and ordered room-service buffalo wings. She asked me if I'm gay. Back then, I said no. That was six years ago."

"Jesus Christ." Colin's dad rolled his eyes and sucked on his cigarette. He looked a bit like an old queen when he did that, but Colin wouldn't be the one to tell him that. "This is supposed to be my son?"

"I don't think there's any question—" Colin grinned. It had always been a running joke how he and his father exactly resembled each other in face, body, even voice, gestures, and walk.

"This can't go on." Colin's dad put out his second cigarette in the same styrofoam cup. This time was angrier than the first. He looked around the conference room. One of his banners caught his eye and he stared at is as if it were a painful reminder. "You realize, people are always watching me? That I'm trying to get re-elected here?"

"I'm quite aware of your re-election campaign, Dad." Colin's word *Dad* struck his father like a bullet. He winced in discomfort. His eyes crawled from Colin's face back to the styrofoam cup. He gazed at the cup longingly, like he was mourning his cigarette.

"What's that saying?" Colin's dad paced around the room. "The only things that could make me lose the election are if I'm a necrophile or if my son's a faggot?"

"I don't think that's how the saying goes." That word hurt. Every time it hurt. Now it hurt more, because Colin knew, and his dad knew, Colin was gay. When Colin's dad had used the term before then, Colin could at least brush it off as a random, one-size-fits-all insult spouting from his father's mouth toward his disappointing son.

"Alright. I've got a campaign to run, and I'm going back to DC tonight." Colin's dad looked at his watch. "You're off the campaign until further notice. Further notice being when you get over this gay thing."

"It's not—" Colin felt like he was in a public service announcement about accepting homosexuality. "It's not a thing I can come out of or get over."

"Colin." His dad sighed deeply. He looked down and shook his head. "I am not capable of policing every minute of your behavior. What that means is that there's a lot you can do that I will never find out about. But I just want you to agree that I will never find out about it. Alright?" He extended his hand to Colin like they were about to make a deal.

"What do you mean, you'll never find out about it?" Colin shook his head. "You're gonna wear earplugs and a blindfold all day or what?"

"Fucking hell." With his right hand, Colin's dad karate-chopped his desk. "I'm trying to be reasonable and meet you in the middle here."

"Reasonable?" Colin's father was a politician, after all. He specialized in claiming that whatever outcome he wanted was the only reasonable option. "You want me to guarantee that you will never find out who I am and who I love?"

"I am saying you can live your life, no matter how much I disapprove of your choices, but I don't want any of it to come back to me."

"Yeah?" Colin stood up. What was galling was not that his father was making such demands. Dad always made demands. Colin's dad had never been easy-going or easy-to-please in any regard. What was galling was that he seemed to think his demands were entirely modest and reasonable.

"How about you can have your gay-hating opinions, the exact opposite of what you tell the voters, by the way, as long as I don't have to bear the brunt of your homophobia? How about that for reasonable -- Dad?"

"Colin, why do you have to make this—"

"I don't have to make this anything. You can have your caveman views as long as I don't have to hear about them. And as long as no one else has to hear about them for that matter. How's that? Reasonable? I think so."

"You're off the campaign, you realize." Colin's dad looked up at his own portrait. Maybe he wondered how such a great man could have borne gay offspring.

"Fine." Colin looked directly into his father's eyes and nodded. He'd never been able to do that before. But then, he hadn't been an adult before. "I'm not going to work for someone who disapproves of my whole life."

"You mean someone who created your whole life?" Colin's father squinted disapprovingly at his son.

"Wow. That's exactly the line that you always mocked." Colin sighed. His father had always scorned parents who thought they had the right to treat their children as they wished only because they'd given birth to them.

"I am free to change my mind." Colin's dad raised his eyebrows in all his senatorial glory.

"And I am free to get the hell out of here." Colin said the words clearly. He filled with pride. He'd never stood up to his father like that. He'd never stood up to his father at all.

Something had changed since he'd fallen in love with Duke and Matias.

Before Duke, Colin hadn't considered himself gay.

Now, living and loving as he pleased, Colin was his own man.

Ten

"Together now. Push!" Standing there in front of the two bench-press stations, arms folded, Duke looked more like a fitness trainer than he ever had before.

Matias pushed. To his right, Duke pushed.

Standard form was to look up at the bar and handles. With a sight like Duke in front of them, it was a little too easy to take liberties. When Duke reminded his charges to look up at the bar and not ahead at him, he said it with a knowingly mischievous grin of a man who knew his power to tempt.

Duke's shorts were just a little too short. His muscle shirt was made just a little too parsimoniously. He looked like a college athlete wearing his high-school clothes, or like a man who hadn't yet realized that his expanding muscles require bigger clothes.

In that trainer outfit of his, Duke's biceps, triceps, and especially glutes were on full display. He wore it only for training Colin and Matias. Duke was hot, and he knew it.

"Down, down easy, down smooth." Duke paced in front of them like a drill sergeant. His glutes were screaming from under the thin fabric of his shorts. Maybe on the front of his shorts that was a shadow, or maybe it was an outline of his big dick. But Matias was supposed to be focusing on the weight, not on his hot trainer. He eased the weight down.

"Try to set it down so it doesn't make a sound," Duke announced to Colin and Matias both. Matias's weight landed back down in its seat with only the quietest clang. Colin's weight, next to him, did the same.

They were good students. Their demanding fitness trainer was the first to admit it. They both went from bench pressing only a bit above a hundred pounds to both comfortably pressing a hundred eighty.

"Alright, guys." Duke announced.

"Whew." Matias dropped his hands down from the handles.

"No, no!" Duke shook his head — his gorgeous head. "Alright guys, meaning next rep is the last rep. Not meaning that previous rep was the last rep."

"Oh shit," Colin whispered from the bench on Matias's right. That was saltier language than Colin usually used in such situations — but he'd grown bolder in many ways since having been fired from his father's campaign.

"I heard that!" Duke shouted, all pretend-indignant.

"Whatever, man." Colin broke out in tired, winded laughter, still lying down, rolling his head left and right under the bench press bar. "I don't work for the fucking Warren Warner for Senate campaign anymore. I'm the fucking black sheep now. I can talk however the fuck I want. I can even fuck however the fuck I want."

"I'm gonna wash your mouth out with soap." Duke wagged a finger at Colin. "Or with my hot cum. Or something."

"Gentlemen!" Matias covered his hand with his mouth in mock shock, still lying back on the bench. "Not at the gymnasium! Not even after closing time!"

"Yeah, tsk tsk." Duke wagged his finger again at the two men lying down on the two weightlifting benches in front of him. "Don't offend our Harvard man here. They don't use that kind of language up in Cambridge."

"Fuck, don't remind me." Colin sighed. He looked over to Matias at his side. "How much longer do we have with you, Matias?"

"Three more grueling months!" Matias said, his head tilted. Leaving Colin and Duke was going to be the hardest thing he'd ever done. Harder than the MCAT, definitely. He tilted his head upright quickly enough so he wouldn't risk suddenly crying like he did last time he contemplated it.

Yes, it was Harvard. It was his dream. But it would still be the hardest thing he'd ever done, leaving his first true loves behind. After moving up to Harvard, Matias could fly down to Miami and visit Colin and Duke — but how many free weekends would he have as a Harvard Med student? Their relationship, their closeness, their lazy

Monday evenings training together at the gym — it could never be the same.

"And Colin? How much longer are you staying on the dole?" Duke asked. He knew perfectly well phrasing the question that way would raise Colin's ire.

Like Matias, Duke found it hilarious that Colin was collecting unemployment benefits. But fired was fired, and Colin was indeed fired, even if he had all kinds of investment accounts to fall back on, and if his trust funds had long fallen out of his parents' control.

Colin got out from under the bench-press bar and stood up. Matias stood up alongside Colin.

Matias tilted his whole body upward, quickly. Everything spun a little: maybe from having gotten up so quickly, or maybe from the shock of what he'd just been contemplating. At least for the moment, Colin and Duke were right there, next to him, standing in the calm air-conditioned air of a closed gym.

Standing side by side, it felt like Colin and Matias were waiting for Duke to give them medals. They deserved some acclaim: their physical progress under Duke's tutelage had been tremendous. Their personal progress was bigger and more important.

If there were medals for learning who they were and for learning how to love, Colin and Matias deserved at least the bronze. Maybe even the gold.

"Well." Colin cleared his throat, sounding a little bit huffy and indignant at the *on the dole* part. "I am actively seeking work, as is required by my unemployment benefits, I'll have you know."

He paced over to the water fountain, leaned down, and drank from it. At the sight of that, Matias couldn't stop thinking about the feeling of catching Duke's orgasm in his mouth: how close it made him feel to this huge bulk of a man who was now standing in front of him as his trainer.

"Yeah, Colin, seeking work as what?" Matias loudly snickered. Snickering under his breath would've been rude. Matias wasn't one to hide his teasing and taunting of Colin. "Your University of Miami degree in political science qualifies you for maybe — standing around and looking pretty?"

"That's my job around here, isn't it?" Colin gave the good-naturedly weary look of a man accustomed to mockery.

Matias's own University of Miami degree in philosophy didn't qualify him for much either, so he was allowed to tease Colin about such things. At least Matias, unlike Colin, had taken the science prerequisites for medical school.

Unlike Colin, he didn't have a family connection to fall back on — but then, Colin no longer had a family connection either. Both of Colin's parents weren't answering his calls. Colin had relayed the information to his roommates in the quietest of mutters one morning.

"Well, on a serious note." Colin cleared his throat and looked around as if he was scanning a legislative committee. He still had his father's rhetorical poise, even if he was now estranged from him. "I have an immediate offer for my dream job in DC. At the Human Rights Campaign. Gay rights campaign management work."

"Oh shit! Your dad would go apeshit!" Duke cough-laughed. "You'd be working for a bunch of queers!"

"Well you know." Colin flicked his eyebrows. He looked totally ready for a Senate hearing. "The irony is that the Human Rights Campaign people think that my dad's the bees' knees. He has their highest approval rating for his pro-gay platform."

"Progressive in the streets, homophobe in the sheets." Matias winked lasciviously at his own joke. It was the best quip he could come up with, even if it didn't really make sense. "I don't even know what that means."

"Hold up." Duke made the perfect hand gesture to accompany those words. "Colin, you're moving to DC?"

"If I accept the job." Colin looked down at the gym floor, a little embarrassed. "And it's my dream job. And it pays as much in real money as I was making at my father's campaign in bullshit nepotism money."

"So theoretically. If you take the dream job." Duke looked down, staring into the gym floor. "How soon would you leave?" He busied himself polishing the metal lift bar on one of the weight machines.

"Theoretically." Colin exhaled very deeply. "If I accept the job. I have two weeks from the offer date before I have to start work. So I'd leave next week."

"Holy shit. Next week you're moving to DC?" Duke looked at Colin, wide-eyed. His eyes roved up and down over Colin, as if it was the last time he'd ever see him.

"Well, congressional primaries are coming up." Colin shrugged. "Elections wait for no man."

"Neither do erections." Matias grinned proudly again.

"I'm gonna miss your lame jokes, man." Colin looked at Matias and shook his head. Colin had been the first, and really only, fan of Matias the Comedian, all the way back in the University of Miami dorms.

"It's sort of hard to digest that this is going to be all over." Matias sighed. "How many years Colin and I have lived together? And how many amazing months now together with you, Duke?"

"All good things come to an end and all that." Duke shook his head. He'd been through a lot more than Colin or Matias. He was inured to disappointment and loss. "And that brings me to a point."

"You mean gym's closed and we should leave?" Matias asked. Duke's trainer pass allowed him to stay inside the facility with his clients well after closing time — but like any privilege, it wasn't one to be abused.

"Don't worry about that. Nobody even knows we're here." Duke looked around. "No, the point I was going to make, is now that I'm no longer sending money to my nonexistent son, I really have no excuse to be mooching free living quarters off of you guys."

"How much were you sending? A thousand a month?" Colin tapped on the keys of an imaginary calculator floating in the air.

"Yeah." Duke walked over to where that imaginary calculator was floating and tapped some keys on it as well. "A thousand a month."

"Can you find a decent apartment in Miami for a thousand a month?" Colin smiled like he'd just swallowed the whole delicious canary of Duke's objections. "I'm thinking *no*?"

"I'm also thinking *no*." Duke covered his mouth with his forearm as he laughed a little.

"Yeah. So don't worry. And you, like, saved our lives when you moved in with us." Colin looked at Duke almost worshipfully. "I mean, where we were then, where we are now — just think about it." Colin smiled.

"Guys." Duke shook his head with a friendly smirk. Only Duke could make a smirk look so benign. "Don't get over-confident about your physical strength. Just stay the fuck away from danger. That's the best defense."

"Not what I mean." Colin folded his arms across his chest, the same way Duke always did as he was watching his charges lift. In that moment, Colin resembled a scaled-down Duke more than he resembled a younger Senator Warren Warner. "I never loved anyone until this all happened."

"I'm no expert in love. I don't know how much I could've taught anyone about that." Duke's face flushed a little. He slapped a weight machine. Its metal shell clanged in response to his palm. "Anyway, I thought love is opening your home to a stranger sleeping in a garage. You guys were already experts."

"Love, and being my own man. Being someone apart from my dad." Colin exhaled and shook his head. "I never felt myself as an independent being until this all happened, until I came out to my parents, until I had to be on my own."

"Speaking of becoming an independent life form." Duke cleared his throat and nodded like he was about to reveal something everybody already knew. "I'm gonna need to find a new place to live anyway, if you're moving up to DC."

Duke looked up with his eyes, as if pointing up to Washington, DC on a map that was centered on Miami. It was dorky and stupid and endearing. It was that much more endearing because this was the Duke that Matias would soon be living apart from.

"Oh no, man." Colin squinted and shook his head as if he was deeply offended by the suggestion. "You and Matias can keep living at the condo even when I'm pimping my ass on K Street up in DC."

"You're just gonna—" Duke smiled and shook his head.

"Colin is like that." Matias was stage-whispering intentionally loudly enough for Colin to hear.

"I'm holding the condo as an investment asset, dudes." Colin clapped his hands together. "Any money I could make from renting it out wouldn't be worth all the hassle, the risk, the taxes, whatever, whatever." Colin sighed and slowly rolled his head on his neck — like a man of a certain mature age, already very much burdened by the world. "You guys will be doing me a favor by living there."

"I guess if I absolutely have to, I could consider doing you such a favor." Duke smiled. He silently mouthed the words *thank you* at Colin. Colin mouthed back *you're welcome*.

"We're practically living at Biscayne Fitness with you anyway, man." Colin laughed and slapped his own biceps and triceps. "Are you sure nobody minds us hanging around here so late?"

"Little secret, guys." Duke held his finger to his lips. "The security cameras at Biscayne Fitness are all fakes."

"No shit." Colin laughed and looked up at the very realistic-looking black cameras in every corner of the gym, sometimes stacked three high. "I guess this place cheaps out where it counts."

"Including cheaping out on paying trainers a decent wage?" Duke grinned.

"Oh yeah. That too." Colin shook his head.

"They had real cameras." Duke looked up at at the ceiling and pointed out the menacing-looking "video cameras" that were pointed down at the gym floor. "But the real cameras kept breaking. Fixing them was expensive. And the security guard they had to hired to watch the video feed was expensive. Fake cameras are a lot cheaper."

"They could just get a love doll in a blue uniform instead of a security guard." Matias nodded seriously.

"Ha!" Colin's amused squawk sounded just like his father's, even if Matias knew well enough not to remind him about the resemblance. "You can't see me, losers!" Colin pulled down the front of his shorts. His trimmed sandy blond pubes looked as if he'd been grooming them all his life for the camera. He waved his semi-hard dick at the faux cameras above. "Look at what's real right here!"

"Speaking of love dolls." Matias smiled and pointed at Colin's crotch with his thumb. "Check out the pencil dick on that blond one."

Colin responded by rolling his eyes. Nevertheless chastised by Matias's observation, he pulled his shorts back up over his dick. Momentarily.

"I admit." Colin pulled down the front of his shorts again. "I've got a pencil dick when compared with Duke's eleven-ouncer. I even pale in comparison to stubby little Matias here, whose dick outweighs mine. There is no shame in any of that. But is any of you brave enough to show yourselves to the ersatz cameras that hover above us like ancient mythical deities?"

He smiled defiantly at the fake security cameras above. He shifted his eyes back and forth between the cameras above and the dick in his crotch, as if confirming that the two existed in the same plane of space-time, and he was indeed waving his thing for the cameras.

His dick was harder now: still skinny, but visibly growing longer. He jerked it again. It was stiff and the veins stood out prominently, running like highways up and down on it. A shiny crown of precum had formed on the tip.

"I've got an ancient deity right here." Matias slipped down the front of his shorts just enough to show off his dick. His own dick had filled out a bit from seeing Duke in his tighty-whitey gym trainer uniform, then filled out some more from Colin's incorrigible penile exhibitionism.

"Gentlemen, gentlemen!" Duke held both hands up in the air, palms outward. He could've been a football referee, except football referees didn't wear tight fabric shorts to barely cover their incredibly delicious asses and cocks. "Did everyone check their email today? See anything interesting?"

"You're on Brandon Cody's mailing list too?" Colin grinned hugely, as though he'd found a brother in arms. "Maybe we can split a subscription to the paid section of the—"

"Um, no, that's not the email I'm talking about." Duke laughed, biting his lower lip.

"Oh. Um." Colin coughed and shook his head. "I was joking."

Duke pointed at Matias and Colin. "Whip out your hot, hard, battery-powered six-inch blowers right now, gentlemen." Matias and Colin already knew Duke's vocabulary. They took out their phones. "Now click on Gmail and see what all three of us just got in the email today from Test Sure Miami."

"Oh, *that*." Matias smiled. He'd already seen that email that morning. It wasn't much of a surprise — he and Colin were pretty much virgins, after all — so he didn't have much of a reaction to it. "We're all tested and certified one hundred percent STD-free."

"Hooray!" Colin waved an imaginary flag and blew on an imaginary kazoo. It might've been a kazoo.

"You know what that means, right?" Duke beamed a big, happy smile.

"That I was just joking about being a regular at the gloryhole at the university library?" Matias asked. He fluttered his eyebrows.

"Well yeah, that." Duke sighed. "But it also means: let's hit the showers!" His grin, and the way his eyes scanned Colin's and Matias's bodies, said very well what he had in mind. In the interests of health and responsibility, they'd stuck to jerking and sucking one another off until the results were in.. But now that their clean test results were in

— and all three of them knew it — there was a whole world of pleasure awaiting the three of them.

"You mean the showers aren't just for showering?" Colin held his hand to his mouth daintily.

"I guess it depends what you include in your definition of showering." Duke laughed so loudly that it was a good thing no one else was at the gym.

"As a philosopher, I'm willing to accept the most inclusive definitions." Matias pursed his entire face, held an imaginary monocle to his eyes, and nodded seriously at Duke. "So let's fucking do it!"

Duke grabbed a towel from the rack next to him. He snapped it at Colin and Matias. "To the showers, boys!"

"Men, men." Colin sighed. "You made us into men already."

"Then it's a good time to check your manliness." Duke opened his locker. With a glance over his shoulder, he slipped off his shorts, giving Colin and Matias another full view of that dick and ass. He threw his t-shirt in after the shorts and locked the locker. He was standing there buck-naked in the locker room, for Colin and Matias to admire his body while acting nonchalant.

No matter how many times Matias had seen Duke naked, the view of Duke nonchalantly exhibiting his body of muscle was always impressive. No one, not even online, had that kind of muscle, ass, and dick. And Duke was so down-to-earth about his physical powers. He knew he had a hot body, but he didn't look down on anyone because of it.

Duke stepped into a shower cubicle. He turned on the water. He didn't close the plastic curtain behind him.

"Get naked and get in here," Duke called out to Matias and Colin. The way he said it was so casual, just like telling them to raise or lower a weight.

Colin, laughing, turned on the remaining lights in the locker room. "I can't believe we're doing this."

Colin took off his clothes and dumped them in a locker. His body was beautiful as always, fair and pink and almost virginal, beautiful in the highly sexual way that Matias had never bothered to notice all those years.

"Hurry up, Harvard boy." Duke's semi-hard dick swung like a pendulum as he snapped a towel at Matias.

There was no need to keep mentioning Harvard, but Matias would be a good sport about it. He slipped off his shorts with a grin. His fat dick was already hard. The bottom of Matias's t-shirt rested up against it. Matias pulled off his t-shirt too.

"Get in here now." Duke shook his head at Colin and Matias. He rolled his eyes with hammed-up annoyance.

"Sure, man." Colin was grinning as he stepped into the cubicle. At least it was one of the big ones. Miami being Miami, it had certainly been used by two men at once. Maybe it had even been designed for that. Whoever designed the cubicle might not have known, however, that three men could be in love with one another.

Matias joined Colin. They were both at the edge of the cubicle, out of the water's reach, while Duke stood confidently under the jets of water from the ceiling.

Duke squeezed body gel from the wall-mounted dispenser into his palm. Matias started to do the same. Duke stopped him: "No, dude. Let me do it."

"You're gonna wash us?" Matias asked with a laugh.

Duke only answered by patting Matias's and Colin's backs so the two stood facing each other under the shower. Matias's dickhead rested comfortably on Colin's abs. Colin's stuff dick pointed somewhere into Matias's inner thigh.

Duke's soapy hand ran all over Matias's back. He squeezed in all the right places. It felt like a sports massage, with extra squeezes on Matias's ass.

Duke's other hand soaped up Colin. Colin's perpetual grin turned into a gasp and mouth-agape enjoyment of pleasure. He was moaning as Duke soaped him.

Duke's hands were pushing Colin and Matias closer together. Colin's blue eyes blazed bright as he stared at Matias. "We've been through a lot together," Colin whispered. His warm breath ran across Matias's lips like tropical wind.

"We've been through a hell of a lot together." Matias smiled and nodded, without taking his eyes off of Colin's eyes. "I'm glad we are where we are now. And that includes you, Duke." Matias glanced past Colin's face to make sure Duke knew he was included.

"Thanks, guys." Duke smiled. "Maybe this isn't very manly, but I love you guys."

"There's nothing un-manly about love," Colin said with an authoritative nod. "I love you dudes." He looked at Matias's eyes and drew his lips closer to Matias.

Colin's chest pressed in and out faster with his breathing. His lips quivered a little.

Matias took the leap. He pushed his lips into Colin's.

Their eyes locked together. The way Colin wrapped his lips around Matias's tongue and sucked on it was like that tongue had all the world's sustenance for him. They stared into each other's eyes. Colin closed his eyes for a half-second, then opened them again. Maybe the view was too intense to miss.

Matias pushed his tongue into Colin's mouth like he was trying to satisfy a century's worth of desire. Colin only opened his mouth wider, along with his eyes. Then Colin's tongue slipped into Matias's mouth: roaming, exploring, licking his tongue and lips.

Matias pushed his dick against Colin, like he was fucking his abs. They wrapped their arms around each other and pressed their chests together as they kissed.

Duke whispered, "I fucking love watching you guys kiss."

Duke's soapy hand was in Matias's ass rim, scrubbing up and down. Duke's thick, rough-skinned finger ran circles along Matias's hole. It only made Matias want Duke's dick instead of his finger. Up until then, he'd been content to play with Duke's cock, suck it, make love to it with his whole body, but never put it inside his ass.

Thinking about Duke's dick pounding his ass, Matias kissed Colin fiercely. It wasn't like one was a substitute for the other. They only enhanced the experience. Colin made Matias hornier for Duke, and Duke made Matias hornier for Colin.

Matias spread his legs wider. Colin's dick lazily pressed farther into the crevice of Matias's inner thigh. Duke grew more assertive at Matias's ass: he was slipping his finger into the region that could only be described as "inside."

Every press of Duke's hand on Matias's rim and every thrust of his finger into the hole made Matias's dick grow harder. It felt like it must've been gushing precum on Colin's abs, even if it was only droplets.

Colin's stomach skin was cool and smooth on Matias's wet dickhead. Colin's mouth was all heat and wet desire, sucking and licking at Matias, accompanied by little moans of satisfaction.

Hot water hit Matias's ass. Duke was spraying water from the detachable shower head into Matias's butthole. Matias wanted to step back to feel the water jets harder in his ass, but he also wanted to step forward and take Colin deeper in his mouth and squeeze Colin's back muscles even harder.

Duke's hands returned Matias's back. He ran his palms down to the ass cheeks, then rested them there, with a gentle squeeze that parted the cheeks.

Tongue. Matias screamed and gasped.

"What?" Colin asked.

"Duke is—" Matias breathed heavily between words. "Duke's licking my ass."

Matias settled into enjoying the sensation of Duke's tongue running up and down slowly, then rapidfire pushing into his hole. He inhaled deeply: as Colin french-kissed him he was definitely emitting some kind of masculine pheromone smell. The smell, Colin's kisses, Duke's licking — it all made Matias that much hornier.

"Oh fuck," Colin mumbled while Matias's tongue roamed over his teeth. Then Matias felt it too: Duke had slid his hands in between Colin's and Matias's bodies and was rubbing and jerking both of their dicks.

Colin's dick lay side-by-side with Matias's in Duke's hands. He'd soaped them up. Every press and rub of dick on dick was sending pleasure through Colin's and Matias's bodies.

"Feels like he's—" Matias moaned again from the rimming and the dick-friction. "Feels like he's rubbing sticks to make fire."

Colin laughed, into Matias's mouth. Those moments of Colin's laughter were always the sexiest, always the moments when Matias most wanted to devour him whole. Matias gently thrust his hips back and forth, like he was fucking Colin's crotch, to rub his dick harder on Colin's.

Duke slapped Matias's ass. It was just hard enough to be erotic without being painful. "Change up!" His tongue drew out of Matias's ass. Matias only sighed in exhilaration; maybe he couldn't have taken more of that rimming without cumming.

Duke shifted his position. He greedily groped all over Colin's and Matias's intertwined bodies as they kissed.

Now Duke was behind Colin. His grin shone at Matias. He was soaping up Colin's ass rim.

Colin sighed hot air into Matias's face. He leaned in further. The flat surface of his tongue scraped the whole of Matias's ear.

Matias grabbed onto Colin's sides harder. Colin prodded at Matias's ear with his wet tongue. It felt like he was going to slide his tongue deep inside.

"Oh!" Colin moaned again between licks of Matias's ear. "Duke's fucking going to town on my ass."

The top of Duke's head bobbed up and down between Colin's ass cheeks. Duke's tongue was long enough for Matias to see it from the perspective of Colin's shoulder as he embraced Colin. Duke's tongue was jackhammering in and out of Colin's ass and Colin was sighing, moaning, and gasping all at once.

"Fuck." Matias gasped. Colin was kissing him so hard and Duke was jerking him so hard that he had to work hard not to cum. "And he's still rubbing sticks to make fire."

"My ass." Colin gasped and winced in intense pleasure. "Feels like his tongue's drilling for water in China."

Matias broke out with a laugh into Colin's face. Colin pressed his face up to Matias's. "I love it when you laugh." Colin kissed Matias again.

"Enough prolegomena!" Duke announced from the crack of Colin's ass.

"I think you sucked that catchphrase right out of Colin's butt." Matias reached out far enough behind Colin so he could give a squeeze to Duke's shoulder.

Duke stood up. He slapped Colin's ass, loudly, and Matias's ass, maybe a little more gently. Or maybe Matias just had more cushion in his ass.

"Don't be selfish," Duke said. He put his face in toward Colin and Matias's faces. Matias reached to embrace Duke and bring his face closer. Colin did the same.

Duke slipped his tongue into the middle of their kiss, first licking their tongues, then pushing his tongue into Matias's mouth, then into Colin's.

"Let's enjoy our test results, shall we?" Duke smiled presciently. "Matias. On all fours. Now."

Matias squatted down, then went on all fours. What was next, he'd always imagined as painful. But after Duke's tongue and hand had visited, Matias's ass wanted nothing more intensely than it wanted Duke's dick.

Matias stared down at the shower floor, warm water splashing down all around, and planted his hands down on it. He spread his legs, thighs, and ass cheeks farther apart. Warm shower water tickled his ass. Whatever Duke's lovemaking would be, even if it was going to be kind of painful, Matias wanted it, badly.

"Alright, man." Duke knelt behind Matias. Thud. He Matias's ass with his dick. It felt like a hard, meaty paddle. Matias clenched his teeth in how fucking sexy this all was.

"Colin." Duke's voice boomed, full fitness-trainer mode. "Isn't your roommate Matias's dick looking a little bit neglected, just hanging there like that? Don't you think you could slide under him?"

Matias moaned, loudly, and involuntarily. Colin lay on his back and slid his way in between Matias's arms and legs. In what felt like less than a second after Duke had said it, Colin's lips were wrapped around Matias's dick. He sucked the entire shaft of Matias's, then let it out of his mouth.

"I really, really, fucking love you guys." Colin moaned and the moan's vibrations coursed through Matias's dick and up through his whole body. "I really don't want to leave you guys."

Colin sucked again. This time, Matias's dickhead was held tightly at the back of Colin's mouth. That must've been what they called deepthroating. Fuck. It felt as amazing in real life as it did for the dudes in porn.

Colin's sucking felt like his love and tenderness for Matias put into action. With every suck and slurp, it felt like Colin telling him not to leave, or himself not wanting to leave.

Duke teased Matias's butthole with the tip of his dick. Colin ran his fingers over Matias's balls while he sucked him off.

Something wet was at Matias's ass again. "I'm putting some soapy water on your ass, man." Duke punctuated his words with a light slap of Matias's ass cheek. "My dick isn't exactly beginner-size."

"Just fucking give it to me." Matias sounded like he was in porn. He felt like he was in porn. Love and lust filled his entire being. Both the love and the lust were feelings he'd never felt until all this had started with Colin and Duke.

Something the size of a boulder pushed up against Matias's butthole. Duke's dick was big, huge even, but it had never looked or felt that huge — not until it was knocking on Matias's ass.

"You may want to reconsider the *just fucking give it to me?*" Duke asked, with a slap of the ass cheek of Matias's that he hadn't yet slapped. "In light of my endowment."

Duke's politely worded question sounded like he was advising a fitness client about a training regimen. In a way, he was.

"Just ease it in. But don't go easy on me." Matias wanted Duke inside him ASAP. He'd thought about it enough, even fantasized about it, over the past weeks and months.

The part that was in his butthole already, the part that already hurt like a motherfucker, was just the tip of the cock-berg. He knew that well enough. Still. The pain would be worth it.

Duke moaned. "Being inside you is so fucking hot."

"You like a nice tight virgin?" Matias made himself laugh with the pseudo-porn talk, despite the palpable discomfort of something the size of a nuclear missile prodding at his ass.

"I admit I'm into virgins." Duke squeezed both of Matias's ass cheeks at once. "But don't worry. I love you anyway."

Colin's laughter down below Matias felt like the most random thing ever on his dick. Matias had never imagined how a laugh would feel on his dick. Until all this happened, he'd also never imagined how Colin would feel on his dick. Duke made it all happen.

With a soft moan, Duke pushed more of his dick into Matias. It felt challenging, but not so terrible. Colin pleasuring Matias's dick must've been helping Matias's ass loosen up

"Enough prolegomena!" Matias pushed his ass back. It took more of Duke's dick in him. Maybe even most of it.

Pushing back onto Duke's cock like that, Matias felt like he was wedging himself open at the ass. But it wasn't a bad feeling overall. The pleasure outweighed the pain.

The discomfort of pushing his virgin butthole onto that that eleven-ounce dick was considerable, but it was nothing compared to how good it felt, now to how hot it was that Duke, muscleman trainer Duke, friend and lover Duke, was making love to Matias's ass — that Colin and Matias were the only men he loved and the only men he'd make love to.

"Oh fuck!" Duke laughed. "You're three steps ahead of me here." He leaned forward and licked Matias's back. He rubbed his facial stubble against the small of Matias's back. Duke's lips pressed hard against Matias's neck, then gave him a long, slurping kiss.

Matias groaned and pushed himself back on the dick again. It was his way of demanding more of Duke inside him. Actions spoke louder than words.

"Fuck, can you take that?" Duke breathed quickly. "Your ass is so fucking tight around my dick."

"Feeling like Kermit the Frog here." Matias was laughing between his groans of being filled up like a Muppet. "But yeah, I can take that."

"I love —" Duke caught his breath. "I love how your ass clenches together in sync with your laughs."

"Move your cock around to loosen me up." Matias had known this day was coming. He'd expected to take Duke's dick one day, or at least try. He'd been reading up on all the gay sex Q&A sites. He just hadn't expected the day so soon. But his knowledge proved useful.

"You're an expert already." Duke laughed as he moved his dick up and down, left and right, inside Matias's ass. He pumped in and out slightly, minutely, just like the online guides said. Duke must've been reading the same websites. Or maybe Duke just knew these things from the real world.

"Can't wait any longer." Matias pushed back again, hard. The dick was in him. Deep in his ass, Colin's dick felt like a giant hot exploding shit — but only in the best of ways.

As intrusive as it was, Duke's cock deep inside him was also comfortable. Cozy even. As tremendously, ridiculously, oversized it was, it felt like it had always belonged inside him.

"Fuck!" Duke yelled.

"Yeah, that's what you're supposed to do now." Matias focused on speaking through his short, quick breaths, and not screaming in pain from the big dick inside him.

"Damn, dude." Duke pushed in and out of him slowly. "You can take a dick." He grabbed Matias's ass cheeks hard, as if they were grab handles.

"That's how I got into Harvard Med," Matias said, purposely making his statement sound mundanely matter-of-fact.

"Wait, what?" Duke's laughter sounded a little bit nervous. He probably suspected Matias might not have been joking.

"Just joking, man." Matias thrust himself back onto Duke's dick. Colin below him seemed agile enough to follow along with his mouth. "I've decided not to go to Harvard Med."

"Wait, what?" Colin had slid Matias's dick out of his mouth momentarily just to ask the question.

"Yeah." Matias thrust backward again and grinded his butthole onto the firmness of Duke's cock. "I can't leave you guys. I know Colin is leaving. But still. I just can't walk away from us."

"Didn't you want to be a doctor?" Duke leaned down again, to whisper the question into Matias's ear, giving his neck another lick. He became more assertive about thrusting into Matias. He wrapped his arms around Matias's hips and got into a slow, steady rhythm of thrusting his dick into him. Each thrust felt like heaven and hell combined.

"Oh yeah." Matias slowly raised and lowered his dick into Colin, like he was lovingly fucking Colin's mouth. Maybe he was. "My safety school is University of Miami. I got in. It's a great school."

"So you're staying right here in Miami?" Duke's voice rose at least an octave at the question. Maybe fucking Matias's tight hole was that exciting, or maybe he was that happy about Matias not leaving for Cambridge.

"If Miami will have me, yeah." Matias bit into his own arm as he started to feel the pain of Duke's dick ravishing him. Maybe initially he'd somehow been blocking the pain.

Duke's fucking still felt great. It just — hurt.

"Miami's having you right now, man." Duke slapped Matias's ass again while fucking him harder. He lowered himself down so his hands were on the shower floor. He breathed in Matias's ear.

"I love you, man," Duke whispered in Matias's ear, while sucking and licking his earlobe and fucking his ass from behind. The dick seemed to be going in a little bit easier when Duke was tilted higher up like that, or maybe Matias's had just loosened up.

"Hey Colin, are you still with us?" Duke called out to the blond figure lying on his back below Matias.

Colin was still bobbing his mouth up and down on Matias's downward-hanging dick. He made a sound like a moaned *yes* — a delicious, sensuous vibration in Matias's crotch.

"You know, Colin." It was Duke's trainer voice again. "My ass isn't gonna fuck itself."

Colin made a sound like "Hmm?"

"I understand the impulse to orally please Matias's wiener," Duke spoke from above both of them. "But I can take care of Matias's cock with my hands. I need you to fuck my ass."

Colin eased Matias's cock out of his mouth. "You want me to fuck your ass?"

"If it's not too much to ask." Duke laughed between thrusts and growls as he pounded Matias's ass.

"I've never — I don't know how —" Colin was shaking his head, staring up at Matias and Duke above him.

"Slot A into tab B, dude." Duke reached down and slapped Colin's ass cheek. "Or watch how I'm fucking Matias if you need advanced-level tutelage."

"I wouldn't mind watching how you're fucking Matias." Colin gave a sensuous squeeze to Matias's dick and balls as he slid out from under him. He stood up, assessing the scene. After a few seconds, he started fotly jerking himself off while watching.

"No lurkers allowed," Duke announced. "Join in. We saved you a place." With his eyes Duke pointed at his waiting ass.

Colin stood behind Duke. Then he squatted behind like he was about to play leapfrog.

"Should I put some lube on my dick?" Colin asked. He sounded every bit the eager student.

"Soap and water is fine," Duke answered, sounding like he'd been answering this question all day long.

Colin lathered up his dick, then showed it off to Duke. "Like this?"

Matias also got a full view of its length. That thing was beautiful and impressive, even if Matias mocked it for being thinner than his own dick. If the dick hadn't had soap all over it, Matias would've reached out to suck it. It looked like pure delicious sex.

"Yeah." Duke spread his massive legs farther apart even as he kept thrusting deep into Matias. Duke's hairy legs and thighs scraped Matias's thighs and ass as Duke repositioned himself. "I'm pretty used to dicks in my ass. You don't have to warn me or anything. Just slip it in and take my hole."

"Uh." Colin grunted. "Like this?"

"Yeah. Now push in and out. Just fuck my ass, man."

"I got you, fam," Colin shouted out from behind Duke. The dick-to-ass action was outside Matias's view, but he could certainly hear it: the sounds of Colin's fucking Duke were louder and more frantic than Duke's gentle fucking of Matias.

Maybe it was the ferocity of Colin's sex that made Duke speed up. He started fucking Matias harder. "Is this hurting you, man?"

"Not at all." Matias clenched his teeth. "Or technically." Matias inhaled and exhaled a few times to catch his breath. "It is kind of hurting, but the pleasure exceeds the pain."

"Spoken like a philosopher." Duke bit on Matias's ear and licked its inside like he was eating it out. "You wanna show me what a good power bottom you can be?"

"How do I do that?" The word appeared on some gay porn sites, but Matias wasn't sure what it meant.

"Just like how you started." Duke brought his lips to Matias's and french-kissed him before continuing his explanation. "Fuck my dick with your ass just as hard, or even harder, then I fuck your ass with my dick."

"I can do that," Matias said. He pushed back with his asshole onto Duke's cock. He went faster and faster to Duke's quickening moans.

He hadn't known he could pulsate his hips that fast. He hadn't known he could take anything that big up his ass. But there he was, and Duke seemed to be loving it.

"Fuck, both of you guys. You're gonna fucking make me—" Duke growled. He licked and sucked on Matias's neck, breathing hot breath over him and giving him small love bites. It was almost feral.

Matias kept fucking back at Duke's dick. He thrust back and forth as fast as he could with his ass muscles. He clenched his ass tighter around Duke's shaft every time Duke withdrew it.

Duke's entire body shook. "Oh fuck," he mumbled. He spasmed like a huge push into Matias.

If there was a danger of Matias being split into two, it would've happened then. It didn't. It hurt a bit, but mostly, it felt amazing. Duke's dickhead and shaft ravished Matias's asshole and prostate.

Duke grabbed Matias's dick and started jerking it, pumping it up and down, squeezing it like a cow udder, and running his finger over the ultra-sensitive cocktip. It didn't take long. Matias's body started spasming and he was cumming in Duke's hand.

Duke growled again and shot a load of hot gooey cum into Matias. He'd never suspected cum in his ass would feel that good. Sure, it must've been some normal male amount of cum, but it felt like gallons of the warm, sticky stuff. Duke kept cumming while licking Matias's ear and jerking him.

"I'm gonna make you cum, Colin." Duke said it like a threat. He must've been clenching his ass on Colin's dick and milking it, because he stopped his thrusts into Matias for a second, then started again.

"Holy fuck, man." Colin's unmistakable voice was shouting. "Feels like you're giving me a blowjob with your ass." Colin's hands from behind Duke were grabbing and groping at any piece of man-flesh he could find, on Duke's body and Matias's alike.

"Ohh. Mmm." Colin's pounding into Duke sounded like a fleshy jackhammer. "I'm fucking cumming."

"Yeah? One-pump chump thanks to my dick-milking skills?" Duke asked, laughing. He was still shooting his last loads into Matias and milking the cum from Matias's dick.

"Man, and I thought you're never arrogant." Colin was laughing. He slapped Matias's ass. That was a heavy, meaty slap.

"I'm only arrogant about two things." Duke embraced Matias's torso and chest from above him.

"Your balls?" Matias asked.

"Not bad." Colin guffawed.

"Well done, my resident comedian." Duke nodded, planting kisses on Matias's neck and cheek. "But I'm arrogant only about my dick-milking skills and about how great you guys are, how happy I am to have met you, how deeply in love I am with both of you."

"Dude." Colin seemed to have suddenly remembered something. "Matias, are you seriously staying in Miami? Or was that just some kind of orgasmic crazy talk?"

"Pretty serious, guys." Telling them made Matias ecstatic. "As serious as my love for the two of you."

Eleven

"I'm honored to have been offered a campaign manager position with the Human Rights Campaign." Colin's linen suit was perfect.

Duke was no expert on suits, but that suit of Colin's was a good suit. Duke hadn't even known that Colin owned a suit. Colin always seemed to be wearing loungewear, the work uniform of the idle rich.

Colin looked around the room. That was politician-in-training Colin's signal for his audience to clap. That much, even Duke knew.

Duke clapped like no one had ever clapped before. He mentally envisioned the North Korean Secret Police making sure he was clapping enthusiastically enough at some missile parade, and himself clapping harder just for them, then proudly wiping the snow off his red-starred fur hat.

He elbowed Matias to remind him to clap too. Even if they, personally, were devastated by Colin's impending departure, the least they could do was be happy for Colin.

"I'm furthermore greatly honored to be invited to speak to the Miami chapter." Colin let his audience catch a glimpse of his brilliantly white teeth as he scanned the room.

Colin wasn't just happy to be there. The dude was *furthermore greatly honored*. Duke's mind slipped to imaginary visions of Colin standing up from sucking off Duke and Matias and holding forth grandiloquently on being furthermore greatly honored to receive viscous oral insemination from his two upstanding colleagues.

"Pay attention!" Matias whispered as he reciprocally elbowed Duke.

"Oh yeah. Sorry." Duke looked around. "I don't often go to a — whatever this is called—" Some kind of fancy party. *Reception* wasn't quite the word. *Fete* maybe.

"I don't know either." Matias shrugged with a grin. "I'm just here for the avocado toast." He bit into a piece.

Duke suddenly remembered. He wrinkled his nose a little bit. "I think it's called a — bris?"

Matias covered his face. He was laughing under his hand. "I don't think it's called a bris."

"I just thought that's the name for a fancy party." Duke whispered and shrugged. Sometimes he was as clueless as Colin, even if about different subjects and for different reasons. Anyway both Duke and Colin needed Matias to keep them on track. They would have been falling into a lot of shit without him.

"Yeah." Matias made the universal gesture for *pipe down*. "I know that you've never had a bris, man." Whatever that meant.

Colin's eyes didn't even flinch toward Matias and Duke's little *bris*-inspired melee. Colin's gaze around the room was perfectly measured. The dude ran his field of vision like his eyes were digitally controlled or something. He gave exactly equal attention to all corners of the room, making no one feel left out or neglected. Duke and Matias got exactly no more and no less attention than anyone else in the audience.

Maybe that was how things would be with Colin from now on. He would be only a polite stranger to them whom they'd only know from afar.

Duke crunched into a piece of toast. The tray out in the reception area had it labeled this one as liver pate toast. It kind of smelled like ass. In a good way.

Silently, Matias toasted Duke with his champagne and orange juice mix. If Colin was going away to DC, at least Duke and Matias could get some bijou food out of it.

"We don't often go to fancy places like this," Duke whispered to Matias. Colin had floated the idea a few times: he could take his roommates to whatever Michelin starred Miami restaurant they felt like visiting. But what was the point? Duke wasn't a fan of that kind of food, and eating pizza at home with Colin and Matias was always the best.

"We live in an even fancier place though." Matias's eyes sparkled with the joy in his response. His smile bloomed as if he'd just confessed to a naughty secret.

Matias glanced up at Colin at the podium in front, as if to remind himself who his benefactor was. Of course, as Colin had always told Matias and Duke, they did more for Colin than he did for them.

"The Human Rights Campaign has always been one of my very favorite organizations." Colin sounded silly saying that at age twenty-three. How long was his *always*? He'd probably unconsciously lifted the phrase from his dad.

"It's especially important in these times." Duke worked hard not to doze off. Colin in politician mode must've seemed highly engaging, to politicians. For Duke, he was just blabbering. "In light of the wave of new young candidates, in light of the Supreme Court decision abolishing the minimum wage for US Congress, we younger people, like me, especially we younger LGBTQ people, like me, need to take the reins of civic engagement for ourselves."

Colin nodded proudly like a rock star who'd just finished a solo. Thanks to another elbow from Matias, Duke straightened himself upright in his chair and clapped loudly for the gorgeous man at the podium.

That was it, of course: the official mark of the beginning of Colin's new life. The sadness Duke felt himself was obvious in Matias's downcast eyes. Matias's forced attempts to smile and be happy about Colin's successes looked like the results of a bargain facelift: a perky smile that just wasn't believable.

"Prospective colleagues. Friends. Supporters. Haters." Colin looked at the audience to wait for the expected laugh. He got it. The dude was smooth.

"In light of my job offer with your organization, I would like to announce, officially—" Some small applause broke out.

"Don't pop the corks until the results are in." Colin smiled at the corner the applause had come from. He got his expected laughs again.

"I would like to announce officially that I respect and support the Human Rights Campaign, and I have been honored to receive a job offer from you, but I am declining the offer."

The audience's smugly nonchalant looks became wide-eyed stares in Colin's direction. Matias grabbed Duke's wrist.

"Even those of us most committed to public life have our private lives also, and over the past months, I have found a romantic relationship that it would not be fair of me to leave — not fair to my partners, nor to myself." Colin pointed at Duke and Matias with his whole hand. Duke and Matias stared at each other in shock, then overjoyed shock.

The whole room was staring at them. Duke tried to give the room a dignified smile, worthy of the event.

"I am, however, announcing my candidacy for US Senate in the Democratic primary election," Colin said loudly and clearly. Matias shook his head and smiled at Colin's words. "For those of you who might not have noticed, my incumbent opponent will be my father, Senator Warren Warner."

"Oh fuck," Duke whispered to Matias.

"Shit just got real," Matias whispered back. "Deadass."

"So — you're staying here with us? And Colin is staying here with us?" Duke just needed it confirmed again. Tears were in his eyes again.

"Deadass." Matias elbowed Duke and pecked him on the cheek.

"I thank the Human Rights Campaign for helping me define my career goals," Colin said up on the podium. He was smooth even in turning down a job.

As awkward and clueless as Colin was, he had a certain grace in these high-falutin' sorts of situations. Colin's savoir-faire was awesome and intimidating and sexy all at once.

"And most of all." Colin cleared his throat very senatorially. "Most of all, I would like to thank my partners in life and love, Matias Estrello and Duke Jones, for showing me who I am, what love is, and what the three of us can be together."

Duke squeezed Matias's hand in his own. Matias leaned in with a small, event-friendly kiss on Duke's cheek.

A happy tear rolled down Duke's face. He didn't wipe it away. He wasn't hiding anything from anyone.

Epilogue

"I'm just Duke though. Just your everyday fuckup. I don't want them to see me as a role model." Duke was stepping out of Colin's Tesla in the parking lot of Pine Crest School just as he'd done that fateful day when they'd discovered the reality of his son "Sam."

"Role models aren't supposed to be perfect, man." Colin clapped Duke's back. Being a trainer must have been helping Duke build up his own muscles. His back definitely felt more ripped than it had just a few months back when Colin had first gone to his DC office. "Role models are supposed to be people who have overcome adversity."

"Yeah?" Duke laughed. "Then what about Matias here?" Duke play-punched Matias. "Born in the hood, now a medical student at the University of Miami? How can I be a role model when we've got dudes like Matias around?"

"Duke. Duke." Matias breathed deeply. He was still very much the grounded one of the three. "We never said that nobody else is a role model. There are lots of role models. We never said you're the only one. But the point is, you're a very decent role model for these kids."

The sun shone hotter now than when Duke and Colin had first come to Pine Crest while Matias was busy with the MCAT. Now Duke was stable in his life and even his finances, and he no longer felt a hole in his heart from the son he'd only been imagining. Tricia had come back and apologized, and was making monthly payments to pay back all the money she'd taken from Duke under false pretenses.

With his personal training gigs for Colin's rich buddies, Duke wasn't hurting for money. His first impulse had been to turn down Tricia's offer to pay him back. But Colin — Senator Colin Warner — had given Duke a better idea, and had contributed his own money to make it real.

"Alright, man." Duke laughed and shook his head. "The only one of us who hasn't overcome adversity is Colin here." Duke ran his huge hand up and down Colin's back as they walked toward the school auditorium.

"Hey, I won a very tough election." Colin clicked his tongue in semi-ironic pride.

"Yeah." Duke rolled his eyes. "After your dad quit the race after being cited for lewd conduct in the airport caverns."

"He just has a wide stance, alright? And he just needed to suck on something salty." Colin burst out in laughter. His father's homophobia made a lot more sense after that very public arrest — and his forfeiting the race gave Colin an easy win in the primary, then in the general election.

Colin just didn't like the implication that it was his dad — even by virtue of dropping out of the race — who'd gotten Colin his Senate seat. Colin was his own man.

The sign outside the school's auditorium said it all: *Honoring recipients of the Duke Jones Scholarship.* Duke was getting back the money he'd been bilked for, and Colin put in another hundred thousand, or maybe it was two hundred thousand, from his investment stash. They were funding prep school education for a bunch of kids. Against Duke's modesty, Colin insisted that the scholarship be named after him, and that he meet the recipients.

Duke was great. Under his muscle he was love and integrity and compassion and everything else good. Colin loved him but also respected him. Deeply.

"Guys," Colin announced to Matias and Duke.

"'Enough prolegomena,' are you about to say?" Duke grinned at Colin.

"No." Colin shook his head a very serious *no.* "I was just going to say that I just want to take a chance while we're out of earshot and eyeshot of the high school kids — just to huddle together and hug right now and be grateful for having one another."

"Weird flex but ok." Matias shrugged. "Not so weird flex, actually. I'm in." He put one arm on Colin's shoulders, and the other on Duke's.

"I'm in." Duke closed the triangle.

"We love it when you're in," Matias said. He laughed at his own joke like a dork.

"Guys." Colin bit his lower lip. He was crying, hard, from both eyes. "I love you. I love us. I appreciate us so much. I want us to be — to be us. Always."

"We will, dude." Duke slowly moved his head in to gently forehead-bump Colin in affirmation.

"Deadass." Matias hugged both of them hard. "Deadass as fuck."

Next in the series...

Rick, Matias's boring, geeky, straitlaced classmate might be getting into bed with a professor. Or two professors.

Boris and and Haley are Miami's best cardiologists. They're sworn enemies, but their best student might be able to turn their hate into love.

Three Hearts

http://amazon.com/dp/B07QRWXGJX

Afterword

Steve Milton writes gay romances with sweet love, good humor, and hot sex.

Sign up for Steve's spam-free insiders' club: http://eepurl.com/bYQboP

We Three is the first book of the series **Three Straight**, where Miami's hottest "straight" guys discover their true selves, and the best things come in threes.

Book 1: **We Three**
https://www.amazon.com/dp/B07QB2W9MG

Book 2: **Three Hearts**
http://amazon.com/dp/B07QRWXGJX

Book 3: **Power of Three**
https://www.amazon.com/dp/B07S6KZ844/

Selections from Steve Milton's other books:

Straight Guys is one book of eleven sexy novellas about straight guys who aren't so straight. Who doesn't love "totally straight" dudes lusting after other "totally straight" dudes?
https://www.amazon.com/dp/B018KNWGC8

Crema is a story of former childhood friends finding love.
https://www.amazon.com/dp/B071D4XQJS

Summer Project is a nerd, a jock, a tropical island, and a shared bed.
https://www.amazon.com/dp/B01I0FRENC

Steve Milton has written about twenty other gay romance novels, all of them full of good humor, hot sex, and lots of laughs:
http://amazon.com/author/stevemilton

Author's note about the setting

In real life, Miami is separate from Miami Beach. A real-life beachfront condo would have to be in Miami Beach, not Miami.

The author, a native South Floridian, is aware of the distinction. He has chosen to incorporate Miami Beach into Miami for the purposes of the story.

Three Hearts

Book 2 in the series *Three Straight*

Prologue

"We're adults." Boris exhaled, with a nod.

As if Haley and Boris's adulthood had ever been in question.

Boris's muscled arms definitely belonged to an adult.

He unfolded those arms and slipped his hands into his lab coat's side pockets.

Boris's cool gray eyes assessed Haley's face top to bottom, as if he was mapping it for surgery. From his thick lips, Boris's breath smelled like good coffee, the kind you have to go out for, not just scrounge up from the hospital cafeteria.

Standing eye-to-eye with Haley, Boris snuck his eyes farther down, about as far as he could while maintaining a veneer of decency. He wasn't very stealthy. He was obviously checking out Haley's chest and arms.

Boris Yorshenko wasn't the only one enjoying the eye candy. Haley enjoyed his share, or even more. He'd been checking out Boris all weekend: the quick dances of Boris's eyes, his eagerness to smile, his tanned arms peeking out from under his ridiculous lab coat.

Who would wear a lab coat to a faculty orientation meeting? That and the wild hair. Yorshenko must've been going for the mad scientist look.

At least Haley was subtle about checking out Boris. Boris's roaming eyes, on the other hand, were blatant.

After a leisurely stroll up and down Haley's body, Boris's eyes jumped up like singed fleas. Boris's face held no compunction or apology. Boris actually grinning for a split second. After that very distinct split second, Boris parked his eyes down on the ballroom carpet, where they could tell no more stories about what a loose cannon he was.

"Nobody is questioning our age or maturity, Doctor Yorshenko." Haley looked into those same lascivious eyes of

Yorshenko's. Maybe Haley's gaze was just as hungry. But at least he wasn't proposing to act on it. "With all due respect, I don't need you to tell me that we're adults."

Addressing Boris as *Doctor Yorshenko* was a planned move. Boris was a newly hired professor, like Haley himself. Any newly hired professor would eat up being called by a title, and then being confirmed as real, actual adult.

That was the irony of medical school, and even more so, the medical scientist track. At thirty-two years old, Haley had been a student all his life: even after graduating from med school, he'd spent six more years in residency and fellowship, basically extended college.

Despite academic acclaim, any thirty-something-year-old who'd spent all their life in school had some doubt about their adulthood. Haley could exploit that doubt of Yorshenko's with a bit of flattery.

Haley would flatter Boris by confirming Boris was an adult. He still wouldn't condone that floppy-haired Russian's rule-breaking.

"Sexual relationships between University of Miami faculty are forbidden. Did you not hear that?" Haley was the face of law and order and sanity. Better to establish himself as such right at the outset, especially if he was going to be working side-by-side with the loose-cannon Yorshenko dude.

Haley had gotten to where he was by following the rules. Some surfer-looking Russian cardiologist in a ridiculous lab coat wasn't going to send everything to hell.

"Is it really such a big deal?" Boris shrugged. He was the kind of guy who didn't consider anything a big deal. He'd probably wave his dick at the cardiology residents and call it not a big deal.

"Boys will be boys, isn't that what they say?" Boris called out, a little too loudly. The crowd had mostly filtered out of the ballroom, but not completely. His eyes seemed to say that his yelling wasn't a big deal. "Learn the rules just so you can break them?" Boris lifted his arms ceilingward, as if asking for divine assistance. "Does a bear shit in the woods?" Boris shrugged. "Help me out here. One of those sayings should fit the situation."

Rebuffed by Haley's refusal to play along, Boris broke into laughter. He gazed up at the ceiling skylights like he was expecting to see a blanket of stars.

Seven P.M. It wasn't even dark outside. Even in the wee hours of night, smog and light pollution would've covered those stars.

That was reality. Boris seemed not to care too much about reality.

Haley shook his head: at the flirtation, at the freewheeling attitude, at the invitation to go fuck. He had to be the adult, the one warning his colleague to be careful because he could put an eye out.

"As faculty, it's our duty to respect the rules." Haley spoke in a flat tone, the same kind he'd use with a patient. Maybe Yorshenko was Haley's near-equal in medicine, but he certainly lacked Haley's discipline. "And Boris, between you and me." Haley looked around discreetly, cloak-and-dagger style. He lowered his voice to a whisper. "No matter what the brochures say about inclusiveness, the old boys at the School of Medicine don't want homos on faculty."

"I'm not a homo." Boris's response was immediate. He stood upright, shocked, as if electricity had just shot into his presumably cock-hungry ass. His face reddened in seconds. That response came so quickly, as if he'd anticipated being called — or being called out on — being gay.

"Yeah? Then I guess a perfectly heterosexual man has been making eyes at me all weekend." Haley shook his head at Boris and added a bit of eye-roll for emphasis. Haley had been suffering Boris's fuck-me eyes all weekend. Closets were closets, but Boris should at least be consistent. He was calling himself "not gay" while begging Haley for a hookup.

The look Haley gave Boris was the same mildly disdainful, slightly exasperated look Haley gave patients who were lying about taking their blood pressure medicine. Haley just sighed and shook his head. "I guess a perfectly straight guy has been telling me that no one will know if we just go upstairs and fuck like hormonal lab rabbits."

Boris laughed, nervously. "I just mean I'm not—" Boris looked like he was tripping over his own words. "—I'm not out. I'm not anywhere near out. And you should hear the things the senior faculty say about the gays."

"No shit. I'm fairly aware of the medical old boys' club." Haley whispered it right in Boris's face.

Haley was never afraid to speak in anyone's face. Haley's oral hygiene was impeccable. He never hesitated talking right at someone's face. He never had bad breath, that much he knew. And everybody listened to him, that much he also knew. "And also no shit, Boris, that you're not out. Like a bear doesn't shit in a tree."

"You also aren't—" Boris looked Haley up and down, his face like he was tasting a glass of port. "A bear shitting in a tree?" Boris's syrupy pronunciation of *bear*, almost like *beer*, gave the slightest hint of a Russian accent.

"Sorry. Best metaphor I could think of." Haley shrugged. He could man up to his faults. Like sometimes employing awkward metaphors about bears shitting in trees.

"You also aren't out, are you?" Boris was whispering, almost mumbling, talking down into his shirt collar, his eyes pointed straight down at his shoes.

"I can see Middle Earth outside my closet window, ok?" Haley shook his head again.

"Your closet has a window?" Boris stared wide-eyed. "Where do I sign up for that?"

"Maybe try graduating from Harvard Med instead of UCSF?" Haley grinned and shrugged. "Anyway, I'm not going to ruin my cushy, comfy gay-free life with a hotel room tryst at New Faculty Weekend for my dream job."

Haley's life was cushy and comfy in that nobody gave him trouble for being a homo. It wasn't so easy, because he had nobody, and it was a lot of trouble "not" being a homo.

"Like I told you. We are adults." Boris spoke quietly. His gray eyes twinkled behind one layer of curly hair falling on his eyeglass lenses, and another layer of the lenses themselves. "We are both highly incentivized to keep it a secret. We both would enjoy doing it. We both might as well—"

"Do you realize, I've never even been with a man?" Haley looked down at his shoes. He'd never been ashamed of anything. His life had been a series of jumps from success to success, in every realm but love. "I'm a thirty-one-year-old virgin. I don't even know what to do." Haley tilted his head back. He laughed, almost maniacally.

Open-heart surgery, he could do. They taught that in residency. But making love to another man, the feeling he'd vaguely craved since high school? He wasn't quite sure about the logistics and mechanics of that, or whether it even felt good.

When he'd been pushed together with women in the past, he'd run away before things got physical. But this was something he wanted.

"UCSF is better than Harvard Med, by the way." Boris said it like it was an established fact. "But I won't hold the Harvard thing over you." Boris grilled mischievously. He was a floppy-haired master troll.

"I won't even dignify that with a response." Haley shook his head. "And by the way, I've really never been with a man. Nothing. Shit. It pains me to say it."

"I haven't either." Boris was almost whispering. "Other than in my dreams. With the man of my dreams. Ashton Kutcher."

"My dick's much bigger than Ashton Kutcher's." Haley looked at Boris directly, watching for him to faint, or at least open his eyes in disbelief. He loved to see his words hit a man like a freight train.

He didn't even know whether his dick actually was bigger. But he could say if it he wanted. There was no law against it.

Haley had never talked about his dick like that, or talked about his dick like anything, to anyone. But he'd always used bold statements to throw his conversational opponents off balance.

154

"And you have empirical data or what?" Boris replied without even a pause. He wasn't thrown off balance. He gave Haley a look of clinical inquiry, the same look Boris had given when asking questions at cardiology conferences.

Sometimes Boris just didn't believe the purported results. Maybe he'd just called Haley's bluff.

Boris was smart. Brilliant.

That brilliance was what made Boris so fascinating — that and the floppy blond hair, the absent minded professor look combined with the razor-sharp presence, and the body that looked like he'd been born a fitness model.

Boris was more than fascinating: he was hot. But it was to Haley's advantage to pretend not to know.

"No empirical data." Haley gave Boris a grin of acknowledgment. Yes, they were both closeted gay men in a difficult situation. Yes, the could share a laugh, maybe. But no more than that. "Unless my masturbatory fantasies count as empirics."

"I don't think those kinds of empirics will pass clinical trials," Boris whispered. His smile was slight, positively subtle, but it still stretched across the width of his face.

"I can let you inspect my dick in person." They'd been talking about Ashton Kutcher, not about Haley's dick per se, but it was a perfect moment to pivot the discussion. "How's that for empirics?"

"I don't know you well enough." Boris drew his face in and shook his head slightly.

"You're looking for red roses and an engagement ring before we fuck?" Haley made himself laugh. "Maybe I can write you a poem?"

"Not that." Boris shook his head. The blond locks flopped a bit. "I mean I don't know you well enough to ascertain whether you're serious about letting me check your dick in person."

"I'm a joker, you know." Haley made some kind of finger-popping gesture of party confetti falling from the sky. He didn't even know what it was supposed to mean.

Boris shrugged. "I'm a midnight toker."

No surprise. Boris Yorshenko was the entire marijuana menace rolled up into one floppy-haired dude.

"That's also against faculty rules." Haley wagged his finger at Boris. Just say no. To drugs at least.

"So if I promise to stay away from the cheeba weeba." Boris made a cartoonish gesture of puffing on a joint. "Can I invite you up to my room for some post-conference discussion?"

"No way." Haley tried to look a lot more shocked than he actually was.

"So it's all for naught, our chat here?" Boris smiled like a man who just didn't want to let go of the small good thing he and haley had that weekend. "We just check each other out, have a nice chat, talk about your dick, then go back to our rooms?" Boris made a childlike sad face.

"I never said that." Haley graced Boris with a smile. "I just said we're not going to your room."

Haley's analytical helped him navigate any situation, even a proposed hookup. Boris was no slouch, but maybe his mind had been more on the anal than analytical.

"My regular suite is not good enough for you or something?" Boris waved his key card at Haley, like waving his dick at passers-by. "Is Mister Harvard Man looking for a full presidential suite?"

"Not that." Haley made an exaggeratedly cautious visual scan of the surroundings. "But you might have hidden cameras up in your room."

"Oh jeez." Boris took off his glasses. He shook his head hard. He'd probably been worried about his glasses falling off. "What do you think this is, *Doctors Gone Wild?*" Boris sighed, as if wanting to ruin a rival's career was absolutely unthinkable.

"I wouldn't put it past you people. KGB and everything." Haley said it in such an exaggeratedly fear-mongering way that he could only hope that Boris understood it was a joke.

"Haley. Doctor Haley Bronson." Boris cleared his throat. "There hasn't been a KGB in Russia in thirty years. There also hasn't been Boris Yorshenko in Russia in thirty years. I am deeply, deeply offended." The pause in his last sentence sounded serious.

"I'm sorry!" Haley done fucked up. He'd just insulted a colleague, in the midst of trying to fuck that same colleague. He'd fucked up big. "I'm really sorry—"

"Got you." Boris snickered. His smile pushed his cheek up into a wink. "I'm not actually offended. I was just fucking around."

"Yeah? I knew that." Haley recovered quickly. He smiled instantly. He could pretend he'd also just been fucking around. "You wanna meet in five minutes and fuck around?" Haley clicked his tongue. "Room seven zero eight."

"Smooth. Very smooth." Boris nodded approvingly. "You could be a heart surgeon."

"And please, for the love of Hippocrates: wear your lab coat." Haley covered his mouth as he whispered. "It's sexy." Haley broke out in laughter and shaking his head. "Just kidding."

"Doctors don't understand sarcasm." Boris shrugged. "See you in 708 in five minutes." Boris's eyebrows jumped up and down to say *goodbye* and with his usual half-meandering walk, he walked out of the ballroom and toward the elevators.

What had Haley just gotten himself into?

Did he really just make a sex hookup appointment with a colleague?

He didn't even know what to do with a man. He'd seen it online, sure, but—

He couldn't even back out or pretend to forget. Boris would be right at Haley's door. In five minutes. Or four minutes by now.

Fucking heart surgeons were always on time. Even the goofy Russian floppy-haired ones.

***

It was unbelievable, even by Boris's standards.

The part about breaking, or at least bending, the rules of faculty propriety wasn't the unbelievable part. That much, Boris could do enough mental acrobatics to weasel out of. He and Haley weren't really faculty yet. They hadn't actually started working. They were only on their orientation weekend.

In terms of breaking the rules, this wouldn't be much different from Boris's occasional rooftop ganja breaks. He and the other residents would sometimes have a bit of a smoke on top of the UCSF Medical Center after a long shift. No harm done, just a few drags on a joint, always days before his next shift. A lot of the faculty at UCSF smoked too, so what was the problem?

The unbelievable part was that he was about to get jiggy with a man. What would be really, totally different. It was what he'd most wanted and most feared.

It was worlds away from Boris's usual meaningless rebellion, a joint here and a surfboard there.

Shit. Gay sex with his future colleague wasn't just against the rules of the University. It was against the law of nature. Or so most of the world believed, anyway. And among them, the Dean of the School of Medicine, and his board of henchmen.

He'd been looking at Haley Bronson the same way he looked at celebrities. Untouchable. Safe to dream about, because it would never, could never happen. A perfectly safe dream to have, because Boris would never have to follow through on it.

He didn't expect Ashton Kutcher to step out of the TV screen and invite him upstairs. There was some security in wanting what you couldn't have. But there it was. There was Haley Bronson, perfect, uptight, previously believed to be straight Haley Bronson, inviting Boris to his room.

That chin of Haley's: that jutting jawline, that strong, masculine chin. Fine, Boris fetishized it. Fine, he knew that staring at it reliable gave him a hard-on. Fine, he had no hope of actually ever feeling that chin rubbing against his face.

Even on Boris's way up to Haley's room, none of it felt real, because it couldn't be real. Reality could never be that perfect.

Maybe it was a setup. Maybe the Hyatt Regency Miami had no seventh floor. Maybe room 708 was an elevator shaft. Maybe Haley had sent Boris up to the Dean's room.

Maybe.

Or even worse, it would be just as Haley had promised. Boris Yorshenko would be sent to collide face-first with his homosexuality.

The door to room 708 was just barely open. Maybe the other side held a robber or a camera crew.

Or a policeman. His parents had told him about that kind of setup in Russia.

His mind was really spinning now. Why though? Going to a man's room for sex was immoral but not illegal. If caught, Boris wouldn't go to jail. He'd only — lose his image, his reputation, his dream job, his marketability. He'd end up being one of those doctors who don't even practice medicine. What the hell was he doing, actually?

Boris just barely knocked on the door. He brushed it with his knuckles like he was debridling the wood veneer. He knocked lightly enough so as not to swing it open any more.

"Yo." That was definitely Haley, Haley being manly enough in his verbalization so as not to freak anybody out.

Slowly, the door swung open. On its own. Boris took a half-step forward.

Steam wafted through the room. Everything smelled like Hyatt toiletries.

And there stood Haley Bronson, MD.

Naked.

Holy fucking shit.

Boris gasped. He slammed the door shut behind him.

The *do not disturb sign*. He took it off the inside door handle, opened the door again, and stuck it on the outside door handle.

No. That would be too suspicious.

He opened the door again and took off the *do not disturb* sign. He hung it fastidiously on the inside door handle, like putting away a surgical instrument — in case he might change his mind again.

Haley was casually toweling himself off. He patted dry his pubes like it was a perfectly innocuous part of the body to pat dry. His blue eyes said, "What are you looking at?" Or maybe they just said, "I know what I've got."

There were men on porn sites. There were men Boris surreptitiously glanced at in the gym locker room. They were ok. They served to remind him that as much as he didn't want to be gay, he was. But they were nothing like Haley Bronson.

Flaccid dicks weren't even supposed to be erotic. But Haley's thick flaccid dick hanging between his legs — it had a certain nonchalant bravado. That dick was wearing mirrored aviators, smoking a cigarette: James Dean The Dick. "Yeah. I'm here. I'm cool. I'll get hard when I want to." It wasn't even circumcised. That was how much Haley Bronson's dick didn't give a fuck about anything.

Up from Haley's pubes, his tight, muscled abs flowed into pecs with big blood-red nipples and a chest with just a few hints of hair. When did a cardiac surgeon have time to work out to get a body like that? Had Haley just been born with a six-pack? Did he also pop out of his mom's womb with a big flaccid dick hanging down between his legs? It seemed like it. Haley's swagger, his cool blue eyes—

"So we're gonna have a meeting?" Haley grinned. Early-evening stubble had formed at the edges of his mouth and at the sides of his jaw: he was perfectly groomed as always, just a little bit scruffier. His nonchalant question was suggestive while retaining deniability. Haley was just talking about a meeting with his colleague, after all. And he was naked.

"Yeah—" Boris was just answering his colleague. About a meeting.

Of course Boris would agree to a meeting with Haley. He needed an excuse to touch Haley. Soon.

Or he didn't even need an excuse.

His eyes on Haley's, looking for an objection or refusal, Boris reached out and put his palms on Haley's hips.

Haley's skin was warm. His hips had barely any fat: it was muscle over bone.

In Haley's eyes there was no objection or refusal. Haley only parted his lips enough for a smile to peek out.

It was surreal: Haley Bronson, in front of him, naked. Boris wasn't even sure what to do. He'd watched gay sex online, but this was — this was real, and the man he'd been eyeing from afar, and a man he couldn't even write off as just a dumb piece of flesh.

Boris stepped closer to Haley. He moved his hands up along Haley's sides, up over every peak and valley of Haley's abs, and up to Haley's hard pecs.

He squeezed at Haley's pecs and nipples, watching again for an objection on Haley's face. Haley would've raised an objection, loudly, about anything he didn't like. Haley threw tantrums at cardiology conferences. But to Boris's hands, Haley brought no objection, only a widened smile.

He nodded at Boris. "Take your clothes off." His voice was low-key and commanding. That must've been how he talked in the operating room. Boris knew it well, as a surgeon himself. Hearing another man talk like that was fucking sexy.

"I hope you don't mind. I left my lab coat back in my room." Boris smiled. Being playful took the edge off of being scared as hell.

"Take your clothes off. Now." Haley's palms pressed hard into Boris's chest through his shirt. Over the shirt, Haley's fingertips ran in circles over Boris's nipples. Even through starched cotton, it was electric.

Boris steeled himself not to scream, or squeal, or ejaculate. Any of those might've been possible. He'd never felt anything like that. A man had never touched him like that.

Haley's hands moved to Boris's top shirt button. With surgical alacrity, one finger maneuvering the button through a hole he held open with two fingers, he undid it. Then the second button. And the third.

Haley reached inside, to Boris's bare chest. Or he tried. He contorted his arms, with a grin, groping at Boris's chest hair and smoothing his palms over Boris's nipples. "Shit. This is fucking contortionism." Haley laughed while looking down at his arms bent to get under the top of Boris's shirt.

"You should've gone for the laparoscopic technique." Boris shook his head in reprimand. "Either that or just take off my shirt faster."

"I'll take door number two." One hand still inside the shirt and one hand outside it, Haley worked open Boris's remaining shirt buttons.

"Let me help." Boris started at the bottom of his shirt and unbuttoned toward the top. Boris's hands met Haley's, the way two surgeons working in a small place sometimes brushed their fingers against each other.

Boris grabbed Haley's palms. He brought Haley's fine-boned hands up to his mouth and kissed them.

"Nobody's ever kissed my hands." Haley shook his head and laughed. Maybe this felt surreal to Haley too.

Still holding his hands up to his mouth, Boris blew air between Haley's fingers. It was ridiculous, but it was all he could think of.

Haley drew his hands away and reached for Boris's belt.

His eyes stayed fixed on Boris's. His hands fumbled with the buckle.

He was a heart surgeon. He could figure it out.

Haley opened Boris's pants and slid his hands onto his boxers. Boris shuddered. Haley's caress was a punch in his thighs all the way to his chest. Boris's whole body spasmed. He couldn't believe a man was touching him: not just a man but the most beautiful man he'd ever seen.

Haley's fingers wrapped around Boris's dick. His grip was firm, his hands warm even through Boris's boxers.

Boris's body froze. Grinding up against Haley's hand would've been the normal thing to do. Or at least holding Haley's dick.

Boris only gasped a little. He wanted whatever Haley was doing, but he was too scared to help it along.

Haley snapped the button on Boris's slacks and pulled down Boris's pants. The boxers slid down right along with the pants. Boris's dick popped out from its boxer short constraints like it was launched from a catapult. The dickhead must've been moist; the room's air conditioning made it feel like ice.

"Kind of embarrassing." Boris looked down at his rock hard dick. "I'm uncircumcised. That big meaty foreskin."

"Yeah?" Haley smiled and looked down at his own hard dick. "Foreskin-having bro checking in here."

"I don't even know—" Boris shook his head and sighed as he stared into Haley's eyes. Were they supposed to kiss? Would that have been gay? Weren't they already gay? Or at least being gay?

"Kiss me." There was Haley's cocky, commanding surgeon voice again.

What Haley ordered was exactly what Boris wanted. Boris wanted to kiss him more than ever. He breathed in deeply, like he was about to dive underwater, deep in the lagoon of Haley Bronson MD.

By the time Boris half-closed his eyes and moved his lips forward, Haley was already ravishing Boris's lips with his own.

Haley's nose pressed into Boris's cheek. Haley's smooth upper lip bumped into Boris's. Haley's tongue ran over the surface of Boris's lips, then pushed shamelessly into Boris's mouth.

Haley's tongue was the intruder that Boris had always wanted inside him: his first kiss by a man, his first moment of staring into a man's eyes, of feeling a man's hardness against his own, of feeling his own lust finally reciprocated. Boris was still shocked into stillness. This was really, really happening.

Boris forced himself to kiss Haley. Exploring Haley's lips and tongue with his own tongue was terrifying and wonderful: exactly what Boris had always most wanted and most feared.

One-two. Boris stepped out of the lowered pants and boxers that lay at his ankles. Multitasking was using his toe to hook off his own socks while still kissing Haley.

Haley's hot breath seared Boris's mouth. Boris could only breathe back his own breath into Haley as he kissed him, licked him, explored him. He made love to this gorgeous man's face, mouth wide open and sucking at Haley's stubbled chin and jaw.

Boris wrapped his arms around Haley's waist. He rested his palms on Haley's butt cheeks.

Was he allowed to squeeze? In porn they always squeezed. Boris squeezed the cheeks. Haley moaned into Boris's face. Those gluteal muscles — that ass — sent another wave of arousal through Boris.

"Get on the bed." Haley was commanding again.

"I thought you've never done this before?" Boris whispered it into Haley's ear like a confession.

"I haven't." Haley's voice was confident, even cocky, like the worst stereotype of an arrogant surgeon. "Get on the bed."

Haley lay his hands on Boris's hips. His grip was firm. He nudged Boris toward the bed. Boris sat on the bed's edge, naked, bare feet on the ridiculous institutional hotel-room carpet. What was he supposed to do now?

Sitting down on the bed, Boris faced Haley's cock. It stood erect, pointing at Boris's face. Haley looked down at his own cock, then at Boris, as if giving another command, this one nonverbal.

Boris breathed deeply. Haley's crotch smelled like soap and a sweet smell like pancake syrup. Cowper's fluid in anatomy class, precum in porn.

Either way, he breathed Haley's aroma like a drug. He brought his lips closer to Haley's cockhead.

"You think I'm giving out free tastings here?" Haley laughed and drew his dick away from Boris's lips.

"I thought you wanted me to—" Boris did his best to sound a little bit agitated but still be friendly. Or even better than friendly.

"If you're gonna get me all worked up —" Haley moved his dick again closer to Boris's lips. "Then you've gotta let me fuck your ass to finish the job."

"I thought you've never—" Boris couldn't resist smiling. Haley was arrogant even about his sexual prowess.

"Yeah, I've never. But I'm gonna." Haley smiled big. His white teeth made him look voracious, like the Big Bad Wolf. He pushed his crotch closer to Boris's mouth. The syrupy smell of precum was irresistible; it had that unsubtle sweetness of a cotton candy machine, as if someone had developed a flavor called Big Sweet Dick. "So you gonna suck it or what?"

After all, it wasn't going to suck itself.

"You take such liberties with your grammar." Boris shook his head in a strong sign of *tsk tsk*.

The closer he brought his nose to the shiny tip of Haley's dick, the more he wanted to suck it. He pursed his lips and opened his mouth wide. He'd do it like in porn: keep his lips tight around the dick to make it more exciting for Haley. The gay sex videos he'd watched between surgical tutorials were proving useful.

Haley's cockhead landed on Boris's lips: slippery-wet, warm and sweet. Boris puckered his lips to kiss the cockhead's very tip, then opened wider and wider to push the cockhead, then the whole shaft, inside his mouth.

Deeper. The tip sliding over the roof of Boris's mouth. Going back to the throat and parts unknown.

For every two pushes against the sides of Boris's mouth, the gums and cheeks, Haley's cock boldly pushed directly toward Boris's throat, toward the core of his being. That was where Boris wanted it to go.

Haley's hot dick took the back of Boris's throat. Boris's gag reflex would set in any time. He'd resist it. He knew how. Medical school was useful sometimes.

Moaning, Haley frantically ran his hands through Boris's hair. Even Haley Bronson had a limit of how much he could feign nonchalance. His face flushed and his lips quivered. He moaned slightly and grabbed and fingered randomly at Boris's ears. Boris sucked more of Haley's dick into his mouth.

It filled and stretched his mouth like nothing else Boris had ever tried putting in his mouth. As a kid he'd tried eating plastic cars. In college he accepted a challenge to wrap his lips around the entire top of a beer can. Haley's dick stretched Boris's mouth even farther.

Haley pulled Boris's face toward his crotch. Haley's dick might've had no place to go inside Boris's mouth, but it found room in there, somehow. The dick veins tickled as it was sliding in, but it didn't even hurt too much. Boris moved his tongue as much as he could to give Haley pleasure.

"I'm gonna take your ass now." Haley stepped back a little, pulling his dick along with him. That dick had pushed the limits of Boris's mouth, but sucking it didn't have to be over so quickly. Boris gave Haley's dickhead a parting lick as Haley pulled it away from him.

Haley threw open the door of the mini-refrigerator. He sighed, shook his head, and looked through the stacks of paper next to the TV. "No fucking condoms in the room?" Haley shook his head like a surgeon whose nurses had just badly failed him.

"This isn't an hourly motel, Romeo." Boris grinned. "Actually there was a study at UCSF about the lack of free condoms in upscale hotel rooms—"

"Can we fuck now and discuss the UCSF study later?" Haley ran his fingertips over the length of his dick.

"Yeah, if you can conjure up a condom for us to use." Boris scanned the room, as if this shelf or that might just have harbored an overlooked box of Trojans. "I don't think there are even any convenience stores around the hotel."

Laughing was allowed. The whole situation was ridiculous enough.

Boris finally had a chance to perform the gay sex act he'd spend his life dreaming about and fearing, and he didn't even have a condom to use. It was like that song: ironic.

Haley exhaled violently, dick in hand, head shaking in disbelief. "There's no condom in the room, is there?"

"There is not." Boris tried to use his best surgically cool demeanor.

"Alright. I'm gonna order a condom from room service." Haley grinned like he'd just invented the wheel.

"That's what I was gonna say, what I learned from the UCSF study—" Boris started to say. People were less likely to use condoms when they had to order them from room service.

Haley was already holding the hotel room phone handset. He tapped the *0* button and gave Boris the look surgeons gave to mean *hold my beer.*

"Yes, hello!" Haley said in a high-pitched squeaky voice. That was probably how he thought a woman would sound. He sounded more like a rodent. "I'm here with Haley Bronson in room seven zero eight and we need a, umm, what do you call it, hee hee—" Haley laughed the way he must've imagined a young woman in need of a condom laughed. Boris's jaw dropped and he stared at Haley.

"A condom!" Haley said into the phone, his voice even higher than before. "Just slide it under the door please! Extra large, because you know Doctor Bronson! Hee hee!"

Boris threw his head into a pillow to muffle his laughter. His dick was still hard, but he was now laughing uncontrollably. Self-conscious Haley was trying to pretend to the hotel reception that a winsome woman was frolicking in his room. And he was trying to somehow channel that imaginary woman's voice.

It was better comedy than any comedy, except their dicks were hard and they both kind of needed to be fucking, not just laughing.

"Thank you! We'll be waiting!" Haley squeaked into the phone and hung up. He looked at Boris and nodded proudly. He looked like a teenager proud of himself for just having ordered a dozen pizzas to his math teacher's house.

"You sounded like fucking Minnie Mouse." Boris took the pillow off his face so he could laugh unrestrained. Maybe his laughs were too loud, but the sight of esteemed colleague Haley Bronson ordering a room service condom in a Minnie Mouse voice—

The hallway elevator outside the room beeped and its door opened. Haley gestured for Boris to be quiet. A ruffle of footsteps walked through the outside hallway, to the room door.

A shiny blue wrapped packet slid under the door and into the room. The footsteps walked away. The elevator beeped again.

"Condom!" Haley whispered loudly. "Condom!"

Eureka! Spreading his legs wide, Haley made a naked ballet-jump toward the door and grabbed the condom — as if room service might change its mind about the credibility of Haley's Minnie Mouse performance and suddenly repossess the condom with a vaudevillian hook under the door.

He held the condom up to his teeth. "How do you open these? Bite the wrapper?" He bit down on the edge and tugged at it.

"No!" Boris shook his head. "I've opened a lot of condoms. In public health studies, anyway."

Boris reached toward Haley's hand. Haley handed the condom to him hesitantly, as though maybe Boris couldn't be trusted with it.

"Like this." Boris carefully tore it open at the edge, then handed the entire packet back to Haley.

"At least this part I know how to do." Haley held the rolled-up condom over his cock. "I crown thee King!" He capped the condom over his dickhead and giggled at Boris.

"Roll it down the shaft, dude." Boris shook his head. It sounded like surfing instructions. Haley, for all his macho bravado as an ultra-skilled cardiothoracic surgeon, had never put on a condom. Not that Boris had room to talk. He'd had a lot more experience rolling waves than condoms.

"Good thing I'm still fucking hard." Haley rolled the condom down the entirety of his veiny shaft. Through the condom's gauzy translucence, Haley's creamy pale dick looked no less delicious.

"Fucking Minnie Mouse act." Boris laughed again and shook his head.

"Get on the bed, on your back." Haley's face was dead serious, as if he had a patient on the table in front of him. He pointed his eyes toward the bed. "And put your legs in the air."

"Shouldn't you buy me dinner first or something?" Boris was still guffawing about the Minnie Mouse voice.

"You want this dick or not?" Haley jerked it up and down, slowly. Even if he was a virgin, he knew very well how appealing his cock was. It was long without being malproportioned, girthy but not fat or stubby. The outlines of prominent veins under the condom's surface gave the dick a primal, almost feral sexual appeal.

Haley's dick didn't point straight ahead. It was hard enough to actually be pointing up. That was fucking hot. That dick was ready to fuck, and so was its owner. Even if it meant lying down on a hotel room without red roses and romance, Boris wanted that dick, and Haley, inside him.

"Is the hotel hand lotion water-based?" Boris eyed the tiny Hyatt-branded bottle on the nightstand.

"It better fucking be." Haley grabbed the bottle and emptied most of it onto his hand. "Cheap watery stuff. No fucking way this is oil based."

Haley slapped the lotion onto his condomed dick. He stared at Boris while lotioning up, like he was jerking off to the sight of his colleague naked in his bed. He *was* jerking off to the sight of his colleague naked in his bed.

"You'll go blind, man." Boris laughed. His stomach muscles still hurt a bit from how much he'd laughed at Haley's squeaky-voiced condom request.

"Is that what they teach at UCSF?" Haley's smile brimmed with cocky mischief.

"At least in San Francisco, even closet cases know you gotta lube the bottom's ass." Boris clicked his tongue. He raised his legs higher into the air and held his butt cheeks apart.

"I don't see any closet cases here." Haley kneeled on the bed's edge. He shook the rest of the lotion from the bottle onto his hands, then palmed Boris's lower thighs and massaged lotion into them.

Haley's fingers, dripping with lotion, tickled at Boris's ass rim. Boris hadn't even known anything touching his ass could be that pleasurable.

Haley patted lotion inside the ass rim. Boris pushed his ass up against Haley's lotioned hand. Haley held his hand still. Boris gyrated and pumped with his glutes, rubbing every part of his sensitive rim up against Haley's long fingers, his gnarly knuckles, and the cool flat palms of his hands.

Haley's lubed finger probed at Boris's ass. Boris couldn't help but squeal, instantly covering his own face with a pillow. That was — amazing and magical and like nothing else he'd ever felt.

It was electric, all tingling and pleasure from Haley's fingers to the surface of Boris's ass rim and all over his body. He'd imagined being filled up deep inside. He hadn't known that a man's fingers playing on his rim felt like that.

"You ready?" Haley kneeled at the bed's edge. He looked down at Boris. Haley's dick aimed at Boris's butt.

Boris had never imagined desperately craving a dick inside him. But after Haley's touches, and seeing Haley's cock right there — he wanted Haley's dick fucking him deep in his ass more than he'd ever wanted anything else, more than it was even possible to want anything else.

"Go slow," Boris whispered up to Haley. His desire was tempered only by his fear. He'd heard how painful it was the first time. "But do it. Fuck me."

Haley kneeled and brought his body down over Boris's body. Boris's legs wrapped around Haley's shoulders.

Haley grabbed Boris's dick. He wrapped his fingers around it and squeezed it firmly. He grinned like a kid playing with a new toy and pumped it up and down a little. Haley played with Boris's dick like he was jerking himself off.

"You like that?" Haley's eyes begged for approval.

"Of I like it." Boris smiled. The room's weak air conditioning, the excitement of the moment, and Haley's body on top of him — it was getting hot.

Haley lowered his face down to Boris. He put his tongue out. Boris stuck out his own tongue.

They touched extended tongues and laughed. Boris felt like a horny lizard sticking out his tongue at his mate.

Haley smelled like sex. Boris brought his face and rubbed his cheek against Haley's. As much as haley always kept a perfectly groomed appearance, his cheek had the slightest bit of stubble. It was fucking sexy.

Boris brought his face across Haley's, then brought his mouth to press against Haley's. He opened his mouth to receive Haley's tongue. Haley pushed his tongue inside Boris's mouth and Boris sucked on it.

Boris couldn't help but moan. He savored Haley's firm back muscles under his probing hands: trapezius, deltoid, teres minor, teres major. It had always just been anatomy.

"Ready?" Still leaning into Boris's torso from above, Haley lay his dick lengthwise on Boris's ass rim. The dick was warm and slippery, like it had been made just for going inside Boris. Doctors weren't supposed to believe in destiny — but it was like that dick's destiny was to be deep inside him.

"Fuck me," Boris whispered. "Fuck me really fucking hard."

"Are you sure I can—" For the first time, Haley looked uncertain and worried. The bravado was gone from his face. He looked down at his dick at the entrance to Boris's ass.

"Just fucking do it." Boris pulled his thighs and ass cheeks so far apart it was like doing a split. His butthole was full of lotion.

Haley's dick was huge to look at. It was the size of a baseball bat just nonchalantly hanging from his crotch. It would be terrifying to feel that thing inside him. But so be it.

"Fucking do it," Boris almost growled at Haley.

Haley bent down and put his lips to Boris's. Boris kissed him, gently. At the same time, Haley's hand aimed his dick.

Haley grunted. He slid his dickhead into Boris's hole. Boris bit down on his own forearm. The bite hurt more than the dick.

The dick hurt, but it wasn't terrible. After the almost thirty years Boris had spent imagining how awful the pain would be when he finally had a chance to be fucked, the actual pain wasn't bad at all.

"Keep pushing," Boris said, between quick breaths. Haley pushed more of his shaft into him and kissed Boris more intensely. Haley's soft, short-trimmed pubic hair tickled at Boris's ass cheeks.

"Are we really doing this?" Haley's face was lit up in mirth and disbelief. He'd initiated it, kind of, but he couldn't believe it was real. The esteemed Doctor Haley Bronson was balls-deep in his esteemed colleague Doctor Boris Yorshenko.

He pumped into Boris, in and out. The pain was tremendous but absolutely bearable: it was the price of being gay, the price of Haley making love to him, and it was totally worth it. The rhythm at least made it predictable and therefore more bearable. Each push in brought an apex of discomfort, and each pull out, Haley's ridged, veined, dick sliding out of Boris's tight hole, was rising pleasure.

"I do believe—" Boris pulled his knees back, almost to his ears. He spread his ass cheeks as far as he could, again. "I do believe we are really doing this."

Every time Haley thrust into Boris, Boris raised his ass in rhythm with Haley's thrusting. However deep Haley went, Boris wanted him deeper.

Haley smiled and kissed Boris again. His kisses roamed from Boris's lips to his cheeks and then his eyes.

Haley slid his hands and arms under Boris's back. Boris sat up slightly to let Haley's arms slide under him and bring him into a close embrace.

They were chest to chest. Haley stared into Boris's eyes. Haley's breathing became quicker, his breath hotter.

Haley's stared at Boris, then exhaled and closed his eyes. He rocked his head with the rhythm of his thrusts. Sweat poured off his face, droplets raining on Boris's neck and chest.

Haley's thrusting sped up. He was fucking like a jackhammer. Boris no longer felt every separate thrust. It was just a vague cloud of intense sexual pleasure. Boris wrapped his arms around Haley's back. He squeezed Haley's pumping, thrusting ass cheeks.

"Oh fuck." Haley frantically pushed his lips at Boris's lips. He pulled his hand out from under Boris's back and wrapped his fingers around Boris's dick, frantically running his fingertips over Boris's slippery cockhead.

The feeling was too much. Boris kissed Haley hard, pounding upward with his tongue into Haley's mouth.

Boris bucked as a climax ran through him. Cum spurted out, up onto Haley's stomach and chest. Boris lifted his legs higher and pushed hard to ram Haley's dick deeper inside. Haley's thighs slapped against Boris's ass cheeks. Another rope of cum shot out of Boris's dick, this time onto Boris's own chest.

Haley softly bit Boris's lip. He pushed deeply into Boris's ass and stopped there — one one thousand, two one thousand — then fucked, pushed, and moaned frantically, thrusting in and out of Boris's ass with his whole body.

The condom was filling up with Haley's sperm inside Boris's ass. Haley's dick ejaculated a few more throbs and spurts. Haley lowered more of his weight onto Boris's torso. Their stomachs and ribs touched.

Still cumming, Haley blinked, staring at Boris, kissing him, filling the condom with cum and grinding his dick and pubes into

Boris's ass. Boris lay back, spent, with the image of Haley on top of him imprinted on Boris's mind even when he closed his eyes.

Haley inhaled deeply. In push-up position, he used his arms to lift his torso up off of Boris. He was kneeling again, and he pulled his condomed dick out of Boris's ass. Haley pulled off his condom, held it up to the light like a lab specimen, and nodded approvingly at what he saw. He tossed it into the garbage basket, then threw some hotel stationery on top of it. Discretion.

The pain deep inside Boris faded away, but so did the pleasure. Haley was standing up now, pacing around his room, a little nervously.

Boris stretched out his legs in the bed. As much as he loved getting fucked, there was a cramp coming on from having his legs raised that sharply for that long. That was the price of losing his virginity only in his thirties.

Haley picked up his phone from the desk. "It's ten P.M. already." He walked to the window and looked out between the window blinds.

"Is it bedtime or something?" Boris smiled. Ten o'clock seemed liked an early bedtime even for a punctilious dude like Haley.

"No, but—" Haley paced from one end of the room to the other. The rhythm of his footsteps on the carpet sounded like a distant train. "I have a career to protect. You need to get out of here."

"Yeah, I'm just resting a bit." Boris moved his pillow up on the headboard. The postorgasmic warm and fuzzies he'd read about in endocrinology textbooks were now all over him. Haley wouldn't be giving him wine and roses, probably, but it felt nice to be in Haley's presence after they'd orgasmed together.

"Seriously, man." Haley hopped into his pants and buckled his belt. He put on his shirt like he had a fire to run to. "We can't be here like this. You can't be here like this. This is my hotel room. You gotta get out of here."

"I—" Boris sat up in the bed. Haley wasn't joking.

"I mean, fun is fun, but you know." Haley shook his head, as if Boris had just done something horrible. "I've got a career, a reputation. Shit, you've got a career and a reputation."

"Yeah, I just thought—" Boris sighed and didn't finish what he was saying. He just thought a few minutes hanging out after sex wouldn't hurt anyone's career or reputation. He must've been mistaken.

"Your shirt and pants are here." Haley quickly picked them up from the floor and halfheartedly folded them. He lay them on the bed next to Boris. Those were Boris's orders to get the hell out of Haley's room. Haley took a silver pen from his pants pocket and flipped it in his hand like he was about to attack Boris with it.

"Alright." Boris's stomach sank. It felt like finding out a patient's condition had deteriorated — except this time, Boris himself was the patient.

He put on his shirt and pants and shoes. Somehow those articles of clothing were a lot less exciting than they'd been about two hours back.

Haley stood in the far corner of the room, tapping idly on his phone. The screen looked dark. He was probably just pretending to be busy with his phone.

Boris said "ok" and walked out the door.

Haley didn't say anything.

Either of them uttering an actual goodbye might've looked too needy, way more than what Haley had been looking for, whatever he'd been looking for.

Every step Boris took from Haley's room to the elevator was its own capsule of thoughts and half-regrets. At least he'd gotten that virginity thing out of the way. At least he'd fulfilled a fantasy. At least he'd gotten his ass filled once.

How could Haley have treated him like that? Who the hell did Haley think he was? Was this how it felt to be used for sex — even if Boris had been the one doing the initial convincing?

Boris stepped into the elevator. What was he supposed to do? Which floor was his?

He'd temporarily forgotten.

The world was wrapped around the experience of sex with Haley, then the stomach-dropping hollowness of being kicked out by Haley. Or maybe that was always how sex went. Boris, as a thirty-year-old virgin, could have just been expecting too much.

Sixth floor. He pressed the button. The elevator still worked. Everything was just the same as it had been before their encounter.

Even if it was the same, it all felt so different.

One

"You're either Doctor Yorshenko's cardiology student or mine." Doctor Haley Bronson flipped his silver pen like a samurai. Its metal sheen flew between his fingers as he spoke. The early morning Miami sun reflected from the pen and hit Rick right in the eye. Like a laser: the pen could inflict more damage by reflecting light than by physical impact.

Doctor Bronson must've known that. Doctor Bronson knew, and controlled, everything. The world was his operating theatre.

Doctor Bronson's voice, too, was like a samurai's: perfectly modulated and authoritative. He might have been hired as the voice of talking GPS, if his twirling pen didn't first decapitate you or his macho jawline didn't chew you into a pulp.

Everything about him was modulated. He was huge, but with no part of his body out of perfect proportion. Even his hair was closely trimmed. Bronson had probably chosen that haircut because it looked perfect even when he emerged from bed or from a twelve-hour shift in the operating room.

Despite his huge physique, Doctor Bronson's fingers were as lithe and fine-boned as a painter's. His arms and wrists moved like hummingbirds. Even when he was just writing on the whiteboard, his hands pirouetted.

Haley Bronson was born to be a surgeon. His aquamarine blue eyes followed the pen's every movement, until they rested on Rick. Rick wanted to run and hide, or to jump into Doctor Bronson's arms, or both.

"Either Doctor Y's cardiology student or mine, Rick. You can't be both." Bronson sighed and shook his head. He wasn't even glancing at the pen flying between his fingers. He seemed to be staring directly at the sun rising over the Atlantic outside his window.

The pen's button top came to a violent collision with Doctor Bronson's Steelcase desk. *Bang. Clang.* Metal on metal. Maybe it was just Doctor Bronson's demonstration of rotational momentum. Maybe it was a warning to the wayward student. Maybe it was both.

"What if I'm just here to learn, and I know that both you and Doctor Yorshenko are excellent teachers? The School of Medicine is letting me take both your elective class and his, right?" Rick stole a glance directly at Doctor Bronson's face. Rick could stand the direct sight of Bronson's eyes only for a few seconds. It was like staring at the sun.

Bronson was that intimidating. Bronson was also that handsome: handsome in a way even a perfectly heterosexual guy could appreciate, handsome without any preening or affectation.

Rick's classmates liked to joke that staring at Doctor Bronson for more than two seconds would make a straight man gay. "Is that what happened to Matias?" some random clown always interjected. ("Naw man, I turned gay after seeing your mom naked," Matias had gotten accustomed to replying.)

Doctor Bronson knew they talked about him, but he didn't care. Doctor Bronson was fuck-you handsome. So handsome that he didn't need to make a big deal about it. He was also fuck-you medically brilliant, and he very likely didn't like to be talked about in that realm either.

"That's all fine." Doctor Bronson suddenly blew air out through his lips, like exhaling cigarette smoke. Except he wasn't smoking anything. "You can take my class and his class and whoever the hell else's class tickles your fucking first-year fancy."

Doctor Bronson spoke as if taking Yorshenko's class were illegal. It wasn't illegal, actually. There wasn't any such protocol. The more classes the better, of course, the official policy went. But then, the School of Medicine had never anticipated enemies like Doctors Bronson and Yorshenko.

"I just feel compelled to take Doctor Yorshenko's class." It was ridiculous, having to apologize to one professor for taking another professor's class. But that was med school: ridiculous. "The American Journal of Cardiology rankings—"

"Not the fucking AJC." Doctor Bronson sighed, gritted his teeth, and shook his head with anger and disgust. "Bunch of magazine editors in New York think they can rank surgeons."

It was the talk of the entire School of Medicine, even among the students. The American Journal of Cardiology had started ranking the top one hundred cardiac surgeons nationwide, every year. And the previous year, Yorshenko had come in slightly ahead of Bronson. Bronson number eighteen nationally, Yorshenko number fifteen.

Doctor Bronson didn't appreciate his ranking. Most doctors, all doctors, would have considered a nationwide ranking in the top one hundred to be a career-defining, life-defining achievement. That's what Rick's other professors always said.

Meanwhile, Doctor Bronson took his own achievement for granted. All he talked about was that Yorshenko had beaten him. And for all his talk about the worthlessness of AJC rankings, Bronson cared about them more than anyone else did.

"Oh. Yeah. I have no idea how valid the rankings are." Rick shook his head, as if to pre-emptively absolve himself of any blame for Bronson's rating. "I just read the AJC for my classes."

"Stick with the medical research articles." Bronson shook his head. "Don't get into AJC's beauty pageant bullshit."

"I'll remember that." Rick nodded, a little blankly.

"What drives you, Sarmenian? Seriously. Why are you here?"

"Here, like in med school?" Rick fidgeted a little in the chair. "Or like here, like *here*, like in the universe?"

"The answers should be the same, shouldn't they?" Doctor Bronson held his coffee cup in both hands. He blew over the coffee in the cup, not into it. His eyes were serious, seemingly watching the coffee's surface for imperfections. He looked like he was performing a holy sacrament.

"My reasons for being in med school should be the same as my reasons for existing in the world?"

"Yeah." Bronson pursed his lips and blew a well-aimed jet of air at the coffee in his cup, sending some of it spilling over the edge.

He smiled, pleased with himself. "Assuming you're here in med school voluntarily. I mean if you're here voluntarily, then this should be what you love, what motivates you, right?"

"Umm." Rick exhaled through his clenched lips. Whether he loved it or it motivated him had never come up as a question. Going into medicine was what his parents instilled in him since birth, he was supposed to, and what he did. That was it. "I don't know. What got you into medicine, Professor Bronson?"

"Saving lives." Bronson shrugged his shoulders like it was the most mundane thing. Of course, when doctors talked about their work, saving lives was kind of a mundane thing. "Getting to be a superhero, basically, Every day. And doing science. Working with my hands." Doctor Bronson gestured at the model hearts, plaques, and electrocardiography diagrams all around his desk.

"Wow."

"But you're the student here, not me. What really interests *you*, Sarmenian?" Doctor Bronson rocked back and forth in his chair, a little maniacally. "What are you really into here? Laparoscopic aortic valve repair? Stem cell therapy? PTEs? What drives you in medicine?"

"Uh. I guess maybe cardiology." It was what his father did. It was what Rick was supposed to do.

"That's not enough. I don't see a fire burning in you." Bronson stuck the tip of his finger into the coffee and wiggled it slightly, as if he was palpitating for a tumor. "You're not gonna get through medicine if you don't have a crazy fucking fire burning in you."

"I—" Rick didn't even know what to say. It was better to stay quiet and not embarrass himself.

Bronson leaned dangerously far back in his chair. He sipped his coffee with a quiet slurp. He winced as it entered his mouth, like he'd just tasted twelve-molar HCl. Clenching his teeth, he jerked his head upright, like waking up from a nightmare of a bad cup of coffee and one truculent student.

Bronson's neck gave a robotic-sounding snap. Sometimes he really was robot-like: a golem, a man created in a medical school's most secret skunkworks, just to do surgery and terrify students. Matias referred to Doctor Bronson as "Spock."

With his fingers dancing out a solo on the air piano, Bronson reached in his desk drawer for a packet of sugar. He tore a surgical incision across its top and sank the white powder into the coffee.

Doctor Bronson looked at Rick. Was he expecting applause? The black coffee reflected his pink lips and white teeth like a lake on a distant planet.

"Find the fire, Sarmenian. The fire."

Bronson stopped flipping his pen. He held it intently between two fingers and dipped it into his coffee, writing end first, up to the tip. Then he stirred with it. He didn't seem to think there was anything wrong with that.

"Did you mean to just—" Rick had blanked out on Doctor Bronson's words. He focused on the small everyday shock of a man, his professor no less, stirring hot coffee with a pen.

Doctor Bronson wasn't one to be absent minded. That would've been more of a Yorshenko thing.

But geniuses were geniuses. Maybe even Bronson had his moments of mistaking his pen for a spoon.

Or maybe he didn't. Bronson never made mistakes.

"Stainless steel." Doctor Bronson smiled proudly. He'd probably been waiting for Rick to question his choice of stirring implement. "The coffee doesn't react with the metal at all. Stainless. Like I said. Metallurgically stable. Try it sometime."

Bronson grinned like a madman. He looked like he knew all the answers — to where the bodies were buried.

"Doesn't the ink — doesn't the ink leak into the coffee, Doctor Bronson?" Maybe Rick was speaking a little too frankly with his professor. But this was relevant to the study of medicine, kind of. "It's the ink I'd be worried out. Not the metal. Isn't the ink toxic?"

"We all die sometime, kid." Doctor Bronson smiled, shrugged, and took a big gulp of hot coffee. That look on Bronson's face must've been what people called a *shit-eating grin*.

Bronson swallowed the coffee. He winced again, this time probably from having scalded himself. Even when he winced, the skin on his face was perfectly smooth.

"Yeah, I guess we do." Rick tried to look thoughtful when saying it. Bronson's comment about mortality was a little bizarre, but he deserved the benefit of the doubt. He dealt with mortality every day. "So you don't mind that I'm shadowing Doctor Yorshenko?"

"You can crawl up Yorshenko's Russian butthole and lay a Faberge egg for all I care, Sarmenian. Just find your fire. Find your passion."

"Thanks. I just wanted to get your ok—" Rick was just going for a more conventional approval than some kind of vague statement about laying an egg up Doctor Yorshenko's ass.

"But remember. You can be my student or Yorshenko's. Not both. Got it?" Doctor Bronson reached to the mini-refrigerator at the side of his desk. He pulled out a mini-bottle of water. He twisted off the cap with ER-level speed, then held the bottle almost perfectly upside-down at his lips. His expression was deadly serious, like he was administering a lifesaving drug. He downed the water like he was trying to cool the burn of the previous coffee, a few minutes too late. Maybe he was just trying to cool his burning dislike for Yorshenko.

"Yeah, I think I sort of understand what you're—" Rick understood only that he was being asked to choose his alliances. That he could be in both of their classes, maybe even shadow them both, but he could be a disciple of only one.

Haley Bronson was a jealous god. Boris Yorshenko was also a jealous god. That much was common sense. The fallout from two jealous gods in one Department of Cardiology at the School of Medicine — it was something Rick would have to survive.

"You're a smart kid, Rick Sarmenian." Doctor Bronson stood up, at sort of an awkward moment. Was Rick supposed to stand up too? Rick stood up too just in case, thereby forfeiting the brief moment of at least being able to look up at his professor. "A kid, but smart. Smart, but a kid. Find your fire."

"Ah, thank you, Doctor Bronson." Rick looked at his professor a little awkwardly. It would've been more comfortable had Doctor Bronson towered over Rick. That would've been natural, in accordance with the professor-student relationship. Bronson certainly towered over Rick professionally, but physically speaking, they saw eye to eye, both right around 6'3".

Rick slouched a little when standing next to any of his professors. It felt so uncomfortable not to be looking up at them. At least he didn't have to look down at Bronson, as he had to look down at a few of his other professors. That would've been more uncomfortable.

"Get out of here!" Doctor Bronson said, in a way that didn't at all sound like a joke. "And quit slouching or you'll spend middle age sucking orthopedists' dicks." That part also sounded more like a threat than a joke.

"Yes." Rick gave Doctor Bronson a nod that bordered between the obsequious and the collegial, and headed out the door. Fast.

That was the thing about medical school. Professors openly referred to their students as colleagues and fellow physicians. But that was never how it worked. Students were by no means professors' equals. They didn't even breathe the same air.

That would've been easy if it could've been publicly acknowledged. But it wasn't. Equals in public, groveling ants in the classroom and especially clinical instruction.

Negotiating a balance between the two was just one of many med-school difficulties way beyond the difficulty of the academic material. Add to all that the social cliques, the wealth differences, the traffic, the hurricanes, the roach-infested campus housing, and Rick's anxiety about sometimes involuntarily staring at guys a little too hard.

***

Rick knocked on Doctor Yorshenko's office door. With every one of Rick's knocks, the bell rang on the door-mounted teddy bear.

No answer to the knock. Rick knocked again.

"Yeah! Please!" Boris Yorshenko's enunciation carried only the slightest burden of a Russian accent. Despite that, he still said *please* at odd moments. He'd hand a colleague a scalpel and mutter *please*. But if anyone wanted to start remedying Doctor Yorshenko's eccentricities, they would have started with way more basic stuff than *please*.

Rick did as told. *Please*. He swung the door open.

The back of Yorshenko's monitor greeted him. *DELL* and a vent grille and a bunch of cables obscured any view of Yorshenko's face. That was the usual sight when visiting Doctor Y. In his office he usually buried his face in his monitor with surgery videos. His visitors knew to expect to see the back of a huge monitor long before they saw any semblance of Yorshenko himself. It was kind of like getting used to the sight of your father's hairy ass.

"Check this out." Yorshenko was still hiding with his face to the screen. His mess of wavy of blond hair just barely rose up above the monitor's surface, like a Russian submarine cautiously surfacing. He held his hand up above the monitor and waved, like he was signaling up over a wall, for Rick to come on over to his side of the desk.

Yorshenko looked like he was trying to teleport into the surgical procedure he was watching. His face was inches from its surface. The monitor showed a scalpel scraping some pink tissue and Yorshenko's gray eyes followed it carefully.

"They're doing a PTE?" Rick asked. The close-up view itself didn't say much to Rick, but pulmonary thromboendarterectomies were Doctor Yorshenko's stock in trade. They were his usual office viewing material, and it helped that each PTE video was a good ten hours long. He watched PTE videos at all hours, on all devices, with the voracious glee of a pervert.

"Are they ever doing a PTE!" Yorshenko momentarily looked up at Rick, then shot his eyes back at the screen. He followed the scalpel on the screen with his finger and smiled up at Rick.

Doctor Yorshenko's infectious smile and white teeth beamed like he was in the middle of watching a video of his favorite fetish. Which in a way, he was.

Pink and red on the screen reflected from Yorshenko's huge gray eyes. "Check this out. They've got the blood flow stop time down to ten minutes. That's all this surgeon needs."

"They stop the blood flow so the surgeon can work in the pulmonary artery?" Rick asked. Asking professors about surgery felt like throwing a dart at a board. Surgery techniques were way above the usual curriculum of the first year of medical school. Rick had been able to gather bits and pieces about various procedures from his professors, but he felt like a novice, even a novice at just phrasing surgical questions.

"Absolutely right! You're a genius!" Eyes still fixed on the screen, Yorshenko held up his hand to Rick for a fist-bump. Rick bumped his professor's fist. "Cool the patient's body, stop the lung-heart machine for ten to twenty minutes, surgeon goes in to the pulmonary artery and wham bam, party time."

"Party time!" Rick felt like blowing into an anticlimactic kazoo. He hadn't yet become conversant enough with cardiac surgery to be able to refer to any aspect of open-chest surgery as *party time.*

"The longer the patient has no blood, no oxygen, more risk of serious morbidity or even mortality. Obviously." Yorshenko sighed a little.

"Yeah." That much, even Rick could understand. A patient without blood or oxygen was at risk of dying.

"So this dude at UCSD I've been watching, he's a rock star." Yorshenko smiled big, looking up at Rick for approval. He nodded his head so violently, so enthusiastically that his flying blond locks made him look like Weird Al Yankovic. "Total rock star. Ten minutes and

he's pulling out a thrombus the size of a calamari. Check it out."
Yorshenko clicked his mouse and the video played.

"Whoa. Damn." Rick's excitement was genuine. The surgeon on the screen had in fact just pulled out a thrombus the size of a calamari. "That thing must not have felt good sitting in the dude's pulmonary artery."

"Rock star! A rock star, I'm telling you. Your future too, Rick. I've got a feeling you can be a rock star."

Yorshenko raised one fist above the monitor. Rick dutifully fist-bumped him. Yorshenko raised his other fist. Rick dutifully fist-bumped that one too.

It didn't even feel weird. Yorshenko didn't do stuff like that to seem "with it" or "cool." He wasn't any kind of tryhard. He was just naturally ebullient like that. And he must've been no older than his mid thirties; that wasn't too old for natural fist-bumping.

"I mean — I appreciate your faith in me. But you know. I'm just starting out. I don't know anything about medicine. Or I know a little bit about medicine. Don't know anything about heart surgery."

"Rick. Rick." Yorshenko glanced up at Rick for a split second before bringing his focus back down to the screen. "The PTE is the Holy Grail of heart surgery. That's why I want you to start out watching one. It's like, start at the top." His *r*s were a little weird, but other than the *r*s and the *please* thing, Yorshenko didn't have a Russian accent.

That was really what separated those who knew Yorshenko from those who didn't know him: whether the speech they imitated sounded like the real Yorshenko or like a cartoon Russian villain. Doctor Bronson, in all his deadly accuracy, was scary-good at mimicking Yorshenko's talk, even the way Yorshenko wiped his falling blond locks from his eyeglasses.

"If one day I wanted to be a surgeon doing PTEs—" Rick started to ask.

"Residency in cardiology, fellowship in cardiothoracic surgery, lots of practice." Yorshenko smiled affably, like he was talking about

Christmas. "Figure no more than eight years after finishing med school. To be a novice PTE surgeon, anyway." Yorshenko looked up at Rick and winked.

"You're eight years out of med school, right?" Rick squinted to try to read the date on Yorshenko's UCSF medical diploma on the wall. The digits *2013* stood out embossed at the bottom of the diploma. He was right.

"Yeah, I'm just eight years out." Yorshenko swatted a few locks of hair from his eyeglasses.

"But I'm no novice. I'm Boris fucking Yorshenko." Yorshenko clicked his tongue, made dual pistol-firing gestures with his fingers, and imitated doing a PTE, with imaginary instruments in his hands.

Someone might've thought Doctor Yorshenko was making a Cobb salad.

Two

Haley Bronson wiped the sweat off his face again. His finger cleared the drops from under his Oakleys, then with his hand he slid the beaded water off the rest of his face. Maybe he'd forgotten about evaporative cooling effects, or maybe he just wanted to look good for the male students.

Typical Haley Bronson: he had to make everything intense, even Saturday afternoon beach volleyball. He stared back and forth across the net like he was quarterbacking the Super Bowl. Below his Harvard School of Medicine t-shirt, Haley's neon-green beach shorts were probably harboring a lecherous hard-on.

Boris wouldn't look. Looking down there would've been letting Haley win. He wouldn't fall into that trap again. He'd just coolly stay on his own side of the makeshift volleyball court and admire the non-human scenery: even on a sunny Saturday afternoon, it was possible to find an uncrowded oceanside beach volleyball court in Miami.

Maybe Bronson thought he had gotten one up on Boris by recruiting Rick Sarmenian for his team — shirtless Rick Sarmenian, the geeky first-year student whose perfect body was the surprise of the century. Was Bronson prescient or something? Was there a CT scanner in his dick? From looking at skinny, nerdy Rick, nobody, not even an experienced clinician like Boris Yorshenko, would have guessed he was hiding that kind of perfectly sculpted physique.

Bronson must have forgotten: human vision is primarily forward, not peripheral. Rick was on Haley's volleyball team, but it was Boris who was getting an eyeful of that student body from across the net.

Every one of twenty-three-year-old Rick Sarmenian's leaps for the net, extensions of his lean arms, even peeks at his underarm hair: it was all for Boris's eyes. Boris was just playing volleyball and looking straight ahead. Meanwhile, Haley Bronson, Mister Harvard Medical School graduate, had to side-eye his young teammate like a homo pervert.

The ball came fast. Boris ran toward it through the sand, arms extended, preparing for certain humiliation. He couldn't get to that ball in time.

"I got it!" a voice roared nearby. A mass of man, like a muscle zeppelin, flew right past Boris, arms extended, and hit the ball just over the net. It hit the sand before Haley's team could hit it. "Ha!" the same voice roared.

The muscle zeppelin was the SS Doctor Ritter Lehman from orthopedics. Ritter stood up on the sand and fist-pumped the air like a brute, then flexed for the nonexistent crowd like he was Popeye.

Ritter Lehman, his idiot fist-pumps and all, was a full clinical professor. Saturday volleyball let him strut around in a spandex thong and show off what he must have believed was his amazing body.

Ritter was so in-your-face gay that the old boys at orthopedics didn't even say anything about it. If only life could have been so easy for Boris with the old boys at cardiology.

But not if it meant being as obnoxious as Ritter Lehman. Even Haley Bronson asn't as obnoxious as that dude.

"Nice work, Doctor Lehman." Haley's teammate Rick smiled and gave a thumbs-up to Boris's teammate Ritter.

Haley scowled at Rick. Ritter answered haley's scowl with an eye roll.

"Send Doctor Bronson over to proctology." Ritter spoke to Boris, but loudly enough for Haley to hear. "Maybe they can pull the bug out from his ass."

"Let's go!" Haley glared across the net, hands on his hips. He had no visible reaction to Ritter's proctology referral. The wind coming off the ocean hadn't even perturbed Haley's hair. He must've used products, lots of products. He must've also thought of hair-gel-free Boris as a floppy-haired slob. Let Haley think what he wanted. Let the AJC rankings speak for themselves.

Boris lay the ball in the palm of his hand. He swung and served. Boom. The ball flew over the net, right into shirtless Rick Sarmenian's arms.

Rick hit the ball straight up. It popped up right in front of Haley and lay in the air like a sleepy dragonfly. Haley's eyes lit up the same way they did in department meetings. He flexed his legs and launched himself into the air, arm pulled back.

Haley swung his arm. He smashed the ball with his hand. The ball crested the net and flew straight down into the sand on Boris's side. Boris's team didn't even have a chance — not on that point, anyway.

The ball's landing created a little sandstorm. Ritter and Matias nodded their respect to Haley. Neither of them had any hope of returning the shot.

"Ladies and gentlemen, Doctor Haley Bronson!" Haley announced, as if his volleyball companions didn't know who he was.

"You'd strut better if you took off that shirt." The sole woman in the volleyball meetup group, Doctor Linda McCall, pointed at Haley with tongue-in-cheek adoration. At least it must've been tongue-in-cheek; not many people thought of Haley as anything other than a jerk. "Showing off muscles would complete the studboy look, Doctor Bronson."

Rick smiled at Linda, then nodded approvingly at Haley. "I believe Doctor Linda McCall just called you a studboy."

"Teachable moment!" Linda called out to Rick Sarmenian. "Not exactly correct. I didn't call Doctor Bronson a studboy. I said *complete the studboy look*. Medicine is all about precision, Rick."

"I thought it's all about the studboys." Ritter Lehman rolled his eyes at Linda. That old queen had certainly had his share of studboys. "Can we get back to volleyball now?"

"I'm sorry." Haley said loudly, his lips shaped into a definite shit-eating grin. "I have a bit of a selective hearing problem. Doctor McCall, did you ask me to remove my Harvard School of Medicine t-shirt? I didn't hear anything else that may have been said."

"Indeed I did." Linda stared at Haley shamelessly. Sure, as a woman in medicine, especially in anesthesiology, she had to deal with a lot of shit. But at least she didn't have to hide being into dudes.

"I can't refuse! It's doctor's orders!" Haley shrugged innocently. Or guiltily. He glanced for a half-second at the blazing sun, as if to give himself a slap in the face. He looked back from it quickly and put his shades back on.

Haley spread his feet farther apart in the sand, like he was about to wrestle. Cross-armed, he hooked his fingers under his shirt and pulled it off, looking at his audience. Was he expecting cat calls?

Linda eagerly smiled and nodded, as if following a Teleprompter. Matias and Ritter, both openly gay, hammed it up, furiously fanning themselves while watching Haley.

Haley had somehow already applied some kind of glistening suntan lotion under his shirt. He'd perfectly anticipated this shirt-removal moment.

"Doctor Bronson already fucking pre-oiled his body," Matias whispered to Boris. "He had this all planned." Matias shook his head, still not taking his eyes off of admiring Haley's physique. "He really is Spock."

Ritter asked loudly, "Finished seductively ripping off your Harvard Med t-shirt there, Haley?" Ritter stared down at his Patek-Philippe that he somehow hadn't taken off for the volleyball match. "It took you only what, twenty minutes to manage to remove your shirt? I can do a knee replacement in that time."

"Sorry." Haley shrugged with a mischievous grin that showed the tips of his white teeth to the blazing Miami sun. "My muscles got in the way." Emulating a basketball throw, Haley tossed his shirt off to the side of the sand court.

"I thought he never takes that Harvard shirt off," Matias mumbled to Ritter. He jumped up and down, practicing imaginary power-spikes.

"It's Haley's version of Mormon undergarments." Ritter laughed at his own joke and rolled his eyes.

"Play ball! Play ball!" Haley shouted out. His neck strained with every word, like he was having an orgasm. "Match point, Team Haley Bronson."

"The team is now named after you, Haley?" Linda McCall shook her head like she knew Haley well.

She did know him well, although probably not as well as faculty rumors alleged. Of course, Haley must have enjoyed the speculation about him having a thing with Linda. At least it kept away suspicion of Haley's homosexuality. Only Boris knew that.

"I'm the captain and MVP, and keep making all the shots." Haley shrugged to suggest he was only being reasonable.

"You're captain, Doctor Bronson?" Rick Sarmenian asked, smiling. That kid had balls to talk to a professor like that, especially to an asshole like Haley Bronson.

"But ACJ still ranks Boris above you, Haley." Linda demurely covered her mouth with her fingertips. Then she stopped trying to restrain herself and burst out in laughter. She lifted her sunglasses up to wipe away the laugh-tears and grinned at her teammate Haley.

"ACJ can suck my dick." Haley gritted his teeth while tossing the ball up and down. Linda knew how to get him upset, at least. "Now play ball!"

Rick Sarmenian took the serving position. Maybe youth was his advantage.

In the classroom, Rick's looks were nothing extraordinary: just your average skinny, nerdy white guy in the first year med school. Shirtless, under the blast of the sun and in the salt spray of the ocean, Rick was a beach Adonis. His skinny build became alluringly slim and his ruffled brown hair became fashionably disheveled.

To the surprise of any self-professed expert in identifying hot guys when they still had their clothes on, Rick was absolutely fucking hot. Of course Haley wanted Rick on his team.

"Match point, team Rick Sarmenian!" Rick laughed. Linda laughed with him. Haley politely half-smiled.

Rick cradled the ball in his palm and wrist, preparing to serve. He swung back his lithe, muscular arm. He swung it forward again, like a baseball bat or a golf club, or a big dick. He hit the ball precisely over the net.

Boris's defense zone.

Boris got under the ball and hit it right back over the net. Take that, Team Haley Bronson.

Linda set the ball straight up. She smiled and glanced over to her teammate Haley. It was his time to shine. As much as she mocked him, he was her knight in shining armor, or glistening body oil.

Haley did his part. Shirtless, he jumped up again. That body was as solid as Haley's ego. Boris carefully kept his eye on the ball instead of staring too hard at Haley's flexing biceps as he slammed the ball over to Boris's side of the net.

It wasn't difficult to anticipate. Linda's setup had given Boris time to prepare. Boris was aloft for his defense before Haley even made hit the ball.

As soon as the ball crested the net, Boris slammed it back toward Haley's side. Rick made a decent play for it, but couldn't reach it before it hit the ground in a flurry of sand.

Haley silently shook his head and rolled the ball under the net to Boris's team, Ritter in serving position.

"Fucking match point!" Ritter announced, a little too loudly.

"There are kids around." Linda shushed Ritter down with her downward waving hand.

"Oh. I'm sorry." Ritter did look genuinely regretful. The guy wasn't a monster. Which was maybe more than could be said about Haley Bronson. "Match point, then!" Ritter announced it in a quieter voice, and absent the side serving of profanity.

Ritter's arm swung like a sledgehammer to serve the ball.

On the other side, Haley shouted to Rick and Linda, "I got it!" and spiked the ball back to Boris.

Boris hit the ball way over the net, soaring over the heads of Haley, Rick, and Linda, all of whom stood at the net. Haley yelled "I got it!" again and jogged backwards quixotically — until he lost his balance in the sand and fell flat on his ass.

Haley's ass kicked up a bigger cloud of sand than the ball ever had. Maybe the only bigger dust cloud was the one hanging over his team's defeat. Sure, it was just friendly beach volleyball. But to Haley, it mattered. To Haley, everything mattered.

"Alright!" Boris clapped. He tried to adopt the countenance of a cheery camp counselor. "Team Boris, Ritter, and Matias wins the day! Until next time!"

"Aren't you gonna help me up?" Haley asked Linda from his ass-in-sand position.

"I was just kind of bracing myself." Linda grinned and sighed.

"For?" Haley took off his sunglasses to shake off the sand. He squinted at Linda.

"I expected an outburst about your team only losing because you had a woman on the team." Linda rolled her eyes.

"Shit." Haley shook his head. "I'm a crazy motherfucker, but even I'm not that stupid."

"Oh." Linda reached out to help Haley stand up. "Sorry. I guess I was the one stereotyping here."

"I'm used to it." Haley took her hand and stood up. Even after he brushed sand off his shorts, he carried the heavy look of a man defeated.

"Great volleyball match, everyone." Boris fast-clapped again. This was supposed to be volleyball, not the crucifixion of Haley Bronson. "Haley, you played great, as always."

Haley stood up, turned his back to Boris, and went to put his shirt back on. Linda shrugged to Boris. Boris shrugged back at her.

Three

Scrubbing in to the operating room was the first skill to master. It was only his first year of med school, but shadowing Doctors Yorshenko and Bronson had allowed Rick to watch more procedures than even most fourth-year students had.

Rick couldn't hope to learn how to perform surgery. He could at least hope to learn how to wash his hands and put on a gown.

Asking for help when he suited up for the OR felt like having his mom dress him for kindergarten. The orderlies and nurses had to help Rick with everything from washing the entirety of his arms to finding a lead coat long and slim enough to fit him. "You'll learn soon," they always assured him.

"Alright!" The chief surgical nurse gave Rick a joking knuckle-pat on his head, like a football coach tapping a player's helmet. "I think you're all suited up."

The nurse opened the door to the operating theatre. A waft of cooled, pressurized air blew over Rick.

He saw the through the plastic splatter barrier over his eyes. He breathed sterilized air through a mask. His hands and lower arms were covered in latex. And worst of all was that heavy lab coat, required when there was a fluoroscope nearby. It was hot enough to sweat before he even walked into the hot, bright lights of the operating room.

"I hope you had a really good pee before scrubbing in." Doctor Yorshenko's voice was recognizable even if, under all the surgical gear, his face wasn't.

"Why?" Rick's eyes opened wide. Had he forgotten some bit of surgical preparation? Was there a urine sample or something?

"PTE is an eight-hour procedure." Doctor Yorshenko laughed morosely. "That's why we call it the *pee*-tee-ee."

"We can't even scrub out to—" Rick started to ask. His eyes went wide with disbelief. He hadn't exactly prepared himself for eight hours without a bathroom break.

"Of course *you* can scrub out to pee." Doctor Yorshenko pointed a gloved finger in Rick's face. "You're just a first-year med

195

student. A kid around here. You're supposed to need your wee-wee pee-pee breaks."

"Oh." Rick tried to feel consoled by that statement. Maybe it was condescending, but it wasn't anything untrue.

"But if a resident steps out for a pee?" Doctor Yorshenko shook his head and made a *yap-yap-yap-yap* gesture with his gloved hand. "They'll never hear the end of it. We'll be gossiping about it for years."

"And the anesthesiologist sticks around the whole time?" Rick asked.

"Oh yeah." Boris pointed with his thumb toward one of his colleagues inspecting an IV drip machine. "PTE is not one you can check out on. Especially when we switch to heart-lung bypass."

"You may recognize me from yesterday's game." That must've been Linda McCall. Her voice was familiar, although Rick hadn't yet learned the surgeon's art of distinguishing colleagues by body size and shape even when they were wearing full surgical gear.

Doctor McCall waved and nodded. "When I'm not playing volleyball, I do a little anesthesiology on the side."

"Oh yeah." Rick nodded back. If he was going to be a surgeon, he might as well learn to recognize his colleagues through their space suits.

"Patient is stable, Doctor Yorshenko," Linda said over the steady beeps from the machines around her. "Anything else you need right now?"

"No, I've just been thinking. Call me Boris." Doctor Yorshenko, Boris, shrugged. "I read something about more collegial, less hierarchical operating theatre environments. All of you. Rick, too. Call me Boris. Alright?"

Linda shrugged. "Weird flex, but ok."

Rick laughed.

"You know how to get to a man's heart, Rick?" Boris asked.

"By slicing his breast bone with a reciprocating-blade saw?" Rick shrugged.

"Please!" Boris laughed. "High fiiiive!"

"Damn, he's good!" Linda spit imaginary spit on her finger, then touched it to an imaginary Rick. Imaginary steam resulted. Linda emphasized it with a sizzling sound.

"Exactly right." Boris exhaled. "Rick is the expert. Although Linda is renowned for her ability to reach a man's heart." Boris smiled like he knew something. Considering the weirdly semi-flirtatious interaction between Doctor McCall and Doctor Bronson during the volleyball game, maybe Boris really did know something.

"Hey hey now." Linda shook her head. "The operating theater costs two dollars a second, gentlemen. Let's start operating."

"Please." Boris nodded. Rick stood back in his usual place, safely back from where the real action was, so he wouldn't get in the way, but close enough to at least see Boris's hands at work. Three LED monitors hanging from the ceiling showing close-up camera feeds of the procedure supplemented Rick's view.

"I'm starting on the sternum here, Rick," Boris spoke louder for Rick's benefit.

"Got it. Thank you. I'm watching on the monitors." It was like watching sports at a stadium: he could choose between the faraway direct view, or a close-up view on the monitors.

"Alright. Let me know if you have any questions as I proceed." Boris's voice was perfectly calm, authoritative, scholarly. He wasn't just the wild-eyed goofball. He was an actual professor of medicine, and a famous surgeon. Maybe Boris's easy-going manner sometimes made that too easy to take for granted.

"Yes, Doctor Yorshenko."

"Yes what?" Boris asked with a small laugh.

"Yes, Boris."

"Please." Boris nodded.

***

Three hours into the procedure, Boris had really hit his stride. He hadn't even said anything for more than an hour. This must've been what they called "the zone" or something like that.

Lesser surgeons got fatigued as they proceeded through a procedure. Practitioners at Boris's level would only grow more energized by the act of surgery itself. That's what it said in the books, anyway.

Boris was working in the patient's heart with the ease and familiarity normal people — not highly ranked cardiac surgeons — know only from brushing their teeth or tying their shoes.

"Is the patient down to eighteen Celsius?" Boris was looking at the body temperature readout on the screen, but Linda McCall — and not the machine — was the anesthesiologist.

"Correct." Linda's scanned the anesthesia machine's rows of numerical displays.

"Rick." Boris spoke up toward the ceiling, so his voice would reflect back at Rick behind him. It was a little like the old-time operating theaters that Boris sometimes talked about — that really were theaters, with tickets for sale.

"Yeah Boris? I'm still watching." For the past three hours, Rick's mind had fused with Boris's stream of action: his hands working in the chest cavity, his small taps and hand signals and whispers to Linda, the way he occasionally chose a new instrument from the cornucopia laid out on the table before him.

"Patient is cooled down to eighteen degrees celsius. That prevents brain damage when we stop blood flow." Boris was speaking up at the ceiling again.

"You guys are gonna turn off the heart-lung machine, right?" Rick asked. That was what they were supposed to do in a PTE operation.

"Yeah." Boris answered. "We don't turn off the machine, of course. Just push the button to stop the blood pumping. Even a Boris Yorshenko level surgeon can't operate on an artery when there's blood gushing out of it."

"Wow." Rick nodded.

"This will be you one day, Rick. I swear." Boris spoke back over his shoulder to Rick. "Except you'll be using surgical techniques old guys like me will have no idea about."

"I— I hope." Rick tried to visualize himself doing all the complex chest-cavity surgical work Boris was doing. That was difficult even to imagine.

"Better believe it, Rick." Boris nodded in Rick's direction.

Boris looked closely into the chest cavity. The fiber-optic headlight mounted on his forehead blazed like the hot sun in the volleyball game. "You can hit the button, Linda. Stop blood flow."

"Stopping blood flow," Linda said. She clicked a touch screen and the machine beeped. The hum of the heart pump went silent.

"I'm taking the pulmonary artery," Boris mumbled, bent over and looking into the chest cavity. "I'm taking the— taking the—"

Boris stood perfectly still.

"Complication, Boris?" Linda peered over the anesthesia machine.

"The—" Boris answered. "The—"

Boris slouched deeper. His arms swayed at his sides. He fell to the ground.

"Doctor Yorshenko!" the surgical nurse yelled out.

Boris lay on the ground.

"I can't turn the patient's blood flow back on." Linda stared at Rick, then at the surgical nurse. "Pulmonary artery is open. That blood would just bleed out."

Rick only looked on, mouth agape. It was like an emergency-room TV drama, but real.

Boris still lay slumped on the ground in a fetal position, drool from his half-open mouth.

"Boris!" Linda yelled down at him. She shook her head and pressed a red button on the wall. A red light flashed outside the emergency room.

"Should I send Doctor Yorshenko down to the ER?" the surgical nurse asked. Linda nodded in response. The nurse took the sterile phone and described the situation. Boris Yorshenko had just fallen down while performing a procedure and needed first aid.

"Are you going to call Doctor Bronson to continue the procedure?" the nurse asked Linda.

"It's his day off." Linda shook her head with a pained look. "He's probably at home, or wherever else he goes."

The outside door swung open and a man entered — bearded, heavyset, in hastily-donned scrubs. Rick had briefly seen him around: Doctor Jones, head of cardiac surgery.

"Haley Bronson's not answering his hospital cellphone," Doctor Jones called out to Linda McCall. "He's the only one who can take over a PTE."

"It's Haley's day off." Linda shook her head.

"Don't you have his personal phone number?" Doctor Jones stared at Linda. Apparently everybody knew that Linda and Doctor Bronson had something going on.

"No I don't." Linda spoke firmly through her mask. "I don't have any contact with Doctor Bronson outside the workplace."

"It's an emergency, Linda." Doctor Jones threw his arms up in the air in exasperation and shook his head. "We're in the middle of a PTE. We don't care what's going on between you and haley. Just call him and get him over here."

Linda raised her voice in return. "I'm not going to escalate this conversation, Doctor Jones. There's a patient on the table I'm taking care of. I don't have any of Doctor Bronson's information other than what's in our staff directory."

"Alright. Alright." Doctor Jones shook his head. He sounded like he still didn't believe Linda.

"I—" Rick raised his hand. "I can probably get in touch with Doctor Bronson."

"He's not in his office, if that's what you mean." Doctor Jones shook his head. "And Bronson won't lift a fucking hairy finger of his if Yorshenko is involved."

"Not his office number." Rick tapped his gloved hand on the pants pocket that held his phone. "He gave me his personal WhatsApp. Gives me school advice sometimes."

"Worth a try." Doctor Jones looked at Rick with a mix of condescension and incredulity. "Scrub out and see what you can do, kiddo. Tell him to call me. Just don't tell him it's Yorshenko. He'd run the other way from helping Yorshenko."

Rick stepped out of the OR. He fumbled to take off his gloves and lab coat. He found his phone in his pocket.

This was important enough for a voice call. Rick pushed the voice call icon. Doctor Bronson's profile picture flashed on the screen as he answered the call.

"Rick Sarmenian! Man of the hour!" Doctor Bronson sounded like he was enjoying his day off.

"You need to come to the hospital, Doctor Bronson." Rick's voice sounded so mechanical when he was trying to convey urgency. He hated that about how he talked. It made him sound like a robot. Or like Spock.

"Yeah?" Doctor Bronson laughed. "First-year med student Rick Sarmenian dictates my work hours now? Do you need me to make you coffee and massage your balls, Doctor Sarmenian?"

"No, but it's—" Rick tripped over his attempt to describe, verbalize, or even vocalize.

"Rick, this isn't the first time I've taken a day off. The hospital has other doctors covering for me. Relax."

"You're needed in the OR." Rick was breathing faster. He paced back and forth outside that same operating room. "Right now."

"I have some magic surgical skill that neither I nor the AJC is aware of? Maybe I can laparoscopically sew my asshole shut with my lips?"

"There's a PTE. You need to do a PTE procedure." Rick tried to calm his breathing. A team of nurses wheeled Boris Yorshenko out of the operating room on a gurney.

"Have them call Yorshenko." Doctor Bronson sounded so perfectly cool and composed. "Yorshenko can do anything I can, and then some. Even the AJC agrees."

"Doctor Yorshenko—"

"Yorshenko is too good to do it or something? He already put in his three hours for the day? What?"

"Doctor Yorshenko suddenly went unconscious while starting the PTE. Fell to the ground. He's in the emergency room. The PTE patient is still on the table in the OR."

"Shit. Which OR?"

"Cardiology West, Room 1." Rick read it off the plaque. "Patient name is—"

"I know. Juan Alvedar." Somehow Doctor Bronson preternaturally knew the patient's name.

"How did you know that?"

"I'll be there in five minutes."

"Five minutes?" Rick didn't want to look like an idiot to Doctor Jones.

"I said, five minutes." Doctor Bronson hung up the call.

Rick walked over to Doctor Jones slowly enough so he could think of what he should say. This was no time to smile or gloat, but he'd just gotten Doctor Bronson to come in, despite no one else being able to even call him.

"Doctor Jones." Rick spoke quietly. Doctor Jones was tapping at something on his hospital-issue iPad.

"Nice try, Rick. Never hurts to try." Jones's face shone with sweat, despite the air conditioning. Sweat stains grew from his armpits like vestigial wings. "We're checking if we can get a cardiac surgeon from Mount Sinai to come in to finish the job."

"Doctor Jones." Rick forced himself to raise his voice just a little bit. To be taken seriously. To have a place in the discussion.

202

"Doctor Bronson is on his way over. He agreed to do the procedure. He said he'll be here in five minutes."

"Don't joke about stuff like that." Doctor Jones shook his head. "Patient lives at stake. This isn't high school."

"Doctor Jones. I'm serious. Doctor Bronson is —"

"Haley Bronson agreed to come in on his day off? When he'd intentionally shut off his hospital phone?" Doctor Jones shook his head. "Does he know it's a Yorshenko job?"

"He knows." Rick nodded. In response, Doctor Jones's face was about halfway between admiration and disbelief.

"Are they ready for me to scrub in?" Doctor Bronson shouted the question before he'd even stepped off the elevator.

"You're already—" Doctor Jones squinted so hard he was almost wincing. He stared at Doctor Bronson like he was a ghost.

"I said five minutes." Doctor Bronson shook his head, apparently exasperated with his colleagues' not taking him at his word. He walked toward the scrub room.

"Doctor Bronson, let me give you the case notes on this one." Doctor Jones followed after Doctor Bronson, waving a manila folder.

Doctor Bronson stopped again, shook his head again, and shot Doctor Jones a *you just don't understand, do you?* look again. "You don't think I'm already familiar with all the PTE cases that come through here? What the fuck you think I do on my days off, golf?" Doctor Bronson rolled his eyes and returned to vigorously scrubbing his hands and arms.

"So you already know the case notes?" Doctor Jones sounded shocked.

"You administrators just don't get it." Doctor Bronson was suiting up in his surgical gown. One of the nurses tied the mask behind his head and led him into the surgical suite. Doctor Bronson didn't even look back at his boss.

Four

"On behalf of the Miller School of Medicine and the University of Miami, it is my honor to award Doctor Haley Bronson the Lifetime Service to Medicine prize."

It was Doctor Jones. Big boss man. Talking up Haley. Giving Haley a big prize.

Applause. Bright lights. A cheering crowd. A trophy. A check for some big amount of money. It was the last place Haley wanted to be.

"Doctor McCall." Doctor Jones was yelling out to the crowd. "Doctor Linda McCall. Come on up here."

Linda gave a confused look before smiling and trudging out onto the stage. Doctor Jones handed the microphone for Haley to say something about her.

"Doctor Linda McCall was the anesthesiologist for Mister Alvedar's procedure. She kept Mister Alvedar alive during the entire procedure, including taking charge of the procedure after Doctor Yorshenko collapsed."

Haley nodded at Linda. She smiled at the audience. "The smartest thing I did that day as the anesthesiologist in charge was knowing that Doctor Bronson was the surgeon to call in to finish the PTE." The crowd laughed politely and applauded.

Haley did his best to look flattered. There was a normal staff succession list. Any dumbshit would've known that Haley was the only surgeon who could take over a complex PTE, because that was policy. But Haley could blush a little and act like Linda was giving him a big compliment.

"Doctor McCall!" The big boss Jones must have really liked the sound of his own voice. "You're known to flatter Doctor Bronson quite a bit."

Doctor Jones looked at Linda as if she was supposed to say something, admit it, blush and deny it, something. Linda's gaze was still, stony discomfort.

Doctor Jones continued. "Folks, colleagues, the whole department knows that Linda McCall and Haley Bronson have a—" Jones was so fucking blatant witht hat shit. He was drunk on the sound of his own voice.

"Haley Bronson, everybody!" Linda spoke into her own microphone while Doctor Jones was still speaking. "Lifetime Service to Medicine prize goes to Haley Bronson! Congratulations!" She shot Jones a look that said she'd drown out any more of his bullshit. Linda McCall didn't need to be shipped with anybody, especially not by a hamfisted idiot boss.

Haley hadn't slept more than an hour since that Monday's impromptu PTE. He hadn't even changed his clothes since he'd walked into the hospital. He'd spent seventy-two hours jogging between the bedsides of Juan Alvedar, the PTE patient during whose procedure Boris Yorshenko had decided to have a stroke, and Boris Yorshenko, the stroke-haver himself.

Hospital rules didn't allow that much work without sleep. But Haley had a little trick: they couldn't know you were overworking if you never clocked in. Haley bummed access passes off of friends and otherwise worked off the clock.

Haley wasn't actually doing anything around Boris that could've been impacted by a lack of sleep. He wasn't providing actual medical care. He was just providing moral support. Having little tantrums at attendings who slacked off about attending. And chilling with Boris's mom.

Who knew that a piece of shit like Yorshenko even had a mother? You'd think a dude like Yorshenko had been shat out by a genetically miscoded dog.

Post-stroke Boris was blurry eyed, a bit confused, but cognizant — but talking. "Haley Bronson and I have been colleagues. Rivals."

Jones was holding up a microphone to Boris's mouth. They'd actually wheeled poor wild-haired Boris in on a wheelchair. "You could even say — Doctor Bronson and I were workplace enemies."

Boris looked at Haley apologetically, as if Boris had been the instigator of all the shitty things Haley had said and done, as if Haley hadn't been the driving force of the awfulness.

There was some laughter in the audience. More than just a little bit of laughter. The enmity between Haley and Boris had apparently become more than a private feud. That in itself was regrettable.

Allowing that petty feud to affect not only Boris and Haley's working relationship, but to actually go public and affect the organization's image, possibly patients' view of the organization — that was fucking shameful. And it was all on Haley.

Boris blinked quickly. Doctor Jones pulled a Kleenex from a box on the podium and wiped a tear from Boris's face. Boris spoke again. "But in all my years as a physician, and also as a patient, I have never been cared for with as much selflessness and dedication as Doctor Bronson has shown over these past few days."

It was an awkward time to be Haley Bronson. All eyes were on him like he was the Sphinx. Haley was a decent surgeon, maybe even an excellent surgeon, but standing on a stage and getting awards was never what drove him. And now the shitty way he'd treated Boris in the past was being thrown directly in his face. It was shit, but shit of his own making.

Doctor Jones passed the microphone to Juan Alvedar. His Hawaiian floral shirt covered what appeared to be a portable EKG. "Doctor Bronson, when you and I first met, I was chilled to eighteen degrees celsius — and not because I'm such a cool guy."

Haley smiled and shrugged at Juan and at the audience. Really, he just wanted to be either asleep at home or working with patients, but these dog-and-pony awards things were a necessary part of the profession. He could ham it up once in a while when necessary.

"Doctor Bronson, I didn't find out much later, but apparently you were not even on duty when my surgeon, Doctor Yorshenko, experienced some sort of health problem while he was working on me, me the very cool guy at eighteen degrees. And Doctor Bronson, you were there. You arrived in five minutes, they tell me. And you have been there. You have been at my bedside for even longer boring periods of monotony than my dear wife."

Juan's wife laughed from the front row. Juan gave her a thumbs-up.

Doctor Jones took the microphone again. He managed a smile. "If we can just ask you one question, Doctor Bronson. Seriously now. On behalf of your colleagues, your patients, the audience here. How the hell did you make it from home to the operating room in five minutes?"

"You didn't believe me." Haley shook his head. It was sometimes the only way he could convey the concept of *please take what I'm saying seriously.* "I told Rick I'd be there in five minutes. Nobody believed me."

"I'm sorry." Doctor Jones smiled, a little guiltily. "I mean — Miami traffic. None of us even know where you live. I assumed you'd be coming in from Coral Gables or Fisher Island or something."

"I don't live in Coral Gables or Fisher Island." Haley stared out blankly at the audience. He was exhausted, but awake enough to at least describe his dwelling location. "I live at the Flamingo. Next door to the hospital."

"Ha ha ha!" Doctor Jones nodded. "Among his many other talents, Doctor Bronson has an excellent sense of humor."

"I'm not joking." Haley was a bit too tired to put much inflection in his voice. As embarrassing as it was to sound like Spock, that was just sometimes how he talked, especially when the point he was making was too serious to spice up.

"The Flamingo is a single-room occupancy—" Doctor Jones said quietly to Haley, avoiding the microphone. "Flophouse, if you don't mind the term."

"Yeah." Haley shrugged. He spoke about halfway between off-record and directly into the microphone. The audience must've heard at least a little of what he was saying. "You think I have a life outside of work? You think I'm hosting dinner parties or something? I just need a place to sleep and charge my electronics. The closer to the hospital the better."

"Well, ladies and gentlemen! That's professional dedication! Another round of applause!" Jones excelled at molding anything in his reach into a smoothly crafted production.

That talent made Jones an administrator with an MD degree, not a clinician.

The clinical world was never that seamlessly assembled. The clinic world was where shit got real. Blood sputtered. Surgeons had strokes. Some men even had the audacity to love other men.

***

"Rick." Haley caught his star student in the hallway, just outside of Boris's inpatient room. The kid hadn't been doing Haley-level hours at Yorshenko's bedside, but he'd been there a lot — and he presumably had classes to attend and studying to do.

Rick Sarmenian stopped in his tracks. "Sorry, Doctor Bronson. I have to go to class." He stood straight up, a momentary freeze-frame, and looked into Haley's eyes. After a delicious few seconds Rick broke eye contact with Haley, and used his eyes to point back at Boris's room. "I'll be back with Boris after class though."

His eyes skitting to avoid eye contact with Haley, Rick bent down to drink from a water fountain. He pursed his lips. Water spurted into his mouth. He was beautiful, with a long, lean, lithe torso. His lips shone glistening wet. He was swallowing his last gulps of water.

"Thank you." Haley said it directly to Rick, looking at his eyes. Rick still didn't seem to understand. "Rick, thank you. Really."

"For visiting Boris?" With the back of his hand, Rick wiped water from his mouth.

"No. Mister Alvedar might be dead now if it weren't for you. I'd still be the world's biggest piece of shit now, if it weren't for you."

"Me?" Rick smiled as if Haley had been joking. "If it weren't for me?" Rick leaned up from the drinking fountain and shook his head. "What did I do that's so great?"

Haley stepped closer to Rick. His personal smell — his pheromones — came like a gut-punch. How could he find a student so attractive? But after that student had saved his life and Boris's, how could he not?

Haley spoke closely to Rick's face. "I never would've answered the phone if it weren't you calling." As Haley spoke, Rick seemed to tremble a little, like Haley's words shook his core.

"But—" Rick's eyes were full of earnest disbelief. The kid wasn't playing at false modesty or fishing for compliments. Rick really didn't know all he'd done, as a mere first-year med student who just happened to have the courage to call in cardiology's number one asshole, Haley Bronson.

Rick had saved not only Juan Alvedar's life, but also Haley's relationship with Boris. Maybe he'd saved Haley's life too. Had Haley not been able to save Juan Alvedar, and had Haley not been able to take care of Boris post-stroke — thanks to Rick, Haley didn't even have to wonder how he would've or could've lived with that guilt.

"I never had an excuse to apologize to Boris." Haley exhaled and shook his head. It was tough explaining patently juvenile behavior, as a professor speaking to a student. "I had to keep playing at that stupid feud with him, with no chance to back down." Haley looked down at the ground. "Not until you brought me in to care for him." Haley was whispering loudly enough to be emphatic, but quietly enough to be out of hearing of Boris's room.

"Apologize to Boris? Why?" Rick looked taken aback. "Why would you apologize? Isn't Boris ranked ahead of you in AJC?"

"Jesus." Haley shook his head and laughed. "Not the fucking AJC."

"You don't care about the—" Rick stared into Haley's eyes. Maybe he understood, a little bit.

If anybody could understand Bronson, it was probably Rick. He was as focused on medicine as Haley. Maybe he was just as lonely and unhappy as Haley.

"I care about the AJC about as much as I care about the weather. Gives me something to talk about. Something to pretend to be angry about." Haley exhaled deeply.

"Ok, you don't care about the AJC." Rick nodded. "But you wanted to apologize to Boris? I still don't understand."

"For treating him like shit. For treating him like shit worse than you could possibly know." Haley shook his head as his mind filled with flashbacks, all starting with that New Faculty meeting at the Miami Hyatt.

"You actually regret—" Rick's face sank. He might've believed that the shitty way Haley had been treating Boris was the right way to be. Teaching a student that kind of shit was even worse than the treatment itself was.

"Rick." Haley shook his head. "Boris is a very decent guy."

"Yeah, when I shadow with him—" Rick broke a small smile as he started to talk about Boris.

"You don't need to tell me. I know it. Boris is a very decent guy."

"This, coming from you—" Rick again broke a smile of disbelief. Rick looked like he was watching Haley roller-skate backwards.

"Boris is thoroughly a decent guy, Rick. Don't believe the bullshit that flew from my shitty mouth." Haley shook his head. It had been, what, three years of him staying away from Boris and playing up the feud? All bullshit. All to avoid facing how badly he'd treated Boris that one night. "And even if Boris wasn't a decent guy, the way I've been treating him is no way to treat a colleague."

"I thought your taking care of him was just you doing your professional duty," Rick said. "Hippocratic oath, stuff like that."

"Sure. Basic human duty, you know."

"Never heard you talk like that." Rick looked up and down the hospital hallway, as if to make sure he wasn't dreaming.

"Even if AJC ranked him ahead of me, Boris Yorshenko is a fellow living creature." Haley forced a smile. Rick stared at him with an ingenue's gaze.

Twenty three years old. He could probably fuck for days.

Haley restrained his baser instincts at the sight of Rick's virile beauty. At least he tried to. He kept his face a respectable distance from Rick, even if sometimes he just wanted to bring his face close to Rick's and breathe in his essence. "Hey. I've got to go say hi to Boris." Haley pointed at the door to Boris's hospital room, as if Rick didn't already know about it — as if Rick hadn't just been in the same room with the same Boris.

"Yeah." Rick smiled. He gave Haley two thumbs up. "Now I know what really drives you."

"Smart kid. A kid, but smart." Haley laughed at his own cheesy saying. He gave Rick a deep nod, or a small bow, like something from a samurai movie — no idea where that had come from — and walked down the hall to Boris's room.

The hospital must've been the same as it had always been. This was Haley's first time going there on personal business. It was his first time visiting anyone in the hospital. He didn't have friends. Except maybe Boris and Rick. Walking through the hospital hallway with skin in the game, something to lose, a patient to visit, a friend recovering from a stroke — that was how patients saw it.

"You're waiting for the welcoming party, or what?" Sylvia Yorshenko's voice bellowed out from Boris's inpatient room. "Come on in here, Doctor Bronson!"

"Sorry." Haley wasn't even sure what he was apologizing for, but meeting Boris's mother always made him feel apologetic. He tapped his knuckles on the door as he walked in, just to be really sure he was wanted there.

"If you want a red carpet, this hospital doesn't provide that." Sylvia looked back over her shoulder at Haley. She was sitting in a chair diagonally facing Boris's face. "Come in, come in anyway!"

Haley stepped into the room. He kept his eyes down. For his visits over the past days he didn't feel worthy of looking Boris and his mother in the eye.

Boris gave Haley a friendly nod — the same nod he'd usually given Haley at department meetings. This time, Haley didn't force himself to believe that Boris's nod held sarcastic ill intent. Maybe it actually never had. Haley nodded back, and added a friendly smile.

Sylvia Yorshenko reached into her brown leather Michael Kors handbag. She fished around with both hands like the handbag had millions of secret compartments and depths that defied the laws of physics.

"Ah ha!" She nodded to Haley and Boris. Out from the purse came her hand, holding a can of V8. She handed it to Haley. "Drink! It's vegetables! Rick just had one, and look how healthy he is!"

"No shit," Boris muttered.

"Thank you. I— " A can of V8 was possibly the last thing Haley had expected to receive from Mrs. Yorshenko, but it was far from the worst possibility. "I've tried V8 before." That was the most diplomatically honest answer Haley could think of.

"Do you know what my darling son Boris confessed to me?" Sylvia leaned in toward Boris, her face inches from his, and shook her head in reprimand.

Had Boris somehow confessed to his mom his homosexuality? Or his fumbling night with Haley? Did Boris even remember that night? He must have.

Boris must've thought he was on his deathbed. Of curse he blabbed all his secrets to his mom.

Had Boris outed Haley too? Would Sylvia spread the word around?

Sylvia's age group was the most dangerous to Haley's heterosexual reputation. Miami's senior citizens didn't know who

Kylie Jenner or Ed Sheeran were, but they sure as hell knew who Haley Bronson was.

They or one of their shuffleboard buddies had certainly had at least an angiogram done by Doctor Haley. Quite a few of them had even pinched his cheeks afterward.

"Haley! Are you awake? Do you know what Boris confessed to me?" Sylvia shook Haley's arm.

"Oh. Sorry." Haley shook himself awake. He'd just play stupid to her. "No. I have no idea. What did he confess to you?"

"Mom." Boris sounded slightly embarrassed. The way Boris drew out the single vowel, together with his shock of tangled blond hair, made him resemble a teenager even more than he usually did.

"Well, I told Rick, and now I'm going to tell Haley." Sylvia shook her head at her son. What a silly boy indeed.

"Yeah, if Rick heard it, I should be hearing it too." Haley laughed, cautiously. He steeled himself into one of the bedside chairs. He grabbed the cushioned armrest as if he was preparing for launch.

"Well. My little boy." Sylvia looked over at Boris. "My little boy hadn't been taking his blood pressure medicine. For years now he ignored it. That's why he had the stroke!" Sylvia shook her head in reprimand.

"Oh. I— I had no idea." Haley sent Boris a small nod of reprimand. Indeed, in Boris's intake sheet, he claimed to be taking his blood pressure meds.

"Those pills make me feel woozy." Boris sighed. "I know it's stupid not to take them."

"Now that you two made up—" Sylvia started to say.

"We made up?" Boris laughed, a little wearily.

"Ok, now that you two made up enough so you are on speaking terms." Sylvia rolled her eyes a little to show her disdain for the technicalities of the matter.

"We did." Haley looked into Boris's eyes when he said it. Boris's eyes had no grudges, no regrets. It was only that deep, curious, loving stare, the same one that had made Boris so intriguing to Haley

213

when he first saw him at a conference, then again at new faculty weekend.

Boris glowed with love for the world. If Haley could only learn to be one half, one tenth, of that.

"So now that Boris confessed his mistake--" Sylvia sighed. She stood up and looked closely into Boris's face, then ran her hand over his arm. "Haley, can you please give him a good lecture about remembering to take his medication?"

"He's a fucking cardiologist!" Haley laughed and shook his head, half-raising his arms in exasperation. Boris cracked a smile too. "What can I tell him about heart meds that he doesn't already know?"

"Language!" Sylvia wagged a finger at Haley.

"Sorry, Mrs. Yorshenko." Haley looked down with compunction. "Anyway, you may have heard: your son is a cardiologist. He knows everything already."

"Oh, he definitely, definitely knows everything already." Sylvia rolled her eyes. "Wouldn't hurt if you reminded him though. That Rick boy already lectured him about it today, and he's not even a real doctor yet." Sylvia smiled as if she'd just revealed a dirty little secret about a mutual friend.

"Alright. If Rick lectured Boris, I guess I can too." Haley grinned and shook his head. It was ridiculous, but then doctors were famous for not doing themselves what they'd told their patients to do. "Boris. You have essential, idiopathic hypertension, which oddly enough, is one of your research interests! Anyway, you are supposed to be taking verapamil and lisinopril every day to keep your blood pressure down. Will you do it, please?"

Boris smiled and looked into Haley's face. "I can't say no to eyes like that."

Boris really said that. In front of his mother. Haley wasn't hallucinating.

Did Boris still—

"Boris, did you take your blood pressure pills today?" Haley had to act cool. Professional. At least around Mrs. Yorshenko.

"Does a bear shit in the woods?" Boris glanced at the two prescription pill containers on the nightstand.

Boris's voice, his breath, the slight stubble around his jawline, the way locks of his hair fell into his eyes — it was all that old desire from the night at the Miami Hyatt washing over Haley again. Not that the desire had ever left Haley, even if he'd spent three years hiding it with a patina of petty hate, until Rick had brought them out of it.

"Oh." Haley breathed deeply as he spoke to Boris. Boris only smiled back.

"Hey!" Mrs. Yorshenko shook her head sternly. "You lovebirds can wait until I'm out of the room at least before your tongues slip over each other like wild dolphins swimming in the ocean."

"What?" Haley burst out laughing. "What— wild dolphins— what—?"

Boris shrugged. "Don't ask me."

"You know that Boris is— likes— is—" Haley stared at Mrs. Yorshenko.

"Does a bear shit in the woods?" She shrugged as she gathered her keys and phone and tossed them into her handbag. "Have fun but don't let hospital security arrest you."

"You're leaving?" Haley asked.

"I don't want to intrude." She held up her bag like an old-time robber and waved to Haley and Boris. "I have to see a dog about a man, or something like that."

"A man about a dog, Mom." Boris's eyes evinced the same fondness for his mother that he had for the world at large. "A man about a dog."

"Please. I just know that a bear shits in the woods." Mrs. Yorshenko shrugged. She stepped out and closed the door behind her.

"She knows?" Haley squinted.

"About what?" Boris's face was pure faux-innocence.

"That you're into— that you like—" It was better not to say the g-word. But there was definitely something that Boris liked.

"That I'm gay?" Boris smiled mischievously. He'd just knocked the wind out of Haley's circumlocutions. "Yeah, she's always known."

"You came out to her?"

"No."

"She walked in on you?" Haley was laughing at the mental picture of it.

"No!" Boris shook his head. He spoke quietly. "Just one day in high school, when I came home from the Homecoming Dance at nine P.M., she gave me this look and said, *Boris, you don't kiss girls, do you? You probably want to kiss a boy, yes?* And I just didn't answer and went to my room. That's the closest I've come to ever coming out. To anyone."

"Do you want to—" Haley breathed in deeply and stared into Boris's granite-gray eyes.

"Does a bear shit in the—" Boris didn't finish the sentence.

Boris pursed his lips. Haley was there for him.

Boris's mouth was warm and hungry. Three years had passed already. And for what?

Haley sucked on Boris's lip. He rushed his own tongue into Boris's mouth. The feeling, the taste were more of a thrill than even they'd been on that night back then.

He'd been dreaming about Boris for three years. Boris was a brilliant scientist, a selfless physician, a dedicated teacher — a man big enough not to engage in Haley's petty warfare. And he was beautiful. Haley mocked Boris's long blond hair falling over his face — only because he thought about it so damn much.

Boris embraced Haley. His hands roamed Haley's back. Were Boris's motions uncertain because he was still recovering from a stroke, or because their recovered closeness was a shock — or both?

Haley had dreamed of a moment like this, a reunion kiss, so many times that it was difficult to believe it was real. The wall clock was running. There were trees outside the window. This wasn't a dream.

Afternoon sunlight coated Boris's face in gold. He leaned his head back and opened his mouth wide. Haley maneuvered so his torso was on top of Boris's. He kissed Boris again, hard. He inhaled Boris's smell like a drug. He pumped his tongue in and out of Boris's warm mouth.

Boris kissed back. His eyes half-closed, his floppy hair down over his forehead, Boris murmured with every kiss and lick he gave Haley.

Lying in his hospital bed, staring up at Haley, Boris breathed fast and hard. His mop of hair made an indentation for itself in the pillow. Haley kissed Boris's lips, then his cheeks, his jawline — with just the right amount of weekend scruff, even if it wasn't a weekend. Haley's kisses on Boris's neck brought Boris to whimper softly. He reached out to Haley's hands, squeezing them in rhythm with Haley's kissing.

A murmur outside. A knock on the door.

Haley lifted himself off of Boris and pulled his mouth away. He instinctively wiped his mouth on his shirt-sleeve, like wiping off stray food, but this time it was stray saliva from making out with this beautiful man—

"Hello?" That voice was definitely Rick's.

"Yeah, come in, Rick." There was no evidence of impropriety, neither on Boris nor Haley. Haley's erection was conveniently pointing down the leg of his slacks. See no hard-on, hear no hard-on, disclose no hard-on.

"Sorry." Rick looked down apologetically. "I just had to go to class."

"That's what medical students do, right?" Boris smiled at Rick. "Go to class?"

"Yeah." Rick sounded unsure of himself. "And what you're doing right now, Doctor Bronson — taking care of people — that's what doctors do."

"Gotta find what drives you, Rick." Haley exhaled. "Taking care of people. Making people healthy."

"You're coming in here on your days off, just to help Doctor Yorshenko, night and day." Rick spoke quietly. He slowly shook his head. "I never — I guess I never expected medicine was about that."

"Did you just think it was about what, chemistry and incisions and lab coats and—" Haley shook his head.

"Something like that. I didn't know that medicine is really about, really about—"

"Yeah, Rick." Boris smiled and leaned his head back as he spoke. He could've been on a beachside lounger instead of on a hospital bed. "Tell us: what is medicine really about?"

"About—" Rick looked at Haley, then at Boris, then down at his hands. "It's about love."

Five

Salty ocean air washed over him. From that high up, breaking waves were almost silent.

Standing on his condo balcony was the closest Boris got to surfing now. He wasn't a rebellious UCSF medical student any more. He could no longer ride the waves to take out his frustrations about his closeted homosexuality and profound loneliness. Miami's waves weren't even surf-worthy, not that a heart surgeon had time for surfing.

He'd floated the idea of taking a surfing trip to San Francisco. Doctor Jones first laughed at him, then threatened him with professional discipline. A surgeon wasn't allowed to risk his hands on an activity like surfing. Surgeons were masters of the universe in everybody's minds but their own.

Forty-eight stories below, Miami looked exactly the same as it had a week before: before Boris had collapsed during a PTE operation, before Haley had saved the day, before Boris's life had flipped upside-down — or maybe right-side-up.

It had been only twenty-four hours since the kiss. Only ten hours since he'd been discharged from the hospital. Of course he was a sociable guy. Of course he invited everyone involved to his condo to celebrate. At least his colleagues were having a good time. Haley especially. Boris hadn't dared to speak to Haley one-on-one, or even to be seen standing near him.

Haley seemed engrossed by his boss's attention anyway. Big Man Jones followed Haley around Boris's four rooms and was constantly whispering something to him, like he was trying to sell him a carpet.

The ocean waves were almost surfable. Bodyboard at least. It wouldn't be epic or gnarly or any of the other terms he used back then, but maybe it was worth a try. Maybe he could even do it without asking Jones for permission.

A gentle tap on his shoulder: maybe Boris's situational awareness was still reduced after the stroke, but even without that,

Linda McCall had a talent. She moved quietly. Anesthesiologists were like that.

"How's it going, Doctor Yorshenko?" Linda was right behind him, just on the other side of the boundary between living room and patio.

"I'm still getting used to everything." Boris shook his head.

"To recovering from your stroke?" Linda stepped out onto the balcony and, like every visitor to Boris's condo, did the usual panoramic right-and-left look.

"That too. But I meant getting used to being the patient, the one being taken care of." Boris smiled. That must've been what they called a wistful smile.

Being doted over by anyone — much less by the previously hostile Haley Bronson, and the previously off-limits Rick Sarmenian — might have too strange to ever get used to. Haley Bronson wasn't supposed to care about Boris. Rick Sarmenian was supposed to ask Boris about angioplasties, not spend days and nights hovering over him.

"Haley is great that way." Linda smiled widely. The way she said it, it sounded like she had some part in Haley's greatness. Her offhand acknowledgment was as if she deserved credit for Haley's caring and love, the same way people said "thank you" when someone complimented their spouse.

Maybe she did. Boris wasn't the boss of Haley. Maybe Linda was the boss of Haley. There certainly did seem to be something between them.

"Linda!" Doctor Jones wagged his finger from across the room, as if summoning a servant. "Come over here with me and Haley!"

"I better go." Linda pointed at Jones with her eyes. "If I know what's good for me." Sure. She had a career to protect. Doctor Jones ran Cardiology like a consigliere.

Linda followed Jones's wagging finger like a homing beacon. Haley made space for her in his huddle-conference with Doctor Jones. It was the three of them now — Haley, Boss Man Jones, and Linda

McCall — but their interactions looked less like an all-sides huddle and more like Jones trying to sell Linda and Haley a dubious Persian rug.

"Doctor Yorshe— Boris!" Rick said Boris's name with all the eagerness of a puppy meeting his best friend.

"I'm glad you made it up here." Boris looked down for some reason, as if they had grappled the building wall, forty-eight stories up to his condo.

"I used the elevator." Rick nodded faux-smugly. The look on his face when he was joking could have cheered up a room of oncologists.

"Oh. Right." Boris allowed himself another look at Rick's face. The balcony's overhead LED lamps illuminated Rick's green eyes, the green eyes that were still staring at Boris. Rick looked like he was expecting a treat. "I meant made it to the building. Like, you found it."

"I've been here already." Rick nodded like a man of the world. It came off unintentionally comical, thanks to Rick's appearance. He was twenty-three but looked about nineteen.

"You get around?" Boris asked with a stupid grin. Had he really just blurted that out? Maybe he'd get some extra leeway for being in stroke recovery.

"Uhh—" Rick turned red. He glanced at Boris's eyes, then quickly looked back out at the darkness on the beach down below.

"I mean, you go off-campus a lot?" Good save. Boris was almost hyperventilating. He was being the creepy professor he never wanted to be — but he could barely control himself, and worse yet, Rick didn't seem to mind.

"Oh. Remember Matias?"

"Everybody remembers Matias." Boris nodded, then retroactively tried to make his nods look less gay.

"Yeah!" Rick got that excited-puppy look again. "Matias lives in this building too!"

"No shit!" Boris smiled and nodded. Maybe he was a little too openly enthusiastic. But Matias, whom Boris had unfairly always thought of as Rick's sidekick, living in that same building as Boris — that was interesting.

Matias's homosexuality was no secret, and not only to frustrated closet cases like Boris himself. The janitors probably knew Matias was gay. He prided himself on being open about it, rainbow t-shirts and all. But Matias's living situation, nobody knew the details of.

"Yeah. I sometimes hang out with Matias and his boyfriends." Rick half-smiled, as if he was checking that Boris already knew Matias was gay.

"Boyfriends?" Boris laughed and shook his head. "Those young dudes get around."

"I mean, they live together. Like, long-term. I mean—" Rick turned red. On the artificially lit balcony, his face shone a deep burgundy. His eyes shifted nervously around, avoiding eye contact, as he stumbled over his words. "I mean it's not like Matias sleeps around. He has two boyfriends at the same time. The three of them live together. They're really happy. I don't know why I just told you all that." Rick turned a deeper shade of burgundy.

"That's pretty open-minded of you." Boris nodded at Rick as if he valued Rick's non-homophobia only in an abstract sense.

"No!" Rick's eyes popped wide open. "I mean, I'm not involved in that. I'm just Matias's friend. I'm not one of his boyfriends. I'm not part of—"

"I know." Boris gently shook his head. Rick stared at Boris's forehead exactly the same way Haley always did: he must've been watching Boris's hair flop around. "I just mean it's open-minded for you to be friends with Matias."

"Yeah. His situation sounds kind of nice." Rick stared off over the balcony. "I mean, like, I think consenting adults should do whatever they want."

Rick was undeniably sweating. Sweat stains pooled in the armpits of his heathered cotton t-shirt. That kind of look, that kind of smell, would have been foul on an old man, but was adorable on a muscular young hunk. Mega-adorable on this specific young hunk.

"Yeah." Boris breathed deeply to smell Rick's body in stress-response overdrive. "Good that you're open-minded."

**

"I'm not some kind of homophobe, Haley. Really, I'm not." Doctor Jones was sweating harder the more pushback he faced. The sweat stains under his armpits only made him less sympathetic.

"So basically—" Linda exhaled deeply and shook her head at Jones. "My job, after four years of medical school, four years of residency, and three years of anesthesiology fellowship, is to decorate Haley's arm?"

"You're all wet for Haley!" Doctor Jones said it without any hint of compunction or irony. "All of cardiology knows it."

"I'm all— " Linda shook her head. She sighed. "So Doctor Jones, you're not only a physician and an administrator, but also a mind reader?" Linda stared at Jones silently for a full three seconds. "And you probably also write porn movie dialogue?"

"How did you know?" Jones winked salaciously. There still wasn't any inkling of irony or self-mocking in his overtures.

"And that's somehow ok?" Haley shook his head. He'd come to Boris's party to celebrate good health, not listen to paranoid homophobic bullshit. "You can be a full-on dirty old man, but if Boris and I don't have girlfriends, it's full fucking rainbow alert, evacuate the whole fucking hospital?"

"Shh!" Jones looked around nervously. True, Haley had spoken a little more loudly than he should have. But maybe that was how loudly he should have spoken in the first place.

If Jones thought the appearance of possible homosexuality was so wrong, then Jones could own that, couldn't he? Why should Haley quiet down if Jones believed himself to be in the right?

"I'm not judging anybody." Jones hunched over again and spoke to Haley and Linda as if they were his willing co-conspirators. "Just that people are talking, ok?"

"People are talking." Haley rolled his eyes and nodded.

"The way you take care of Yorshenko." Jones pointed with his thumb at Boris out on the balcony, as if Haley might not have known who Yorshenko was. "The way you look at him, talk with him. Just recently, now."

"Uh huh." Haley nodded blankly.

"It doesn't help that the two of you are lifelong bachelors who play shirtless volleyball on Saturdays, ok! That's how people talk, ok!" Jones was almost-yelling. He realized it and covered his mouth, then looked around at who might have heard.

"And this all relates to the job offer how?" Haley calmly asked. When Jones had brought him into a huddle in the corner of the room and told him he'd like to make him head of Cardiology, Haley knew there had to be strings attached. Nothing was easy with Jones.

"We can't have a head of cardiology who's a — you know —" Jones raised his hands and fumbled in the air with his fingers. "A member of the GLTBQ community, you know, what they call it, we can't have someone like that as head of Cardiology. People *talk*, is all I'm saying."

"I see." Haley nodded. He couldn't stop the smile of absurd amusement that was breaking across his face. Jones wasn't just your regular homophobe. The dude was batshit. "So when you were offering me the job, you were just trying to find a way to contain my rumored homosexuality?"

"I just thought." Jones held one finger up in the air. He looked like a football kicker checking the wind. "I thought I'd introduce you to a nice lady."

"Dude." Haley shook his head. He'd just called his boss *dude*. "I've been working with Linda for what, three years now? In what universe are you just introducing her to me?"

"But I mean you're only working with her." Jones nodded as if he'd said something brilliant. "You don't see her as a woman."

"Do go on." Linda wasn't even mad. She was only grinning. She was as interested in seeing the rest of the show as Haley was.

"Everybody knows you two have the hots for each other!" Jones raised his arms to show his exasperation, and his sweat stains.

"Didn't you say everybody knows that I'm a flaming homo?" Haley raised his eyebrows for effect.

"Yes." Jones nodded thoughtfully, like a Freudian psychoanalyst. "And no. I mean, everybody knows. But everybody talks."

"And just to clear up any confusion here." Linda's grin was still only amused, even if anyone less patient would have been — less patient. "You're essentially trying to marry me off to Haley, and the dowry is going to be the job as head of cardiology. Am I getting it correct here?"

"So you're not hot for Haley?" Jones stared quizzically at Linda.

"Dude." Linda grinned at Haley. It must've been only the second time Jones had ever been called *dude*. "I'm not looking to be auctioned off at the cow and bride market."

"A lady doctor can't forget about her biological—" Jones started to say. The thing about medical education was that it was so devoid of context and the rest of the world. Jones wasn't even that old. Maybe sixty. He'd just never emerged from the medical cave.

"Alright." Linda sighed. "Haley, great party. Please thank Boris. I'm tired of this conversation though. Gonna go home and read some anesthesiology journals." She glanced at Jones with a smirk. "Or review the latest *Good Housekeeping* for how to cook meatloaf for my husband. Either one."

"You never know." Haley shrugged, grinned and waved.

"Linda." Jones called out after her. His plaintive voice was the auditory version of a sweat-stained shirt. "I— I have to join Doctor

McCall now," Jones called out to Haley. "Nice party thank you very much."

"Alright." Haley nodded and gave Jones a thumbs-up. As in, *thumbs-up to you getting out of here.*

Boris and Rick stood chatting on the patio, their backs turned to Haley. The party's only two other attendees had just departed.

"So is this still a party?" Haley called out to Boris and Rick. He walked over to them. They each took a half-step apart to make room for him to stand between them. That was the thing about Boris: he'd never leave anyone out of anything. The way Haley had treated him for the past three years was beyond shitty.

"Whoo!" Rick blew on an imaginary kazoo in his hand. "I guess it's still a party!"

"Be careful blowing on any kazoos when you're hanging out with Matias is all I can advise you, Rick." Boris laughed.

"What's wrong with Matias?" Haley asked.

"Rick said he hangs out at Matias's place." Boris made a vague downward-pointing motion. Did Matias live under the floorboards? "And you know how Matias is."

"How?" Haley asked. He was bristling. Maybe his homophobia immune system had been primed by Jones.

"Well, it's no secret Matias is openly gay." Boris shrugged. "So I guess if Rick blows on a kazoo at Matias's place—" Boris's face deflated with the agony of having to laboriously explain a joke. " — then that kazoo Rick blows on might turn out to actually be a dick."

"That's cool with me." Haley nodded dat Boris and then Rick. He'd just had enough of being prodded with homophobia, and of course Boris was the last place where he'd expected to hear it. "If people are happy in a relationship, then great for them." Haley smiled. If it was true what the rumors said about Matias — that he had two boyfriends at once — it sounded idyllic actually.

"Yeah. Whatever makes them happy." Boris sounded as if he'd just gained permission to say that.

"Now you guys are the open-minded ones." Rick smiled at Boris, then at Haley. He was beautiful. Why did Haley have to fight Boris over him though? Why couldn't they just— just—

"Three men in a boat, three men in a luxury condo, whatever makes people happy." Boris smiled. Under the balcony lights and set against the inky blue ocean behind him, Boris's calm smile was almost beatific.

"I'm glad I'm not the only one. I mean, I felt embarrassed about how I felt—" Rick was tripping over his words, as he sometimes did.

"How did you feel?" Boris smiled big, like an invitation for Rick to not just tell the whole truth, but maybe even spice it up for Boris's amusement.

"I'm sorry. I hope you don't think less of me." There went Rick, bright red again. "I just think the way they live is kind of perfect. Like they're so happy together. I never even thought that was a thing."

"Yeah." Boris shrugged. "Humans find happiness in all sorts of different situations." Standing with his stubbled face and locks to the ocean breeze, Boris looked like a hippie sailor greeting the night over his ship's bow.

"You know, thanks to you guys—" Rick shook his head. "It sounds cheesy. Or too forward. You guys are my professors. Never mind."

"I don't give a fuck that I'm your professor." Boris shook his head, blond locks flying all over the place. "Gimme the tea."

"Like, thanks to you guys, I'm learning about — I mean medicine essentially is — I'm learning a lot about love." Rick lay his palms and thin, delicate fingers on his cheeks, ascertaining how hot he was blushing.

"That *is* the ideal of medicine." Haley folded his hands behind his back. Maybe he was self-conscious: Rick's hands were beautiful, in a fine-featured standard Haley's own hands never could reach. "Medicine is supposed to be bringing love and caring to all humans.

Maybe we lose sight of that sometimes, often, because nobody's perfect, but that's the basic idea, you know." Haley rarely had a chance to wax so philosophical about medicine in any place other than his own mind.

But then, Haley really didn't have anyone to talk to about anything, not even for small talk. Good thing that Miami weather was never really discussion-worthy.

"Shit, man." Boris nodded approvingly. "I didn't know Haley had it all figured out like that."

"I was telling Rick, one of the first times I met him: you gotta find what drives you in medicine. It's gotta be more than just making incisions or calculating flow rates. You gotta be doing what you're passionate about, because this job is hard work." Sure, when Rick was sitting in front of Haley in his office that day, Haley was trying to contain his hard-on. But the points he'd made about medicine were valid, even if his hard-on was equally valid.

"Would it be cheesy?" Rick's green eyes shone in Haley's direction, then Boris's. He was something like a young prophet. The way he spoke was almost religious. "Would it be cheesy if I said that the most important thing I learned so far in medical school is about love?"

"Not cheesy at all." Haley spoke firmly, directly at Rick. What his critics called his Spock voice. He needed to emphasize, though, how important this point was. "If you've learned that lesson, then you've learned the most important thing here."

Rick sighed. "When I watched you taking care of Boris." Rick looked down on the floor, obviously embarrassed. "It was like watching love. The purest love."

"Maybe your eyes weren't fooling you." Had Haley really just said that? Rick's expression was between shock and wonder.

"You— " Rick smiled, a little bashfully. "You love Boris?"

"Whatever makes people happy, right?" Haley nodded at Rick again. Rick looked like he still couldn't believe what he was hearing. "If that means I love Boris, then so be it."

"Wow— I—" Rick shook his head.

"Maybe Haley revealed a little too much." Boris wiped the blond locks off his forehead. Now Boris was the cautious one. "But you're a friend to us now, not just a student, not even just a colleague. So yeah, Haley and I — long story — but yeah."

Boris smiled a little bit uncomfortably. That was the continued irritation of three years of Haley's ill-treatment toward him, after that one an amazing night when Haley had first treated Boris like a day-old pizza.

"Rick, you see—" Haley laughed. He did his best to shift his voice to sarcastic instead of just serious. But then, people sometimes thought he was sarcastic when he was just trying to be serious. "When a man and a man love each other, they sometimes show that love."

"I know, I know!" Rick waved his hand in the air like the eager schoolboy he was. "When two men love each other, they get jiggy with it. Is that the right term?"

"You're quite precocious for your mere twenty-three years." Was this the right time to smile back at Rick? Haley smiled back at Rick.

"Yeah, man. Haley and I love each other." Boris nodded. "That's facts."

"But for the past three years, this stupid rivalry thing kept us apart, in addition to my assholish behavior, in addition to a specific incident of my assholish behavior from three years ago that I would really very much prefer to forget." Maybe Haley was sounding robotic again, but everything he said was true.

"That and the fear for our careers has kept us from getting jiggy with it." Boris made something like a jazz-hands gesture to indicate *jiggy with it*.

"Until you brought us together." Haley sighed. "It's so fucking ridiculous that a student of ours, an M1, knew more about what's good for us than we did. Or at least than I did."

"You guys are only supposed to be experts in medicine, not anything else." Rick's eyes darted between Haley and Boris. He did his best to be complimentary toward his professors, the same professors he'd exposed as fools, at least in life and love, if not in medicine.

"But remember the lesson we just covered?" Haley stared into Rick's face, obviously awaiting an answer. "That medicine *is* love?"

Boris stepped closer toward Haley and Rick. He was almost touching them. Haley's cock felt like it was about to jump out of his pants.

Never, ever. Not a gazillion quintillion years.

He'd never expected he'd be standing on a balcony with his two favorite professors — those supposed arch-enemies — and talking about love.

He'd never even expected to become passionate about medicine. Before those talks with Doctor Yorshenko and Doctor Bronson, medicine was only what his parents had dragged him into.

Rick's teenage kicking and screaming had turned into fatalistic acceptance after college: he was going to be a doctor because that was just how the world worked and that was his designated place in it.

He became passionate about medicine when he realized that it's a form of love. Medicine was Doctor Bronson's and Doctor Yorshenko's way of loving the world.

Rick took a big gulp of air. In the movies, they'd take a big gulp of whiskey to steel themselves for making an announcement. Rick didn't drink alcohol, so it would only be air. "I never thought I'd be able to tell you this, Doctor Bronson, Doctor Yorsh— Boris."

"You cheated on the MCAT?" Boris snapped his fingers in the air.

"You should call me Haley, Rick. We're friends now. Alright?"

"Yeah. Boris. Haley." Rick smiled and looked at the two of them. Then he did more than looked: he put his two arms around these two gorgeous, perfect professors, physicians, teachers, and men.

"And what did you not expect to be able to tell us?" Boris leaned in to Rick's embrace. "If it's anything other than cheating on the MCAT, I want to hear it. Haley does too."

"The way you guys take care of your patients. The way you take care of each other. Even the way you take care of your student, me." Rick could say it, even if he couldn't make eye contact while saying it. He stared down at his feet so hard that he was almost looking behind.

"That's a list of noun phrases, not a complete statement." Haley smiled self-consciously. His small smile sat like a crown atop his manly, chiseled jaw. Rick really had no idea he could find men so attractive. "You know how I'm Spock and stuff."

"Yeah, we want the deets." Boris clicked his tongue and snapped his fingers again. He was the cleverest impromptu comedian Rick had ever encountered. He was so much funnier than all the supposedly funny friends Rick had back in undergrad. "And we want those deets with verbs and shit."

"Alright." Rick stared out into the now-black night sky, and the ocean rolling and swelling below it. "I'm attracted to you guys. To both of you. Even though you're my professors. I'm — I'm sorry."

"I don't mind." Boris laughed and shook his head.

"Dude, I don't even complain when women are into me." Haley laughed, then swung his arm around, to embrace Rick. "I'll take all the compliments I can get."

"Is Linda McCall your girlfriend?" Rick asked. Boris coughed and gagged like he had a hairball. Except he was laughing and looking at Haley's face for presumably an extreme reaction.

Rick backtracked a little: "Maybe it's a sensitive question. I'm sorry." When Boris was done shaking his head and laughing, he also put his hand around Rick's back. Maybe Boris's and Haley's hands were even touching as they both lay on Rick's back.

"She's not my girlfriend." Haley laughed and shook his head. "She's a great physician and a great friend. But really, honestly, I've never found a woman romantically attractive. I think at some level even Linda knows that."

"You guys are —" Rick was scared to say the g-word, but but they'd been talking about everything so openly; maybe even that word wasn't off-limits. "You and Boris — I mean the way you love each other — is it, like, a gay thing?"

Boris smiled. "Bear. Woods. Shits in. Yes no?"

"Uh. Yes?" They really were gay? "A bear shits in the woods. Yeah."

"Well there's your answer." Boris shrugged.

Rick forced himself to hug Boris and Haley tighter. He'd never been so scared to do something he so badly wanted. He closed his eyes a little, as if it would physically hurt. Then he hugged them tighter — both of them. "It's getting kind of chilly out on the balcony."

For the first time ever, Rick didn't feel a desperate longing. Those two warm bodies in his double-armed embrace were everything he needed. Boris and Haley were both breathing, glancing at him, looking out at the blackness of the night ocean — together. His dick was standing up hard enough to tent his gray sweatpants. But these guys were doctors. They must've seen dicks before.

"So are you guys into—" Rick's breathing sped up.

"Not without you, Rick. Only you brought us together. You have to be part of this." Boris smiled. "Assuming you swing that way, and from the support pylon standing proud in your crotch, I assume you do."

"Boris is pretty smart." Haley clicked his tongue. "Even if he didn't go to Harvard Med."

"Yeah." Boris nodded. "Haley is pretty modest, at least for a guy who did go to Harvard Med."

"Maybe it's just because of the chilly breeze—" Rick tapped his foot nervously on the balcony.

"Are your nipples erect?" Boris laughed and pretended to stare at Rick's chest. A micro-mini daydream flashed through Rick's mind: Boris ripping his shirt off, Boris having a look for himself whether his nipples were erect, Boris having his way with Rick's ass.

This daydream, though, Rick had the power to make real. Somehow he was emboldened.

"Maybe." Rick tried to give Boris his most flirtatiously mischievous, impish look. He'd never done anything like that before. Maybe he'd seen it in movies. "Maybe you should perform the examination yourself though."

Haley stage-whispered: "That's pretty fucking hot."

Boris's steady surgeon hands moved over to the buttons on Rick's button-down shirt. He could definitely hold his hands steady when unclogging an artery or repairing a valve. But now, when he palmed Rick's chest, Boris's hands were shaking.

"Can you handle undoing those buttons?" Rick asked Boris, a little shamelessly. He had no sexual experience of any kind. He was the little twenty-three-year-old virgin. He had little place to mock Boris's awkward way of unbuttoning Rick's shirt buttons.

"Only slightly more demanding than a PTE." Boris smiled. He'd undone the first three buttons already. His face was moving in— closer— until his warm breath was on Rick's chest.

"By *more demanding*, you mean *more exciting*?" Haley asked.

The tips of Boris's lips hovered over Rick's chest. They touched. Rick's knees shook. He was hot all over, then cold all over.

Boris opened his lips. He kissed with wet, warm lips, all over Rick's chest. Those must have been the same places, the same pectoral muscles and sternum, Boris had cut into so many times on so many people — was that why Boris was shaking as he kissed Rick's chest?

Boris looked up at Haley. "How about a little less conversation and a little more action, Doctor Bronson?" Haley stared at Rick's chest like he'd just been given permission to rest his mouth where he'd all along wanted to rest it.

"Oh my God," Haley whispered to himself. "I can't believe I'm—"

Then Haley's wet lips were on Rick's chest too. He went faster than Boris, kissing and slurping. Haley undid two more buttons of Rick's shirt. Haley's — Doctor Bronson's, his professor's — lips wrapped around Rick's nipple. He slurped it into his mouth.

Rick made a sound that must've been a yowl. He'd never felt anything like it. His thighs trembled.

"Doctor Bronson?" Boris traced tongue-tip figure-eights down the middle of Ricks's chest. While Boris ravished Rick's chest with his tongue, Rick grabbed at Boris's hair: soft, wavy. He ran his fingers through Boris's scalp.

As Rick rubbed his fingers on Boris's scalp, Boris kissed his chest. Rick grabbed frantically at Boris's locks, as if he wanted them for himself.

He'd never felt a man's hair. How could plain, simple hair feel this amazingly good and make him so fucking horny? Why hadn't he thought to do this earlier? It probably wouldn't even have hurt his GPA if he'd had an actual boyfriend in undergrad, instead of jerking it to man porn whenever he had a free minute. But those days and opportunities were lost; he only had today, and the future, to make amends.

"This feels amazing," Rick whispered. It was just in case Haley and Boris didn't already know how good it felt for Rick. His purpose was entirely selfish: he didn't want them to stop.

"I repeat, in case you're too caught up in the act: Paging Doctor Haley Bronson." Boris crowded his words in between licks of Rick's chest hair.

"Yes, Doctor Yorshenko?" Haley gave Rick's nipple a momentary respite from his lips and tongue.

"I was just wondering if I can assist on this procedure."

"What procedure did you have in mind?" Haley asked, while still half-sucking Rick's nipple. Haley's speaking voice vibrated the nipple. Rick moaned in sexual ecstasy. Rick's dick must've been dripping precum into his briefs.

"I was just wondering if I can assist on your nipple-sucking, to make the procedure bilateral." Boris put on a totally believable surgical voice. Rick had to remind himself that Boris wasn't actually talking about a medical procedure. Or maybe he was — if medicine was love, and the three of them were healing their hearts.

"You wanna suck Rick's other nip is what you're saying?" Haley laughed. His laughter again vibrated and stimulated Rick's entire sexual being.

Boris answered Haley's question by pressing his moist lips to Rick's left nipple. He sucked it into his mouth, while running the entirety of his flat tongue over it. He slurped and sucked at it while

Haley worked on the right nipple. Rick felt like he was going to launch into space.

With his surgically precise hands, Haley undid the other four buttons on Rick's shirt. Haley's lips and Boris's were still ravishing Rick's nipples.

Haley wrapped his arm around Rick, his hand squeezing and groping at Rick's back. Boris followed suit, running his fingers lightly from Rick's shoulder blades down to the waistband of his sweatpants.

Maybe those extra deltoid exercises in Rick's workouts were all worth it. He had nothing to be embarrassed about as far as the state of his back. He'd just never expected that his professors would be lovingly groping it.

Rick kept his left hand in Boris's blond locks. He slid his right hand into Haley's hair. Trimmed short, Haley's hair felt like touching a putting green, or Astroturf. Mini golf was the only time Rick had ever touched Astroturf.

"Doctor Yorshenko." It was difficult to distinguish Haley's mock-serious voice from his real-serious voice. Doctor Bronson always sounded deadass serious, even when he was trying to joke. "I suggest we continue this exploratory procedure."

"I don't think anyone will argue with that." Boris's mouth sounded wet. He was still slurping at Rick's chest. As he sucked Rick's nipple, he pulled Rick's shirt off and tossed it inside the condo.

"Rick." Haley's blue eyes looked up into Rick's eyes. His huge manly jaw looked almost as red as his lips. He'd been orally busy. "You're fucking tented." Haley stared at Rick's dick tenting his sweatpants.

"Is it alright if we help you out with that swollen penis?" Boris blew warm air on Rick's wet nipple. After his licking and sucking, the sensation of warm air on a wet nipple was — whatever it felt like to have an orgasm without actually cumming.

"My God." Rick breathed faster.

"Doctor Bronson." Boris spoke like a hospital public address announcement. "May I palpitate the patient's pelvic region?"

"Oh shit." Rick laughed. He was no surgeon but he knew what that meant. "It's getting chilly out here. Can we go back inside please?" He must've sounded like a teenager to them.

"Your wish. My command." Haley might've been hamming up the Spock voice. Or maybe that was just how he talked.

Haley and Boris pulled their mouths away from Rick's nipples. They both embraced Rick, hugged him closely, held his hands and arms in their palms — maybe they were everyday gestures, but they meant a lot. Rick had never received that kind of physical affection: not from anyone, not even his parents.

In Haley and BOris's embraces, enjoying their occasional pecks on his cheek and neck, Rick followed them indoors.

"That's a nice looking sofa." Haley pointed to the expanse of white leather standing in Boris's living room. Rick hadn't seen any sofas like that outside of furniture stores.

"Let's go to the bedroom." Boris pointed the way, still embracing Rick, walking with his own torso touching Rick's. If Rick was going to be held and loved like this, he'd go anywhere.

Boris pushed open the bedroom door. Inside, the bedroom shone white-hot: white LED lights, stark white painted walls, and a bed outfitted completely in white.

"You miss operating rooms that much when you go home?" Haley laughed.

"Shit, man." Boris shook his head. He used the motion of his head as an excuse to nuzzle his face in the crook of Rick's neck and bathe Rick's shoulder in kisses. "At least, unlike you, Haley Bronson, I have a home away from the hospital."

"My room at the Flamingo is a home too." Haley shrugged.

"You gotta invite us over sometime." Boris laughed. "You're probably the only resident who doesn't pay his rent from a panhandling jug?"

"Nah. I do a free clinic for the building residents once a week." Haley's eyes lit up. "On the downlow. They don't have an actual clinic or anything there. In exchange, they don't charge me rent."

"Medicine is love, right?" Rick asked.

"I—" Rick had no idea what to say. The whole experience was overwhelming. It was as if he'd lived his whole life with emotional volume maxed out at five, and now it was on eleven. These feelings were all new. This intensity was ravishing him, together with Boris and Haley's kisses.

Boris whispered in Rick's ear: "Lie down."

Rick sat on the bed, then lay down. The bed felt like an ocean of feather down. HIs head sank into the pillow.

"Guys, I've never — I mean I've never done anything." If they were expecting Rick to be a skilled fuckboy, he was nothing of the sort. "I'm actually a — I'm actually a virgin."

"We all learn together," Boris whispered into Rick's ear. Boris pressed his scraggly chin into Rick's cheek, his blond locks falling everywhere. His tongue made soft, slow circles in Rick's ear.

"Can I take off your pants?" Haley whispered in Rick's other ear.

"Yeah." Rick was saying it to one of the two most beautiful men he'd ever seen. He was saying it to his professor. He was finally, for the first time in his life, experiencing love.

Haley tugged on Rick's waistband. It didn't take much for them to slip off, together with his white briefs. His dick popped out, like a bird out of a cage.

Rick's dick smelled like precum; the smell hit his nose. He did his best to not be embarrassed by the smell, nor by his dick being uncut. They were doctors. They must've seen uncut dicks before. It wasn't a disgusting tube sock, no matter what Rick's high school PE classmates had said about his uncircumcised dick.

"That sweet precum smell. Oh man." Boris shook his head, then unbuttoned his own shirt.

Shirtless, he kneeled at the side of the bed and kissed Rick's inner thigh. His tongue roamed up and down on Rick's thigh, with small, furtive jumps over to his pubes.

"You wouldn't mind if we have a taste, Rick?" Haley's manly jaw was already near the base of Rick's cock. He ran his tongue around the base of the cock. It felt like pure sex, especially when his face rubbed against the shaft and the dickhead.

"Ever heard of FOMO, guys?" Boris asked quietly, between kisses and slurps. He was on all fours on the bed, sucking on Rick's pecs. His hair tickled as he moved his head around Rick's chest. "Fear of missing out. Because I definitely do not want to miss out on this."

Boris moved his face in closer to Rick's crotch — where Haley was already running his tongue up and down Rick's shaft.

Boris stuck his tongue out toward the dickhead, just short of touching it. He looked like he was awaiting a sacrament.

Haley moaned, closed his eyes, and moved his lips in toward Boris's lips, and toward the tip of Rick's cock.

Boris and Haley's lips and tongues met at the very tip of Rick's cock. Their lower lips rested on his dickhead while their upper lips came together. With their tongues, they licked each other while licking Rick's dickhead.

Not cumming from that sensation was the most challenging thing Rick had ever attempted. The only thing that had touched his dick previous to that had been his own hand, sometimes through underwear or a sock. Now it was Haley and Boris's lips and tongues wrestling on his dickhead.

"I can't hold off any longer." Haley wrapped his fingers around Rick's dick and swung it out of the way. He pushed up to Boris's face and kissed him passionately. It was beyond amazing or unbelievable. Boris kissed back and they stared at each other.

"Sorry for excluding you for a second there," Haley said. He pursed his lips, held Rick's cock pointing up, and lowered his tight, wet, pursed lips onto Rick's dickhead, then his whole shaft.

"Fuck fuck fuck." If Rick previously felt like he was launching into space, now he was going into another dimension. So this was why guys loved blowjobs so much. It was so totally different from the feeling of groping his own dick. And it was his gorgeous professor giving him that pleasure, but Rick tried to put that out of mind. Otherwise, he might've cum way too early.

Boris kissed Haley's face, down to his jaw. He must've appreciated that beautiful jaw too. He put his lips to Rick's balls and sucked. Rick moaned-screamed. The suction on balls hurt, but it hurt in the most amazing way possible.

Boris popped Rick's balls out of his mouth one by one. "Are we serving you well here?" Boris asked Rick.

"My God." Rick's head was already in another dimension. All the blood that should've been in his brain was either in his dick or somewhere in that other dimension. He could barely speak.

"Raise your legs up." Boris gave Rick's ass a light slap. That must've been how he slapped a surfboard before riding it.

Rick raised his legs. His pinned them back, his left thigh resting on Haley's shoulder.

"Are you going to a M&M conference or something?" Boris looked up at Haley. Haley was still on all fours, bobbing his head up and down on Rick's cockshaft. "Take off your fancy party shirt and put on your birthday suit."

Haley used his hand to slip Rick's dick out of his mouth. "Birthday suit?" He looked at Boris like he wasn't getting it.

"The clothes, or lack thereof, that you were born in." Boris shook his head. "Take off that shirt, dude."

"Mmm." Haley bobbed his head up and down on Rick's shaft, then used one hand to support himself on all fours, the other hand to unbutton his shirt. He awkwardly pulled off the shirt.

As much as Rick enjoyed seeing Haley's physical beauty, he had to close his eyes or look away. Every time he looked at Haley's musclebound torso and his own dick disappearing in Haley's mouth, it was sexually too much like looking at the sun. He felt his cumshot stirring if he glanced for more than just a second. The sight of Haley shirtless, sucking him off, was too fucking hot, especially when Rick was already enjoying all the sensation of his dick in this beautiful man's warm mouth.

"Hold on a second," Boris called out to Rick. "I need to grab some supplies."

"Don't fuck my ass!" Rick almost screamed it. He laughed a little at how urgent it sounded. But it was an urgent request. Rick was all sorts of virgin, and especially an anal virgin.

"I'm not gonna fuck your ass," Boris said, grinning and low-key. "Just gonna eat it out, if that's alright with you."

"Oh shit." Rick breathed faster.

"Yeah, exactly." Boris stood up from the bed, then smiled. "I'm getting some wet wipes just to make your ass extra-clean before I go down on you."

"Oh — I didn't — I didn't even know —" Rick had no focus to comment on what he knew or didn't know, other than that Haley was slurping and sucking at Rick's dick, and Rick wasn't sure how much longer he could hold out without blowing a huge load.

Boris appeared with blue latex gloves, a stack of baby wipes in one hand, and a trash can in the other hand. "I just want to make it extra clean before I feast."

"I guess you have experience—" Rick started to say. Sure. Boris was in his thirties. He must've had experience.

"No." Boris laughed and shook his head. "I only learned from the porn I'm always watching on that big monitor in my office."

Boris spread Rick's ass cheeks and wiped and cleaned with a few baby wipes. Even if Rick's ass already had been clean, being coddled and pampered like that — it was love, even if it wasn't even the sex act itself.

"That ass is, like, so fresh and so clean." Boris announced it to both Rick and Haley. "In fact, so fresh and so clean that I'll eat it out." Boris gave a long, gentle lick to Rick's rim on one side, then the other side. "Which of course was my plan from the very beginning."

Lips puckered and tongue erect, Boris kissed deep inside Rick's hole. Nothing had been there but toilet paper, until today. He followed up with tongue, licking, tongue-caressing, and slurping all over Rick's butthole.

"I really — this feels so good — I don't know how much —" Rick put his hands to his face. His cheeks were scalding hot like irons. All of his sexuality was about to leap out. His dick, despite his attempts to calm it, was about to shoot a fat load of cum anywhere it was pointing. "Shit, you guys, this feels too fucking good."

Boris pulled Rick's ass cheeks farther apart. Smiling up at Rick, he changed his slow licks to vigorous tongue-fucking. He plunged his rolled-up tongue into and out of Rick's hole.

"Fuck, fuck fuck." An orgasm was taking over Rick's body. It was like he was possessed. The more he tried to calm himself down, the more Boris's and Haley's love for him brought him up to sexual ecstasy, and that much closer to orgasm.

"Mmmhmm." Haley moaned and groaned on Rick's cock. The vibrations coursed through Rick's dick all the way up to his brain. If something was going to send Rick over the edge, this was it.

Haley sucked hard on Rick's dick. He flicked his tongue like a hummingbird along Rick's shaft and dickhead.

Haley groaned and sucked harder. Haley was holding Rick's dickhead tighter. That must've been his throat. He was trying to take it deeper still. Meanwhile, Boris plunged his tongue deep into Rick's ass and slurped at it, running his tongue up and down the rim.

"Sorry!" Rick moaned as his whole lower body bucked upward. Sexual ecstasy was pumping through his crotch. He was cumming. The cum stored up deep in his crotch was now shooting out his dick.

He bucked upward again. Haley moaned and sucked harder. He swallowed the first gob Rick sent into his mouth.

Boris tongue-drilled Rick's butthole while pulling his cheeks apart for deeper penetration. He must've been intentionally blowing hot air on Rick's rim. It all felt amazing.

Every time Rick shot another gob of cum into Haley's mouth, Haley smiled up at him. He swallowed each rope of cum slowly and sensuously — savoring his lover's taste, not disgusted by it. Did Rick really deserve all this?

Rick spread his own ass cheeks to take Boris's tongue deeper inside his ass. He gyrated his rim against Boris's tongue and face. At the same time, he was gyrating his dick inside Haley's mouth.

The idea of ass play actually feeling good was pretty new. He'd just kind of assumed gay men agreed to get assfucked because it made their partners happy. He'd had no idea, none, how on-top-of-the-world it felt for a man's tongue to tickle the entrance to his ass.

Haley raised his head, letting the base of Rick's cock emerge from his mouth. He was still sucking hard on it, even if Rick was no longer shooting ropes of cum. Haley very slowly let Rick's dick fall out of his mouth, licking and slurping every drop of cum from it.

"What a fucking feast." Boris was laughing, his mouth just outside Rick's butthole.

Haley let Rick's cock completely slip out of his mouth. Still on all fours, he crawled up so his face was next to Rick's.

Haley brought his face down, his blue eyes like white hot flames, staring down into Rick's eyes. His face was flushed. HIs lips were moist. He brought his mouth closer and closer to Rick's.

Haley moaned and kissed Rick — urgently, furiously, almost angrily. He was pressing down into Rick with his mouth, taking small side breaths himself, and exploring all of Rick's mouth with his tongue. Haley's mouth tasted salty and sweet: an aroma Rick had previously only smelled, never tasted.

Looking at Haley right there, the here-ness and this-ness of the whole thing, was always a surprise. That was his professor.

"Can I join here, guys?" Boris said it like he was about to get on a three-man sled. In a manner of speaking, he was. He brought his mouth toward Haley and Rick's lips, half closed his eyes, opened his mouth, and put out his tongue. Rick's and Haley's mouths found Boris's mouth.

In regards to Boris's question, Haley only nodded. His eyes were half-closed.

Rick had gone from never having kissed anybody to making out with two men at once. Haley and Boris's mouths fought like hungry guppies at Rick's mouth, for his kisses and licks, as if his hot breath was vital to their lives. Maybe it was.

"I have a question." Rick lay his hand on his half-hard dick, just for emphasis.

"Yes, Doctor Sarmenian." Haley was dead-serious again. "Uh, I mean Rick."

"Don't you guys wanna get off too?" Rick had cum hard, so much harder than anything he'd achieved with his own hand. But he wanted Haley and Boris to cum too. And Rick wouldn't mind cumming again.

Boris piped up: "Recall the adage of the bear in the woods, young master."

"Yeah." Haley nodded, all professor-like. "Two heart surgeons in a bed. Do they want to cum?"

"Uh, Professor Bronson—" Rick smiled. "Would the answer be *hell yeah*?"

"Correct!" Boris broke in. "Definitely correct!"

"So you guys wanna—" Rick lifted his head, raised his legs, and glanced down at his rim. It looked like there'd been a man just feasting on it. It didn't look ready to get fucked by two big dicks, even though it kind of felt ready.

"Haley." Boris started laughing and shaking his head. "You wanna call down to room service for a condom?"

"Hello!" Haley held an imaginary handset to his ear and spoke in a squeaky high voice. "This is Stacy McLabialips! Can I have a condom sent up to Haley and Boris's room, I mean Haley and Stacy's room?"

"Fucking Minnie Mouse voice." Boris shook his head. They seemed to have some kind of an inside joke about it.

"At least I got the condom slipped in under the door, did I not?" Haley was laughing. There had to be a lot to the story — a lot that Rick didn't know.

"That's not all that slipped in." Boris was nodding. There was obviously a lot that Rick didn't know.

"That's what *he* said." Haley was laughing like a frat boy catching a comedic wind.

"Do you guys have — something in the past between the two of you?" Rick asked. It was a little bit painful to say.

"Do we ever!" Haley's laughter grew ribald, almost obnoxious. This wasn't fun anymore.

"That poor condom they slipped under the door got a lot of use." Boris shook his head with faux-sad eyes.

"Yeah." Haley was grinning, arrogantly, the way jocks grinned when they were making fun of you but didn't want you to know exactly how and why. "That condom belongs in a museum or something."

"I think there's a fossil remnant of it somewhere in my ass." Boris grinned just like the jocks' accomplices would have grinned.

"More like all up in your small intestine." Haley smirked and grabbed at his crotch.

"Haley, if your dick was any bigger, it would've come out the other end." Boris coughed and pretended like he was pulling something up out of his throat.

"Yeah." Rick glanced at the two of them as he spoke. They seemed to be having a good time. "I guess it would have." Rick looked down, at his own naked body, a lot skinnier than Boris's and Haley's. Had he just been used by those two? Was he the boytoy they'd found themselves for the evening?

"Oh man. Haley and I have a bit of history together." Boris shook his head, laughing. His locks didn't look cool or beautiful or alluring. Those floppy blond locks were only off putting, silly, bordering on stupid.

"I guess you guys do." Rick rose from the bed and put on his pants, then his shirt. "It's kind of chilly here."

"Aren't we going to—" Haley started to say.

"Yeah, aren't we going to fuck Rick's ass?" Boris asked.

"Nah." Rick kept his gaze fixed down while talking. "I've gotta go back to my room, get back to studying."

"Hey! Rick man!" Boris beamed a big smile at Rick. It was all so artificial. Of course he and Haley wanted to keep their young fucktoy around for the evening. How had Rick ever managed to tell himself that he was anything more than a third wheel?

"Great party." Rick said it so flatly. He hadn't even intended it to be derisive. That was just how he spoke when he was being serious. "See you around."

Rick put his socks and shoes back on. He took out his phone and ordered a Lyft back to his room at graduate housing.

The "love" he'd found was a chimera. There was a reason students weren't supposed to have relationships with their professors, and that was exactly it: professors would use their students as disposable fuck toys. Of course. That was a privilege of power, especially in the world of medicine, especially with two medical superstars like Bronson and Yorshenko.

He'd be back to being only their student, nothing more.

Just another face in the crowd. Just regular, lonely, weird, geeky old Rick Sarmenian. That was all he wanted to be anyway.

Seven

"Just a couple of minutes left. Let's wind up." The class's seventy students sat intently in their seats. Their hands were on their laptops, iPads, or notebooks, and their eyes focused on Boris. He was proud of not having missed even one day of teaching due to his stroke. He wasn't fully recovered enough to be doing procedures, but at least he could teach.

Teaching was uniquely rewarding. Boris could only imagine the patients who might one day be helped by what Boris taught his students — or the patients, or the young careers, that might be hurt if Boris slipped up in teaching something.

Rick was in the audience too. Or he was, but wasn't. When he'd first started Boris's class, Rick was by far the most talented and quickest-thinking, even if not the most interested or passionate in medicine. In the past few weeks, though, it seemed that Rick had become passionate about the study of medicine. He breathed, ate, drank, probably shat medicine, at least during those previous few weeks of close acquaintance with Boris and Haley.

Boris walked to the row of whiteboards and tapped his fingers proudly on each one. "Today we've covered some surgical treatments for atrial fibrillation, most importantly, Maze surgery. On Thursday we'll cover what's known as mini Maze surgery. Anyone care to guess what that is? Why it's called *mini*?"

Rick's hand had always been the first to fly up. In a class of seventy, he was the only student who had carefully reviewed the reading every single time.

"*Mini*." Boris shouted out to the roomful of his charges. How could they possibly not know? "Come on, when we're talking about *mini* what are we usually talking about?"

Matias's hand shot up. Boris pointed at him with a nod.

"I was expecting Rick Sarmenian to get this one." Matias glanced and smiled at Rick. Rick stared ahead, as if he couldn't care less about Matias. "If Rick's not gonna get it, then I'll say it: *mini* means minimally invasive. Endoscopic ablation. Just like Maze, but without the big skin incisions."

"Perfect answer, Matias. Your Nobel prize is on the way from Stockholm. Come back on Thursday and we'll see if it's arrived yet." Boris clicked off the projector and capped his whiteboard pen. That was the classroom equivalent of taking off his surgical mask after finishing a procedure: show's over, at least for that session.

The students stood up and started gathering their things. Rick sat a few rows farther back than he'd normally sat.

Boris stood in front of the rows of seats, a spot Rick would have to pass to leave the room. Maybe it was just a little bit shitty to corner Rick like that, but Boris was a professor. Rick's professor. He could ask to have a chat with his student, couldn't he?

Rick stared directly ahead, directly past Boris, as he walked down the auditorium steps. Boris stood in wait like a hungry tick. What was a fully grown thirty-four-year-old man doing, acting so thirsty toward his poor M1 student?

He wasn't going to be hungry, though. He was just going to casually ask, offer help—

"Hey, Rick!" Boris called out to his student walking past him. He tried hard not to sound hungry, even if the whole thing was hungry as fuck.

"Yes?" Rick stopped on the step directly in front of Boris. "Doctor Yorshenko?" Rick's gray eyes stared at Boris. His glasses were perfectly propped up on his nose, the way they always were in class.

"Just wondering." Boris had to invent some kind of professionally reasonable excuse. "I'm just wondering whether everything is ok with you. You seemed less enthusiastic in today's class."

"I'm alright, Doctor Yorshenko."

"Aren't you supposed to call me—" Rick was looking at Boris with eyes of incomprehension and maybe a little bit of pity, as if Boris had just arrived from Planet Boris. It would've been useless to try to press the issue, any issue, with Rick. "Yeah, it's good that you're alright. Let me know if you need anything."

"Yeah." Rick walked out of the classroom as fast as it's possible to walk without breaking into a jog or looking like Mister Bean. His ass was beautiful, but looking at it was very much inappropriate.

Boris tried to inhale Rick's scent. That was stupid. There had been seventy students in that room just during that one class session. And no matter how much he tried to sniff like a dumb dog, he wouldn't be able to bring back the way he'd felt being close to Rick and Haley — before Rick had come to his senses.

One one thousand. Two one thousand. Three one thousand.

Boris counted out a slow ten seconds.

He wouldn't run out after Rick like a horny bloodhound in pursuit. He'd wait a full ten seconds, at least, before emerging from the auditorium.

Satisfied with his ten-second waiting period of deniability, Boris walked up to the auditorium's exit door. He swung it open.

"You jack off in classrooms after you lecture, is that it?" Haley shook his head at Boris. It was Haley's day off. He stood there in his Harvard Med t-shirt, worn like a talisman, as if it was totally normal for him to stalk the outside of Boris's lecture.

Haley was blowing onto his styrofoam cup of coffee as if he was trying to make an air-spout, not cool the coffee. Maybe he was.

"No. No. I just—" It was actually pointless to attempt to fish for an excuse. Haley was in the same shitty situation with Rick as Boris was. "I mean, you know. Rick was in this class. I didn't want it to seem like I'm running after him."

"It's that bad, huh?" Haley sighed. "Then it's not just me Rick is ignoring."

"He's fed up with the bullshit coming from the both of us." Boris looked down at the ground. "Yeah, I guess it is that bad."

"It's like I didn't learn anything I was supposed to learn, from treating you like shit that night three years ago."

"That?" Boris shook his head and waved at the air. "Long time ago."

"Well, not so long ago, as far as Rick is concerned. I think we freaked him out pretty good. Same way I freaked you out pretty good that night."

"Kid probably feels like a third wheel."

"Sure." Haley shook his head. "So do you think we should — try — somehow?"

Haley took his gleaming silver pen from his shirt pocket and stirred his hot coffee with it. It wasn't even worth making an issue of it. Haley would act as if it was the most natural thing in the world.

"Yeah, we should try. Somehow. I gotta admit, I've fallen in love with him." Boris sighed. "You probably have too."

"Probably." Haley nodded. "Just a little. Or more than just a little."

"Maybe we can beg him for just one meeting where we can state our case, admit fault, beg for forgiveness?" Boris sighed.

"Yeah. I'm guessing you want me to be the one to reach out to Rick and extend the invitation?" Haley stared past Boris, into the darkened auditorium, as if Boris might've been hiding Rick in there.

"Since I already tried to talk to him after class today, yeah, I think it's your turn."

"Oh. You approached him today?" Haley's eyes grew wide, like he was so eager to hear any news at all about his crush — which actually kind of was the case.

"Just after class. Just asked him if anything's wrong." Boris shrugged. "He just acted like he didn't know what I was talking about, like I was just some random professor of his."

"Which, I guess you now are. Boris Yorshenko. Just a random professor of his."

"So you're gonna help me out and talk to him, right?"

"You forgot to say *pretty please*." Haley smiled. He was adorable even when he was upset.

"Haley. Help me talk to Rick. *Pretty please.* Alright?" What the world had come to: not only was Boris begging, but he was begging Haley Bronson. Maybe rivers would start running backwards.

"Alright. Anything for you, Boris." Haley smiled his usual dead-serious, dead-literal smile.

Boris grinned, the way he did when he'd just solved a moderately challenging puzzle. "And I know that you want Rick back just as much as I do."

"That might be the case. I might want Rick back with us just as much as you do." Haley smiled. He was probably trying to look coy or coquettish. "Or maybe — have you ever considered this possibility? — I want Rick back even more than you do."

Eight

"No. Now is not the time." Haley shook his head at Doctor Jones.

"I just wanted to remind you of the tremendous opportunity." Jones's breath was foul, like week-old ham sandwiches.

"This is really not a good time." It wasn't. Haley was expecting Rick in his office any minute. Jones's carpet-salesman schpiel was not conducive to a star student, maybe star love, definitely star lover, feeling comfortable in Haley's office.

"The position has a very competitive payscale—"

"Jones! Get the fuck out of my office. Jesus fucking Christ. Really. In all your years in this universe, did no one really teach you the fucking meaning of *no*?"

"What?" Jones looked at Haley in shock.

"I said it." Haley pushed Jones out the door, tossing him out into the outside hallway, using only his eyes.

"You — you —" Jones might never have been talked to like that. At least not to his face.

Rick walked into Haley's office just as Jones walked out. His facial affect was uncomfortable, almost pained. He looked like someone presenting at Urgent Care with a splinter: not having kittens, but definitely agitated.

"Mister Sarmenian. Rick. Thanks for coming into my office."

"Yeah. I got your message. What are we meeting about?"

Haley stood up. He closed the office door behind Rick. He then sat back down, and looked around as if to check whether anyone had seen him..

That looked shady as all fuck. Or maybe it was only Haley's prejudiced knowledge that made closing the door shady. Didn't professors usually meet with their students behind closed doors? There was nothing intrinsically shady about it, not unless Haley chose to make it so.

"Rick. I'm really sorry." Haley stared down at the textbooks on his desk: all about how to operate on a heart. Any heart but Rick's, it seemed.

"That doesn't make sense." Rick shook his head. He was famous for being as *Spock*-like as Haley. Was Haley really this bad though? "You shouldn't have to apologize for being in a love relationship with Boris. A love relationship that predates your having met me. There's nothing wrong with that."

"So you'll come back?" Haley reminded himself of the patients of his trying to grasp for a sliver of hope in their otherwise grim diagnoses.

Rick rolled his eyes, sighed, and shook his head all at once. Apparently Haley — much like his boss, Jones — just wasn't getting it. "I'm not coming back anywhere or to anything, Doctor Bronson." Big, adult words came from Rick's boyishly small mouth and lips.

"I'm not pressuring you into anything, Rick—"

"I appreciate that, and I expect nothing less from a professional physician and faculty member such as you." Shit. This kid knew that stuff. Maybe a PR executive or a lawyer lived in Rick's shirt pocket, just to be closer to those tight little pecs and juicy young nipples of his.

"I'm going to offer only once. And you can reject it."

"Offer what?" Rick's eyebrows flew up, together with his piqued interest. At least he didn't reject Haley's offer without hearing it first. That was one great thing about young dudes like Rick: they didn't believe themselves to have figured out all of life's answers already, so they actually listened to apologies, instead of firing off a prepared answer.

"Basically—" Haley inhaled deeply and sucked up his pride. "Basically, Boris and I, but especially I, want to grovel and apologize to you. And beg for you to take us back."

"If you haven't noticed." Rick shook his head with a world-weary grin. "I don't know how I can take you back if I never had you in the first place. You guys have your own thing without me."

"We both love you, Rick."

"Translation: you need me to spice up your sexual relationship, right?" Rick smiled like a detective. "I know. Two dudes in their thirties always think it would be hot to get a firm little college-aged fucktoy in their bed."

"Rick." Haley shook his head. He never actually thought what Rick was accusing him of thinking. But it was true: Haley was maybe one step away from it, especially the way he and Boris were treating Rick that evening.

"I've never had a relationship. I've never done anything with anyone, other than with you guys." Rick rocked back and forth in the chair. How far things had progressed from when he'd sat in that same chair in Haley's office as mere student. "But I've gotten lots of those daddy type offers. I'm pretty accustomed to it."

"Oh." If there was such a thing as pure, unmitigated shame, Haley was feeling it in that moment.

"StudentDoctor, MedStudentsOnline, all those websites." Rick shook his head with a bit of disgust. "As soon as I mentioned in my profile that I'm a single male med student, boom, pairs of, you know sixtysomething orthopedic surgeons, or a psychiatrist and a pulmonologist, or two ER doctors — all those guys want a young med student to spice up their bedroom. And that's the end of it."

"Rick. I'm sorry." Haley's nose was already running. Tears would be next.

"You're still not getting it, Doctor Bronson, Haley if you prefer." Rick looked directly at Haley. "You don't need to be sorry. It's a perfectly normal desire to get a fucktoy in your bed. I just don't want to be that fucktoy."

"I, we—" Haley couldn't even come up with words to defend himself and Boris. Maybe they weren't as guilty as Rick alleged, but they weren't innocent. "Rick, will you teach us how to love you?"

"What?" Laughter erupted from Rick's mouth, together with a spray of spit. He wiped his mouth with his shirt sleeve.

"Rick. Boris and I have spent our lives in medical training." Haley pointed with his eyes at the diplomas and certificates on the wall, then at the shelves of journals and textbooks. "You're getting to see the beginning part of that kind of training, but I don't think you quite appreciate how isolated we've been from normal human life."

"So that excuses you treating me like a sex object?"

"It doesn't excuse shit, Rick. Not that I even think we quite treated you like a sex object. But it doesn't excuse shit." Haley tapped his fingers on his desk as if playing air piano. He nodded his head a little with the music in his head.

"If it doesn't excuse shit, then why are you even bringing it up? Just so emphasize that you are the superior professors of medicine here and I'm just a little M1 twink?"

"Your gay vocabulary is good." Haley smiled.

"I don't have a boyfriend. I do have the internet." Rick smiled back.

"I'm not trying to have us excused or forgiven or whatever. I'm just trying to tell you it's something we need to learn. You need to show us. Neither of us has ever had a boyfriend either, you understand?"

"Then what about all the little, you know, the stuff about the Minnie Mouse voice—" Rick looked like even saying it hurt him.

"Boris and I hooked up once. Alright? Three years ago. We didn't even finish what we set out to do, sexually speaking, by the way, and I treated him like crap that night, by the way. And we never spoke about that night until recently."

"So you guys weren't boyfriends all along?"

"Fuck no. You think we're such amazing actors that we could've pretended to be enemies for three years while carrying on a relationship?"

"Well you guys are both geniuses."

"Want some coffee?" Haley clicked his espresso machine to make him a cup. Using his best emergency-room hands, he tore open a packet of sugar and managed to distribute it evenly over the bottom of the cup before the machine could even start pouring.

"Are you going to stir it with your pen?" Rick laughed. He knew Haley too well. But then, it wasn't difficult to spot Haley's tics.

255

"That's the other thing, Rick."

"I have to teach you how to use a spoon like a normal person?" Rick smiled and bit his lower lip. The sight of Rick's affect brightening almost brought Haley tears of joy.

"I've never spooned in my life." Haley laughed.

"I mean using a spoon in your coffee. Instead of a pen." Rick nodded like he was lecturing Haley. It was adorable.

"That's the other thing, Rick."

"What now? Your medical education made you excessively fond of pens?"

"You're not that far off." Haley blushed a little. This was shit he never brought up to anybody. He'd heard his classmates being called "ass pies" in junior high and that was enough.

"Do tell." Rick leaned in toward Haley. In all his twenty-three-year-old gravitas, he looked like some old-time TV interview host.

Haley whispered: "I'm on the spectrum."

"You're on the—" Rick stared at Haley and started breaking into a smile. Maybe he thought it was some kind of sci-fi term.

"Autism spectrum. Ever heard of Asperger Syndrome? Something like that." Haley was still whispering conspiratorially.

Rick leaned back in his chair and laughed. He leaned his body back, then up again. He covered his mouth and laughed some more. "You—" Rick shook his head.

Haley exhaled. He knew this dance. It was the standard thing he heard at any mention of a doctor who was on the spectrum. "It's really surprising that a person with autism went to Harvard Med, has a job, is even usually capable of tying his own fucking shoes?"

"No, dude." Rick put his palms on his cheeks, like he was trying to warm his hands. "I'm on the spectrum too. Asperger." Rick shook his head.

"No way." Now Haley felt like a fool. It was he who hadn't considered the possibility of not being the only one in the room.

"Yeah way. You didn't even think that was possible, right?" Rick smiled triumphantly. It was that particular smile of his — when he'd just beat the supposed master at his own game.

"I didn't even consider—"

"Well, you know." Rick grinned. "I'm no neurologist, but that's part of Asperger too, isn't it? Not even realizing that other people might have Asperger?"

"Shit." Haley inhaled deeply and could only look at Rick. This kid — no, this man — was amazing. "If I tell you that you're spectacularly intelligent and even more spectacularly wise, will you accuse me of trying to lure you into bed?"

"Nope." Rick grinned. "Sex in bed is boring anyway."

"Wha—" Haley looked at Rick with eyes agape. "I thought you never—"

"I have the internet, remember, Gramps?" Rick leaned back in the chair, put his hand in his crotch, and pantomimed jerking his dick.

Knock on the door. "Haley. Please?" That was definitely Boris.

"Hide the nuke secrets!" Haley stood up and shouted out toward the door. "The Russians are here!" He swung the door open.

There stood Boris in full: blue scrub shirt, gray UCSF Med sweatpants, weirdo hippie Mephisto sandals. And Boris always had a quip. "I guess hide the pee tape, the Americans are here?" Boris shrugged and wiped some locks of hair from his face. "Anyway how you guys doing here?"

"Better." Rick smiled. "Definitely feeling better. Doing better."

"Well." Haley cleared his throat. "I think I've convinced Rick to at least allow us to attempt to apologize to him."

"Good progress." Boris nodded.

"And I'm sorry too." Rick looked at Haley, then Boris.

"You're a kid." Boris grinned. "Or a young man at the very least. You don't need to apologize for anything."

"Maybe I don't need to, but I want to." Rick looked down. "I'm sorry for acting impulsively and running away instead of just talking things out."

"I don't think I can ever have any room to talk about acting impulsively." Boris shook his head.

"At least you don't stir your coffee with your pen." Rick smiled at Haley.

"Yeah, Haley — really." Boris stared at Haley like a very concerned doctor. Which he was. "Why the fuck do you do that?"

"Haley is au—" Rick started to say.

"Hey! Hey!" Haley barked at Rick. "Boris doesn't know."

"Boris doesn't know? But I do?" Rick looked in disbelief.

"Why do you think that's weird?" Boris asked. "I don't know shit about this dude."

"Yeah, so." Haley inhaled deeply and looked around at his two best friends, the two people he could trust with anything. "When I was a little kid, I had a favorite spoon for stirring stuff. I stirred anything. Juice, soda, water, anything."

"Okay, and?" Boris smiled, like he knew a good story was coming. There actually wasn't much of a story coming, but it was still a story.

"And one day, the spoon disappeared. I might've thrown it down the garbage disposal or something. Who knows."

"So you started stirring with a silver pen?" Boris asked, shaking his head with an amused grimace.

"Yeah." Boris took the pen out of his pocket, stirred his espresso with it, then held it up in front of his face. "In fact, with this very silver pen. I carry it everywhere with me."

"Oh shit." Boris nodded.

Haley lowered his voice and looked at Boris. "And I'm on the spectrum, by the way. That's why I do weird shit like that."

"I think we already kind of knew that, dude." Boris laughed. "It's pretty much a requirement for admission to Harvard Med, isn't it?"

"Maybe that's how I got into med school too." Rick smiled.

"Oh you ate one too?" Boris asked Rick.

"What?" Rick stared at Boris.

"You know. OU812. Oh you ate one too. Like—" Boris sighed.

"Joke's not funny if you have to explain it, Boris." Haley drummed his fingers on his desk again. "Are you guys free for the rest of the day? So we can talk somewhere a little better than my office."

"I don't have any classes." Rick tapped on his phone to confirm, then nodded at Haley and Boris. "I mean, I have to study, like always, but no classes or meetings or anything tonight."

"I'm just a cardiac surgeon and a professor of medicine." Boris shrugged. "I always have all the free time in the world."

"Is that sarcasm?" Rick asked.

"Kind of. But what I really mean is I'll make time for you guys. I have articles to review and PTE videos to watch and insurance write-ups to do, but that can wait for a day."

"So?" Haley smiled. "Are we out of here?" He dangled his office keys.

"Let's go." Boris nodded. "I'm the only one here with a car, so let me appoint myself driver."

"Before stepping out of this room though." Rick stood between Boris and the door. "It just feels like we've built something really special here, our closeness." Rick breathed deeply in and out, and looked at Boris, then Haley, for a full two seconds each. "Can we like — try to take that with us wherever we go?"

"Of course." Boris smiled.

"Deadass." Haley nodded. "That's what the kids say nowadays, right?"

"Yeah, yeah it is." Rick shook his head and laughed. "Deadass."

Nine

"Gentlemen, will you forgive me?" Boris's gray eyes glanced at Rick next to him, then to Haley in the rear-view mirror.

"Not this again!" Rick laughed. "You're forgiven. I fucking swear."

"I don't mean relationship stuff." Boris opened the center console, pulled out a University of Miami cap, and donned it — backwards of course. He must've thought it made him look cool. It actually did though. "I mean driving."

Boris drove the way he operated: the utmost precision, with occasional interludes of yee-haw rebellion. Or whatever the Russian version of *yee-haw was*.

"Your driving's been fine so far." Rick glanced at the speedometer. Eighty MPH: by no means excessively fast for an evening on I-95 in Miami, and perhaps downright suspiciously slow for a red Bentley convertible with three goofy dudes going to some kind of mystery location.

"Yeah, but I'm requesting penance in advance." Boris passed over the solid yellow line to get into the carpool express lanes.

"For that? Getting into the carpool lane over a solid yellow?" From his back seat perch, Haley glanced into the rearview. "I don't see any cops. I guess that transgression can be forgiven."

"No, that was only the lead-up." Boris shook his head, already full of faux shame. "It was only preparation for the major sin."

"There's three of us in the car, dude." Haley pointed at the three of them, one by one, then held three fingers in the air. "If my math skills haven't deteriorated since the MCAT. No carpool violation here as far as I can see."

"That's not the sin in question." Boris sighed, a little heavily.

"So?" Rick asked, half-smiling.

"So. The Bentley user manual, even all the Bentley owner forums, all say you've gotta let this thing run for just a bit, a few times a year." Boris pointed at the Bentley logo on the steering wheel, just in case Rick and Haley had forgotten what kind of car they were riding in. "To get it, like, lubricated and cleaned out and stuff."

"I think I see where this is going." Haley sighed. "How high does the speedometer need to go if you are vowing to quote unquote run it for just a bit? To lubricate its ass or whatever."

"I'm flexible." Boris laughed. "Top speed is electronically limited to one seventy or some shit like that. But I'm not that crazy."

"Only, like, half that crazy." Haley sighed. "Dude. Be careful."

"Am I a terrible person if I take it up to one twenty? In the empty carpool lane? For like a second?" Boris looked over at Rick for moral guidance.

"Yeah. It's putting innocent lives in danger." Rick sighed. "But then, everybody does it. And then, all the lives you've saved. Oh shit, I don't know. We can ask Matias sometime. He's the philosopher."

"Alright. Enough indecision. Unpopulated stretch right here." Boris put his hands on his wheel at the perfect nine and three positions. The Bentley's engine roared. The wind roared even louder: it ripped at Rick's face, his eyes, all over him. Boris laughed maniacally.

The buildings outside went by like a blur. Boris's eyes were fixed on the road as if it was a pulmonary artery he was opening.

Suddenly, the road, the buildings, even Boris in the driver's seat — it started to go wavy and spin. Rick was dizzy. Very dizzy.

Something was coming up in Rick's stomach.

Boris was still laughing. He was enjoying triple-digit speeds for more than just a bit.

Rick tried to tilt his head down — why, so he could hurl all over the precious leather interior? — but when he salivated and his mouth trembled and the hurl finally came up, it flew out of his mouth and went everywhere.

That must've been what vomit did in a Bentley convertible at triple-digit speeds. Despite the air rushing by, everything smelled like the inside of a Porta Potty. All thanks to Rick's throw-up.

"You alright there, Rick?" In the rearview mirror, Haley was trying to look unperturbed by the vomit all over his face.

"I'm sorry, guys. I'm sorry." The world was un-spinning, the car was back down to double-digit speeds, and Rick was feeling mostly kind of ok in his head and in his stomach.

"I have to say." Haley was laughing. "This is a fun bit of nostalgia to working in the ER. I'd get vomited on every night."

Boris held one finger in the air. "Some people pay big money for that, you know." He quickly glanced over at Rick. "Rick, how are you doing? Was that just a bit of car sickness?"

"Yeah. I'm sorry. I'll pay to have the car cleaned. I mean, I'll clean the car myself. I mean—"

"Rick. Don't worry, alright?" Boris smiled at Rick, as if both of them didn't have vomit all over their faces and shirts.

"I fucked up your car." Rick sighed.

"Rick. I'm a lot more worried about your car sickness than about the leather of my Bentley, alright?" Boris looked over at Rick and nodded for emphasis. He was driving at nearly legal speeds, but he still had that Miami hat on backwards, with blond locks strategically falling out. "Your health is more important than this dumb car."

"Yeah. I've just never felt — I mean, I guess I've never really felt loved before." Rick sighed and shook his head. "And you guys are my professors."

"Oh yeah." Boris held up a finger again. "Since you just threw up on us, please name the four major classes of antiemetics."

"Eeeeaaasy!" Rick laughed. "Antihistamines, dopamine antagonists, serotonin antagonists, and Scopolamine, which is an anticholinergic."

"Daaaaamn!" Haley shouted from the back seat. "I'd reach out to fist-bump you, but my hands are full of throw-up."

"There are better things to do with fists anyway," Rick said, quietly. He'd been watching videos. For years, actually. And if they were being honest with one another — maybe Rick could be honest too.

"Whoa, Rick is pretty hardcore." Boris laughed and nodded. "Never tried it myself, but for those who are into it, I'm a firm believer in the Fist Amendment."

"The Society of Righteous and Harmonious Fists, you mean?" Haley was laughing like a teenager in the back seat, shouting to make sure Boris and Rick could hear his joke over the wind noise, and holding his two fists up toward the rearview mirror and laughing.

"I've never — I've never done anything. I mean you guys know I've never done anything." Rick did his best to speak loudly enough to be heard over the wind noise. "But that just seems so exotic and so hot."

"I'll try anything once." Boris grinned at Rick, then at Haley. Boris's blond locks fluttered in the wind under his cap — he looked like a Ralph Lauren ad. "Or twice or whatever."

Haley laughed. "Shit, Boris, you're forgetting that you're as much of a near-virgin as I am?"

"Not forgetting anything." Boris tapped his fingers on the steering wheel the same way Haley sometimes played air-piano on his desk. "Just saying I can try."

"Uh, guys." Rick spoke in his best official-announcement voice. "Whatever secret favorite hangout of his Boris is taking us to, shouldn't we stop and shower or something before we go there? Or at least wash the throw-up off our faces?"

Haley leaned forward to talk to Rick and Boris. "As much as I love Rick's vomit all over me, I vote for a stop at a gas station."

"Nah." Boris smiled proudly and shook his head. "Not needed."

"The fuck?" Haley yelled from the back seat. "Are you taking us to some kind of vomit fetish club or something?"

"Maybe." Boris shrugged.

"You sick fuck." Haley shook his head and laughed.

"It's just up ahead." Boris waved vaguely in the same direction as the Bentley's nose pointed.

"What, a condo building?" Haley scrunched his nose in disapproval. Rick only wanted to kiss him again, maybe after the vomit was gone from his face.

"Nope." Boris was beaming proudly, like a dad showing his family a favorite camping spot. He suddenly braked and pulled into a small beachfront hotel. "Right here!"

An attendant jogged out with a valet parking tag. "Doctor Yorshenko!" Boris sighed as if he didn't in the least enjoy the ritual. He pointed out the throw-up in the interior and handed the attendant a hundred-dollar bill. The attendant looked like he was ready to jump off of a cliff for Boris, or at least for Boris's money.

"That attendant really respects you, even though I came out ahead in the new AJC." Haley laughed. It was true, although Haley had promised not to care about it anymore: Haley was now third in the country, while Boris was fifth.

"So you suddenly start caring about the AJC once you rank higher than me?" Boris smiled.

"Nah. I'm just kidding. I stopped caring about all that shit." It was true. Word had gotten around the School of Medicine about Boris and Haley's new 2019 rankings, but neither Boris nor Haley had mentioned it themselves. "More than I care about the AJC, I care about the RTB. The Russian and Turkish Baths, right?" Haley looked up at the sign on the building the three of them were about to enter. "I've seen this place."

"Yup!" Boris beamed a huge, vomit-stained smile.

"Boris, are you—" Rick tilted his head a little to show just how puzzled he was. He made his best innocent face. "Are you taking us to a bathhouse?"

Haley burst out laughing. "You sure you're only twenty-three, Rick? And you know what a bathhouse is?"

"Maybe going on fifty, thanks to the internet." Rick shrugged. He definitely knew what a bathhouse was, even if he also knew they were mostly extinct.

"I've always wondered about this place." Haley led the way toward the entrance. "Too embarrassed to ever be seen here, so never checked it out."

"Yup." Boris nodded. He knew exactly what Haley was talking about, apparently. "I'm Russian, so I have an excuse if anybody sees me here."

"And me?" Rick laughed.

"No excuse." Haley made an exaggerated frowny face. "None whatsoever. Everyone will know you're just here to get some dick."

"To wash the vomit off my face. That's my excuse." Rick nodded proudly.

"Oh yeah. Not bad." Haley nodded.

Boris had already planted himself in front of the front desk, gesticulating at Haley and Rick behind him and speaking to the attendants in some kind of mashup of Russian and English.

They got their towels and locker room keys as if they were soldiers preparing to war. Boris led the way to the locker room. "Shower first, guys. That's the rule here, even if we didn't have throw-up all over us."

The toiletries in the shower smelled amazing. Getting lathered up with that stuff, the smell was like an actual forest — not the regular grocery-store toiletries Rick had spent all his life using.

Rick washed his hair and body twice, just because it felt so good. The vomit was definitely gone from his body. Rick now fully and totally smelled like some kind of forest herbs or some shit like that.

"No jerking off in the shower!" Boris said loudly into Rick's shower cubicle. There didn't seem to be anybody else in the shower area, so Rick would've considered jerking off — if he hadn't been in the company of two beautiful men who'd sort of made masturbation obsolete for him.

"Steam room one!" Boris called it out like a football quarterback calling a play. Boris led the way to a wooden door, his perfectly round ass thrusting and gyrating as he walked, as if he were power-fucking the air in front of him.

They filed into the steam room.

"Shit, the bench is hot," Haley said, in a semi-whiny voice of complaint.

"Is that your excuse for your shriveled dick?" Boris guffawed.

"It's my excuse, at least." Rick's own flaccid dick was cocktail-weenie size. But he was always more of a grower than a shower.

"How long are we supposed to stay in this room?" Haley asked. He sounded as if any amount of time would be much too long.

"The crazy old Russians stay for like an hour." Boris shook his head. "That's nuts, and probably dangerous. I'd say ten minutes is good enough."

The wooden door opened again. Two buff, naked, buzz-cut dudes walked in and sat down on the bench.

"It's always good to be protected by the local constabulary, even when I'm naked in the sauna." Boris smiled at the men. "Nice to see you."

"Always a pleasure, Doctor Yorshenko," one man said.

"You know, our daily patrol through here, making sure nobody's naughty." The other man shrugged and smiled. "Good way to get a free daily sauna, but you didn't hear me say that."

"Your secret is safe with me." Boris grinned and zipped an imaginary zipper across his lips.

The two cops made took some deep breaths in and out. Then they stood up in unison and walked out. "See you next time, Doctor Yorshenko."

"Keep fighting crime, guys!" Boris sent them off with a laugh and a tongue-in cheek thumbs-up. The cops walked out the door and meandered toward the locker room.

"They do a patrol through here every day to make sure nobody's having too much fun." Boris gestured jerking off with his left hand and giving a blowjob with his left hand.

"Sounds like you're quite a regular here, man." Haley nodded in admiration.

"A bit. Good place to think. And I've got a bit more time recently since I'm not cleared to perform surgery yet after my TIA."

"So does it get cruisy?" Rick asked, laughing. He kept his eyes on Boris to emphasize that he really wanted an answer to his question. He wasn't making an idle joke.

"I've seen some shit." Boris laughed. "Haven't been involved in it."

"And the police patrol?" Haley asked.

"I've seen them arrest two dudes who thought it perfectly normal to sixty-nine in the cooling-off room." Boris clicked his tongue in disapproval and shook his head. "But generally as soon as the cops leave, you know it's safe for the rest of the day."

"Or so you've heard." Haley grinned.

"Or so I've heard." Boris nodded.

Rick couldn't restrain himself any longer. He'd been watching Boris and Haley during the entire car ride, missing their kisses, their touches, and their smells.

"Boris." Rick brought his face closer to Boris's. Boris half-closed his eyes. Rick pushed his lips to Boris's lips. Rick slipped his tongue into Boris's mouth. Boris kissed back. He ran his soft hands over Rick's arms.

Rick's dick instantly rose up, erect. Boris's dick followed, standing like a pink-gray bowling pin in Boris's lap.

Haley embraced Rick from behind. His pecs and erect nipples pressed into Rick's back. Haley pecked at Rick's neck, then licked and sucked on Rick's ear and embraced him closely.

French-kissing Boris while being held and kissed from behind by Haley — it was the feeling of love again. And this time it wasn't an illusion.

"You guys—" Rick had to try hard not to burst into tears when saying it. "This sounds pathetic, but you guys love me, right?"

"Rick. I love you. Boris loves you. We love you." Haley slurped at Rick's ear. It was just his ear, but the erotic feeling was amazing. It felt as good as getting his dick sucked.

"Rick. I really couldn't live without you, man." Boris spoke between deep kisses on Rick's mouth. "Seriously."

"Deadass?" Rick asked. He glanced behind at Haley; the question was for Haley too.

"Deadass, Rick." Haley sucked on Rick's back shoulder blade, then moved his tongue to the small of Rick's neck.

Rick leaned far down, almost like a yoga pose. He opened his mouth wide. He took the tip of Boris's fat cock into his lips.

"Oh fuck," Boris groaned. His nipples stood up hard. He grinded his crotch upward, at Rick's mouth.

Rick licked a circle over Boris's dickhead. He let the dick slip out of his mouth, then leaned over to the right while leaning down. He couldn't leave Haley out of the action.

He lowered his head onto Haley's cock. Haley's purple dickhead glistened with sweet precum. Rick took his time in gently, lovingly licking off the precum, then swallowing it, drop by drop.

"Oh fuck." Boris shook his head while watching Rick pleasuring Haley's cockhead. Rick reached for Boris's dick and held onto it like a grab handle. He slowly pumped Boris's thick cock with a firm grip while he made oral love to Haley's dick.

"You guys wanna chariot race?" Rick laughed knowingly. They'd know the term if they'd watched a lot of gay porn, like Rick had. If not, Rick could teach them.

"What the fuck?" Haley asked, still moaning and gyrating his crotch into Rick's face.

"Chariot racing?" Boris laughed. "Is that like something from *Spartacus*?"

"Get on all fours," Rick said. He'd been practicing that voice — that firm, assertive voice of unabashedly giving his professors a command, at least outside the classroom. "On the bench, on all fours, side by side."

Haley and Boris did as told: two grown men in a steamy sauna, crouching side-by-side on all fours on a wooden bench.

"Is this the chariot race?" Boris asked.

"Yeah." Rick spoke quietly. He was still a little ashamed of his fantasy. "I guess your asses are clean after the shower. And with all this steam and water, it's gonna be wet enough."

"I think I know where this is going." Boris looked back at Rick with a laugh.

Haley looked to the side at Boris, then back at Rick. "Yeah, I think I can guess where Rick's fist is going."

"Two fists." Rick held up two fists. "That's why it's a chariot race."

"Holy fuck." Boris laughed. "That's kind of hot."

"I fist you two guys. Both at once. From behind. You guys make out with each other and shit. You can both suck my dick too. But whoever cums first from fisting doesn't get to assfuck me. Whoever doesn't cum first—" Rick smiled at Haley, then at Boris. "Whoever cums second gets to plow my ass."

"I'm not sure I want to win this race." Boris grinned. He spread his thighs and ass cheeks apart. "But let's fucking go. I'm ready."

"Ok. Umm." Rick struggled to maintain his facade of being the authority on fisting, even if all he'd known about it was from online videos and his own fantasies. "This is how I've seen it done in porn. I'm just gonna start real slow with my fingers and knuckles."

"Sounds like a plan." Boris raised his beautiful, muscular ass, as if it to beg for Rick's fist in it. Rick rested his fist on Boris's hole. He maneuvered it slightly inward. Boris only grunted and pushed his ass back farther onto Rick's fist. Rick couldn't help but use his other hand to fondle Boris's heavy, hairy, meaty balls. Boris's balls looked like they could breed the entire world, or at least the entire male world.

"Wake me up before you go-go," Haley said. "Or fist me before I cum-cum. Or something like that." He spread his legs, thighs, and ass cheeks the same way Boris did.

"Got it," Rick said. He put his fist toward Haley's ass. That ass had more muscle and less fat than Boris's. It would be a tighter fit, but he couldn't imagine anything more erotic than putting his fist in his professor's ripped muscle ass.

Haley glanced behind at Rick and raised his eyebrows. His face dripped steamy sauna sweat. "I'm not afraid of it, dude. Just put it in."

Rick's left hand was already halfway in Boris. Haley's balls were hard and hairy, as beautiful as Boris's. He had to fondle them with his right hand before he could fist him.

Rick tugged on Haley's balls and massaged them with his right hand. He ran his extended fingertips over Haley's hard, downward-pointing dick.

Then he pulled his right hand away from Haley's balls, made it into a fist, and proceeded to the main event: he made his right fist tight and and slipped it into the ass crack, between the globes of muscle that were Haley's glutes. Rick's knuckles ran over the inside of Haley's ass like a super-mega-vibra-ribbed condom.

"Fuck." Haley's voice sounded like he was impaled on something.

"You alright there?" Rick leaned down and kissed the small of Haley's back, just where his spine rose and his ass cheeks began.

"Very much alright." Haley was speaking through clenched teeth.

Rick was crouching on the floor behind them, the big bench in front of him — and two absolutely gorgeous asses pretty much in his face, with his fists in both of them.

Rick moved both fists farther in. He twisted and turned a little bit with the curvature of Haley's and Boris's ass canals, to make the entry a bit easier. His knuckles and fingers pushed up against the ass insides and both dudes were only throbbing and moaning. Both of their ass canals felt like wet socks inside: not dirty or disgusting at all.

"Fuck," Boris said. His teeth chattered a bit. "It's like having a fucking bulldozer driving in me. Feels great though." He turned his head toward Haley on his right side and puckered his lips while looking into Haley's eyes. It was so fucking hot to watch that from behind.

Haley rushed in toward Boris's mouth with his own lips and frantic kisses. Their heads angled sideways, Haley and Boris made out with deep kisses.

Steamy drops of water poured off of both of their beautiful asses. Rick only moved his fists inside them ever so slightly, until they both moaned harder. Their balls were as rock hard as their dicks, and both of their bodies were flushed red in hot steam as they made out with each other.

"Fuck, man." Boris breathed heavily as he spoke. "I didn't know this would feel this great. I thought everything these days is supposed to be *minimally invasive*."

"You didn't watch enough porn, I guess." Rick slightly opened his hand inside Boris's ass, letting his fingers fold out to pleasure Boris deeper.

"I don't know the right websites, I guess." Boris pushed back with his butthole, impaling it farther on Rick's fist. "Fuck fuck fuck, this feels amazing." Boris pushed down with his ass so his dickhead touched the wooden bench below him, as if he was thrusting into the bench.

"You don't need to fuck the wooden bench," Haley said. As he spoke he kissed Boris's cheeks and neck. "Let me help you out."

Haley reached back and took Boris's dick in his hand. He pumped it up and down as if he was awkwardly milking a cow, using his other hand to support himself in the all-fours position.

Rick pushed his fist farther into Boris's ass. He touched some kind of nub — that must've been the prostate. Boris screamed in pleasure for half a second. Then Boris buried his mouth in his own shoulder.

"Must feel great, but keep it on the downlow, dude." Haley laughed while he kissed Boris and jerked Boris's fat dick. "We're still in a public place, you know."

"Fuck." Boris gyrated his ass on Rick's fist, rubbing his prostate against Rick's finger. "Fucking fuck." The sauna stunk of sweat and precum.

Boris's whole ass clenched hard on Rick's fist. It felt like Boris's ass would just swallow Rick's arm.

Haley jerked Boris's dick faster, more frantically. He stuck out his tongue to push in Boris's mouth. They were making out as if they'd missed each other for years — though that was probably kind of true.

Rick bent down to get his face near Boris's ass. He gave Boris's rim a long, slow lick.

"Oh fuck Rick!" Boris shouted. He stuffed his mouth into his shoulder again. He shook all over.

Haley held Boris's dick in both hands, milking it like an udder. Boris must've been cumming: the sauna room filled with the hot stench of fresh cum. Rick breathed it in. It was the nectar of sex and love.

Boris groaned. His last ropes of cum must've been shooting out onto Haley's hands.

Rick readjusted his whole body. His fists still inside Haley and Boris, he sat between them on the bench and slid his legs forward then folded them up, so his dick was at their mouths.

Haley and Boris knew what to do. Their lips and tongues fought over the prize that was Rick's dick, taking turns pleasuring Rick's dickhead and his shaft.

Boris took Rick's entire dick in his mouth and sucked on it hard, moaning softly. Rick felt the vibrations of Boris's moaning through his whole body. Boris had definitely cum.

"You won the chariot race, Boris. Congratulations." Rick laughed. "That means Haley gets to assfuck me."

"This is like the AJC surgeon rankings, isn't it." Haley was laughing. "The winner is really the loser."

Rick cleared his throat and pulled his dick out of Boris's mouth. "How about less chatter and more fucking my ass?" Rick laughed. Talking like that to his professors — to anyone — was novel as fuck, liberating as fuck, hot as fuck.

Rick made one final push of his fists into Boris and Haley, one final turn around, one final tickle of their prostates. Then he pulled his fists out of them.

Rick turned his body around so his head was at the wall and lay face up on the same bench, his legs up, almost at his shoulders. "Fuck me now, Haley — Professor Bronson."

Haley's dick was rock hard, gleaming with veins, dripping condensed steam. His balls were just as firm as when Rick had fondled them.

Haley stood between Rick's open thighs. He lay his palms under Rick's ass cheeks. He squeezed Rick's ass cheeks in rhythm with his fundamental inquiry: "You ready, Rick?"

Rick breathed deeply. "My first time, but I'm ready." There were worse ways to lose his virginity than in a sauna with two brilliant, caring men who loved him. In fact, there were no better ways, none that Rick could think of; this was all better than any of his fantasies about how his first time would be.

Starting with playing at Rick's rim, Haley pushed his dick all the way into Rick. It wasn't painful at all. The long, pointy dick went deep into Rick and it only felt like pure love. Haley brought Rick's legs and feet to his mouth and kissed them while he fucked Rick faster and faster.

Rick lay back. Boris was sitting next to him, half-exhausted, dick half-flaccid, watching the action.

"Hey Boris." Rick spoke as best he could while pumping and turning his ass to take Haley's dick deeper into him. "This isn't a peep show. Get on your knees and fucking lick Haley's ass. You don't need a hard dick to do that." His own dirty talk made Rick hard.

Boris's mouth dropped agape, with a smile. It must've been novel hearing Rick order him around like that.

"And you." Rick looked up at Haley. "Fuck me harder. Fuck me like I'm your little fucktoy, even if I'm not." Rick grinned. He was secure in that knowledge. These guys really loved him. But that shouldn't stop them from plowing his ass hard.

Haley bent down, his beautiful blue eyes approaching Rick's face like twin UFOs about to make a long-anticipated landing. Haley's lips and tongue touched Rick's. They kissed, deeply, while Haley kept fucking Rick, pulling his ass cheeks apart with his hands to get his dick deeper in.

Boris kneeled behind Haley, his mouth right at Haley's ass. He wrapped his arms around Haley's powerful legs and thighs.

Rick couldn't see the action on the other side as Haley fucked him, but Haley moaned faster and fucked harder while Boris's blond locks were moving around behind his ass. Boris must've been tonguing Haley's ass.

"Fuck. I never thought I'd. Fuck." Haley breathed quickly and spoke between his breaths. "Getting rimmed is gonna make me— make me— fuck!"

Haley pushed hard into Rick, then withdrew and fucked him fast and hard like a jackhammer. Rick lifted his legs higher in the air. The sauna was filled with the smell of cum and sweat and the sounds of Boris's slurps of Haley's ass and Haley's and Rick's moans of pleasure.

"Oh fuck." Haley clenched his teeth. He leaned down again and kissed Rick's lips. Haley's whole body shook. His dick filled Rick's ass with a gob of cum, then another, then a third.

Rick was shaking. Haley took Rick's dick in his hand while he kissed him. One squeeze, one small motion of Haley's fingers over Rick's dickhead and Rick exploded in orgasm. He sent hot cum all over Haley's muscled pecs and abs. Rick even managed to shoot cum on Boris's arms that were wrapped around Haley's thighs.

"Oh fuck." Rick inhaled deeply.

Haley bent down again to french kiss him. Haley's hands fondled Rick's pecs and nipples.

Boris stood up behind Haley and moved over to the bench, next to Rick. "I just ate Haley's ass. I hope you don't mind kissing."

Rick didn't mind at all. He pulled his mouth away from Haley slightly and moved in to kiss Boris, then drew both Haley and Boris into a three-way french kiss.

Rick had never felt anything like that: not just physical satisfaction and sexual satiation, but pure love. The men with him were his professors, but also his lovers and best friends.

"I think our ten minutes in the sauna is just about up, guys." Boris laughed. Boris sounded just as exhausted — and satisfied — as Rick felt.

Haley stumbled to the wooden door. His legs seemed weak from all the fucking. "I love you guys," he said to Rick and Boris.

He opened the sauna door. An ocean of cool air washed over them like an after-sex cool shower. Rick still felt aftershocks from the orgasm he'd gotten from Haley's fucking.

"I love you too," Rick said. "I love the three of us."

Haley, then Boris, then Rick stumbled out of the sauna room into the main bath area. The two cops hadn't left; they sat naked in a hot tub just outside the sauna area.

"Looks like you guys had a good sauna," one of the officers said, his eyes obviously scanning Rick's, Haley's, and Boris's exhausted bodies and spent, flaccid dicks.

The other officer grinned and put his finger to his lips. "But we didn't see, or hear, anything."

Epilogue

"Point, set, match, team McCall!" Linda had just made the winning over-the-net spike.

It was a loss for Team Boris, but at least it was over. Running full-speed against Linda's sets and spikes in ninety-degree afternoon heat wasn't exactly Boris's idea of a pleasant afternoon.

Haley was using his usual Harvard Med t-shirt as a sweat rag. Ritter Lehman was cracking morbid jokes about an hour in the blazing heat being a preview of Hell. Even the young bucks Rick and Matias were crouching more often than standing.

Meanwhile, Linda hadn't even broken a sweat. She looked fresh enough to have just stepped out of a Summer's Eve ad.

Suspicions confirmed: anesthesiologists weren't even human. They always looked like they'd just walked out of a fresh-feeling field of daisies in a douche ad.

Rick called out to the group: "Hey, does anyone else watch The Backyardigans?"

Boris energetically raised his hand. "Uh, Haley and I do, thanks to you."

"Ok, anyone other than my condomates and boyfriends watch The Backyardigans?" Rick looked around at the group.

"Condom mates?" Ritter snickered.

Linda shook her head at Ritter. "You always live up to the stereotype of orthopedists being dirty old men."

Ritter laughed and nodded. "Thank you, come again!"

"Guys, guys!" Rick called out. "Anyone watch The Backyardigans?"

"I admit I've watched an episode or two. Or a season or two. Or three." Matias smiled. "I don't live with Rick, but I do hang out with him."

"Good!" Rick pointed at Matias. "And at the end of every episode, what do they say?" Easy question. Boris knew the answer, but he wasn't going to admit it.

Matias shouted into the air like a wild man: "Let's go to my house for snacks!"

"Thank you, Matias." Rick nodded. "I knew I could depend on Matias to fill the gaps in my colleagues' knowledge."

Ritter wrapped his huge torso in a towel while snickering. "Those Colin and Duke dudes depend on Matias to fill something else."

"Hey!" Rick snapped his fingers in the air. "Keep your dick in your pants and your mind out of the gutter. This isn't an orthopedists' meeting."

"Ouch." Ritter laughed. He reached behind with his big hairy hand demonstratively spanked his own ass a few times.

That dude really was as fucking dirty as everybody said. Too bad he was a hell of a surgeon, and actually a great guy if you didn't let the salty language offend you.

"So Rick, are you actually inviting us up to your house for snacks?" Linda looked up in the direction of the balcony. She had a preternatural ability to know exactly which one of the identical balconies was Boris's — and now also Haley's and Rick's.

"Yes he is," Boris said.

"Yes I am." Rick nodded. "Uh, let's go!"

"Are we eating day-old medianoches or cold pizza or Doritos or what?" Linda grinned and looked at the trio: Boris, Rick, Haley. They were a good-looking bunch, even if Boris said so himself. "I can't imagine you guys cooking."

"We kind of have a cook next door. Kind of." Boris smiled at Haley and Rick. They'd grown accustomed to Boris's mom, even if most of his colleagues had never met her.

Ritter squinted and shook his head. "What, you kidnapped Wolfgang Fuck and keep him as a scullery maid?"

"No." Boris sighed and shook his head. "And that's not Wolfgang's name, as you know full well."

"Sorry." Ritter made an exaggerated sad face. "I must've been thinking of Gordon Rimjob." He sped up his walk, directly behind Rick on the way to the condo building.

"Ritter." Linda shook her head at Ritter while still walking and bouncing the volleyball up and down.

She could do at least three things at once. Not human, really.

"I'm fifty years old." Ritter shrugged. "I don't give a fuck anymore."

"I don't think you ever gave a fuck." Linda smiled.

"Oh shit. I forgot you've worked with me before."

"Sure did." Linda nodded knowingly.

"Patient was a jerk. I would've preferred to rip out his knee without anesthesia anyway. But you know, laws, cops and other bullshit like that." Ritter shook his head.

"Rick." Linda gave Rick an older-sisterly smile. "You know we're just fucking around, right? And this is not what medicine is supposed to be like?"

"I don't see or hear a thing." Rick shrugged. "Actually, you know, if you see who my boyfriends are — Haley and Boris — it's pretty obvious I know about joking around, even in serious medicine."

"Good." Linda sighed with relief. "Who's got the building access code?" She tapped the access pad.

"No access code!" Boris proudly stepped up to the entryway and lay his finger on the access pad. "Fingerprint based!"

"God, I can't imagine leaving my fingerprints anywhere but a twink's ass." Ritter shook his head ruefully.

"Alright, Doctor Ritter Lehman." Linda looked at him sternly. "You're gonna be meeting Boris's mother. Be on your best, alright?"

"Or his worst." Boris shrugged. "I don't think my mom gives a fuck."

"She's the cook?" Ritter asked.

"Yeah. De facto."

"I can't imagine any woman wanting to live with the three of you." Ritter shook his head at Boris.

"Oh, yeah. I bought the condo next door. She lives there. She's technically working as our cook to pay the rent on her condo." Boris smiled at his friends. The thing with his mom was an arrangement to make her feel better about her son buying her a condo, of course.

"Oh yeah." Ritter nodded. "Sounds like a fair deal. What do the units here rent out for? Twenty K a month or something?"

"Hey, hey." Boris smiled at Ritter. "I thought you're the only one here who's into renting units." Boris grinned at Ritter, like he'd one-upped him at his own game of double entendres.

The whole group stepped into the elevator. Up they went.

"Been years since I've rented a unit. I've got a husband now." Ritter smiled.

"The surgeon and the mechanic." Linda shook her head. "Who would've fucking believed it."

Haley cleared his throat and glanced at Linda as the elevator shot up. "About as many people as would've believed in the Haley Bronson - Linda McCall dream relationship Doctor Jones had planned for us?"

The elevator door opened. Haley led the way out, then stopped short of his condo door and looked at Linda for an answer.

"Jones dude trying to ship us like we're fanfic characters. Fucking nutcase." Linda shook her head.

Haley snapped his tongue. "Funny how Jones still made me Head of Cardiology, even after I came out as gay. Like he suddenly came to his senses."

"Even caveman Jones is scared of the University getting sued under his watch." Linda smiled, a little coyly. She started walking toward the condo door. The rest of the group followed behind her.

"Hold up!" Haley called out to Linda. He hadn't moved one step. "The University getting sued? Is there something I don't know?"

"How do you open this damn door?" Linda asked Haley, like she was ignoring his question.

"Here." Boris stepped forward laying his finger on the touchpad until the door swung open.

"Nothing much, Haley." Linda shrugged. "Just that I scared the shit out of Jones by showing him the university policies and state regulations about discrimination — gender, marital status, sexual orientation, what have you."

"You did that for me?" Haley opened his blue eyes wide at Linda. "For insufferable fucking jerk Haley Bronson?"

"You're not so insufferable." Linda waved her hand. "And I didn't like being auctioned off like cattle either."

Linda stepped in to the apartment ahead of Boris. Boris followed. He turned around behind him to invite the whole group inside "Come on! Don't act like you haven't been here before!"

"Nice apartment you've got here, Boris." Linda grinned as she hammed up the compliment. "You must be a doctor or something."

"Good guess." Boris nodded. "Not as overpaid as anesthesiologists though."

Linda whispered to Boris: "After the little arranged-wedding debacle, Jones pushed me up to five hundred K a year."

"Holy shit!" Boris showed Linda a thumbs up. "Give me a call when you're at at six hundred fifty thousand like me, but not bad at all, for a poor." Linda knew him well enough not to be offended by that shit.

"Not everyone can be The Amazing Boris Yorshenko." Linda shrugged. "I guess I'll just have to stay in the poorhouse."

"Hello, excuse me!" Rick walked between Boris and Linda. "I make six fifty a month in my research internship. Like, six hundred fifty dollars a month. Can I even breathe the same air as you?"

"Whatever." Boris laughed. "Don't close the door. Mom's bringing us some snacks or something."

Linda smirked at Boris. "Six hundred fifty K a year and your mom still cooks for you. Nice, Yorshenko. Nice."

"We love her cooking," Rick said. "Even if she has some fun with the visual presentation."

"Booooris!" That was Mom at the door. She walked in, holding a tray. "My dear stupid Boooris, my always-serious Haley, and my cute Rick! And all your friends!"

"Ah." Boris's face flushed a bit. "That's my mom, everybody. Sylvia Yorshenko. Give a round of applause or something."

"First dish! Yum yum! Eat!" She lay the platter on a coffee table. "Dessert is on the way as soon as the oven cools down!"

Rick looked down at the platter. "Is that a plate of sausages?" He covered his mouth as he cough-laughed. "With loose foreskins?"

"I believe it is." Boris cringed and nodded.

"And oh look." Rick shook his head. "A nice bowl of nuts."

Sylvia jogged back into the apartment. "Cookies haven't cooled down yet! But here's some fruit for you first!" She set a fruit platter down on the table.

Boris shook his head. "Bananas stuck in peach halves. Nice, mom. Nice."

Mom shrugged. "I know what you guys do. Don't pretend I can't hear from the next apartment!"

Boris stared at her. "We always use the room farthest from your wall—" He stopped himself. It wasn't an explanation worth going into.

Mom smiled at Boris, Haley, and Rick. "Oh, your tongues playing like slippery dolphins in the sunlight, your eager buttholes puckered to receive love — I know how it goes! I've watched *Queer as Folk*!"

Ritter silently mouthed at Boris: "What the fuck?"

"Mom." Boris sighed. "It is true, but—"

"Thank you for the wonderful snacks, Mrs. Yorshenko," Haley said. "I, for one, appreciate your cooking. Even your cocking." Haley pointed down at the fruit platter. "Seriously, did you just go to Publix and buy a bunch of bananas and peach halves, all nonchalant like that?"

"Why not?" Mom asked. "Checkout clerk laughed at me, but he's a big leather daddy. He knows the score." She shrugged.

"Facts." Rick nodded.

"Alright. Alright." Boris slurped at both tips of the banana, then the peach half, before biting in to both. "That's actually good. You guys should taste."

Rick's hand reached toward Boris. He held Boris's hand and whispered, "I think I have some idea of what the cookies are gonna be."

"I don't even want to predict," Boris whispered back. It was true. It was more fun if he just let it happen. His mother loved and accepted him and his two boyfriends. If that came with a bit of juvenile culinary humor — so be it. It would only make gatherings more fun for Boris, his boyfriends, and all their friends.

The smell of fresh chocolate chip cookies preceded Mom's appearance in the doorway. After a second, she appeared, and announced "Cookies are here!" and set the tray down on the main dining table.

"Why is there—" Linda started to ask.

"Is that intentionally—" Matias stared at Mom with a bit of shock.

"Mrs. Yorshenko, did you—" Ritter started to ask.

Boris stepped in to confront her directly. "Mom, you put a few dollops of Cool Whip on the cookies because— is that supposed to be what I think it's supposed to be?"

"Does bear shit in woods?" Mom asked.

"I guess so." Boris sighed. "I love you anyway, Mom. And I love Rick and Haley."

"Now if you'll excuse me." Mom nodded confidently. "I don't want to cramp your style. So I'll be going to see a man about a dog."

"You get an A-plus for your colloquial English, Mrs. Yorshenko." Rick nodded and gave Mom a thumbs-up.

"As weird as it is." Linda put her hands on her hips and breathed in deeply, looking at Boris, Rick, and Haley standing together. "You guys are really a perfect match, the three of you."

"No shit." Boris grinned. "We are. And yeah, it's weird, for some people maybe. So what?"

"Thanks for understanding, Linda." Haley sighed. "I'm sorry that I didn't tell you earlier that I'm gay. I'm sorry if I led you on or something. I was just trying to keep my job, my reputation, all that stuff."

"It's cool." Linda smiled. "Don't worry about it."

Haley patted Linda's back. "We're here to support you once you find your true love."

"How do you know I haven't already?" Linda grinned. There was that coy grin of hers again. She never let out everything at once. Just like an anesthesiologist.

"You've found your true love?" Haley asked Linda, wide eyed.

"Maybe." Linda shook her head side to side. "And it's the kind of *maybe* that's actually a *hell yeah*."

"Whoa." Haley smiled. "Good work. Who is he?"

Linda shook her head. "I think you mean *she*."

"Woo hoo!" Boris laughed and shook his head, eyes staring wide open at Linda. No one had even quite thought of her orientation, other than the vague assumption that she was into Haley. "Damn. We had no idea."

"Seeing you three guys — how open you are — how in love you are — it's what inspired me." Linda smiled. "You guys will be getting the wedding invitations next week."

"Wow!" Boris laughed and clapped. Haley cheered like he was at a football game.

Mom appeared at the open doorway again. "Did I miss something?"

"Watching your son fall in love with Haley and Rick, it inspired me to follow my true love too. I'm getting married soon!" Linda shouted to Mom. "To a woman!"

"Oooh!" Mom nodded thoughtfully. "Have fun scissoring!"

Boris cringed like he'd just swallowed a whole lemon. "Yeah, Linda. I'm glad we inspired you. Have fun scissoring."

Next in the series…

Cops need love too, and patrolling the baths can pique a "straight" guy's desires.

Asher and Dane are Miami's finest. Maybe they've gotten a little complacent on their daily patrol of the beach resorts and the baths.

A million-dollar private security job protecting a billionaire might break them out of their routine — and show them something completely new.

The Power of Three
https://www.amazon.com/dp/B07S6KZ844

Afterword

Steve Milton writes gay romances with sweet love, good humor, and hot sex.

Sign up for Steve's spam-free insiders' club: http://eepurl.com/bYQboP

Three Hearts is the second book of the series **Three Straight**, where Miami's hottest "straight" guys discover their true selves, and the best things come in threes.

Book 1: **We Three**
https://www.amazon.com/dp/B07QB2W9MG

Book 2: **Three Hearts**
http://amazon.com/dp/B07QRWXGJX

Book 3: **The Power of Three**
https://www.amazon.com/dp/B07S6KZ844

Selections from Steve Milton's other books:

Straight Guys is one book of eleven sexy novellas about straight guys who aren't so straight. Who doesn't love "totally straight" dudes lusting after other "totally straight" dudes?
https://www.amazon.com/dp/B018KNWGC8

Crema is a story of childhood friends finding love.
https://www.amazon.com/dp/B071D4XQJS

Summer Project has a nerd, a jock, a tropical island, and a shared bed.
https://www.amazon.com/dp/B01I0FRENC

Steve Milton has written about twenty other gay romance novels, all of them full of good humor, hot sex, and lots of laughs:
http://amazon.com/author/stevemilton

Author's note about the setting

The Miller School of Medicine at the University of Miami is a real institution, but it has been entirely fictionalized for the purposes of this novel.

None of this novel's characters are meant to resemble any real people. None of this novel's characterizations of discriminatory and unprofessional behavior at the Miller School of Medicine are meant to represent the reality of the Miller School nor any other institution.

Some details of medical practice and medical education have been altered for the purposes of this story.

The American Journal of Cardiology is a real publication, but it does not publish rankings of surgeons.

The Russian & Turkish Baths in Miami is a perfectly non-sexual establishment. Most of the time.

The Power of Three

© 2019 Steve Milton

Book 3 in the series *Three Straight*

One (Dane)

"I didn't know a fist could do that." Mouth agape, Asher stared inside the steam sauna window. He was absentmindedly splashing bubbling hot water on his six-pack.

"It's rude to stare." I shook my head. Mustering my best politeness, I tried to keep my eyes off of what was happening inside that steam sauna. I wasn't a voyeur. Or at least I didn't want to be thought of as one. "It's rude to stare at people making love." I gave Asher a look that was a silent *tsk tsk*.

"We're cops, man." Asher laughed. He leaned his head back against the hot tub's ledge. "We're supposed to watch all the action."

Asher splashed hot water on his hairy chest, like irrigating a forest, or putting out a fire. The twin bonfires of his nipples only grew brighter from the hot water.

"Yeah." I whispered down into the water, in my best police officer insider-talk voice. "We're supposed to make an arrest if we see illegal activity. Not watch it for our own amusement."

"Amusement?" Asher grinned. He lay his hands behind his head and leaned back again, showing his muscled triceps and his hairy armpits to the world — or at least to me. "What makes you think I'm finding their homosexual activities amusing?"

"Physical evidence, dude." I glanced at Asher's engorged purple dickhead just barely rising out of the water, like a lazy turtle. I wasn't into checking out dudes, but when Asher got hard in the hot tubs — the size of that thing made it impossible to ignore.

"I'm just—" Asher smiled, or maybe smirked, just a little knowingly. He'd been caught checking out the show, and enjoying it. "I'm just admiring the talent involved here."

I let myself glance inside the sauna porthole. At least for a second. Collecting reconnaissance, in police-speak.

In the heat of the steam sauna, three dudes were playing hopscotch, or something like it. Two of them stood on all fours. A third dude crouched behind them. He was doing something unholy to

291

the other two dudes and I didn't really want to see more than that. I looked away.

"I— I guess it's a talent. But we shouldn't be treating it like a live sex show." I said the last two words a full few notches quieter, with an abundance of caution.

We were the law, after all. Not just any part of the law, but supposedly the finest the law had to offer. Highly decorated. So highly regarded that nobody asked any questions about our daily afternoon patrols of the Russian bathhouse in South Beach.

Dane Wurlitzer and Asher Lane: absolutely unimpeachable as the Miami PD's finest. And here we were, staring at a gay sauna orgy like it was a peep show.

Not only that, but Boris Yorshenko was — if not my friend, then at least my acquaintance. Staring at some dude railing Boris's ass felt doubly rude.

"Maybe we should, umm—" I slid down to submerge my whole body in the hot water. I opened my eyes for just a second in the stinging hot water. Asher's upward-pointing dick stood out in the water like a big beige column. I quickly shut my eyes and slid up again, hot all over, flushed, and somehow reinvigorated. "Maybe we should say something to those guys. Give them a warning."

"Yeah?" Asher laughed. He mimicked my move and slid himself way down. He pushed his legs out. He blew bubbles under the water's surface and his muscular, hairy legs brushed against mine. Maybe he was also staring at my dick. "You first, man. You go tell your buddy Boris that the party's over. Or that he's under arrest. Shit."

"I don't think I'm gonna be having that conversation with Boris." I shook my head. I'd have had no problem arresting friends for serious crimes. But Boris having a little fun in the sauna — it just wasn't handcuffs-worthy. "You know I respect him."

Asher laughed at me. His white teeth spread everywhere, like a shark's just before the moment of ripping into the prey. "Would it be awkward to talk with your buddy Boris in that condition?" Asher grinned, satisfied with where he was leading the discussion. "You know, when he's got some dude's fist coming out of his mouth?"

Asher pantomimed. He held his right fist up to his mouth and wagged it around. Like it was saying hello to me.

I laughed and slapped the surface of the hot tub water like it was a tabletop. "Asher, what the fuck—"

"Yes, Dane we call this a Russian dental exam." Asher stared at me. "Keep your mouth closed when you visit the dentist. Only open your ass wide for the fist." He wagged his fist out of his mouth again.

"Dental exam?" I tried to sound reproachful but I ended up laughing, splashing water all over Asher's body and mine. Like always, the more I tried to reprimand Asher for his filthy sense of humor, the more I let on that I was enjoying his jokes.

Asher wagged his fist and mumbled in a nasal voice: "Urrgghh, Dane's fist is inside me, and it came out the other end!"

"What the fuck." I shook my head. "Are you fucking Kermit the Frog or what?"

"No, man. I'm not Kermit the Frog." Asher shook his head with a serious look. Then he pointed with his eyes inside the steam room. He wagged his fist again. "But some dude's still puppeteer-deep in Boris. Full-on *Muppets* revival in there."

"You're kind of sick." I fake-winced at Asher. It wasn't the first time I'd told him that. The part I never mentioned was how much I enjoyed his kind of humor.

"Am I making you uncomfortable?" Asher asked. His lilting voice didn't sound apologetic. It sounded triumphant.

"Maybe." I sucked air through my teeth and splashed water on Asher's hairy chest in front of me.

"Am I making you uncomfortable? Am I?" Asher put two fists up to his mouth and gyrated them around like some kind of weird boxing exercise. "Oh my God, two fists popping out of my mouth! It's Boris's threesome!"

"Yeah, man." I sighed, keeping my latent laugh under control. "You're making me uncomfortable."

"So tell me the surprise you have for me." Asher clicked his tongue. I'd mentioned the surprise to him and he hadn't let go of it. I'd been hoping to make the million-dollar security job more of a surprise. "The thing you mentioned when we were parking here and you said you'd tell me more about it later."

"Oh shit, man." I splashed more hot water at Asher's chest. "I guess I can tell you a bit."

"Let me guess." Asher flashed his permanently mischievous grin. "You and Boris are inviting me to a threesome?"

"No!" I sighed. "It's not that kind of surprise."

"Foursome?" Asher smiled wider.

"No, man." I shook my head and tried to look exasperated, though I was mostly just amused. "It's a business opportunity kind of surprise."

"I'm not sending any money to a kidnapped Albanian prince." Asher's head disappeared under the waterline again. He blew bubbles up through the bubbly hot tub water. He tickled my shins with his toes.

"Nope. Not that kind of opportunity." I splashed hot water on my own chest. Somehow on my own hairless, tattooed chest, the water wasn't as fun to watch as it was when it splashed on Asher's jungle of chest hair. "Private security job kind of thing."

"You gonna send me to make twelve bucks an hour patrolling for shoplifters?" Asher rolled his eyes. "We're a little too senior to be taking those kinds of jobs, aren't we?"

"How about a million bucks for a year-long job?" I dropped the *m*-word. It was an easy way to make anybody pay attention.

"The fuck?" Asher shook his head. "I don't wanna go work oil security in Iraq. My dad needs me here. You know that."

"Naw, I'm the military dude here." I shrugged. "This job doesn't involve any serious risk of violence."

"And it pays a million dollars a year?" Asher wiped water out of his eyes as he shook his head.

"Half a million, actually." I lowered my voice a bit, like I was revealing a secret — because I kind of was. "Half a million per man per year. And you know I don't need the money. You can have it."

"No, no." Asher sighed and shook his head. That was always an undercurrent of contention between us: my billion-dollar trust fund, his million-dollar medical debt. His refusal to allow me to use part A to clear out his problem with part B. "I told you I don't want your money, Dane."

"Not giving you any money, man." I smiled. "I negotiated it with the bankers already. You get paid nine hundred ninety nine thousand and nine hundred ninety-nine dollars per year. I get paid a buck. Just a matter of salaries, you know. I'm not giving you anything."

"Bankers? This a bank guard job?" Asher scrunched his nose just a little. That was also one of his classic calendar poses. Every Christmas, our benefit calendar had Asher scrunching his nose at a bowl of cranberry sauce, and every summer, it was at a glass of lemonade. That scrunched nose thing — Asher knew how to work it.

"No. We're not protecting a bank." I shook my head, imagining all kinds of Keystone Cops scenarios. "But there are bankers who want to protect a rich dude who's got himself a stalker."

"And how did these bankers magically find us? They liked my calendar photoshoots or something?" Asher wasn't shy about his claim to fame. "They wanna make a deposit?" He stood up in the tub, held his arms above his head, and shook his ass side-to-side.

"No, man," I loudly whispered. "And sit the fuck down. You're an officer of the law."

"But a damn good looking officer of the law." Asher nodded with a smug grin. "Is that how the bankers found me?"

"No. The bankers in question don't browse muscleboy catalogs." I sighed.

"Well, maybe they should." Asher nodded earnestly.

I tried to look like I was regarding Asher with pity. I loved this ridiculous back-and-forth with him.

"Our prospective client's family uses the same private bankers as my family." I was definitely in for some ribbing saying that, but Asher already knew all my financial secrets.

"Oops, sorry, Mister Wurlitzer billionaire!" Asher used his right hand to squirt water in my face. He leaned back in the tub and with his left hand pretended to jerk his dick. He even made an orgasm face just for my benefit. "So this dude is also Billiony McBillionface, like you?"

"I guess." I sighed. "His bankers at Goldman Sachs know my family and know that I'm a cop. Even know that I'm a pretty good cop."

"Golden Cocks?" Asher grinned.

"Yeah. Goldman Sachs." I took the chance to lean back in the hot tub. Under the waterline, my shins grazed against Asher's hairy legs. "So apparently the bankers were like, *Yeah, we know somebody trustworthy who can protect Blair. Not gonna be after his money, because his family banks with us too.*"

"Blair?" Asher made a swooshy hand gesture. "This guy's name is *Blair?*"

"Yeah."

"*Blair?* Is he hiring us to go elbow-deep in him or what?" Asher held up his two fists again and wiggled them again. I had to laugh again. A lot.

"If you've kept up with the latest science, Asher, and I'm sure you have." I splashed more hot water in his general direction. My sweeping hand almost hit the tip of his dick sticking out of the water. "Sexual orientation is not determined by being named *Blair.*"

"Alright." Asher shrugged, still grinning. "Just wanted to make sure we're not hired to be the million-dollar assboys."

"Not that there's anything wrong with that." I tried to look serious.

"Right." Asher laughed. "Not that there's anything wrong with million-dollar assboys. Still. Just the name. *Blair.*" If there was a way to give a homosexual air to a monosyllable, Asher did it with the way he said *Blair*.

"Ever heard of—" I looked around to make sure nobody could see or hear. Boris's threesome was still doing whatever the hell they were doing, and there was nobody else in the bath house but those three and us. "Blair Hamilton? Canadian billionaire?"

"Yeah, the dude with that stupid ASMR app." Asher rolled his eyes.

"That stupid ASMR app you and I both bought?" I smiled at Asher. Getting automated ASMR on my phone was worth five bucks.

"Yeah, that ASMR app, I guess. What about Blair Hamilton though?"

"That's him." I clicked my tongue. "That's the dude we're protecting."

"The guy nobody's ever seen? How the fuck can we protect him?" Now Asher looked earnestly concerned.

"Apparently he's in Miami, and going out in public now. Cutting the rug."

"Rug?" Asher stared down at his pubic hair. He went digging through his pubes with his hands, as if his joke hadn't clear enough.

"Figure of speech—" I shook my head disapprovingly. "Anyway, Blair Hamilton, that Blair Hamilton. If we can get the contract. It'll be a nice thing." I pulled myself up out of the hot tub and stood above Asher, talking down at him.

"Why I gotta look at your hairy ass though?" Asher asked.

"Get up out of the tub, Asher, so you can look at my face, not my ass." I clicked my tongue.

"Good idea." Asher stood up in the tub. Hands on his head, he did a side-to-side dance and gyrated and pumped his ass. He always got into a stripper act when naked, or even half-naked.

He knew he had fans, and the whole department teased him enough about whether he was auditioning to strip. Having to watch Asher's gluteal gyrations must've been the natural consequence of how much we teased him for being a showoff.

I grabbed a towel and wrapped it around my waist. My dickhead dangled just below the towel's edge. At least I wasn't perpetually hard like Asher. The shower towels always looked fucking ridiculous wrapped around Asher's waist; they should have had a hem for his stiff dick.

"Putting on a towel already?" Asher grinned, then pointed toward the sauna room with his eyes. "Aren't we going into the sauna to pay a visit to Boris?"

"I don't think they need any help in there, man." I shook my head and looked down at our feet. Asher was moving his feet in rhythm with an imaginary something. "Are you fucking dancing again?"

"You know, dancing because I'm happy."

"Yeah, put your clothes back on, Asher, and let's get out of here. We've got a patrol shift to finish."

Asher's dick swung left and right as he shook his ass and flexed his arms like a bodybuilder. He didn't even bother to wear a towel. He leaned in closely to my face. Water droplets only made his face more radiant, more uniquely handsome. He spoke softly and confidently: "I don't need a patrol shift. I'm the million-dollar ass boy."

Two (Asher)

Key West: a hell of a drive. A hundred twenty miles. At least nobody knew me there. Other than Brooks.

Three hours' drive in the evening to get to the nine P.M. show. Three hours' drive back to Miami in the wee hours.

And three hours of whatever the fuck you called what I'd been doing on stage and in the back rooms of Meat Market every weekend night.

Five hundred bucks on a good night, meaning a night when Brooks was there. Maybe with the extra cash I could somehow catch up on six months of late mortgage payments and get my shitty-but-mine condo out of foreclosure.

At least the driving didn't feel as fucking weird as the other stuff did. The other stuff, the dancing and whatever else happened afterward, was — whatever it was, it made money, and I was doing it voluntarily, so how could I complain?

Miami had those clubs too. But it was too damn close to work. Maybe the female officers were having a girls' night out? Maybe some of the non-closeted cop dudes were having a guys' night out? Maybe some fuckhead wanted to take video?

I couldn't risk any of it.

Cops were allowed to moonlight as security guards or Uber drivers or maybe even respectably clothed fashion models. Not as thinly disguised prostitutes.

I parked my ratty Prius behind the Meat Market Club, under the sign reading *Please Enter From The Rear*.

I checked in. "Checking in" meant paying boss man fifty dollars for the privilege. For the privilege to dance there that night.

"Asher Lane, checking in," I said to Arnold, the boss man sitting at a decrepit wooden coffee table in the corner. I sat down in a chair across from him at the same coffee table, the one with the female anatomy cataloged with knife-scratched diagrams. It was like at the police station: don't ever be physically talking down at the chief, because he might feel challenged and do something stupid to assert his authority.

"Checking in, schmecking in," the boss man cawed. His bad breath permeated the already putrid club air in the small space between us. "Pay your fee if you wanna work tonight."

I could take bad breath when there was money to be made. Any money-making venture involved contact with something unpleasant.

"You know I don't make much here, Arnold. I didn't even make back the fifty last time." I was lying. Brazenly. Last time I took home over five hundred bucks of Brooks's money. But another dancer had warned me that if boss man found out how much money Brooks was giving me, he'd raise my fifty-dollar fee to more like a few hundred.

"Pay your fifty buckaroos or go find another job." Arnold sighed. His sigh came up from the most putrid cavern of his halitosis.

"I just don't know if I can make it back." I was lying. But it was the only way to protect myself from that fifty going up to five hundred. I'd heard enough stories.

"You're welcome to go dance on South Beach by yourself and see if you do any better." Arnold laughed uproariously. He'd apparently made a funny.

"Ah. Ok. I think I can come up with fifty dollars." I pulled out the notes as if they were my last. Arnold took them from me giving me a look as if I was severely underpaying him.

I'd told Dad I was working as a bouncer to make extra money for his cancer bills. I thought of that term, *bouncer*, every time I bounced my ass and dick on stage. This kind of bouncer paid better than that kind of bouncer. At least I wasn't trying to pay off a million-dollar medical debt by working as a ten-dollar-an-hour type of bouncer.

My kind of bouncing paid a lot better. Especially when Brooks was there. He always wore the same fucking pink Oxford shirt and khaki shorts.

Who was I to complain? In that shirt and shorts he had stacks of ATM-fresh twenties he stuffed in all my orifices. He dealt in twenties, not hundreds; that's how I knew he wasn't some kind of gangster.

He was always in the front row. He always tipped every other dancer a polite twenty. He must've considered that a consolation tip. Shit.

Then I came on. Macklemore, "Thrift Shop." It was always my first song. I wore my best vintage-style New Balance sneakers. My hipster-ironic Christmas sweater. My plaid pants. Even pink-hearts underwear.

Not that I was any kind of genius at stripping, but nobody else put that much effort into their costumes and producing their whole show. But then, the other strippers were just Key West beach boys and barflies looking for extra cash. I was a real professional, driving three hours down from Miami Thursday, Friday, and Saturday nights—

"Private dance?" Brooks asked me when I lay on the stage with legs in the air, pulling off my pants. It was the same every time.

"Of course. I missed you." I smiled as best I could. I missed Brooks's money at least.

Still lying on the stage, I pulled my pants ceiling-ward. Off they went. I kicked my legs in the air like I was doing the bicycle in high school gym.

Only pink-heart tighty-whiteys covered my ass. That bit of the costume, I'd had to actually buy, not just fish out of the police station's unclaimed-clothes box.

Brooks's right hand held a thick stack of twenties. His left hand was running along the waistband of my briefs. As I lay on the stage gyrating my body and ass, each bill went in under my waistband. Each insertion was aided by Brooks's hand: he was getting a bit of a feel of my waist and pubes. That was justified, considering how much money he was giving me, and what he'd be getting later anyway.

The twenties peeking out of my briefs looked like tassels. Me decorated like that, Brooks would be getting his Christmas.

The way he arranged them in my waistband, he seemed more interested in the decorative aesthetics of the bills decorating the entirety of my waistband and his hands arranging those bills, than in how much money he was spending — just that waistband bit he did every time he saw me was a good five hundred bucks in twenties. That kind of money went a long way when I had collection agencies on my ass.

Still on my back, I wriggled my whole body like a snake. My ass high in the air, I snapped off my briefs. Twenties went flying. No matter where they flew, they were all mine. Brooks smiled like he was perfectly confident of what would happening next.

Of course what Brooks wanted to happen, happened. I got totally naked on stage and he was able to stick a few more twenties in my ass crack before I gathered up my cash from the stage and announced I'd be available for private dances.

In theory, private dances were for anyone who had sixty dollars to their name. Of course I'd only go with Brooks. He made it rain so hard in that private room—

To the sound of "Walk This Way," I danced on the tiny stage in front of him. Naked. Swing left, swing right. Let my dick fly through the air with all its force. Thrust, thrust, thrust, like I was fucking the air. Step hard. Look down and smile at Brooks.

He crowded his tall, slim body onto what looked like a wooden kitchen chair. With all the money the club made, could they really not afford better furniture?

I'd get a payday. Again. Thinking about the money made me hard. There was a little more making me hard: there was the Viagra the manager dispensed to the dancers as we showed up for work. That was partly what the fifty-dollar house fee paid for.

I couldn't believe it when they first made me the offer, that I'd have to pay to work there. It all worked out. As long as Brooks was in the house, I easily made a thousand dollars a night.

Brooks stood up. He wrapped his arms around my lower back, his palms on my ass. He loved worshipping my abs. I knew that. I pumped my six back for him and gyrated and flexed all my core.

His lips and tongue traced every muscle in my abs, like he was drawing a map. Maybe it would've felt good, if I was gay, if it was my boyfriend or whatever doing it. But this was just getting licked and fondled for money, and that's all I'd let it be.

Brooks's lips moved down to my pubes. He always pushed his nose into my pubes and sniffed, hard, and muttered something about how much he loved my "man sweat."

Man sweat, I had plenty of. I was working a full-time police job, then driving six hours round-trip for my second job. I had no problem producing man sweat.

My dick was already hard from the mandatory start-of-shift Viagra. Brooks's lips moving down to the base of it — it was a physiological reaction, not a gay thing, just a simple matter of stimulus-response. I was fucking hard.

Like always, I eased myself down to lie at the edge of the private room's mini-stage. I rested my back on the cool linoleum floor of the stage. It must've been dirty, but dirty was my business now. My legs hung over the edge of the stage. My feet rested on Brooks's chair.

My dick pointed at the ceiling, awaiting the inevitable grasp of Brooks's warm, wet lips. The song changed to "Come As You Are." Shit. I couldn't help but think of double entendres.

His lips gripped my shaft, tightly. His teeth must've been resting on my balls. Lying back on the stage, looking up at the filthy ceiling, I wasn't really looking. My dickhead grazed the roof of his mouth.

In sync with the Nirvana song, I slowly pumped upward to fuck his mouth. Up and down. He bobbed his warm, wet mouth up and down on my dick about twice as fast as I could thrust with my hips.

His cool hands palmed my ass cheeks. Somehow that always drove me to orgasm. I didn't dare ask whether I took long enough or whether he wanted to suck dick fast or slow, but when he lay his palms on my ass was always when I came. Maybe he knew that was our signal.

The cold of his hands and the heat of his mouth — I shook. Even my thighs and knees shook. My hands tried to grab at the linoleum floor.

My crotch felt like it was on autopilot. I bucked up into his mouth. A gob of thick cum shot out of my dick and deep into Brooks's mouth. *Gulp*: he swallowed it all, like always.

He squeezed both my ass cheeks and I shot another rope of cum. He gulped and swallowed again.

I let myself relax and let go of the rest of my load into Brooks. He loved swallowing my cum, so why not give it to him? My leg muscles relaxed. My stomach muscles. I was all-over relaxed. Even my mind was relaxed: this was the dude that would give me a fat stack of twenties for that climax into his mouth.

I breathed deeply and lay back on the linoleum floor, as if I was doing a relaxation exercise. My cum was cleared. My money was made. I didn't even really have to dance the rest of the night. And this Brooks dude was still nuzzling my fat dick in his mouth, like he always did.

I went softer. He slurped the last drops of my cum off of my dickhead, then slowly licked it clean. When he let my dick out of his mouth, he caught it into his hand and looked at it, then looked at me, with a satisfied smile.

He'd always put a stack of twenties under my ass cheeks and disappear somewhere. This time though — he stood looking over me: tall, slim, perfectly upright, with a head of wavy light-brown hair above a boyish face.

He was a good-looking dude, actually. He could've held his own on the gay circuit in Key West or even Miami. I'd peeked into the bars. Those guys were intimidating, but still no more handsome than

Brooks. Maybe Brooks was married or closeted or shy or something. Like me. I was "or something."

I lay on the stage, looking at him and at the ceiling, my eyes half-shut. He stood next to the stage, positioned himself between my legs, and leaned down toward my face.

His lips were approaching mine. His breath smelled like mint. His breathing was steady. His eyes were looking directly into mine. HIs eyelashes were more beautiful than any woman's I'd seen.

I panicked.

This was the best-paying gig I'd ever had, but I wasn't gay. I wasn't going to kiss this dude. I was— whatever I was, I wasn't gay.

Panic ran through me. I turned my head abruptly to the side. Brooks landed a soft kiss on my cheek.

That didn't feel so terrible. It was just a kiss on my cheek.

Even the blowjob he gave me hadn't felt so bad. Physical reactions. Neurotransmitters and all that. Just a physical response, not a gay thing. So what if I had that kind of physical response to men? Maybe after some more practice-dating, I could have that sort of response with women too.

Brooks stood over me and whispered: "You're beautiful. See you tomorrow." Fine. He could call me beautiful if he was paying me.

I nodded. I kept my eyes away from his eyes. I didn't want to invite anything else.

That kiss on the cheek was enough. More than enough.

Three (Dane)

"Come on, Asher. Hurry up. This is a job interview, not Miami's Next Top Model." I sighed into the phone. But my sigh was more like a growl. I didn't want to sound like a whiny little bitch.

Asher came running down the outdoor concrete stairs of his low-rise condo building. He looked way too well-dressed to be living in that dump of a condo building. But then, the condo was his, and he was proud of it. Dressing like a superstar didn't cost as much as a an upscale Miami condo would have.

Asher must've spent all morning upstyling his hair. It looked like an illustration of tempestuous sea waves, as if he'd just walked out of a mousse commercial.

In the late-morning Miami sun, his pressed white shirt looked like hot flame. Even his shoes: the dude couldn't wear plain old Nikes or something. He had his fucking Donald Pliner driving slippers that he was so proud of. He could've been a costume designer. Even when Asher was in police uniform, he was so proud of it — it felt like he was showing off a costume.

Asher pulled open the door of my old Mercedes and slid his six-foot-three frame into the seat.

"Were you bleaching your asshole?" I asked, with a grin. "Is that what took so long?"

"Sugaring my taint." Asher nodded seriously. "When I get a Brazilian, it just isn't smooth enough. And you know our new client likes taints to be super-smooooooth." Asher made a gliding motion with his hand.

"You always take this kind of talk to the next level, Asher." I had to laugh and back down from any attempt to match his level of graphic sex talk. Getting into a gross-out contest with Asher was like bringing a knife to a gunfight. I knew better than to attempt it.

"I'm still not getting how Blair Hamilton is planning to pay us a million dollars without us sucking his dick." Asher shook his head and looked at me like I was concealing something, maybe a secret prostitution task that I wasn't telling him about.

"Have faith, man. There's no fellatio required." I started the engine and pulled out into traffic.

My hand-me-down Mercedes growled deeply. That growl was the only tangible memory I had of my grandfather. My billion-dollar trust fund was from him too, but it wasn't something I could touch and hear.

"Alright, I trust you." Asher nodded. He put up his palms in front of him and wagged his tongue out. "There's no fellatio required. We're only required to provide our good man a few friendly rimjobs, and a little felching."

"No, dude." I laughed. "No rimjobs. No ass-licking. Nothing like that is required. I promise."

"Mmm!" Asher shouted. He put his tongue out so far it almost touched the windshield. Then he grabbed his tongue with his fingers. "If I can stretch out my tongue a bit more, it can reach Blair Hamilton's prostate! Maybe there's a bonus for that! Look, I stuck my tongue so deep in his ass that I licked his prostate!"

"You're sick, man." I used the back of my hand to cover my laugh.

"Only getting ready to be a million-dollar ass boy."

"Sure, sure." I nodded at him. I tried to be the stable, responsible one, even if in reality I often felt like Asher was the more grounded one of us. I weaved through the Miami traffic in my ancient Mercedes coupe and caught glances of Asher in his reflection on the windshield.

"Where are we meeting Richie McRich, anyway? You driving us to fucking Fisher Island or Coral Gables or something?"

"Just on his yacht. Dinner Key Marina."

"Oh! His yacht! So faaahncy!" Asher again put up his hands to his mouth. He used his hands to part Blair's imaginary ass cheeks, then stuck out his real tongue and licked inside the imaginary ass. "Blair Hamilton is so rich that his prostate is actually a five-carat diamond!"

"Dude." I shook my head. "I hope you tone that talk down for our meeting."

"Of course." Asher nodded and adjusted his hair in the visor mirror. "Perfectly calm and professional. That's me. Lieutenant Asher Lane, Miami PD."

"Seriously, man." I took my eyes off the road for a second and stared directly at Asher. "I worry about you. About your money situation. I hope we can get this security gig going."

"My fault for co-signing financial responsibility for my dad's cancer treatment." Asher sighed. "And I'd do it again in a second."

"I know, man. I know. I just hope this thing can help you out. Since you won't let me help you directly."

"I'm not taking your money, Mister Wurlitzer billionaire heir, no matter how many times you offer it to me." Asher laughed and shook his head. "Your grandpa made that money for you, not for me."

"The offer's still open." I looked at Asher's blue eyes to remind him sternly, as I did every once in a while, that I was capable and willing of writing him a half-million-dollar check for that medical debt and my trust fund wouldn't even feel it. "I know you turn it down, but it's still open."

"I'm not taking any of your Wurlitzer family money." Asher smiled. His voice turned to a whisper. "I do tremendously appreciate it. As much as I give you shit about your offering to pay off my debt. I do really appreciate. The answer is still *no*."

"Yeah." I sighed. I'd once surreptitiously slid a check for half a million dollars, payable to Asher Lane, into his police station locker. The next day I found the same check, torn up, in my own locker. "At least I'm hoping this security job will solve your money bind."

"Seriously, man?" Asher looked at me. "I really want it to. I feel like shit being a cop chased by bill-collectors like a fucking criminal."

"Marina slip number sixty-nine." I pointed up ahead into the marina parking lot. Rows of yachts bobbed slowly in the water. The air smelled like ocean salt. "We're supposed to meet Blair Hamilton on his yacht at slip number sixty-nine."

"I promise not to comment." Asher cleared his throat while staring into the visor mirror to examine a blackhead on his nose.

"This isn't time for your facial." I looked over at him. I knew him too well, including his habit of playing with his pimples on patrol duty. "Playing with your blackheads will only make them stand out more. Let's go." I grinned. Even beautiful perfect Asher had his moments of silly weakness.

Asher popped his passenger door open. He was first out of the car. I was still messing with the parking brake and sun visor while he stood next to the car, assaying the land. Our feet stirred up small clouds of Florida gravel dust in the parking lot.

"So, seriously?" Asher asked. "Slip sixty-nine?"

"The slip numbers are not assigned randomly, Asher." I shook my head. I also had rich relatives who'd do shit like that. "There's probably a waiting list for number sixty-nine. I know rich people."

"You *are* rich people." Asher clicked his tongue at me.

"And you *are* smartass people." I pointed at Asher and clicked my tongue right back at him.

"The million dollar smartass boy, you mean." Asher nodded proudly.

"Yeah. I hope we can get it. Let's go." I led the way down the line of boat slips.

Sixty-three. Sixty-five. Sixty-seven. The yachts were all pretty much the same.

Then there was sixty-nine. It was bigger. Much bigger.

"I'm thinking of that meme," Asher whispered.

"Which one?"

"Put the regular yacht at sixty-seven next to the mega yacht at sixty-nine. And it's like *Meet my son.*"

"Yeah. Blair Hamilton's boat is the dad here I believe." I gave the boat an approving nod. As if the boat cared about my nods. As if anybody at Dinner Key Marina cared about what Asher and I thought about anything.

"Yo!" Asher shouted out toward the boat at slip sixty-nine.

"Professional, Asher. Be professional." I regretted the spittle I sent into Asher's face with those words. "We're interviewing for a job with a billionaire, not looking for a game of pickup basketball."

"You don't have to fucking spit in my face, man." Asher smiled at me. Then he waved his perfectly manicured hand toward slip sixty-nine. "Mister Hamilton! We're here to meet you regarding the job opportunity!"

It sounded thirsty and stupid and awkward, like we were about to meet a school principal to beg forgiveness for some escapade that included toilet paper and spray foam. Not that I was capable of coming up with any better approach to Blair. My family was as rich as his, but I'd spent my life pretending otherwise, being a regular cop, and only knowing to address billionaires as *mom* and *dad*.

We kept walking toward the boat. Nothing was happening around it. It was just — there. The windows all around it were tinted black.

"Hello!" Asher yelled again. I was usually the first one in to dangerous situations, but Asher was definitely the PR man of our duo. "Blair Hamilton! We're here to meet with you!"

On the yacht's top deck, a door swung open. It flapped a bit in the ocean breeze.

Out stepped a tall, lean man, with sandy brown hair. Bright sunlight hit his face. He winced and retreated back inside the cabin.

"Blair Hamilton!" Asher yelled up at where that door had closed. "We're your security detail, man! Or we want to be, at least." The last part sounded a bit deflatory.

The tall man emerged again on the top deck. He nodded at us. He jogged down the stairs to the bottom deck. He wasn't nearly as graceful as Asher in running down stairs, but he still very much radiated his own confident style: the sort of man whose eyes tell his servants *well, what are you waiting for?* without even saying a word.

Having descended the stairs, Blair walked on the bottom deck, toward the gate to the gangplank that would take him out to the slip.

He stopped. Hard. Cartoonishly hard. Like he'd hit a glass pane.

Standing at the lower deck railing, he stared down at us. He stared more at Asher than at me. But he stared. Hard.

He must've infected Asher with stare-itis, because Asher was staring back at him just as hard.

Blair looked at us, then looked down at the water below his yacht. He took a step forward and peered again over the deck's edge.

He jumped. Off the yacht's deck. Down. Toward the water.

Blair flew through the air haphazardly, hands and arms flaying, like a man who all his life had never jumped off anything. His shirt sleeves flapped like a flag in the wind. He hit the water. He flapped around for a second. Then he disappeared somewhere under the yacht's hull.

"Shit." I looked to Asher like he could do something about Blair being in the water.

"Shit," I repeated. Asher was still staring blankly into the water, like Blair Hamilton's diving skills had him under a spell.

I repeated myself: "Shit shit shit. Shit. Shit shit shit." As if my first two shits hadn't conveyed the message clearly enough.

I didn't have any choice. We were supposed to protect this dude. Even if we weren't contracted to protect him, we were off-duty cops. And even if we weren't off-duty cops, although we were off-duty cops, rescuing a hapless and helpless dude doggy-paddling in the marina water was a matter of common human decency.

I started to jump. Then I remembered: my clothes, my shoes. I kicked off my shoes, threw down my pants, nearly tore off my shirt, and dropped them all on the pier.

Was I supposed to take off my underwear in these situations? What did they do in the movies? Or at least in the cartoons? I wasn't sure. But I took off my underwear. I could use it later. If I survived this.

"Watch these," I said to Asher. That must've been the most ridiculous request I'd ever made of my patrol partner. But he didn't even notice. His eyes were stuck on the water, the same way they were previously stuck on the boat's tinted windows. It was like the sight of Blair Hamilton was hypnotizing, or terrifying.

Without any acknowledgment from Asher, I jumped into the water. It was warmer than I expected. But it smelled a lot worse than expected. The aroma was a mix of gasoline, algae, and sewage. And there I was, ass-naked, absorbing it all.

I paddled in the same direction as Blair had gone.

Blair was there, under the hull. He treaded water. Occasionally he reached up toward the boat's hull, as if it had grab handles for him to hold on to. It didn't have any grab handles for him to hold on to. He was palming at smooth fiberglass. He most likely hadn't done this too often.

"Let me rescue you." I said. It felt stupid. I was naked. There wasn't anything better to say to Blair. "I'll get you out of this mess."

"Who's that dude with you? What's he doing here?" Blair cocked his head in Asher's direction.

"That dude? He's my partner on the force." I must've forgotten I was in a nasty urban marina, not a swimming pool, because I let water into my mouth. I spat it out violently, trying not to register the toxic taste.

"Partner? On the force?" Blair looked up toward the dock."That dude — he's a cop?"

"He's a good-looking cop, isn't he?" I smiled. I felt like Asher's pimp. It wasn't particularly the most appropriate thing to say.

"Shit. Yeah. I guess." Blair shrugged while treading water.

I swam close enough to touch him. How exactly was I supposed to rescue him? I awkwardly made a motion like I'd put my arm around him and he looked at me like I was a serial killer about to drown him.

Blair looked toward the dock. "Are there stairs here or something?"

"I don't think so." I looked around. "I don't think the marina's designed for swimming." I swam in semi-circles around Blair. I was looking useful. "I can — I can help you — I don't know how."

"Fucking hell." Blair spat some of that same marina water out through his mouth. If it tasted horrible for me, I could only imagine how horrible it tasted for Blair Hamilton.

"I could rescue you. By. Um—" I looked around. There had to be a flotation device of some kind at a marina. At least that was how it worked in the movies. "Asher! Dude!" I yelled, and Asher looked in my direction with some pain in his eyes, like maybe just the sight of Blair Hamilton hurt his delicate constitution. "Asher, can you throw me, like, a floatie ring? I need to rescue Blair Hamilton!"

"A floatie ring?" Asher asked. His voice was blank, like he wasn't really paying attention.

"Like in the cartoons!" I screamed. It wasn't the most professional thing for a guard to be yelling. "The floating ring they always throw to the man overboard in cartoons."

"Oh!" Asher speed-walked up and down the dock. He approached a post and a booth with an emergency phone. He looked around it. There seemed to be some kind of flotation ring there. "Got it!" Asher yelled. "We've got this, Mister Hamilton!"

Asher took it off the post. He held it in his right hand. He stood to the side and put his arm back, like he was going to throw a frisbee. He threw. The heavy flotation ring went *thud* a few feet in front of Asher.

"Dude!" I yelled at him. I paddling hard to raise myself slightly in the water. It would make my yelling more authoritative. No one took reprimands seriously from a man who looked like he couldn't even tread water properly. "Put some more feeling into throwing that ring over here. You're saving our lives, man. Don't phone it in."

"Yeah," Asher said. He was still looking blankly. He picked up the flotation ring off the ground in front of him. He stood at the boat slip's edge and looked down on me and Blair flopping around in the water.

Asher squatted down, holding the ring in his arms.

"Asher!" I shook my head and winced. "Throw that ring over here. This isn't squats or whatever."

"Yeah." Asher nodded. He tiptoed to the dock's very edge over the water and twisted his whole body like a wind-up doll, ready to throw that flotation ring hard.

He threw it hard, twisting through the whole motion, putting all his muscle into it, just at the dock's edge.

He tumbled face-first off the dock and into the water, ring still in his hand.

At least he wouldn't drown.

He hit the water and looked over to me like it was all my fault.

"Shit!" I had to say it again, even though the more I said it, the worse things became.

"What the fuck?" Blair Hamilton, pink oxford shirt at all, was shaking his head in reprimand at us. "You guys are supposed to be rescuing me?"

"We are." I nodded vigorously at Blair. Maybe if I could make myself believe it, I could make Blair believe it too. "We're performing a two-man rescue."

"Fuck." Blair shook his head. He reached down below the waterline and took the shoes off his feet. He threw them and they actually landed on the dock. "Two man rescue — Is that the one where the two men protecting me need to be rescued? Sounds like a fucking joke."

"Asher is just in the water to assist with the rescue," I lied. "Together with the flotation device." I continued swimming semi-circles around Blair, like a hapless moon orbiting a billionaire planet.

"That dude's name is Asher?" Blair glanced in Asher's direction for a half-second, as if looking too long at Asher's perfect face and body would burn his retinas. "And he's supposed to protect me?" Blair smirked and shook his head.

"I brought the safety device!" Asher announced. He slapped the flotation ring with his hand.

"Yeah, you're the expert on bringing a safety device." Blair smirked again at Asher, then shook his head. Whatever the hell that meant.

"I've surveyed the rescue scenario here," Asher called out. He was shameless. He was as clueless as I was, but he'd apparently just found his authoritative public-safety voice. "And it seems that we do have a flotation device, but we have no actual means of levitating ourselves out of the marina."

"Levitating?" I squinted at Asher.

Blair wasn't even squinting particularly at Asher. He just seemed entirely amused by the entire situation.

"Fuck! I just remembered!" Blair said. He lay back and floated on his back and put his hand in the pocket of his shorts. He fished out something that looked like a miniature TV remote control. "I paid fifty thousand dollars for this fucking man overboard system." Blair held up the remote control in the air and held down the red button on it.

As smugly satisfied with his gesture as Blair seemed, nothing was happening. We were still three idiots bobbing like apples in the marina water next to Blair's yacht.

The wind was picking up. The storm clouds above were closing in. it was about time for a regular Miami twenty-minute rainstorm.

Man overboard! a computerized female voice boomed from the yacht. *Man overboard rescue initiated!*

"See? It works. It fucking works." Blair waved his remote control in the air triumphantly, still treading water.

Something like a turret popped out of the yacht's top deck. It folded out into a crane holding what looked like a small cannon.

Man overboard located! the same computerized voice boomed.

"No fucking shit," Asher shouted back at the yacht. "We're right fucking here."

"It's meant for more perilous—" Blair started to say. Boom. A sound like a balloon popping. The cannon shot a floating three-seat raft into the water, attached to a rope. It looked like a playground ride: three seats attached to a floating ring around a central pole that the crane's rope was attached to.

"The system is meant for more perilous conditions, as I was saying." Blair nodded proudly at the bobbing rescue raft that had cost him more than some people's luxury motorboats. "I'm glad I got the three-person version. I don't really have any friends, so I was gonna just get the one-man version."

Here he was, explaining his life-raft shopping choices. While we were in this marina water. He was adorable and precious and out-of-touch, kind of.

Were Asher and I any better? We doggy-paddled right alongside Blair in the murky marina water. We couldn't even get out of the water without Blair's help.

Still a cop, still ostensibly responsible for making this a rescue, I took the initiative and swam to the raft. I clung to one of its seats, my bare ass exposed for the entire sleepy marina to see. My flaccid dick hung just barely above the waterline, like a vestigial anchor.

Naked or not, I still felt responsible, and the very idea of a rescue primed certain instincts in me — ones I'd seldom used since Afghanistan. As Blair swam toward the rescue craft, I grabbed him and brought him closer to the three-man rescue contraption, and sat him down into the second seat. He grabbed hard on to the central grip. Every time he looked at my naked, wet body, he grinned, like he was getting a free show. Nobody had looked at me like that before. I'd thought only Asher got looks like that.

Asher took a few extra seconds to swim in the raft's direction. "We got you, Blair! Rescue time!" Asher yelled, with no sense of irony. He grabbed lifted himself into the third seat and hung on.

Blair took out his remote control and showed it off to both of us, like a bar douche showing off a Maserati keychain. He pressed a second button on it.

The computerized voice on deck answered: *Rescue crane operating. Stay clear.* The raft moved up, inch by inch. It lifted the three of us. Dripping wet like overcooked pasta, we were being lifted out of the water.

We were suspended, dangling, wet, taking a computer-controlled course on the crane lift up from the water and to the yacht's deck. Blair and Asher looked ridiculous in their completely soaked-through shirts and pants. I was bare-ass naked, but somehow it was easy to forget that.

Like the Apollo astronauts on a moon landing, we were set down cautiously on the ship's surface. *Rescue operation completed,* the voice announced. The crane folded itself up like origami and retreated into its turret-like receptacle, which itself retracted back somewhere into the yacht.

Now what?

We still had to sell ourselves: as the people who could protect Blair Hamilton, who were responsible, who would let no calamity befall him.

After he'd just rescued us from marina water with his own yacht's robot-voiced crane.

It was a soft landing. We all stayed on our feet when being set down by the crane. Asher and I were able to maintain that bit of our dignity. I was actually able to think about dignity, despite the cool marina air blowing over my ass cheeks, between my dick and balls, and through my taint.

"I guess I should invite you in?" Blair nodded and walked toward a door to the yacht's interior. Other than the wetness of his outfit, Blair sort of looked like a British gentleman inviting new acquaintances into his drawing room. He tapped his finger on a pad and the door opened.

"Welcome, welcome!" Blair said. The words were so well-modulated and well-rehearsed they could've been coming from a computer. Water was dripping every part of him, even his wet socks, but he hadn't lost any of his poise.

Blair stepped inside the yacht's cabin. Asher and I followed.

"A bit chilly." The air conditioning breeze flew across my body. I folded my arms across my chest.

Blair looked me up and down with more than just a casual glance. "You're more than a bit naked." His eyes definitely stopped at my pubes and dick. It was nice to be admired. Even if my dick wasn't hard, at least it didn't shrink in cold water. I still had a nice dangling piece of man-meat between my legs — nothing like Asher's dick, but then, I never sought to compare with Asher on looks.

"Take off your clothes." I said it to Blair as nonchalantly as I could manage. "You must be freezing."

"For a second I thought you—" Blair smiled at me. He reached to undo his pants.

"You're dripping wet and the A/C here is super cold." I tried really hard not to smile at all, not to let a twinkle out of my eyes. I was perfectly straight. Standing naked in the cabin of this dude's yacht didn't make me gay.

Blair pulled down his jeans. Damp, they required a lot of pushing and pulling on his part. His white ass cheeks hung out naked and exposed — perfectly pale, perfectly globular — while he contorted and strained tugging down at his jeans.

"I guess it's cold here." I looked up at the air conditioning vent and down at my hardening dick. With my hands, I covered my erection.

Blair grinned again — like he knew something. Finally under all his pushing and pulling, his jeans slid down, his briefs together with them. His long, skinny dick popped out like a spring. Uncut, it was as tall and handsome as Blair himself.

Blair looked at my fat, hard dick. "You've got nothing to be embarrassed about there."

"What? Embarrassed?" I tried to act stupid.

"You don't need to cover that big fat cock." Blair's eyebrows danced. "You should be proud of that thing, especially coming out of cold water."

"I need my clothes!" I realized they were outside, on the dock, where I'd torn them off. I jogged down the yacht's interior stairs. Then I stood looking for where to go next.

Naked, Blair leisurely descended the stairs after me. His dick looked like it hardened with his every step down his yacht's spiral staircase. His dickhead glistened with precum. "I need to open that door for you."

Blair scanned his palm across some kind of fingerprint reader. It beeped. The door popped unlocked, like a submarine pressure chamber.

When Blair leaned in to open it completely, his glutes squeezed and contracted like he was pumping and fucking — was that always how dude's asses looked from behind, or was Blair putting on a show for my benefit?

Even more conscious about my erection, I covered it with both hands. I jogged out of the door, onto the lower deck, and across the plank-ramp, into the cool breeze and light drizzle.

Just retrieving my clothes.

While not wearing any.

A police officer galloping, naked, with a hard-on, from Blair Hamilton's yacht at Slip 69 at Dinner Key Marina, grabbing a stack of clothes lying on the dock, and galloping back to the boat. Still obviously erect.

Nothing to see here.

Oh shit.

Clothes under my arm, I leapt back into the air-conditioned confines of Blair's yacht.

The worst part? That somehow being naked in the cabin of Blair Hamilton's yacht felt like refuge.

Blair had already removed his shirt and laid it casually on a table. Tall, lean, and proud, nearly hairless, he seemed to be presiding over the proceedings.

Asher was quietly removing his sopping wet clothes in the mini-bathroom, door wide open.

Asher came back, naked. He was holding his pile of wet clothes under his arm the same way I was holding my pile of dry clothes.

Asher whispered to me: "I can't believe this is our job interview."

"I can't either," I whispered back. "Roll with it."

Who was I even talking to? My superego maybe?

Was I trying to summon the Dane Wurlitzer who would never be naked on a billionaire playboy's yacht? That Dane Wurlitzer still existed. He was naked on a billionaire playboy's yacht.

Four (Asher)

I was on Brooks's yacht. Or Blair Hamilton's yacht. Whichever name that dude went by that particular day.

And this time around, shaking my dick and ass wasn't enough. But the stakes were bigger.

Blair definitely recognized me. His little grins and head-shakes were telltale. I was never the smartest face-reader, but this shit was obvious.

So there we stood: naked and wet on Blair's yacht. I wasn't exactly unaccustomed to being naked in front of strangers, or even strangers staring at my body.

But now Blair and Dane were with me.

Dane shouted from the pantry: "Holy shit, you have like twenty types of organic gourmet tea in here!"

"I don't even know," Blair mumbled. "Somebody stocks that stuff for me."

"Is it alright if I make us three cups of warm-up peppermint tea?" Dane shouted again.

"Fuck if I care," Blair said.

"I'll take that as a qualified *yes*," Dane answered. "Did you know there's a clothes dryer here?"

"Not really," Blair shouted. "I get my laundry picked up."

"Alright." Dane entered the living room again, thick semi-hard dick swinging like a clock pendulum. He jogged up the staircase. After some muttering upstairs, he jogged back down. He held an armful of Blair's wet clothes. "I'll dry these for you."

"Why?" Blair asked. It was oddly blunt from a man who radiated grace and panache.

"Uh, because dry clothes are better than wet clothes?" Dane smiled. "And the only alternative to dry clothes or wet clothes is no clothes. And the novelty of that wears off quickly."

"Does it ever?" Blair laughed and looked at me and Dane. His eyes obviously sized up our dicks.

"Whoa, whoa." Dane shook his head. "We're here for a work interview, nothing more."

"Work interview?" Blair asked. He strolled the length of his nautical living room.

With his long strides and confident glances side-to-side, Blair resembled Napoleon strolling through Versailles, planning his attack.

Allow some differences. Napoleon, at least in the history books, wasn't tall, skinny, and beautiful. Napoleon in the history books definitely wasn't naked.

As Blair walked, his ass cheeks pumped with every step, power-fucking the air. His hard dick swayed right and left as if it hadn't really expected to have so much freedom on a Tuesday afternoon.

"You, or your bankers, are going to hire us as your security contractors, right?" I asked the naked Blair Hamilton, our possible future boss. "Something about a stalker?"

"Really, why are you guys doing this?" Blair asked.

"Doing what? Trying to get the security job?" I laughed. "Because we need the money? Or I need the money." Blair already knew what else I was doing to try to make money.

Dane walked in. He carried a marine-looking piece of plastic that he'd converted into a serving tray, three porcelain mugs of hot tea standing on it. He also had a plastic mini-box of Oreos.

"Tea is served!" Dane called out. "It'll warm you up, Blair. You still look like you're freezing cold. Eat some cookies too."

"Why are you doing all this?" Blair asked Dane point-blank, staring directly at him. I was used to Blair/Brooks from the club in Key West, but even I was a little freaked out by his questioning.

"Rescuing you from the water?" Dane shook his head. "Because I'm a cop, formerly an Army search-rescue specialist in Afghanistan, a human being — trying to help you out?"

"Why did you jump into the water like that?" Blair asked.

"To help you." Dane nodded calmly, as if speaking to a child. "To rescue you, get you out of the water, to provide assistance to a fellow human being. Isn't it obvious why someone would do that?"

"What if — what if I didn't want to be rescued?" Blair suddenly stopped his back-and-forth pacing through the living room. He turned and stared at Dane. His slim figure always looked artistically chiseled; in that moment, he only looked fragile, like a willow branch against the world.

"Blair. Are you — are you saying — am I hearing what I think I just heard?" Dane stared right back at Blair. He had that helpfully clinical gaze, like the best counselor or friend anyone could have ever hoped for.

That was how Dane looked at me when I told him about my money problems, about my loneliness — anything. That was how he looked at me when he told me he'd be setting me up with this million-dollar contract.

"You didn't hear." Blair shook his head, almost violently. "Just a question. A hypothetical. Never mind." He stepped on and kept walking. With each step of his bare feet the yacht's hardwood floors squeaked so slightly that we could hear it only in perfect silence. The marina was dead on a weekday afternoon, save for the distant hum of a generator and squawking seagulls.

"Blair. If the idea of people wanting to help you makes you feel uncomfortable, then—" Dane sighed. "I can play make-believe and tell you that we jumped in to save you because you're a rich guy who can pay us, alright? That's not true, but if it makes you more comfortable, we can play along."

"I mean, like—" Blair shook his head. This perfectly composed, capable man was radiating confusion. "Why are you giving me hot tea and cookies? Why are you drying my wet clothes? Because I'm cold? That doesn't make sense."

"Sheesh, dude." Dane shook his head at Blair.

"Don't *sheesh, dude* me." Blair pointed his finger at Dane almost violently. "I'm not stupid."

"Blair." I wasn't the smart one, but I needed to at least say something. "Dane is like that. He takes care of people. He helps people. Paid or not."

"What's in that tea, dude?" Blair stared at Dane. He leaned down and smelled the tea Dane had made, the way cops would smell a suspicious substance. "I'm not stupid."

"It's tea." Dane sighed and shook his head. "I got it from the cabinet right here on your boat. So unless you've corrupted your own tea, I don't know what to say."

"And you're just making me tea just because?" Blair stared eye-spears at Dane. "I don't believe that."

"If you want. Like I said. If you want, it's because I'm sweetening you up for us to be your security detail. For a million dollars. That's not the reality. The reality is I'm just trying to help a human being who went for an involuntary swim."

"Involuntary?" Blair asked. "I jumped in, didn't I?"

The conversation wasn't going anywhere good. "Maybe we can discuss the employment matter," I said. "My partner Dane and I are prepared to accept a contract to work as your security detail. Maybe we can limit the discussion to that matter under consideration."

"Alright." Blair raised two hands in the and snapped his fingers. "Then there's no discussion, because there's no matter under consideration. You two aren't getting the job. Closed. End of case. Alright? Finished." He looked seriously at both of us. He wasn't fucking around.

"You're sure? It's off?" Dane asked. As grounded as Dane always was, this caught even Dane Wurlitzer off-balance.

"I'm not somebody who fucks around." Blair spoke in a monotone. He wasn't avoiding our eyes. He was looking right into Dane's eyes, then mine. "You guys can make your leave now. Go."

We did.

I put my wet clothes back on.

Dane put his dry clothes back on.

I looked straight ahead as Blair led us off the yacht. I was scared to look in his eyes. He closed the pushbutton vacuum-lock door behind us. He didn't say goodbye.

Dane turned his car's air conditioning to full blast. It looked and felt like a chilly day, but I felt flushed hot, even in my dripping wet clothes.

Gravel rumbled and cracked underneath as Dane pulled his car out of the marina parking lot. He didn't say anything.

"I'm sorry about the—" I started to say. My wet jeans dripped dirty marina water on his vintage car's interior.

"Don't worry." Dane exhaled deeply. "I'm sorry Blair sketched out on us. I really thought I could make this come together for you."

"You don't need the money, Dane." Every time I told him that, every time I gave him the knowing smile that accompanied those words, I wondered what it would be like — just having a secret stash of more money than any person could ever spend.

"Yeah?" Dane laughed and shook his head. "I'm pretty happy being a cop, actually. This deal was for helping you. You know that. I didn't need it for myself."

"So let's be cops then." My shrug squeezed more water off of my shoulders and onto his vintage car's interior. "Let's go back to being cops. What we both know we can do."

Like everything else, it would be easier for Dane than for me. I had that other job besides being a cop, and that other job might not even have been worth it without my regular customer "Brooks." That and my bills and debts. Always that. But none of it was Dane's fault. Dane was the best partner and friend I could've imagined — or even better than that.

"I'm worried about Blair, though." Dane exhaled as he pulled out onto the highway, heading west, away from the marinas and the respectable parts of town, to drop me off at home. "The guy seems like — I mean, who just jumps off his yacht into the marina water like that? I mean, what the fuck?" Dane scowled at me.

325

"I honestly don't know." I absentmindedly squeezed some water out of my wet jeans, onto the car seat. "I just think rich dudes are eccentric."

"Paying to dock at Slip Sixty-Nine, sure. That's normal rich-guy eccentricity." Dane squinted into the sun setting over the swamps in the distance. He pulled down the sun visor and put on his aviators as he wove his lumbering Mercedes coupe through traffic. "But even rich people aren't supposed to be doing and saying stuff like what we saw. I mean, no matter how rich. Sickness is sickness, you know?"

"Yeah." I shook my head. "I mean — I guess maybe I was making excuses but yet. Now that you say it, I'm concerned too. I don't know what to do."

"If this was TV, we'd fucking stage an intervention or something." Dane fidgeted in his seat and shook his head. He fidgeted when he couldn't do enough, as much as he wanted to.

Dane fidgeted when we got a repeat call for a domestic violence, or when a "rehabilitated drug addict" was crouching in an alley with a needle, or when we got to a standoff when the bullets had already flown and the ambulances had already come. We, and especially Dane, sometimes could not do as much as we badly wanted to do.

"You care a lot." I looked out my passenger window, away from Dane. I pretended to be occupied with staring at the cars in the right lane. "That's really what I love about you, Dane. You care so much. About everybody. About me. About the world. About the cat we found in the station garage."

"Oh shit. One Facebook post with that cat and your duck face and how many adoption offers did we get?" Dane smiled and shook his head. "All I did was the post. It was your looks that got the cat adopted."

"Sometimes I wish I had more than a nice ass." I broke out laughing at the sound of my own words.

"You realize that's just a joke, right?" Dane pulled the car onto Ponce de Leon Drive, just down the street from my ratty condo.

Dane steered at five miles an hour through the quiet of my unimpressive neighborhood. The street was quiet, without any traffic coming in the opposite direction. People were eating dinner now in their downmarket condominiums that they, like I, must have been struggling not to have taken away from under them.

"What's a joke?" Sometimes I needed reassurance. "That I've got a nice ass?"

"That's definitely not a joke." Dane's smile was more calmly appreciative than jocular or mocking. "But you've got a lot more than that, man. You're an amazing dude."

"Because of my mad open-water rescue skills?" I squeezed more water off my shirt, just to emphasize my point. "Or my mad job-interview skills? Or what?" I sighed.

"Come on, man. You know. You know how great you are." Dane slowly brought the car to a stop across the street from my condo, behind a ratty Coco Furniture delivery truck that hadn't moved in years.

"Not particularly." I wasn't just fishing for compliments. I didn't go around with a list of my good qualities in my head. "I know I'm competent enough as a police officer not to get fired. I know I've got a nice enough chest and ass to sell calendars."

"Dude. Fucking hell." Dane laughed while shaking his head and looking down, the way he laughed when he wanted to compliment me without becoming a sycophant. "You're at least fifty percent, probably more, of everything we do as a team. I couldn't fucking do anything without you — without how grounded you are, how smart you are. And how much you care. Man, how much you care."

The engine was running. The air conditioning was blowing ice cold, cold enough to keep me comfortable even when my face was suddenly flashing hot. Cold air running over my wet clothes felt like swimming in ice, but it was what I needed. Maybe my knees were trembling. Maybe it was because my clothes were wet.

"I care?" I shook my head and stared down at my wet knees. "I wish I could be like one percent of you."

"Dude." Dane sighed. "I'm sorry if I don't say this often enough, but I look up to you. To how much you care. To how dedicated you are to this work. I'm sorry if that gets lost in all the dumb jokes about your good looks."

"Well, I do have a nice ass." I grinned. "Not gonna lie."

"I prefer your eyes. The color of water under Seven Mile Bridge." Dane was staring blankly through the windshield. He grabbed the car's gear shifter as if he was holding on to something, about to be thrown off.

"Did you just say that?" I smiled. It was all I could do.

"Asher. Not just your ass. Not just your eyes." Dane breathed faster, quick enough so I could hear it against the humming of the engine and air conditioning. "Your personality, your dedication, your, what's the word, what's the word — shit, I'm all verklempt or whatever they say — your conscientiousness. Conscientiousness. That's the word. In the five years we've worked together, you've never been late for a shift. Not once. Do you know that?"

"Doing my job. That's all." I looked in Dane's gray eyes for a half-second, then rushed to look away.

"We've been — I mean — how closely we work together. Every day. Overwhelming, you know?" Dane turned his head to the side. The car smelled like marina-water stench, mixed with our sweat, and maybe something like pheromones. "To the point that — to the point that jumping into the marina with you, having some kind of weird half-naked water rescue, meeting Blair Hamilton — it just feels like another day in the life for the two of us, you know?"

"Yeah. Just another day in the life. Not too different from patrolling the Russian baths." I laughed and shook my head at the ridiculousness of it all. "Wurlitzer and Lane. The new buddy-cop bromance in theaters near you. People always say I should be an actor, right?"

"Some things are—" Dane breathed in, gulped, so hard that I heard. People in the condos outside might have heard. "Some things are too real—"

In the car's tight interior, Dane's buff shoulder was almost touching mine. He half-closed his eyes. He leaned closer toward me.

We were in a cocoon all our own. The whole world was only us. Outside this car, these seats, these windows, nothing else mattered.

He looked at me, paused for a half-second, then again moved his head still closer toward mine.

He lay his hand on my hand. His hand was trembling. I felt his heartbeat in his wrist. My hand trembled too, and my heart beat like I'd never felt it beat before.

His lips were full, pink, as if he'd prepared them just for this occasion. His lips trembled even more than his hand. He breathed quickly and looked in my eyes, at my mouth, then looked away out the windshield.

He exhaled softly, then gulped air again. His lips were almost at my lips. His long eyelashes fluttered above his gray eyes.

"See you tomorrow!" I blurted. I drew my head away. With whatever strength was left in me after that moment, I pulled the interior door handle and pushed the car door open.

Ponce de Leon Drive was just outside, awaiting me. My body felt frozen in place. I was too overwhelmed. Dane and I had never talked about or done anything like that. I knew I always thought about him, but I didn't think it was like that.

My body could move only on manual mode, every muscle contraction requiring conscious effort and even some patience. I'd lost all the innate knowledge of how to do normal things. That moment had been like a nuclear blast: obliterating.

I had to move my legs out, out of the car. Stand up. Shut the door. Wave a little bit with my left hand, a normal goodbye.

Look away. Never look at the car pulling away. Speed-walk toward the building, jog up the stairs. Hope, know, it would be a fresh new day with Dane tomorrow, and there would be no more of that sort of explosion.

I stood on the concrete outside hallway, just outside my apartment. The window-mounted air conditioner beckoned with rust and mold. The green painted wooden door in front of me looked wavy, almost rounded, like it was undulating together with the waves of an unseen ocean. My legs felt unsteady, like I was standing on a rocking boat.

I breathed the sopping wet inland Florida air. I grabbed at the thighs of my wet jeans to ground myself in reality.

Strips of tape held a yellow envelope to the door.

It was stamped *Notice of Eviction*.

That was that.

I was a cop. I knew how eviction worked. I knew my condo was in foreclosure. The news didn't come at the best time.

I went inside. I took off my wet, dirty clothes. Their stench was stronger than it had ever been on the yacht or in Dane's car.

Naked, I took a one-minute shower to smell a little less, and went to bed. I fell asleep to the humming of my air conditioner, imagining the sight of Dane driving away down Ponce de Leon drive, and Blair sitting on his yacht alone, too scared to eat those Oreos.

Sometimes you just go to sleep and hope for a better day.

Five (Blair)

"When I Fall In Love," in E-flat major. Originally performed by Miles Davis. That Wednesday morning, it was performed soulfully, with Dinner Key Marina and the Atlantic Ocean dawn as a background, by solo virtuoso Blair Hamilton. Standing alone on the bow of the *Power of Three*, playing a trumpet into the Miami sky — I looked like a cartoon.

When the phone in my pocket rang, I sleepily assumed it was the marina. Only they would call at seven A.M., and call at seven A.M. they did. Every day they found some new fee I had to pay or service I should use or delivery I should accept.

That was fine. The marina was a business. Their motives were clear. I got their laundry service and bottled water delivery and wifi hotspot and farmer's-market vegetable delivery and whatever other bullshit. It was easier than saying *no*.

The number wasn't familiar, and the voice on the other end was only half-strange. Before he could finish stumbling over his phone introductions, I recognized Dane Wurlitzer's voice.

He was the unfortunate whom my bankers had sent over as a spy or a Trojan horse or whatever other motive they had — or maybe the bankers really did believe my "stalker" story, but they probably knew it was bullshit just as well as I did.

"Deal's off," I said: calmly, politely, but authoritatively. "Don't waste your time. I'm not hiring any kind of security detail." It was the same voice I always used when telling off well-intentioned salespeople of things I didn't want. It was no fault of theirs that I didn't want a Key Biscayne condo or a McLaren 720S. But it was also no fault of mine that I didn't want extended conversations with them.

"Not that." Dane exhaled so loudly that I could hear him on the phone. "I'm just worried about you."

"Shit. Fuck." I gritted my teeth to stay polite. "I understand selling me shit. Fine. Everybody makes a living. But don't do this *I'm just worried about you* bullshit. I've seen it so many fucking times.

Every salesman quote unquote *just worried* about what will befall me if I don't buy their shit."

"Not that either. Seriously." Dane left a silence.

"I'm waiting for your sales rant, Dane. Go ahead. I've heard it. I'll be nice. I'll give you the courtesy of listening. The bad things that will befall me if I don't give you a million dollars to protect me. Probably with a few hundred K extra for security modifications to my yacht and another hundred K for some of your buddies to be backup security, right? Fucking hell. I hate this fake-concern shit—"

"You're the one with a sales rant." Dane's voice was calm and precise. The bankers had mentioned something about him being ex-Army. "Can you hear me out for a second without preemptively dismissing what I'm saying? Can you?"

Dane sounded like he was about to rescue me from a burning building. Maybe he was.

"I can." I almost regretted just assuming that all Dane had to tell me was another sales rant. But that was all I'd ever heard when someone called me and told me they were worried about me. "Bring it. I'm listening." I sat down on the boat's bow, trumpet at my side. Now I really looked cartoonish — like a lamentful young boy. Maybe from a *Peanuts* cartoon, or *The Sorrows of Young Werther*.

"Blair. You have a problem." The way Dane said it sounded like every sales pitch I'd ever received. "And before you interrupt me: it's not the kind of problem I or Asher can solve. I'm not selling you anything. I accept you won't hire us for security. Fine. I just want to make you aware of something else."

"The fuck?" I laughed. "You're calling me on behalf of a boat rust-proofing company? Marine engine overhaul? Selling satellite phones? Which one is it?"

"Blair. The stuff you said yesterday. The way you jumped into that water and said maybe you didn't want to be rescued. The way your mood turned. It's about that."

"Are you a doctor or something?" I shot back. This might've been some sort of psychological-conditioning cult scam.

"I'm not a doctor, Blair." Dane was still calm, despite my series of mini-outbursts. "I've just seen bad stuff. And I don't want bad stuff to happen to you. Ok?"

"Yeah. Ok. You don't want bad stuff to happen to me. Great. Thanks. Wonderful." What a nothing statement. Fine. It sounded nice: he didn't want bad stuff to happen to me.

"Blair. I need you to do something about it."

"And this is when you tell me to wire the money to an account in Croatia?" That was the other possibility: Dane was telling me he cared about me in order for me to reciprocate with money.

"Stop, Blair." Dane's voice showed a tinge of frustration. "I want you to go to a doctor. A counselor. A psychologist. Psychiatrist. Some help. Whatever you're comfortable with."

"You think I'm crazy?"

"You're smarter than that, Blair. Come on." Dane made another exasperated sigh. "You need professional help. You freaked me out the other day. You probably freaked yourself out too."

"Maybe I do." I was proud, but not delusional. "But what am I supposed to do: walk into some Miami psychiatrist's office and ask her to help me?"

"Yeah. More or less." Dane didn't seem shocked by the idea.

"No way, Dane." I contorted my whole voice into a rejection: the whole idea of *no*. "I don't roll like that. I don't just go to strangers and ask for help like that."

"I can help you. I can refer you. Or I can set you up with the referral office at the PD."

"I'm a crazy man, not a criminal." I laughed loudly into the phone. Maybe I played the *crazy man* role a little too enthusiastically.

"I can—" Dane started to say.

"No, and no. No with a side dish of no." That was my usual conversation-ender with these salesman types. "I'm hanging up the phone now. Bye." I instinctively followed those words with a motion of my thumb toward the big red button to disconnect the call.

At least I told him *bye*. I wasn't rude at all.

334

I breathed deeply and stood up and looked out across the water. Had I really jumped into the water from up above? Just because I was directly confronted with my homosexuality, in gorgeous, perfect-assed form, walking down the boat slip?

I held up the trumpet to my mouth. "In My Solitude." Duke Ellington. Lips pursed. *Mmm* position. Fingers on the valves. Blowing loud.

At eight A.M. I played with less restraint. There wasn't any shame in waking up the marina neighbors at eight, the way there was at six. My whole trip to Florida was about living less with less restraint. Doing what made sense for me. Not anyone else.

I breathed deeply and took out my phone. I called back Dane. He didn't seem surprised.

"If I agree to get help — will you take me to the doctor? Go with me?" I couldn't believe I was saying it. If he'd gladly jumped in a toxic waste marina to fish me out, maybe I could trust him to take me to get help.

"Of course I will." He could've run away calling me an overbearing freak. But he wasn't even perturbed by the request. "I'm on duty now. I'll be done at noon. I can come over and pick you up then."

"Today?" Suddenly it was all immediate. "Like, we can do this today?"

"Yeah." Dane didn't seem perturbed.

"You're, like, working now?"

"If that's what you call driving around South Beach and chatting with Asher, yeah." Dane laughed. He made it all sound so easy.

"Is Asher coming with us?" I felt twelve years old, but there was no better way to word the question. "Asher can come with us."

Those two had a special chemistry together. I hated to admit it, hated to admit badly wanting to be part of anything, but I badly wanted to be part of it.

Asher had seen me at my seediest. So what. He could see me actually trying to do something about my demons, instead of trying to cure my homosexuality with stacks of twenties in Key West.

"You betcha." Dane laughed. "Is that ok? If Asher comes with us? Doesn't this sound like we're sixth-graders going to the arcade?"

"Yeah." I sighed. "They had arcades back then."

"Good point." Dane hummed. "So we'll pick you up at the marina around one P.M. and mosey on over to the counseling center."

"It's that easy?" I asked. I seriously had no idea.

"I can get you a same-day appointment. I'm a cop, you know." Dane laughed.

"Yeah. You are. More than that. But yeah. You're a cop."

"Now if you don't mind." Dane cleared his throat on the other end of the line. "Asher and I have to go back to patrolling the mean streets and looking respectable and stuff."

Asher's voice chimed in: "It's not easy being the face and ass of the law!"

"Alright. Thank you. One P.M." I sighed, with relief. A little bit of apprehension, but mostly relief. "See you at one P.M."

Six (Dane)

The patrol shift with Asher was normal. Just normal.

I'd let a little too much of myself slip the previous evening, but Asher didn't act any different.

He was happy to help Blair get help. So was I.

With a little extra throttle, Asher and I were at Dinner Key Marina ten minutes early. The sun burned hot fifty minutes past noon. The marina wasn't dead the way it had been the previous day. People were going to and from their boats, carrying things, doing things; maybe I was just noticing it better with the improved mood.

"Ready for sixty-nine?" Asher asked.

"Slip Sixty-Nine? Yeah." I smiled, then averted my eyes. After what I'd let show the previous night, our homoerotic banter landed too heavily and felt too real.

We stepped out of the car. I un-contorted myself to fully-standing after the hour's drive in the constraints of a thirty-year-old two-door Mercedes.

I shut my door and Asher shut his. Asher looked back at the car and winced a little. "I'll sit in the back on the way over."

"Oh yeah." I smiled. "Three six-foot-plus dudes, one cute little coupe."

"Tight." Asher said it with a deadpan salaciousness.

"Hey hey now." I looked over toward the yacht slips. "Let's go get Blair. Make sure he hasn't bailed on us again."

Asher shielded his eyes from the overhead sun and looked down the boat slip toward Blair's yacht. "Feels so different from how it was yesterday."

"Yeah." Of course I had to agree. "Everything. I mean, everything feels different."

That previous evening, on Ponce de Leon Drive, I'd shown Asher a tiny window into my feelings. Even if it didn't go anywhere from there, at least now we were squared up. I didn't carry the guilt of hiding anything from him.

"What's that?" Asher shielded his eyes with both hands and squinted even harder down the dock. Something was bobbing and hopping down the path.

"Miami Kangaroo?" I laughed.

"Fucking hell." A smile broke across Asher's face. "That's him, isn't it?"

"I do believe so." I stared in wonder at Blair hopping toward us. Wearing the pink oxford shirt and khaki shorts. Riding a pogo stick.

"I didn't know—" Asher shook his head, still shielding his eyes from the sun. "I didn't know those can be used for forward motion."

"You think they're just for hopping in place, huh?" Blair asked, loudly, while breathing hard and hopping in place.

"Yeah. Forgive my ignorance." Asher walked closer to Blair's resting spot. "You were getting a pretty good forward hopping speed on that thing."

"You're not riding this to the appointment, are you?" I whispered to be semi-discreet, although Blair must've known that Asher already knew where he was heading.

"I'm eccentric, not batshit crazy." Blair laughed. "I'm not riding my pogo stick to the appointment. But it's related"

"How?" I frowned a little and stared at him. I feared there was confusion about what sort of appointment I'd booked for Blair, if he though a pogo stick was related to it.

"Oh." Blair stared down at his resting spot as he still bounced up and down. "Just that being myself, pursuing my interests, should be good for me. I've always wanted to ride a pogo stick. So I went out and bought one today."

"The wonders of being rich." Asher grinned. "You want a pogo stick? You just go buy one. You probably paid cash, too."

"I did, I did." Blair laughed. "And now I'm coding an app for pogo stick sharing. You know, like—"

"Like those fucking e-scooters?" I turned up my nose.

"Yeah, I guess, kind of like e-scooters." Blair nodded. His eyes looked a little embarrassed of his highly insignificant admission.

"Cops fucking hate e-scooters." Asher nodded authoritatively.

"Thanks for revealing all our cop secrets, Asher." I shook my head in reprimand at him.

"Dudes. Dudes." Blair stopped hopping. He climbed off his pogo, still breathing hard, and then lifted it into his hands, the way old men carried their golf clubs. "We've got an appointment to get to, don't we?"

"Yes we do." I nodded. "Let me put your pogo stick in the trunk."

"As long as you promise to give it back to me later." Blair nodded eagerly, awaiting approval. I nodded back at him.

I dutifully lay the pogo stick down in my trunk. It filled the space. It shimmered a few times in the early afternoon Miami sunshine before I closed the lid.

Asher already lay across the back seat, his head propped up against the rear corner window. Imitating the position of the pogo-stick, he fit width-wise, folding his legs up and splaying his body out across the back seat like it was a lounger. There was no way a guy his height, or any of our heights, was fitting into that back seat the regular, sitting-up way.

"Shotgun!" Blair called out. He looked at me for approval, as if he was unsure that he was allowed to do that. I nodded my approval.

We pulled out onto the road. The car felt like it had finally found itself a full load to carry: it carried the three of us dutifully, fully, like it knew that our group of three was complete, full but not overfull.

"You guys listen to jazz?" Blair ran an idle finger over the car's stereo controls. His manicured fingernail reflected the sunlight.

"I'll listen to anything." I shrugged.

"Yeah, he'll definitely listen to anything." Asher snickered.

"Yeah." I confirmed. "Asher is pretty glad that the stereo died in this car. Saves him from listening to my stuff."

"So we're not gonna listen to jazz?" Blake tapped his finger on the stereo controls again.

"Not this time. Not today." I gave a small apologetic nod, like a Japanese dinner host telling his guests that this will have to be their last flight of sake.

"How am I gonna get back home from the counseling place?" Blair asked.

"I'll leave your pogo stick chained to the bike rack there," I said. I looked over. Blair's face turned from shock to mirth.

"Now I know when you're joking." Blair sat back in his seat and leaned his head back. His skin was perfect, as if it had been airbrushed. He smelled as if either he'd applied just the lightest touch of woody, musky cologne to himself, or as if he naturally just had that kind of delicious aroma.

When we pulled into the counseling center's underground parking garage, Blair undid his seatbelt before the car was even fully parked. He was like a dog eager to go to the vet. Just after I turned off the car and unlocked the doors, he whispered to me, "I know I need this. Thank you."

We jogged up two flights of concrete stairs to a pastel-decorated waiting room. "Officer Wurlitzer," one receptionist after another greeted me. "This is the place where everybody knows my name," I whispered to Blair.

Blair laughed. "You should see the places where everybody knows my name!"

"What kind of places is that?" I asked.

Blair looked at Asher's face. Asher was looking down, suddenly very interested in his own shoelaces.

"Oh. I don't know," Blair said. "A joke. Just a joke."

A woman came out from behind the counter and motioned to us. "Mister Blair Hamilton, please?"

Blair followed her.

"We're not going anywhere without you," I said to Blair, as if he didn't already know that.

Seven (Blair)

Blair Hamilton: the app developer, the billionaire heir, the closeted homosexual, the trumpet player, and now, the psychiatric patient.

It was just counseling and therapy. They didn't lock me in any padded rooms. But the questions the psychiatrist was asking me — it was like she was carrying a cheat sheet of my deepest subconscious rumblings.

I'd be going to counseling twice a week. It would be good for me.

I'd be taking Prozac every morning.

And maybe I'd be seeing more of Asher and Dane.

I still had my unease around them. Nobody had ever reached out to help me like that without an ulterior motive. It didn't help that they were cops: *ulterior motive* in uniform.

I unscrewed the prescription pill bottle. I gently shook it so one of the green-and-white capsules slid out into my hand. *Prozac 20 mg.* I threw it in my mouth as if I was taking a basketball shot.

Trumpet-playing had taught me how to summon up saliva without any drinking water. I swallowed the Prozac without even needing to take a drink.

I chased it with a whole bottle of water just for the sake of thoroughness — and because I wanted to play trumpet that morning. At eight A.M. I didn't have to worry about waking up boat-neighbors, but I could still enjoy the morning cool.

I fluttered my fingers on the trumpet valves. Herbie Hancock, "Cantaloupe Island," or at least the trumpet part. A good five minutes of blowing on that thing. At least the tune was familiar enough so any boat-neighbors I might have disturbed would recognize it and maybe even appreciate it.

Dane and Asher — they hadn't mentioned anything about their security work when they took me to the counseling center. Not even once.

Were they rubes who'd forgotten about the possibility a million-dollar payday? Did they have some other, bigger payoff in mind?

They had driven me back from the counseling center to the marina, and given me back my pogo stick, without any mention of a future meeting or interview.

It would've been normal if they'd mentioned the million-dollar job. It would've even been normal if they'd requested a fee for helping fish my stupid ass out of the marina water, and another fee for chaperoning me to a counseling appointment. But they didn't. They hadn't even implied or hinted.

It was too weird. It made me itch — itch to find out what was going on.

I called Dane.

"Blair Hamilton. Man of the hour. Man of the week." Dane was as cheery as the cheeriest yacht salesman, which was indeed very cheery. "How's your first day of your new dawn?"

"My new dawn?" I knew exactly what he was talking about, but I allowed myself to play stupid.

"Don't play stupid, man." Dane laughed loudly into the phone. "I'm a cop, you know."

"Oh yeah. I forgot." I was deadpanning it. "Anyway, feels good. Yeah. Took my Prozac. Played some trumpet. Feeling good."

"Wonderful. Awesome. Spectacular." Dane must have been about to pivot to the sales pitch for the security gig. Except he never did. The silence was a bit awkward.

"Hey, Dane. Asher." I cleared my throat.

"Yeah! Asher here too!" Asher's voice bellowed through what must've been speakerphone.

"Would you guys be available for some security work?" I cleared my throat again. "This weekend."

"Yeah, just let us know," Dane said.

"Uh — if we can get time off from the Department," Asher interjected.

"We can get time off from the department," Dane said to Asher. "Sorry about that, Blair. My handsome partner here is a little more scared of the Chief than he needs to be."

"So you guys can do it?" I asked to confirm.

"We can do it." Dane said. Hearing only his voice, I could still visualize the smile breaking across his face. "As long as we know what *it* is. Like from when to when? Where? And so on."

"Oh. Yeah." I cleared my throat again to give myself a few seconds of thinking time. "Start Friday morning. Until Sunday night. I'm leading a weekend cruise for some friends. I need security."

"Sure," Dane said. "We'll be at the marina on Friday morning."

"Aren't you going to ask about the pay?" I asked. I was laughing. These guys were either complete rubes, or they had a much more sinister plan.

"Uhh." Dane grumbled. "I'm sure we'll figure that out. You can pay us whatever is fair."

"And you're just gonna trust me?" I asked.

"Yeah, Blair." Dane sighed. "I'm just gonna trust you. We're both just gonna trust you. Ok?"

I spoke quietly into the phone: "I think so."

Eight (Asher)

I cracked one egg and dumped the contents into the bowl. Then a second egg. A third. And finally a fourth.

I stuck a fork into the bowl and stirred it around.

"Whisking?" I asked Dane. "Whisking the eggs I think they call it."

"Shhh. You'll wake him up." Dane flapped his hand at me in the universal gesture of *shush*.

"If you wanna make an omelet, you gotta break some eggs." I smiled triumphantly at Dane. I'd kept that line in store for when it was omelet day again.

Dane usually warned me not to wake up my sleeping father when we cooked for him on Sunday mornings. French toast, pancakes, oatmeal, even steak and eggs — all perfectly fine breakfasts, but only omelet day let me crack that joke.

"You've been waiting to use that line, haven't you?" Dane asked me. He shook his head in mock exasperation. He could always see through me.

"No, man. All my humor is spontaneous." I cleared my throat. "Anyway, have you cut the cheese yet?" I giggled.

"Are you, like, twelve?" Dane sighed.

"Mentally. Maybe. Sure. Yes."

"Alright." Dane nodded. "That clears it up at least. And yes, I have already sliced the mozzarella. Or, as you put it, cut the cheese."

I poured the eggs into the frying pan and stirred a bit. When they were firming up, I sang out to Dane, "Pour some mozzarella on me, baby!"

"Fresh mozzarella from the Coconut Grove farmers' market," Dane said. "Only the best for your dad's breakfast."

"Whoa, whoa, Mister Trust Fund Man has just bought some mozzarella! Did you have to liquidate a few diamond mines to buy that cheese? Maybe sell a few thousand shares of Berkshire Hathaway?" I laughed, but at the same time, I knew that Dane lived off of his police salary, just as I did, and that making a run down to the

344

farmers' market was a commitment — not to mention Dane's weekly commitment to come up to my dad's retirement home with me and cook the guy breakfast.

"This cheese is very affordable." Dane nodded, deadpan. "I swear it didn't cost a penny over twenty dollars."

"Shit, man." I shook my head. "If you didn't spend all that money on heritage-grade hipster cheese, maybe you could buy a newer car."

"Badaboom!" Dane said, and flipped the omelet over in the pan. "Don't make fun of my grandpa's nineteen-eighty-two Mercedes. You got the magic mushrooms though?"

"Sure do." Unpacking and washing pre-sliced button mushrooms from Publix, that much I could handle. "Got the magic mushrooms. Or at least the mushrooms." I dumped them into the pan.

"Step aside, Asher. Wurlitzer's gonna do the finishing touches." He actually brought his own cooking utensils to our little Sunday morning cookathons.

"Someday you gotta teach me." I made puppy-dog eyes at Dane. He stared down into the pan, playing with separating the omelet from the frying pan.

"One day in the far future, Grasshopper. For now, I have bought ultra-hipster hot sauce for your father's Sunday omelet enjoyment." Dane reached into the pocket of his dad jeans and pulled out a tiny bottle of some kind of red sauce. "Artisanal, small batch, whatever. I hope he likes it."

"You sure you weren't a cook in Afghanistan?" I gave Dane a sideways look.

"Yes and no, actually." Dane shrugged. "It wasn't my official job. But I was so fucking bored ninety-nine percent of the time that I took up cooking for my whole unit. Plate, please!"

"Plate, sir." I said obediently, putting a plate in front of Dane. He flipped the omelet out of the pan and into the plate.

Dane poured a glass of orange juice and carried it in one hand and the plate in the other hand.

345

"Good morning, Mister Lane!" Dane said. "We heard you ordered some breakfast?"

Dad lay half-awake. He wasn't the same after the most recent three cycles of chemo, but he had a definite smile breaking across his face. "Breakfast?" Dad squinted at me. "I thought I asked for a hooker."

"Dad." I winced, then broke out laughing. Dane grabbed the Amazon in-bed table he'd bought for my dad and set it up. I put the omelet, utensils, and orange juice on it.

"As an officer of the law—" Dane saluted my dad. "As an officer of the law, I will assume you're talking about TJ Hooker."

I nodded. "Right. About TJ Hooker. Or about fishing."

Dane leaned down to mock-whisper to Dad: "Mr. Lane, I have no idea where your son got his risque sense of humor." Dane coughed. "But I do have some idea." He laughed.

"Ah, Asher. Don't mind Asher." Dad shook his head. "I've been telling dirty jokes before Asher was even swinging from his mom's pussy hairs."

"I'll keep that in mind." Dane made a shocked deadpan expression at my dad. I tried not to imagine the hair-swinging scene.

"Dad. Dad. Serious matters now," I said. The security job wasn't a lock yet, but it felt like close enough to a lock that I could tell him about it. "Dad. I might be able to pay off the thing we're not supposed to talk about. Like, soon."

"Bank heist?" Dad asked without a pause.

"No. Private security job. Maybe. Not confirmed yet."

"That will pay enough for that whale of a debt?" Dad furrowed his eyebrows a bit — the same way he always did when he thought I was full of shit. "How can you make a million dollars that fast? I don't want you to do anything illegal, no matter how much I hate the bill collectors."

"It's more like— the situation is more like--" Dane made a face like he was crawling out of a swamp. "A friend is going to help us out."

"I don't want you guys involved in any John DeLorean type deal, you know?" Dad shook his head. "And I don't want you to lose your condo to pay off my debt. I know how much you worked to buy that little shoebox."

"No, no. Just—" Dane was obviously looking for the right words to describe it. "A good friend. A close friend. Is going to help us out. We'll do some private work for him. Nothing illegal. He'll help us, alright?"

"I hope it's alright." Dad shrugged, still lying in bed. "Not like one of those shady money-making opportunities you police officers sometimes get."

"You know I always turn that stuff down." I sighed. "Honestly, as tempting as it is sometimes. As tempting as it would be. I turn that stuff down. Dane keeps me on my toes."

"I sure do." Dane reached out a fist toward Dad's bed for a fist-bump. Dad brought up a frail fist toward Dane. Dad was only seventy, but looked worse; he seemed to have aged a decade in the two years since the cancer diagnosis.

Dad fist-bumped Dane. Dane enthusiastically acknowledged him, as he always did. "Alright, Mister Lane!"

"You can legitimately get that kind of money?" Dad asked. "Pay off everything? Not just keep them away for a month?"

"Give us a week or so," I whispered. "I'm pretty sure."

"Shit." Dad shook his head. "I'm gonna be lonely every day."

"Lonely?" I asked. He didn't exactly have a bustling social life bedridden, but he'd never complained of being lonely. "You know I visit you every time I get a chance."

"You ruined my joke, Asher." Dad sighed. He turned to Dane. "I raise my son right, do what I can, but he ends up lacking comedic timing."

"I feel your pain, Mister Lane." Dane looked down and scowled.

"The joke I was going for." Dad looked at me as if I should've already known it. "Is that I'll be lonely without the bill collectors knocking on the door every day."

"Badaboom!" Dane announced. "Score one for Mister Lane!"

"Alright." I smiled at the two of them. Dane was like a brother to me, coming up with me to cook for my dad every Sunday. "Decent joke."

"Speaking of things that are a joke." Dad forked some more omelet into his mouth and looked at me with his usual worried smile. I knew it was going to be the usual topic. He was just concerned about me.

"Yeah, Dad?" I looked at him as if I had no idea what he was going to talk about. Dane was pretending to busy himself with something on his phone: maybe an ASMR app.

"Asher, you're twenty-eight." Dad shook his head and moved his hand up and down to massage his throat. "You don't have a wife. You don't even have a girlfriend. You've never even had a serious girlfriend. It's your love life that's the joke I'm referring to."

"Yeah, Dad." I sighed. I'd give him the stock answers, the way I always did. He'd find them mostly unsatisfying, the way he always did. "You know how hard I work."

"So does every other twentysomething, Asher." Dad leaned his head back, exposing his jaw and neck. He must've cut himself shaving more than a couple of times, but I was adamant that he keep doing personal hygiene tasks himself, and so was he. It was his dignity. "Every guy, every girl your age works hard. But damn, Asher, they're all matching up and getting married."

"Yeah. I know." I sighed. I sat down on the chair next to his bed. I cradled my chin in my hands.

"I'm worried for you, Asher. Not for me." Dad spoke quietly. "Sooner or later, I'll be gone. I want somebody to always be there for you, the same way I've always tried, at least tried, to be there for you."

By the time I knew to check my eyes for tears, I was already crying. I wiped them away, doing my best not to let Dad notice. Maybe he did his best to act like he hadn't noticed.

"You always *have* been there for me, Dad." Awkwardly, I squatted next to his bed and leaned in for a hug, my shoulder touching Dad's shoulder, my arm resting behind his neck.

"I just don't want you to be all alone in the world." Dad shook his head and looked out the window. "Being single is fun for a while, I know. But then — around twenty-eight maybe, right where you are — maybe it's really time to settle down, you know?"

"Yeah." I nodded at Dad. "I mean — yeah. I'll try. I'll — do what I can." What else could I have said? At least Dad was no longer trying to introduce me to his neighbors' daughters.

"Asher, what I'm saying here, ok." He took a deep breath. "I'm seventy years old and maybe I don't know about these things, but Asher, if it's not a lady that you want to settle down with, you know, that's alright by me too."

"What?" I was shocked. I also, as a matter of self-defense, had to pretend to be shocked. "What are you talking about?" I played up the *shocked* part, because I knew what he was talking about, but I wasn't sure whether I'd let him know.

"I don't know much about these things." He shook his head. "I just know if my son doesn't seem to be interested in finding a girlfriend, didn't even call the very attractive girls I tried to set him up with, has not even once brought a girl over for me to meet—" Dad shrugged.

"Yeah," I said. I wasn't admitting anything. I wasn't committing to anything. But I was crying again, because Dad's understanding of the situation was, as always, way beyond what I had any right to expect, way beyond what I had any right to think myself entitled to. He was that kind of father.

"You and Dane are pretty close." Dad looked at Dane, then back at me, and breathed deeply. "I have no idea what the situation is.

Maybe Dane. Maybe someone else. Maybe not necessarily a girl, alright?"

"I think I understand." I nodded. Of course I understood.

Dane held his phone in his hand and was staring at us now. He, too, was either crying or about to cry.

"Everybody needs love, Asher," Dad said, definitively. "I loved your mom until she passed. I love you as my son and always will, until I pass. You're a great man, Asher. There's a lot of love in the world. I— I don't know what I'm saying here—"

Dane spoke up in a vocalized whisper. "You're speaking truth, Mister Lane."

"What I mean, Asher, is don't let me stand in the way of you finding love, alright? I don't know who it's going to be with, and I apologize for taking some mental shortcuts and always asking you about girls, ok? That's all I'm saying, Asher. I want you to be happy, no matter how exactly it happens. I want you to find love, no matter exactly how it happens. Alright?"

"I think so." I sat back in the chair. The wave of his words and his near-infinite understanding had just hit me. That was Dad. He knew everything. And he was there to support me.

"How's the omelet?" Dane asked Dad. He was an expert at lightening the mood; no surprise, given all the moods that needed lightening during his time in Afghanistan.

"I have seriously never tasted mozzarella like this." Dad forked another piece of omelet into his mouth, the mozzarella strings extending from his mouth all the way to the plate, as if he was the smiling man on frozen pizza box.

"It's super-hipster mozzarella," I said with a nod.

"Then probably Dane bought it?" Dad laughed. "Dane always buys me the good shit."

"Maybe." Dane looked up at the ceiling coquettishly. "I might have also put some hipster hot sauce on that omelet."

"I taste it!" Dad nodded. His eyes lit up. "That shit must be, what do they call it, artisanal and small-batch!"

I laughed. "Maybe you've been going to hipster language school."

Dad shook his head. "I have the fucking internet, Buckaroo." He looked over to Dane. "Kids today. I tell ya."

"Yeah." Dane said. He stealthily rubbed his cheek against his shoulder to wipe off a tear. "Dads today. I tell ya too."

Nine (Dane)

"Rise and shine, million dollar ass-boy!" I muttered into the WhatsApp voice message to Asher.

He came jogging down the stairs of his building, in police uniform, lugging a big backpack. Peeking upstairs inside his condo, everything was stacked into boxes.

I popped open the car trunk and asked Asher, "What's in the backpack? Cosplay gear?"

He laughed, at least, standing outside my driver's side window, looking at me uncomfortably. "Something like that."

"No, seriously dude." I shook my head from my driver's seat, still looking at him standing next to me. "It's a three-day job. What the hell are you bringing? The backpack looks like you're trekking through the Gobi Desert for a month."

"Electronics. Passport. Social security card. Insurance records. Family heirlooms. Stuff like that." Asher looked down on the ground as he spoke.

"What the fuck?" I cocked my head back. "For a three-day boat trip?"

"Can I just leave it in the trunk of your car?" Asher asked.

"You can do anything you want, but a car parked in Miami for three days isn't a safe place for valuables." I laughed "A cop should know that."

"Oh yeah. Um, I guess I'll take it onto Blair's yacht." Asher spoke quietly, a little bit ashamedly.

"I'm sure Blair won't mind." I looked the backpack up and down again. It looked like its weight was going to overpower Asher and plummet him into a sinkhole. It looked like it had everything. I hopped out of the car and lifted the backpack off of Asher's back and put it in the trunk. "But why are you bringing all this stuff?"

"Eviction stuff." Asher stared down at the trunk lid. "They finalized foreclosure. Now it's eviction."

"Your condo? You're losing your condo?" My stomach tightened. My knees were weak. What I most hated about Asher's money problems is he wouldn't let me help him.

"I've packed up everything into boxes already." Asher got into the passenger-side seat. "They might lock the place up anytime, so I'm taking my valuables with me."

"Asher." I started the car engine again and shifted into drive.

Asher answered before I could even offer: "Thank you, but I won't accept your money."

"Asher. My money is not doing any good just sitting there." That was a weak argument, but it was the best I could think of.

"Donate it to charity then." Asher shrugged. "Seriously. I'll figure this out. And maybe something will work out with this Blair guy."

"I hope so, man." I sighed. "I hope so."

"Does Chief know we're wearing our uniforms on this job?" Asher asked. Moonlight in uniform was a sensitive point: not explicitly forbidden by department regulations, but sort of discouraged.

"Yeah. He Ok'd it."

"Oh. That's kind of a surprise." Asher nodded.

"Well, I reminded him we'd only be on a boat. There wouldn't be other people seeing us in uniform, other than whoever's on the boat. It's not like the assholes who have uniformed cops stand outside their houses."

"We do look good in our uniforms, don't we?" Asher grinned.

"A lot better than in wet street clothes, yeah," I said. I looked at Asher every day in his police uniform and every day he seemed to look more beautiful. It was most likely my knowledge and appreciation of him that was always improving.

I'd grown to love him. Even if we didn't do anything about it, at least now he knew it. And if the Blair Hamilton job worked out, at least I could do something for Asher's money problem.

"Not that there's anything wrong with jumping into toxic marina water. Or getting kicked off the yacht and wearing wet street clothes," Asher said. "Shit. That whole mess seems like it was ages ago."

"Yeah. A week ago." I laughed. "Maybe that's ages in Blair Hamilton time."

When we showed up at Slip Sixty-nine, the gangplank was already out, and the door to the interior cabin was open. For once, Blair was expecting us.

"I see my security detail is here," Blair announced to nobody in particular. Maybe he was speaking to the yacht's voice-control system, or maybe to an onboard servant we hadn't yet seen.

"Y-yeah." Asher nodded at Blair. "Your security detail is here."

"We have food and water on board." Blair pointed at Asher's huge backpack and laughed. "No need to bring your own."

"Oh. Yeah. I just brought a backpack." Asher flushed red. "I mean, I just brought it. To store it for the weekend."

Blair shrugged and nodded. He led us into the boat's living room, two long white leather couches parallel to the boat's hull. The dark tinted windows let in a hint of the blazing morning sun. "You guys are wearing your police uniforms." Blair nodded at both of us. His gaze came in just a little bit lascivious. "Hot, isn't it?"

"No problem. You've got onboard air conditioning." I smiled at Blair and looked up at the A/C vents. I wasn't clueless, but I could pretend to be. "For hotness, you know."

"It's definitely — it's definitely hot." Asher grinned for a half-second, then immediately un-grinned. His breathing was fast enough to hear.

"When do the guests arrive?" I asked. "How many people are we supposed to be protecting you from anyway?" I grinned. Maybe we were already comfortable enough with Blair to be able to joke a bit.

"We don't carry our weapons off-duty, by the way," Asher said to Blair. "I know some clients complain about that. But for your party, you probably prefer not having guns scaring your party guests."

"My party guests are pretty fearless." Blair clicked his tongue. "I don't think they'd be scared of police-issue handguns."

"How many guests are there—" I was getting some hunch of the number of guests for Blair's cruise being lower, much lower, than I might have previously expected.

"Just two guests." Blair pointed two fingers, at Asher and me. "And they're fearless."

"We're the only guests on your cruise?" I laughed. "And we cops, by the way, are more scared of guns than the average person is."

"The more you know!" Asher chimed in. "Seriously, though, we're the only seamen going on this cruise?" He giggled like a junior high kid who'd just made a naughty joke.

"Seamen?" I shook my head at Asher. "Your humor never grows up. And that's what I love about you."

"Alright. I won't say *seamen*. How many dudes are going on this cruise?" Asher looked around at the three of us.

"Do I get to count as a dude?" Blair made a puppy-dog face. He had dimples. He was beautiful. "If I do, then it's a three-dude cruise."

"You are—" Asher leaned in toward Blair. He inhaled all of him deeply. His lips quivered. He leaned back again, away from Blair. "You are definitely a dude."

"I hate to get bogged down in practicalities here." That was always my job: getting into the practicalities. Even in the Army, the place that attracts and cultivates people who love practicalities, I was the practicalities guy in my unit. "But just a minor question. Who's driving the boat?"

"I am." Blair smiled. He wasn't joking.

"You don't have someone doing that for you?" I asked. "A charter captain or something?"

"That's what everybody asks." Blair shook his head. "I don't trust anybody on my boat. I learned to drive it myself. Navigation, radio calls, all that stuff. It's not a big deal."

"Cool." Asher nodded.

"Yeah. Cool. And where are we going? Where are you driving us?" I asked.

"A favorite place."

"Well that narrows it down." I looked at Blair, expecting more detail.

"Sometimes I take this thing down to Key West." Blair looked off into the distance, as if he was already navigating his way there.

Asher suddenly coughed. Then again. He sounded like he was coughing up a hairball.

"You alright there, Asher?" I asked.

"Yeah. Yeah." Asher stared straight ahead, steely-eyed. Something about the mere mention of Key West seemed to set him off. Him and maybe Blair too.

"But on the way to Key West, there's a little unnamed, unpopulated island where I like to stop." Blair smiled. His eyes lit up. "You know, my happy place."

"Swimming and snorkeling and stuff?" I asked.

"Yeah." Blair nodded enthusiastically. "That island. That little place. It's like ASMR without my app."

"Oh shit, Blair. Don't ruin the market for your app." I laughed. "People might start buying yachts and traveling to unpopulated keys off the coast of Miami instead of paying five bucks for your app."

"It's alright. I'm in the pogo stick sharing app industry now." Blair hopped up and down on an imaginary pogo stick. His legs — I'd never noticed his legs. They were like a bicyclist's or a rock climber's, chiseled with muscle.

"You admiring my legs, dude?" Blair asked. He pulled the lower edge of his shorts up a little to show more hair, more muscle. No matter what, it was sexy. "Pogo-sticking built up my leg muscles."

"Didn't know that." I nodded.

"And." A smile broke across Blair's face. "And, I have awesome, muscular glutes."

I gulped in shock, then forced myself to calmly nod and smile.

"Shall we?" Blair asked, and pointed with his eyes to the stairs going up to the captain's bridge.

"Shall we what?" Asher looked upstairs like there were demons up there.

"Shall we proceed up to the best seats in the house, I mean. The captain's bridge." Blair nodded confidently.

"Fuck, yeah." I said. It somehow felt like we deserved it — after all the effort and back-and-forth, even if we weren't going to make a million dollars for Asher, after all the effort and back-and-forth with Blair, we could enjoy a nice boat ride.

The captain's "seat" was more like a half-moon-shaped sofa, upholstered in smooth, cool white leather. Blair naturally sat down in the middle, at the controls.

"Gonna have them untie me," Blair muttered, typing text messages into his phone.

"Sexy!" I answered, not even thinking. Maybe I'd spent too much time with Asher and that sort of comeback just came to me naturally.

Asher filed in and sat next to him on Blair's right. I sat on Blair's left.

Blair reached into a compartment and pulled out sunglasses. They weren't drugstore glasses, and they weren't even random aviators: they were high-style glasses of some kind, ones he'd kept in that compartment just for this purpose.

"Are those your boat-driving shades, Blair?" I asked.

"Why yes, they are." Blair took a second to turn in my direction and smile.

Even through his oxford dress shirt, his taut triceps rubbed against me. I didn't want the feeling to end. I sat so that my arm was just barely touching his. Just barely, but still touching. Because not touching Blair would have been too painful.

He started the engines with push buttons. Everything was silent. He pulled slowly out of the marina. It wasn't too different from pulling out of a parallel-parking spot, especially when I was driving our lumbering patrol SUV.

Eyes scanning the horizon, sometimes scanning the GPS displays in front of us, Blair steered the yacht toward open water: infinite crests of blue stretching out into the horizon. It felt like we could go anywhere. It felt like we were going everywhere.

Not just the Caribbean. Not just Cuba. It was a spiritual sort of freedom, looking out onto the open ocean. It looked and felt like we could travel to different states of being, different planes of existence—

Seagulls soared overhead in formation. We passed the buoy marking the marina's exit. Not even looking, Blair reached down and put on a headset with attached microphone and said some nautical-sounding things to the marina, exchanged some pleasantries, and put away the headset again.

"So from now on." Blair stood up. His legs stood long and lean like lighthouses framing the infinite ocean outside. "We're going out into the open ocean."

"That we are." I nodded. It was an oddly obviously true statement.

"I hope you don't mind." Blair unbuttoned his dress shirt's top button.

"It's your yacht, man," I said. "You can get comfortable."

"Yeah," Asher said. "Unbutton your shirt if you want. It's your yacht, not ours."

"I mean when I'm on open water—" Blair opened a few more buttons. He opened his shirt. His chest was perfectly toned, with lithe, powerful pecs, nowhere an extra hair nor an ounce of extra fat — nothing like my own dad-bod.

"Oh I think I know what you're getting it." I nodded at Blair.

"Yeah, guys. I hope it doesn't interfere with your ability to perform your duties as the security detail." Blair looked at Asher, then at me, like he was completely serious about this point. "But when I go out on open water, you know, it's just me out here."

"Yeah, and?" I was quite sure I knew what he was getting at, but I still didn't want to assume the nude hypothesis without hearing it directly from Blair.

"So when I'm out on open water." Blair took off his shirt, folded it up, and put it away on a shelf off to the side. His back muscles were textbook-perfect trapezoids. His arms were impossibly ripped for such a slim guy. "I go totally naked when I'm on the boat in open water."

"That's fine with us," Asher said. "I mean, I don't speak for Dane, but—"

"Yeah, it's fine with both of us." I stared at the pink nipples atop Blair's pecs. "Totally, totally fine."

Blair took off his shoes and put them to the side of the cabin. He pulled off his khaki walking shorts.

There wasn't any underwear to restrain his dick. When he slid down his shorts, his cock popped out, already perfectly hard: long, pink, uncut. It looked about twice as big as it had looked after our accidental marina swim.

I tried to control my breathing.

Blair stood up and calmly folded up his shorts and lay them on a storage shelf. He pumped his muscle ass like always: just the way he walked was so nonchalant, but you knew that he knew that his ass was beautiful, every bit of him was beautiful, and he was working it.

"So I guess what I'm trying to say." Blair looked at me and Asher. "Is there's no dress code on this boat. For anybody. Including you guys."

"Is that an invitation to get naked?" I asked. I burst out laughing. I couldn't believe I'd actually said that. To a dude. To a potential client. While wearing my police uniform.

"Do you need an invitation?" Blair asked. "I like being naked even without an invitation."

"Excellent point!" Asher said. He unbuttoned the shirt of his police uniform. "It's pretty warm here." He folded up the shirt and put it exactly where Blair had put his own clothes.

Asher's pants were still on him. He wore his police uniform pants so tight: he must've known how they complemented his beautiful, muscular ass.

The sight of Asher's muscular back and six-pack, his naked torso while he still wore his police pants — I wasn't proud of it, but I was rock hard. If I didn't have my image and dignity to maintain, I might've started jerking off to that sight of half-naked Asher.

We cruised far out enough that the marina disappeared behind us. Blair followed the coordinates from his navigation computers. I thought to myself that his dick looked like a directional pointer.

"It is getting toasty here, isn't it?" I did my best to act nonchalant as I unbuttoned my shirt and peeled it off, then took off my shoes and police pants.

"Fucking hell," Blair muttered with a smile. "Check out the dad bod."

"Is that a bad thing?" I shrugged.

"Fuck no." Blair shook his head while staring me up and down. "That hairy chest, those six packs with a belly. Oh fuck."

"I concur on that one," Asher said. "Dane Wurlitzer does have a perfect dad bod. You know, Steve McQueen dad bod."

"Oh yeah, totally." Blair nodded while staring at my chest. "We're talking Steve McQueen dad bod, not Chris Farley dad bod."

"I'll take the compliment," I said. I took off my shirt and folded it away. I went with the flow and stood up, facing the open ocean through the tinted windows, and took off my pants too. My fat, hard dick popped out like a lighthouse. Blair didn't even pretend not to stare.

I didn't know how or why, but I was fucking horny.

Ten (Asher)

It wasn't like on stage at Meat Market in Key West. The way Blair looked at me was totally different now. In Key West he had been "Brooks," a desperate, hurried, and very thirsty pervert, a man who grabbed at whatever he could get.

Here on the boat, he was the man who knew me, who appreciated me — and wanted me. I hadn't even taken off my pants, but he looked like he could have taken me right there, pants or not.

I was rock hard inside my pants. Even Dane was naked, and his dick was fat and hard and reeked of precum. He looked like he was itching to at least jerk off.

I was waiting for a signal from Blair. I wasn't going to jump on him, or let him jump on me — but I knew we could make each other happy.

Blair pushed some buttons on the control panel. The backlighting of the keyboard went dim, and the central display flashed *AUTO*.

"The boat's totally on autopilot now," Blair said. "That's when I get to relax. Just keep an eye out for any obstacles. Out here, we've got like half an hour of lead time to see them."

"I guess you've already waited your half hour." I laughed and pulled down my pants. I knew how much Blair and even Dane wanted to see my dick. I let them see it. My ass too.

Putting away my uniform pants on the shelf gave me an excuse to spread my legs for Dane and Blair and give them a good show from behind: my ass crack and the big balls that hung below them, "horse balls" as the not-so-subtle manager of Meat Market called them.

"Fuck." Blair sounded like he couldn't breathe. He looked at me and Dane self-consciously, then gave a look of *well, what the fuck* and grabbed his dick and started slowly stroking it, looking back and forth at me and Dane on his left and right.

"You guys know what I learned on Tuesday?" Blair asked.

"That psychiatrists aren't evil?" Dane offered.

"Yeah, ok that too." Blair nodded. "But most importantly, I learned to ask for help when I need it."

"Yeah, you did learn that." Dane gave Blair a double thumbs-up. Fuck, Dane's massive arms were sexy — his biceps and triceps had that solid strength of an ex-military man. Those dudes trained a lot harder than we cops did.

"So." Blair cleared his throat and stared down at his shiny, glistening cockhead. "I think I need some help here."

That was what I'd been waiting to hear. I got down on my knees and pulled myself over so I was between Blair's spread-open legs. His hard dick was almost directly in my face.

Next to us, Dane started slowly stroking his own dick. The mix of Dane's and Blair's precum smell with my own was the hottest musk I'd ever smelled.

The foreskin atop Blair's dick fascinated me. I had a dick too, but Blair's didn't look like mine, at least at the tip. I hadn't seen any dicks that didn't look like my own circumcised cock.

I moved my lips closer to Blair's cock. I sniffed the full length of his shaft: the aroma wasn't the same as Dane's or my cock.

I opened my mouth. "I've never done this before," I said to Dane and Blair. Blair pushed his dick closer to my face. I opened wide and let it slide in.

It felt girthier in my mouth than I expected. I'd never sucked a dick. I'd never done anything with a man. Blair's dick looked slim, like Blair himself, but when it was in my mouth, it pushed at my teeth and gums.

Dane was staring at us and jerking his own dick without any of his usual modesty.

"That's a beautiful thick, fat cock," Blair whispered to Dane. "Matches your gorgeous dad bod."

"Suck it," Dane said. It was a sharp command, and the hottest thing I'd ever heard.

Blair did as told. He guided his own dick into my mouth, then leaned over to Dane's dick. He started with Dane's big hairy balls, popping them into his mouth one by one. "Fuck, your balls are huge," Blair mumbled.

Dane's dick disappeared in Blair's mouth. Blair moaned and sucked and pulled and pushed trying to fit Dane's dick all in his mouth. He looked like he was holding his mouth open to its very limits. But he was taking all of Dane's fat cock in his mouth. I envied that Blair was tasting Dane's dick, Dane's thick, veiny dick that I'd frantically dreamed about tasting so many times.

But I wasn't going to give up sucking Blair's dick. Dane's dick could wait. Dane threw his head back in pleasure as Blair sucked him off.

"Fuck. I can't believe this is happening," Dane said. "I always dreamed about you guys."

"About me too?" I asked. Maybe I was a little insecure.

"Definitely about you too." Dane laughed. I reached over to do what I'd always dreamed of — I slid my palm under and squeezed at his meaty ass. It was an awkward position, but Dane's meaty ass was a prize almost as much as his dick. I moved my hand up from his ass to squeeze at his balls, then run my hand over his hairy stomach and six pack, then to paw at his pecs and nipples.

Blair bobbed his head up and down on Dane's cock. Dane softly moaned with pleasure every time Blair took him deep in his mouth.

I was licking Blair's long, slim dick from the very base to the foreskin. I slurped at the dickhead every time my tongue rose to it. I nuzzled my lips up to his foreskin. I sucked on the foreskin like it was candy and licked its interior at the same time I licked the tip of his cock. Blair frantically ran his hands through my hair as he sucked Dane.

"Fuck, that feels good." Dane's voice sounded like a growl. He lay back in the seat, his muscular arms propping up his body. Every square inch of his body was masculine and sexy: the hairy chest, the hairy armpits, the solid muscular stomach, the dark-blood-red nipples, and especially his fat dick and ass.

"Good," Blair said to Dane, between pushes of Dane's dick down his throat. "It's supposed to."

"What I mean is—" Dane gulped down air and moaned. "Guys, I haven't done anything with anybody, not a woman, man, anybody, in years. Many years."

"That's cool," Blair said. "I haven't done anything either in a long time. Kind of." He glanced at me. I looked away.

"What I mean is." Dane moaned. He gyrated and pumped his ass as he fucked Blair's mouth with his dick. "I'm gonna cum pretty easily."

Just the sound of that word, and Dane saying it, made me harder.

"Cum, baby," Blair whispered up to Dane. He slurped and danced with his lips and tongue on the tip of Dane's dick. Blair's hands massaged and jerked Dane's shaft and balls. Blair looked up at Dane again with his beautiful eyes. "Cum. Cum for me."

"Arghh." Dane growled. His body shook. His stench of sweat and musk was suddenly overpowering. He pumped his crotch at Blair's mouth. "Ohhh." Dane growled again.

I sucked hard on Blair's dick and bobbed my head up and down on it. With one hand I reached out to manhandle Dane again, to feel his shuddering stomach and biceps and pecs in the throes of orgasm.

"Urgh." Dane rose his whole body up. He'd just shot his first rope into Blair's warm mouth. I knew that mouth well. Blair's face showed satisfaction; he smiled even with the dick in his mouth, and he looked up and nodded at Dane. His throat bulged hard every time Dane pumped another rope into him. Blair swallowed it all.

With my other hand I clumsily fingered at Blair's ass — I'd never done it before, but when I poked at his rim, he gasped with pleasure, and his dick throbbed in my mouth. He was suddenly grabbing and frantically squeezing at my face as I sucked him off.

Blair's cum was syrupy-sweet. It didn't smell as strong as my cum smelled when I jerked off. It smelled like cum lite. Maybe at his wealth level, he had some special cum fragrance — or more likely, at his wealth level, he had a cleaner diet than I did.

Blair moaned as he released his third rope into me. I swallowed it all, even after he mumbled "You don't have to swallow" to me. Of course I wanted to swallow — I wanted all of him, not just his dick but also his cum, inside me.

"Oh fuck that felt great," Dane whispered to me. Despite the boat's air conditioning blowing cool air on us, Dane's hairy, manly body was soaked in sweat.

"You're not having any post-orgasmic regrets?" I asked Dane, with a laugh.

"My only regret," Dane said. "Is that you haven't cum yet."

Wordlessly, Dane slipped his dick out of Blair's mouth, and got down on his knees next to me. Blair saw what he was doing and followed along.

Dane wiped sweat off his eyes and said to me quietly: "You can't imagine how long I've been dreaming about sucking Asher Lane's dick."

He ran the wide, flat surface of his tongue from the base of my cock all the way to the tip. He stopped at my circumcised cocktip to plant soft, playful kisses on it, while smiling up at me.

With his usual practiced touch at everything he did, Dane put my cockshaft lengthwise along his lips, like a corncob. He looked over at Blair. Blair knew what to do immediately: he put his lips to the other side of my shaft, so Blair and Dane could kiss my dick together while they kissed each other's lips.

My dick felt so much pleasure I thought I was in space. I'd never felt anything like it. The two men — the two men I now loved — kissed each other and kissed my shaft and dickhead while I watched from above. I ran my hands through their hair and over their shoulders and biceps. I reached down and grabbed their asses as much as I could.

Wordlessly, they coordinated and took turns. Blair sucked my dick hard, and Dane's mouth went to work slurping on my balls, moaning with pleasure. Dane was the most unselfish lover I could imagine, but I would've guessed that from all I'd ever known of him.

Dane let my balls slip out of his mouth. He moved his lips up on my shaft to tongue-kiss Blair, then focus on me again. His tongue alternated between pushing inside Blair's mouth and pleasuring my shaft. Then — like the partner and best friend that he always was — he focused on sucking my dick, running his tongue up and down the veins, slurping and lapping at my full purple dickhead.

He and Blair kneeled face-to-face, closer to each other. The boat pitched only slightly as we crested some waves. Autopilot kept us moving Blair and Dane leaned in to each other for a passionate kiss, both of their mouths wide open, two grown men moaning and gasping for air like horny teenagers.

They both moved their heads down, staring at my dick, like worshipers paying homage to a sacred chalice. They brought their bodies down slightly to be both face-level with my dick. They kissed each other and they kissed my dick at the same time, making out with each other's mouths and with my cut dickhead in the midst of their tongues and lips.

Dane — partner, old friend — smiled at me and drew my cock entirely into his mouth. He fluttered his tongue along its length as he sucked it into him. My dickhead bumped into something firm; that must've been his throat.

Dane gyrated his face while sucking my dick, deepthroating it, moving it in circles, and humming and moaning to vibrate it with his throat. He slurped with his lips, and his hands roamed up and down on my thighs and legs.

Blair ran the flat surface of his tongue over my balls. He was licking at my taint. When he pushed down on my taint with his tongue it felt like he was deep inside me. If all this were not new enough already — Blair started flicking the tip of his wet tongue against my assrim.

Dane groaning and moaning on my dick and Blair tonguing my ass, I couldn't take it anymore. My feet were the first to feel unsteady. Then the feeling spread up to my legs.

I grabbed onto Blair with one hand and Dane with the other. Orgasm took over my body. I pumped and thrust with my dick upward. Dane was slurping the thick cum I was shooting out. With all the stimulation I'd had, there was a lot — more than I'd ever seen come out of my dick any other time.

Blair responded by tonguing my ass deeper. His probing wet tongue was everywhere in my butthole. That felt like a second orgasm that traveled my ass to my cock. Another wave came over me. I came hard, again, in ropes and ropes into Dane's mouth.

Dane held my dick steadily in his mouth while looking up at me with a smile. I looked back at him and returned that knowing smile.

Blair slowly licked his way from my ass to my balls, then kissed Dane again.

I sat back in the chair, spent and yet still excited. I'd never done anything like this — not with guys I'd cared about, not with my partner Dane, and certainly not with two guys at once. Not only didn't I want our little boat cruise to end, but I didn't even want the sexual moment to end.

Dane rose up from the floor to kiss me. He half-stood-up and then stood in front of me. It was less standing and kissing me and more mounting me.

As I looked at him wide-eyed, leaning back in the seat, he widened his stance, held my legs up, and somehow mounted me, his knees on the seat. His dick was only rubbing against the outer edge of my butthole.

"Can I—" Dane started to ask, streams of sweat running off his face. He was jerking his dick up and down along the entrance to my ass. His dick glistened with cum and precum and everything else slippery, and I was so horny that my own ass felt like it was full of natural lube.

"You can, but may you?" I smirked as I teased Dane.

"May I?"

"You can," I whispered. "You may. You have to."

He pushed the tip of his cock into me. It felt full, but not horribly painful. It only felt full.

He leaned in and breathed in my smell and moved his lips to mine. It was what we'd always wanted: with his thick, manly lips, he kissed me. His tongue pressed into my mouth and I kissed back, exploring his hot, wet mouth, hearing his fast, excited breathing.

Dane pushed his dick farther into me. It didn't hurt as much as I'd expected. There was some pushing and discomfort, but the physical and mental pleasure of having Dane inside me was a lot stronger than any minor physical pain of his fat cock pressing up against the physical limits of my ass.

He extended his manly tongue into my mouth, so far back I thought he could reach my throat. "Is this alright?" he asked.

"Fuck me hard" was all I could answer.

Dane smiled. He drenched my face and jaw and neck in small kisses. He lifted himself up higher, then pushed hard into me.

I clenched my teeth. The pain still wasn't too bad.

He pulled out a little, and put back in. He had a rhythm going.

It hurt a little, but it felt good a lot.

He embraced me from behind and dug his fingers into my back. My view was his beautiful face, and the yacht's skylight behind it. He sped up more with his fucking, until all I could feel in the world and all I cared about was his dick moving in and out of my ass and his lips making love to my face. Everything else disappeared.

He grunted and groaned and fucked faster and harder.

He stopped for a second. "Hold up a sec," Dane muttered. I opened my eyes wider. Blair was behind Dane, getting ready to fuck his ass as Dane fucked my ass.

When Blair entered Dane, Dane howled in the usual mix of pain and pleasure, and he gyrated his dick and moved it sideways inside me, as he tried to get comfortable with Blair's dick inside him.

"Alright." Dane smiled forward at me, then back over his shoulder at Blair. "Let's do this."

Dane fucked me hard, running his hands over my legs raised in the air and kissing my face. Meanwhile, Blair was fucking Dane in the ass, feasting with his tongue in Dane's ear.

Both of them reached around and played with my dick and balls with their hands. Even after all the hard cumming I'd done, I was rock hard, and ready to cum again soon.

Dane and I stared into each other's eyes and kissed. I imagined the lost time since our first non-kiss on Ponce de Leon Drive, or maybe all five years of lost time when we'd been working together without knowing what we wanted or needed— but until now, until all this, we had no way of knowing, and no impetus for trying.

We had what we had, nothing more. The foreclosure papers existed. Maybe my things were already gone. That was real. But Dane's kisses, his breaths, his tongue exploring the crevices between my teeth as he stared into my eyes — that was also real.

Blair was sucking onto the back of Dane's neck like a vampire as he fucked Dane's ass. My eyes met Blair's, and Blair leaned his head forward so he and I could kiss — softly and passionately, in a way we'd never done at that stupid club in Key West.

Blair grunted hard as he fucked Dane faster. His face turned red. He and Dane sped up their jerking of my dick.

Blair moaned. He kissed me hard, then bit into Dane's neck, without even leaving a mark. He was trembling, shooting cum into Dane's ass.

Dane pushed harder and deeper into me than I'd ever felt. His dick felt like it was splitting my ass cheeks in two. His dickhead was definitely tickling my prostate. I lowered my body to impale myself deeper on Dane's dick.

His dickhead pressed against my prostate hard. He squeezed my dick and lapped his fingertips softly over my dickhead. I came hard, bucking up with all my force. I thrust my dick into Dane's hand and stomach so hard that I almost knocked Blair off of Dane.

I contorted my body to point up and shoot my cum on Dane's pecs and nipples. I loved the sight of that.

He started to cum inside of me. He looked me deep in my eyes as he came and unleashed hot creamy loads in me. It was what both of us had always wanted.

Blair backed off and pulled out of Dane. He sat with me and Dane, cuddling on the "captain's seat" that was effectively a three-man love seat.

We cooled down in comfortable silence. Blair grabbed three small bottles of water from a hidden mini-fridge and passed them around. We hydrated, staring at our flushed red, sweaty, exhausted bodies as that day's greatest accomplishment — because they were.

I caught my breath. Stretching my arms and legs, I sat up straighter.

The autopilot was still controlling the boat. Blair retook his position in the middle of the three-man seat.

I was on Blair's left, and Asher sat on his right. Sort of. It was more like we were an entwined web of legs and arms and torsos and faces, hugging and cuddling, with only a vague correspondence to our official positions on that seat.

"That was awesome." Blair laughed and nodded. "I've never had an experience remotely like that."

"*Awesome* doesn't even begin to describe," Dane said.

"I think—" I paused a second to think— "I think I've just spilled more cum now than I've cumulatively spilled in all the fantasies of the people who buy the Asher Lane police calendars." I laughed at my own convoluted comparison.

Dane nodded at me. "And they say I'm the weird one."

"Nobody says you're the weird one, Dane." I shook my head. "I'm always the weird one."

"I guess that's true." Dane nodded. He gave me a small mouth-kiss.

It was alright now. We were over that boundary. Dane didn't need special permission or planning or shame to kiss me. He could just kiss me. It was a new world, a new dawn.

"Damn, this security detail." Blair looked at me and Dane. "I sure got my money's worth." He nodded smugly.

"What?" Dane asked.

"Yeah, what?" I squinted at Blair.

"I mean—" Blair calmly explained to us, as if we hadn't understood the meaning of his words. "Even if I pay you guys a million bucks, or whatever I pay you— I've never had sex like this before. Any amount I pay you for this is well worth it."

"Um." Dane looked at Blair and shook his head. "Are you sure about what you just said?"

"Pretty sure." Blair nodded casually. "Did I ever tell you I got a perfect verbal SAT? I don't make mistakes in what I say."

Dane's body tensed up. He sat up straight, no longer resting his head on Blair's shoulder, no longer casually wrapping his arms around Blair.

I knew what was wrong. Dane's face showed hurt like I'd never seen him show. Dane Wurlitzer was famously impervious to physical pain, and stayed free of any relationships that might cause emotional pain. Dane's face looked like a knife was twisting in his heart.

Eleven (Blair)

The shipboard mood had changed faster than a sudden open-water storm. I was just babbling about how great the sex had been, and suddenly Dane and Asher got up and walked down by themselves.

I knew normal people like those guys don't change their moods so suddenly for no reason. I knew that my own mood swings were abnormal enough for Dane and Asher to send me to counseling. So there had to be something behind it. Normal people didn't just snap.

It took me fifteen minutes sitting alone at the captain's bridge to figure this out. Like before, I needed to ask for help. I needed to let them help me.

We'd reached the secret islet anyway. But if the tense mood continued, it would be just me skinny-dipping there — and it would no longer feel like my happy place.

I cut the throttle, set the electronic anchor, and went downstairs to the living room.

"Guys."

Dane and Asher sat on a sofa, naked, staring out the window and looking somewhat uncomfortable.

"Yeah." Dane nodded.

"Guys, I'm sorry. I must've said something. I just don't know what."

"You don't know?" Dane smiled wryly. It was a smile, but his lips stayed closed and lay perfectly horizontal.

"I didn't get a perfect verbal SAT," I said, preemptively. "I didn't even take the SAT. Didn't even go to college. I know you'll call me on that stupid thing I said."

"Oh." Dane shrugged. "Really doesn't matter who did and didn't go to college. I mean, not unless you're hiring somebody. If you're hiring somebody to do a job, then it does matter."

"And we consider you a friend and a lover. Not our employee." Asher looked directly at me and smiled. "Are you getting it?"

"Was I ever supposed to be your employee?" I stared blankly. "I'm not getting it."

"The analogy is still too remote," Dane said to Asher, with a calm, knowing, Dane-like smile. "Let me try to explain to him."

"Blair," Dane said to me. "Blair, if we're hired to be your security detail, that's fine. But if we're messing around and having sex, that's something else."

"It's definitely something else." I grinned stupidly at Dane.

Dane sighed. "No, Blair. Let's put this very bluntly: we aren't prostitutes. At least not right now, not anymore."

"I told Dane about Meat Market in Key West," Asher said to me. "I told him everything."

"That's in the past," Dane said. "I don't stigmatize it. Whatever. People need to do what they need to do with money. But now, here, now if we're with you, if we're doing stuff that's naked and sexual, I don't want it to be part of our job. I don't want it to be about payment."

"So you don't want to have sex with me anymore?" I asked. "That's fine. I'm sorry if I overstepped."

"I do want to have sex with you. A lot." Dane laughed. "It's life-changing. I love it. But I don't want it to be part of our job. I want it to be for— for—" Dane took a deep breath. "I want it to be for love. Ok? I want us to be your lovers, not your prostitutes."

"I didn't know that was an option," I said blankly. "I didn't know you, or anybody, would offer me that."

Asher stared at me, closely, with his huge blue eyes. "Blair. We're in love with you. Both of us are."

"We don't mind working for you." Dane reached out and held my hand. His own hand was mottled, scratchy, but still soft at its core. "In fact, Asher really needs the money, ok? We don't mind doing work and being your security and being whatever else you want. We just want that to be separate from what we do in bed."

Asher piped up: "Or on the sofa. Or anywhere else." He laughed.

"I'm sorry." I breathed heavily and shook my head — shook my head contemplating my own nearly infinite stupidity. "I didn't think you guys would want me. I didn't think anybody would want me like that."

"You can bring that up with your psychiatrist next week." Dane nodded with a smile.

Asher asked in an impish voice: "Can we kiss and make up now?"

I sat down next to Asher and Dane. We were still all naked. I embraced them: Asher directly next to me, and Dane next to him. My hands and arms at least reached both of them, even if I couldn't wrap my arms around both of them at once.

Our faces came together in a three-way kiss. It was like an equilateral triangle. I'd never imagined a three-way kiss would work so perfectly, but it did. I plunged my tongue into Dane's mouth, then Asher's mouth, then just explored and wasn't even sure whose lips and tongue were on my lips and tongue.

It was all good. It was all love.

"We're already at my secret little island, by the way," I said. I pointed out the window with my eyes. It didn't look like much: an islet with a sandbar and very shallow-water beach. But Dane and Asher nodded toward the view outside with eager eyes.

"I must say." Dane grinned and looked at the three of us, naked. "I wouldn't mind some three-man skinny dipping."

"That's definitely on the agenda." I gave them a thumbs up.

"The *gay* agenda," Asher said, with a big smile.

"Yeah. I guess we all learn something about ourselves. The *gay* agenda. I'd never thought of that word — gay — applying to me." I sighed.

"Samesies over here." Dane sighed and shrugged. "I always thought I wasn't gay, even if I knew I wanted to be close with Asher, and then once we met you, well— it's just so crystal-clear."

"Samesies!" Asher giggled.

"Well. There's no dress code. But everybody needs to put on sunscreen." I clicked a button to open the vacuum-lock door to the outside deck.

"You're gonna help us apply sunscreen, right?" Asher giggled more. "I'm not sure if I can do it myself! I'm kind of clumsy!"

"Of course." I took one of my bottles of sunscreen and squirted a few goops of creamy white onto my hand, then rubbed it into Asher's chest.

I made no secret of making sure his gorgeous pink nipples were very well protected from any minute risk of sunburn. I applied sunscreen to his erect nipples three, maybe four times, as he moaned in pleasure.

Then I rubbed it everywhere else on Asher, starting from his biceps and triceps, and moving down over his six-pack to his ass. And I certainly didn't want his beautiful cock or balls to get sunburn.

When I gently slapped his ass to let him know I'd finished with the sunscreen, Asher's dick was totally erect and glistening with precum. I got down on my knees, and wiped sunscreen off his dick.

"You just put sunscreen on my cock, and now you're wiping it off again?" Asher asked me, somewhat indignantly.

"I just noticed your erection. Can I help you with it?" I asked Asher.

"Help?"

"Like, you know. Swimming with an erection is dangerous." I laughed because we both knew it wasn't true. "I think I read that in *Boy's Life* or something."

"Yeah, sounds pretty dangerous," Asher said in agreement. His dick was already throat-deep in me. I gave him a workmanlike BJ performance, slurping at the tip and bobbing my head in standard fashion to produce an explosive orgasm of Asher's all over my lips.

Dane stood nearby watching us, and jerking his cock. "Are dad bods eligible for assisted sunscreen service too?" Dane asked.

"Oh yeah." I squirted more sunscreen onto my hand. "Fuck yeah." I relished rubbing sunscreen into the forest of Dane's chest hair, his fat cock, and especially his meaty ass. Maybe it wasn't part of the official instructions on the bottle, but I made out with Dane while I covered him in sunscreen. While we kissed, I jacked him off to a hot, spurting orgasm shot into the ocean.

"Now that everyone's wearing sun protection." I announced like some kind of low-budget camp counselor. "There are lots of swim fins, masks, snorkels, towels stuff like that in one of the chests out on the deck."

"Did you buy that stuff?" Asher asked, laughing. "I can't imagine you, loner man, shopping for a dozen snorkels."

"It came with the boat." I shrugged. "I really never had any friends who'd come on the boat and use it with me."

"I'm not here to chat," Dane announced. "I'm here to skinny-dip!"

Dane took a running start and jumped off the deck and into the shallow water below. He stood up on the sandbar and the water was only up to his stomach. He lay back on his back, swimming with his dick sticking up in the air like a safety flare about to launch. Or like a pogo stick waiting to be ridden.

"Hey, Blair." Dane shouted from behind the boat, looking up at the markings on its back. "Why is your boat called *Power of Three*?"

"Back in Canada, I grew up with two older brothers." I smiled just imagining them. "They loved boating. The three of us always called ourselves The Power of Three."

"Cool." Dane nodded.

"Well, and—" I sighed and fumbled with my hands a little bit uncomfortably. But I didn't have any secrets with these guys, and the story needed to be told. "They died in a plane crash. Family private jet crashed trying to land in Key West, five years ago."

"Oh shit. I'm sorry." Dane winced. "I remember that news story. Canadian family on vacation. Gulfstream jet crashed when landing in a storm."

"Yup." I bit my lip. I'd been wary of planes since then. Logically, they were safer than boats. But still. I had my fears. "And I wasn't on that plane because I was in Fort Lauderdale, taking delivery of this yacht."

"Oh man." Dane shook his head.

"Yeah. Survivor's guilt and all that. Yet another reason I appreciate you sending me to therapy."

"You're not the only one with survivor's guilt." Dane stood up in the water and shook his head. "I fought in Afghanistan. Probably don't need to say any more."

"I'm sorry. I'm sorry, Dane." I shook my head. I did all I could do: I hopped into the water and stood with Dane. I embraced him tightly. We kissed. "I hope you and I and Asher can always take care of one another."

"Hey dudes!" Asher emerged from the boat's interior wearing mismatched neon flippers, snorkel, and mask.

"Check it out! Fashion man is here!" I yelled out. Asher hadn't heard our conversation. That was for the best. We could tell him later. For now he could cheer up the mood.

Asher shouted: "Wearing an outfit by Asher Lane, is Asher Lane!" He turned his ass cheeks to us and pumped them like he was dancing. "Welcome to the world of haute couture!"

"Dude." Dane was laughing and shaking his head. "You look like a Russian tourist just back from the gift shop at a Sandals resort."

I burst out laughing. Dane and Asher did too.

Swim fins and all, Asher jumped into the water. On his back, he swam toward us in the shallow water.

He joined our embrace. It felt good to hug. It felt good to hug anyone I loved, but hugging two men I loved felt amazingly great.

"Check it out." I pointed down at a school of blue-and-yellow fish swimming past us in the crystal-clear shallow water. "Angelfish."

"I thought fish like this were only in the movies." Dane shook his head. "Lived in Miami all my life, never had a chance to come down here."

"Yeah. This little islet. Like I told you. My happy place." I squirted ocean water up into the air with my two hands, like a toddler.

"Our relationship." Dane's huge arms wrapped around me and Asher both. He held us both to him closely, and looked back and forth between my eyes and Asher's. "Our relationship is our happy place."

I kissed Dane's cheek, then his huge, manly jawbone. I put my lips to his and we made out. We pulled Asher closer to us and he joined our makeout, holding his hard dick like a wand and rubbing it on Dane's belly.

"Manatee!" Asher yelled out, pointing in the distance. A fat, slow manatee waddled its way toward us, then swam away. "Cow of the sea."

"Good job." I nodded. "West Indian Manatee. The only kind in the Keys. Not the same manatee that hangs around in the Intracoastal."

"Are you a wildlife biologist or something?" Dane laughed.

"Nope." I shrugged. "I just come out here by myself and watch the animals and look stuff up if I don't know what it is. I've gathered a bit of a mental list."

The afternoon sky burned dark red. We frolicked in the water until evening. It was all a blur: the swimming, the fish-spotting, the snorkeling, the games of tag, the beach naps, the sex.

When darkness fell, we went back to the boat for showers. Dane found some questionable spaghetti and Ragu sauce in a cabinet. That was dinner. I played them some Herbie Hancock on my trumpet too. The angelfish must've loved it.

I'd never had anyone else in my bed. Yet inviting Asher and Dane into that bed came so naturally. It was difficult to believe I'd spent thirty-one years without them.

The three of us fit perfectly, entangled in one another's limbs and faces and chests, quietly whispering "I love you" as we drifted off to sleep.

Twelve (Asher)

"Rise and shine, gentlemen!" I felt awake enough to yell it loudly, but I didn't want to actually wake up Dane and Asher. So I just whispered it, crawling in bed and whispering "Good morning, guys!" It didn't have any result, besides Dane muttering, "Be quiet, Asher," and covering his face with another blanket.

I lay back in bed and enjoyed the view. Inside the bedroom, there were the three of our gorgeous naked bodies, with three very virile dicks. Outside the bedroom, just outside the window, was the uninhabited islet where we'd spent the previous evening. Waves lapped at smooth white-sand beach, its smooth surface interrupted only by a few sand crabs and stray jellyfish.

Azure water stretched seemingly to infinity. A few random boats and airplanes dotted the sky and sea in the distance.

The ocean was ours. The weekend was ours. Our lives were ours.

"Alright." Blair sat up in bed and cleared his throat. His glance outside seemed only precursory: he was pretty confident that the ocean was there, and he just needed to quickly make sure. He cleared his throat some more. "The ship's captain is officially awake."

"Stardate— I don't even know what the fuck," Dane announced groggily.

"So we're going to Key West, right?" I asked, a little eagerly. I'd always wanted to go there for some reason other than my previous experience with Key West. In fact, I'd chosen to strip in Key West because I"d never been, and was sure nobody would recognize me.

"Well, we are gay, right?" Blair laughed. "Yeah, we're going to Key West. Finding Key West should be even within my navigational abilities."

"Confirming that we most definitely are gay." Dane laughed. "Especially after last night. Holy fuck." He rolled over onto his stomach. I pulled the sheet off his ass and palmed and squeezed at its — its hefty, substantial meatiness.

The three of us laughed. It could be the new normal for us, sexually. It would be.

"I know it wasn't your primary intent or anything." Blair stared out through the window. "But thanks for convincing me that it's not just a fever dream or a transient mood — that I really am a full-time, full-tilt homosexual."

"Homosexual throttle set to maximum thrust!" I shouted, and flapped a sheet in the air.

"Oh please! Activate the afterburners," Dane chimed in, affecting a queeny voice.

"Seriously though. You guys changed my life." Blair looked to his left and right, as if to confirm Dane and I still existed. He grabbed another pillow and propped it behind his head.

"Pretty sure you changed our lives too," I said. "I was about as clueless about being gay as you were.

"Which is sort of ironic—" Blair started to say, looking my way from atop his pillows.

"Yeah, I know, I know." I nodded enthusiastically. "The Key West strip club thing. I thought I was just being gay for pay."

"Hello Boris!" Dane was laughing. "I'm Asher Lane and I'm only gay for pay! There are three fists coming out of my mouth because it pays so well!"

"*Three* fists?" I laughed.

"Poetic license." Dane shrugged.

"Speaking of pay." Blair spoke a bit quieter. "Suppose I told you that the security job is off. Suppose I wanted to renege on that announcement, and make the security job back on. I mean, suppose I wanted to pay you guys a million a year just to keep me safe, keep me in line. Is that a possibility?"

"It's more than just a possibility." Dane smiled. "I think we can do it."

"The same way you learned to ask for help, Blair." I stared down at the sun reflecting from the bed's satin sheets. "I'm in a bad place financially. I could definitely use the cash."

"I was wondering about that." Blair shook his head. "Miami cops make what, eighty K a year?"

"Yeah, something around there," I said.

"And you were also doing the Key West gig, for however much extra."

"That I was." I sighed.

"So I'm just wondering how as a single guy without a family to support you can be in financial trouble?" Blair squinted a little.

"Ah, yeah." I sighed. "I co-signed on some medical debt for my dad's cancer treatment."

"Like, a lot of money?" Blair asked.

"Like, half a million bucks." I sighed. "Which maybe is not a lot for you, but is a lot for me. And has by now grown to almost a whole million."

"Oh fuck." Blair winced as if it was hitting him personally.

"Yeah, not to be a downer, but I just had my condo foreclosed on and repoed. I shouldn't be talking about that stuff on a nice vacation, but you asked. I'm sorry."

Dane silently mouthed "He won't accept my money" to Blair and threw up his arms in frustration.

"What, Dane?" Blair wasn't much of a lip-reader.

"*Asher won't accept my offers to give him money,*" I said. "I've tried to give him a million or to take over his condo payments, but he's turned me down."

"Oh yeah." Blair stared directly at Dane. "I forgot that you're rich, Dane."

Dane burst out laughing. "That's a nice direct way of putting it. Yeah, I'm happy living on a cop salary, and I don't touch that Wurlitzer money. But yeah, I do have that Wurlitzer money." Dane shifted his gaze and spoke directly at me. "And which Wurlitzer money I wouldn't mind using to bail you out, Asher."

"Actually. I've kind of been thinking." I sighed. I pulled the sheet up over my head, like a kid.

"I know, I know. You won't take my money." Dane snapped his fingers in defeat.

"I mean, I've been thinking. How Blair wasn't scared to ask for help."

"You'd actually accept help?" Dane smiled wider.

"Maybe asking for help isn't always such a terrible thing. I learned from Blair, by the way."

"Maybe it isn't, dude."

"Do you think you—" I breathed deeply. This was something I'd never done before. Like Blair, I'd assumed anyone wanting to help me out was going to try to take advantage of me. "Maybe you and Blair can go halfsies on helping me out? Something like that. Whatever works for you guys."

"We can buy your condo back from the bank and then give it to you, if that's what you want." Dane said it so nonchalantly, like it was buying a pack of gum.

"Although if the three of us stay together, move in together—" Maybe my fantasies were running away from me, but I imagined myself, Dane, and Blair, living together happily ever after.

"I was kind of hoping. Or maybe more like dreaming." Blair sighed. "Hoping, dreaming that the three of us could live together. High-rise condo on the Intracoastal. We'd still have this yacht too, of course."

"And why is that only a dream?" Dane asked. There was his clinical helper voice again.

"I guess until now I never thought you guys, or anybody, would want to be with me just to be with me."

"Yeah, dude." Dane shook his head. "If you don't actually need security from a stalker chasing you, which it doesn't sound like you do, then there's no reason for you to pay us to protect you."

"I admit—" Blair sighed.

"Dude." I chimed in. "You don't have to pay us to hang out with you. We'd love to hang out with you, spend time with you, whatever, without having to officially be your security guards."

"Yeah, the stalker thing was something I made up." Blair bit his lower lip in shame. "For an excuse to get out of Canada, and an excuse to get some dudes to protect me, take care of me, be nice to me."

"We want to take care of you, Blair. And remember? Not for money. But because you're a fellow human." I reached out and squeezed Blair's hand.

Dane whispered: "And because we love you, Blair."

"I— I can't believe I'd ever say this." Blair smiled. "But I love you guys too."

Thirteen (Dane)

"Fuck!" Asher yelled. "This is a lot of more difficult than it fucking looks!"

"Refuckinglax and follow Blair's lead," I yelled up to Asher. He wasn't doing too bad. He had the balance part in check. He just needed to lean a bit more to achieve more forward speed. Otherwise, he'd be more or less just hopping in place.

"Hey guys." Blair glanced back over his shoulder at the two of us. "What is the gayest thing you can possibly imagine?"

"That's easy." I knew the answer. "Three gay dudes on pogo sticks."

"Nope." Asher called out behind me, timing his words between his bounces. "Three gay dudes on pogo sticks, *hopping through Key West.*"

He used that word. *Gay.* That word that I never thought could possibly apply to me. I was a soldier, a cop, a Wurlitzer. I had some thoughts and desires and so on— it took a change, a hard knock on my head, to let me realize the obvious.

"Oh yeah." I could always concede intellectual victory to a superior argument. "Good point."

"I do know something gayer, though." Asher held up one finger as if he were an oracle.

"Nuh-uh," I called out. "Nothing can possibly be gayer than we are." There. I was using the word. I was owning it. *Gay, gayer, gayest.* That was me. That was us.

"Except for something else." Asher held up his finger again and cleared his throat. "Except for one thing you forgot."

"No way. You're not serious about that, are you?" I laughed.

"I have the connections at Key West Meat Market, dude." Asher sure sounded totally serious. "It's on for tonight."

"Not a joke?" I asked.

"Trust Asher. It's not a joke at all." Blair beamed a bright smile.

"So…" I looked at Blair. "You're willing to join?"

"Of course!" Blair called out. "Three-man naked pogo. Why the fuck not?"

Epilogue (Blair)

"You know that one?" Mister Lane's face beamed with joy. I answered with a nod his way and a thumbs-up. I played the hell out of that song.

"I can't believe a young dude knows Clifford Brown," Mister Lane said to Asher and Dane.

"Blair Hamilton isn't the typical young dude." Asher smiled at me.

I was never the world's best trumpet player, but that morning, in that retirement-community apartment, every note I hit was a fucking homerun. It was like all my teachers had said: you can play better if you have feeling, and love is the most inspiring feeling of all.

"That's 'Cherokee' by Clifford Brown," Mister Lane said to Asher and Lane. "You two have no idea, I'm sure. And Blair is knocking it out of the park."

"Blair gives us jazz music lessons at home." Dane shrugged. "It's good stuff, though we're not anywhere near his knowledge level."

"Yeah." Asher nodded at his father. "Dane is still working through Kenny G's greatest hits." Mister Lane broke out in laughter. I laughed along, at least with a wink toward Mister Lane as a I played through the final bars of "Cherokee," then added a few of my own variations to the ending.

I gave Mister Lane a thumbs-up as the song wound down.

I took a deep breath and proceeded right into "Cantaloupe Island."

Mister Lane broke out laughing. "Oh man. Haven't heard Cantaloupe Island in ages."

"Oh yeah!" Asher said. "I know that song. Us3, right?"

"No, man." Dane lightly punched Asher's shoulder. "Us3 was the remake back in the Nineties. The original was Herbie Hancock. Nineteen sixty-three."

"I just like the group name, then." Asher smiled. "Us3."

"Yeah." Dane gave a thumbs-up. "I like that concept too."

I played the shit out of "Cantaloupe Island," just for Asher's dad. I'd practiced that song solo hundreds of times, but I'd never had an appreciative audience like Mister Lane.

"The three of you guys." Mister Lane smiled and shook his head. "I apologize: I'm an old guy and I don't understand everything."

"Dad." Asher squeezed Mister Lane's arm. "You understand everything perfectly well. Everybody needs love. That's all you need to understand. That's all any of us understand."

"As much as I claim I don't understand." Mister Lane laughed. "How much you three love one another, I can see."

I went into a sizzling trumpet solo. Mister Lane laughed and applauded. Asher and Dane joined the applause.

"You're cooking on that thing," Mister Lane yelled out to me.

"If he could only cook when he's actually cooking," Dane said to Mister Lane, pretending like he was whispering a secret.

"Yeah." Asher winced theatrically. "Blair's cooking is — uh, a work in progress."

"It's jazz, man." Mister Lane laughed. "Always a work in progress. Always improving. Three guys working together to make something good — you guys see the analogy here."

I finished the last notes of my scorching take on "Cantaloupe Island." My audience clapped loudly. I held my trumpet up like it was a trophy.

"I heard you guys talking about my cooking?" I asked them.

"Everybody has a weak point." Asher smiled at me and shrugged.

"Hey." Mister Lane raised his hand in my defense. "Blair is not just a talented jazz musician, but also a brilliant businessman."

"Oh, fuck." Dane shook his head and laughed.

"Well, it is the environmentally friendly alternative to golf carts, isn't it?" Mister Lane asked.

"Exactly! Exactly!" I answered him. "Would you like to go out to enjoy the sunshine a bit, Mister Lane?"

Mister Lane lifted himself out of bed without me even prompting.

"I haven't seen my dad this enthusiastic in years, seriously," Asher said. "It's given him a second wind."

"Gentlemen!" Mister Lane already had his helmet on. He stepped first out of his townhouse, onto the concrete walkway encircling the retirement community.

"I see you've already prepared your trusty steed," I said to him. "Good work."

"Grab your own rides," Mister Lane said. "Unless you want me to leave you in the dust."

Mister Lane locked the door behind him. The four of us set off for the community clubhouse, on our pogo sticks.

"I'm a little too old to give a fuck about what anyone thinks," Mister Lane shouted out, as he hopped forward on his pogo stick — the prime development model from my new company.

"You're a role model, Mister Lane," Dane said. "For living well."

"Living well and not giving a flying fuck," Asher interjected.

"Do what makes you happy." Mister Lane nodded at me before returning his attention to his pogo stick. He led the way, first in front of the three of us. He definitely had more time for pogo-stick practice than the rest of us did.

"The three of you guys already know it—" Mister Lane was breathing quickly. Sweat beaded down his face and neck.

His breaths came quickly, but he still comfortably spoke to us behind him as he pogoed down the concrete path, toward the community clubhouse where we'd play dirty pool.

"The meaning of life is do what brings you love and what makes you happy," Mister Lane said. His words came in rhythm with the squeak-thuds of his pogo stick as he accelerated away from the other three of us.

"Find love and be happy," Mister Lane said. "The three of you guys know that all too well."

Afterword

Steve Milton writes gay romances with sweet love, good humor, and hot sex.

Sign up for Steve's spam-free insiders' club:
http://eepurl.com/bYQboP

Power of Three is the third book of the series **Three Straight**, where Miami's hottest "straight" guys discover their true selves, and the best things come in threes.

Book 1: **We Three**
https://www.amazon.com/dp/B07QB2W9MG

Book 2: **Three Hearts**
http://amazon.com/dp/B07QRWXGJX

Book 3: **Power of Three**
https://www.amazon.com/dp/B07S6KZ844/

Selections from Steve Milton's other books:

Straight Guys is one book of eleven sexy novellas about straight guys who aren't so straight. Who doesn't love "totally straight" dudes lusting after other "totally straight" dudes?
https://www.amazon.com/dp/B018KNWGC8

Crema is a story of former childhood friends finding love.
https://www.amazon.com/dp/B071D4XQJS

Summer Project is a nerd, a jock, a tropical island, and a shared bed.

https://www.amazon.com/dp/B01I0FRENC

Steve Milton has written about twenty other gay romance novels, all of them full of good humor, hot sex, and lots of laughs:
http://amazon.com/author/stevemilton